Loving

Loving

Danielle Steel

THORNDIKE
WINDSOR
PARAGON

This Large Print edition is published by Thorndike Press, Waterville, Maine, USA and by AudioGO Ltd, Bath, England.
Thorndike Press, a part of Gale, Cengage Learning.

Thorndike Press® Large Print Famous Authors.
The text of this Large Print edition is unabridged.
Other aspects of the book may vary from the original edition.
Set in 16 pt. Plantin.

LIBRARY OF CONGRESS CATALOGING-IN-PUBLICATION DATA

Steel, Danielle.
Loving / by Danielle Steel.
p. cm. — (Thorndike Press large print famous authors)
ISBN-13: 978-1-4104-2921-6
ISBN-10: 1-4104-2921-0
1. Large type books. I. Title.
PS3569.T33828L6 2010
813.'54—dc22 2010029303

BRITISH LIBRARY CATALOGUING-IN-PUBLICATION DATA AVAILABLE

Published in 2010 by arrangement with Bantam Books, a division of Random House, Inc.
Published in 2011 in the U.K. by arrangement with Little, Brown Book Group.

U.K. Hardcover: 978 1 445 85391 8 (Windsor Large Print)
U.K. Softcover: 978 1 445 85392 5 (Paragon Large Print)

Printed in Mexico
3 4 5 6 7 14 13 12 11

TO BEATRIX

May you always be
proud to be
yourself,
because you
happen to be
the loveliest lady
I know.

With all my love,
Mommy

Ever hopeful
filled with dreams,
bright new,
brand-new
hopeful schemes,
pastel shades
and Wedgwood skies,
first light
of loving
in your eyes,
soon to dim
and then you flee,
leaving me
alone
with me,
the things I fear,
the things you said
burning rivers
in my head,
bereft of all
we shared,

my soul
so old,
so young,
so bare,
afraid of you,
of me,
of life,
of men . . .
until
the bright new
dreams
begin again.
the landscape never
quite the same,
eventually
a different game,
aware at last
of what I know,
and think,
and am,
and feel,
the gift of love
at
long
last
real.

DANIELLE STEEL

1

Bettina Daniels looked around the pink marble bathroom with a sigh and a smile. She had exactly half an hour. She was making remarkable time. Usually, she had much less time in which to make the transition from girl, student, and ordinary mortal to bird of paradise and hostess extraordinaire. But it was a metamorphosis she was thoroughly used to making. For fifteen years she had been her father's aide-de-camp, going everywhere with him, fielding off reporters, taking telephone messages from his girl friends, even sitting backstage to lend him support as he did late-night talk shows to promote his latest book. He scarcely needed to make the effort to do the promotions. His last seven books had automatically spiraled up *The New York Times* Bestseller List, but still, promotion was something one did. Besides which, he loved it. He loved the preening and parading, the food for his ego, and the women who found him irresistible, confusing him with the heroes in his books.

It was easy to confuse Justin Daniels with the hero in a novel. In some ways Bettina herself had done it for years. He was so blatantly beautiful, so unfailingly charming, so witty, so funny, so delightful to be with. Sometimes it was difficult to remember how selfish, how egotistical, how ruthless he could also be. But Bettina knew both sides of the man, and she loved him anyway.

He had been her hero, her companion, and her best friend for years. And she knew him well. She knew all the flaws and the foibles, all the sins and fears, but she knew too the beauty of the man, the brilliance, the gentleness of his soul, and she loved him with every ounce of her being, and knew that she always would. He had failed her and hurt her, he had forgotten to be at school for almost every important moment, had never shown up for a race or a play. He had assured her that young people were boring, and dragged her along with his friends instead. He had hurt her over the years, mainly in the pursuit of his own shimmering dreams. It never occurred to him that she had a right to a childhood, and picnics and beaches, birthday parties, and afternoons in the park. Her picnics were at the Ritz or the Plaza-Athénée in Paris, her beaches were South Hampton and Deauville, her birthday parties were with his friends at 21 in New York or the Bistro in Beverly Hills; and rather than afternoons in the park he would insist she accompany him on the yacht cruises he was constantly being invited to share. Hers was hardly a life to be pitied, and yet Justin's trusted friends often reproached him for how he brought up his child, what he had deprived her of, and how lonely it was to tag along constantly with a bachelor father eternally on the prowl. It was remarkable that in some ways even at nineteen she was still so youthful, still so innocent, with those enormous emerald eyes; yet there was the wisdom of the ages lurking there too. Not because of what she had done, but rather because of what she had seen. At nineteen she was still in some ways a baby, and in other ways she had seen an opulence, a decadence, an existence that few men or women twice her age had ever seen.

Her mother had died of leukemia shortly after Bettina's fourth birthday and was nothing more than a face in a portrait on the dining room wall, a laughing smile with huge blue eyes and blond hair. There was something of Tatianna Daniels in her daughter, but not much. Bettina looked like neither Tatianna nor Justin. She looked mainly like herself. Her father's striking black hair and green eyes were partly passed down to his daughter, whose green eyes were not wholly unlike his. However her hair was rich auburn, the color of very old, very fine cognac. His tall angular frame was in sharp contrast to Bettina's, which was narrow, minute, almost elfin in its delicate proportions. It served to give her an aura of fragility as she brushed the auburn hair into a halo of soft curls, as she did now, looking at her watch once again.

Bettina made a rapid calculation. Twenty minutes. She would be on time. She sank rapidly into the steaming water in the tub and sat there for a moment, trying to unwind as she watched the snow falling outside. It was November, and this was the first snow.

It was also their first party of the "season," and for that reason it had to be a success. And it would be. She would see to that too. She mentally checked over the guest list again, wondering if there were some who would fail to arrive because of the snow. But she thought it unlikely. Her father's parties were too celebrated, the invitations awaited too breathlessly for anyone to want to miss the occasion or risk not being invited again. Parties were an essential part of the life of Justin Daniels. When he was between books, he gave them at least once a week. And they were noteworthy for the people who came and the costumes they wore, the incidents that happened, the deals that were made. But above all they were special, and an evening at the Danielses' was like a visit to a faraway, once-dreamed-of land.

The parties were all spectacular. The luxurious surroundings sparkled in seventeenth-century splendor, as butlers hovered and musicians played. Bettina, as hostess, floating magically between groups, always seemed to be everywhere that she was wanted or needed. She was a truly haunting creature; elusive, beautiful, and very, very rare. The only one who did not fully realize how remarkable she was, was her father, who thought every young woman was naturally as gracious as Bettina. His casual acceptance of her was something that had long since irritated his closest friend. Ivo Stewart adored Justin Daniels, but it had irked him for years that Justin never saw what was happening to Bettina, never understood how she worshiped him, and how much his attention and praise meant to her. Justin would only laugh when Ivo made comments, which he did frequently, shaking his head and waving a well-manicured hand at his friend.

"Don't be ridiculous. She loves what she does for me. She enjoys it. Running the parties, going to shows with me, seeing interesting people. She'd be embarrassed if I made a point of telling her how I appreciate what she does. She knows I do. Who wouldn't? She does a marvelous job."

"Then you should tell her that. Good God, man, she's your secretary, your housekeeper, your publicity girl — she does everything a wife would do and more."

"And better!" Justin pointed out as he laughed.

"I'm serious." Ivo looked stern.

"I know you are. Too much so. You worry too much about the girl." Ivo hadn't dared to tell Justin that if he didn't worry about her, he wasn't sure if Justin would himself.

Justin had an easy, cavalier way about him, in sharp contrast to Ivo's more serious view of the world. But that was also the nature of Ivo's business, as publisher of one of the world's largest newspapers, the *New York Mail.* He was also older than Justin, and not a young man. He had lost one wife, divorced another, and purposely never had children. He felt it was unfair to bring children into such a difficult world. And at sixty-two he did not regret the decision . . . except when he saw Bettina. Then something seemed always to melt in his heart. Sometimes seeing Bettina, he wondered if remaining childless had been a mistake. But it didn't matter now. It was too late to think about children, and he was happy. In his own way he was as free as Justin Daniels.

Together, the two men went to concerts, operas, parties. They went to London for an occasional weekend, met in the South of France for a few weeks in July, and shared a remarkable number of illustrious friends. It was one of those solid friendships that forgives almost all sins and allows the free expression of disapproval, as well as delight, which was why Ivo was so open in voicing his opinions of Justin's behavior with his child. Recently the subject had come up at lunch at La Côte Basque.

Ivo had chided Justin, "If I were in her shoes, old boy, I'd walk out on you. What's she getting from you?"

"Servants, comfort, trips, fascinating people, a twenty-thousand-dollar wardrobe." He prepared to go on, but Ivo cut him off.

"So what? Do you think she really gives a damn? For chrissake, Justin, look at the girl — she's lovely, but half the time she's in another world, dreaming, thinking, writing. Do you really think she gives a damn about all the showy bullshit that means so much to you?"

"Of course she does. She's had it all her life." Her childhood was completely different from Justin's, who had grown up poor and made millions on his books and movies. There had been good times and bad times, and some very hard times, but Justin's spending had only gone in one direction over the years: up. The opulence he surrounded himself with was vital to him. It reassured him of who he was. He was looking at Ivo now over a demitasse of strong coffee at the end of lunch. "Without all that I give her, she wouldn't be able to make it for a week, Ivo."

"I'm not so sure." Ivo had more faith in her than her father. One day she would be a truly remarkable woman, and whenever he thought of it, Ivo Stewart smiled.

Drying herself off quickly with a large pink monogrammed towel, Bettina knew she would have to hurry. She had already laid out her dress. It was a beautiful watered-silk sheath of the palest mauve, which fell from her shoulders to her ankles like a soft slinky tube. She slipped rapidly into the appropriate laces and silks, climbed into the dress, and stepped carefully into the matching mauve sandals with tiny gold heels. On its own the dress would have been splendid. She admired it again as she fluffed her burnt-caramel hair for the last time, making sure that the mauve on her eyelids was exactly the same as the dress. She clasped a rope of amethysts around her neck and another to her left wrist as tiny diamonds sparkled in her ears. And then, carefully, she lifted the heavy green velvet tunic from its hanger and slipped it over the mauve silk of the dress. The tunic was lined in the same shimmering mauve, and she looked like a symphony in lilac and deep Renaissance green. It was a breathtakingly beautiful outfit, which her father had brought her from Paris the winter before. But she wore it with the same ease and unaffected simplicity that she would have worn a pair of old faded jeans. Having paid the outfit due homage in the mirror, she could forget that she had it on. And that was precisely what she was planning to do. She had a thousand other things on her mind. She cast a glance around the cozy French provincial bedroom, made sure that she had left the screen in front of the still roaring fire, and glanced out the window for the last time. It was still snowing. The first snow was always so pretty. She smiled to herself as she made her way quickly downstairs.

She had to check the kitchen and make sure everything looked right for the buffet. The dining room was a masterpiece, and she smiled at the perfection of the canapés that marched along countless silver platters like overgrown confetti scattered everywhere for a holiday feast. In the living room everything was in order, and in the den the furniture had been removed as she'd ordered and the musicians were tuning up. The servants looked impeccable, the apartment looked divine, with room after room of museum-quality Louis XV furniture, marble mantels, overwhelming bronzes, and inlaid wonders at which one could only stare in awe. The damasks were in soft creamy colors, the velvets leaned to café au lait or apricot and peach. The whole apartment was a splendor of warmth and loving, and it was Bettina's taste that was exhibited everywhere, Bettina's caring that so lavishly showed.

"My God, you look pretty, darling." She wheeled at the sound of his voice and stood for a moment, her eyes warm and smiling. "Isn't that the thing I got you in Paris last year?" Justin Daniels smiled at his daughter and she smiled back. Only her father would call the exquisite Balenciaga he had bought her for a king's ransom "a thing."

"It is. I'm glad you like it." And then, hesitantly, almost shyly, "I like it too."

"Good. Are the musicians here?" He was already looking past her, into the wood-paneled sanctum of the large den.

"They're tuning up. I think they'll be starting any minute. Would you like a drink?" He never thought of her needs. It was always she who thought of his.

"I think I'll wait for a minute. Christ, I'm tired today." He sprawled for a moment in a comfortable bergère as Bettina watched him. She could have told him that she was tired too. She had gotten up at six that morning to work out the details of the party, gone to school at eight thirty, and then rushed home to bathe, dress, and see that everything was just right. But she didn't say anything to him about it. She never did.

"Are you working on the new book?" She looked at him with devotion and interest as he nodded and then looked over at her with a smile.

"You always care about the books, don't you?"

"Of course I do." She smiled gently.

"Why?"

"Because I care about you."

"Is that the only reason?"

"Of course not. They're wonderful books, and I love them." And then she stood up and laughed softly as she bent down to kiss him on the forehead. "I also happen to love you." He smiled in answer and patted her arm gently as she swept away at the sound of the door. "Sounds like someone's arriving." But she was worried suddenly. He did look unusually tired.

Within half an hour the house was jammed with people laughing, talking, drinking, being witty or amusing or unkind, and sometimes all three. There were miles of evening dresses, in rainbow hues, and rivers of jewels, and a veritable army of men in black tie, their white shirts studded with mother of pearl and onyx and tiny sapphires and diamonds. And there were almost a hundred well-known faces in the crowd. Aside from the hundred of relative celebrities were another two hundred unknowns, drinking champagne, eating caviar, dancing to the music, looking for Justin Daniels or others they had hoped to glimpse or even meet.

Through it all Bettina passed unnoticed, darting, moving, watching that everything went smoothly, that people were introduced, had champagne, had been fed. She was careful to see that her father had his Scotch, and then later his brandy, that his cigars were always near at hand. She was careful to keep her distance when he seemed to be flirting with a woman and quick to bring him an important guest who had just arrived. She was a genius at what she was doing. And Ivo thought she was more beautiful than any woman in the room. It wasn't the first time that he had wished she was his child and not Justin's.

"Doing your usual number, I see, Bettina? Exhausted? Or only ready to drop?"

"Don't be silly, I love it." But he could see that beneath her eyes there was the faintest hint of fatigue. "Would you like another drink?"

"Stop treating me like a guest, Bettina. Can I interest you in sitting down somewhere?"

"Maybe later."

"No, now."

"All right, Ivo. All right." She looked up into the deep blue eyes in the kind face that she had come to love over the years and let him lead her to a seat near a window, where for a moment they silently watched the snow, and then she turned her eyes back to him. His full white mane looked more perfectly groomed than ever. Ivo Stewart always looked perfect. He was just that kind of man. Tall, lean, handsome, youthful, with blue eyes that always seemed about to laugh and the longest legs she'd ever seen. She had called him Ivo Tall when she was a child. Slowly she gave way to a small worried frown. "Have you noticed that Daddy looks very tired tonight?"

Ivo shook his head. "No, but I notice that you look tired. Anything wrong?"

She smiled. "Just exams. Why is it that you notice everything?"

"Because I love you both, and sometimes your father is a complete moron and doesn't notice a damn thing. Writers! You could drop dead at their feet and they'd march over you, muttering something about the second part of chapter fifteen. Your father's no different."

"No, he just writes better."

"I suppose that's an excuse."

"He doesn't need an excuse." Bettina said it very gently, and Ivo's eyes met hers. "He's marvelous at what he does." *Even if he isn't the most wonderful father,* she thought, *he's a brilliant writer!* But they were words she would never have said out loud.

"You're marvelous at what you do too."

"Thank you, Ivo. You always say the nicest things. And now" — she stood up reluctantly and smoothed her dress — "I have to get back to playing hostess."

It had gone on until four in the morning, and her whole body ached as she walked slowly upstairs. Her father was still in the den with two or three of his cronies, but she had done her job. The servants had already whisked away most of the mess, the musicians had been paid and sent home, the last guests had been kissed and thanked before they departed, the women bundled in their minks as their husbands led them to limousines waiting outside in the snow. And as she walked slowly to her room Bettina stopped for a moment and looked outside. It was beautiful; the city looked peaceful and silent and white. And then she went to her room and closed the door.

She carefully hung the Balenciaga back on its hanger and slipped into a pink silk nightgown before sliding between the flowered sheets that one of the maids had turned down earlier that night. And as she lay in bed a moment later she ran over the evening again in her head. It had gone smoothly. It always did. She sighed sleepily to herself, wondering about the next party. Had he said next week, or the week after that? And had he liked the musicians tonight? She had forgotten to ask. And the caviar . . . what about the caviar . . . was it as good as . . . ? Looking very small and fragile, she sighed once more and fell asleep.

2

"Care to join us for lunch today? Twenty-one, at noon." She read the note as she finished her coffee and picked up the heavy red coat she wore to school. She was wearing navy gabardine slacks and a navy-blue cashmere sweater and boots that she hoped would resist the snow. Quickly she picked up a pen and jotted a note to him on the other side of his.

"Wish I could, but I'm sorry . . . exams! Have a good time. See you tonight. Love, B."

She had been telling him about her exams all week. But he couldn't be expected to remember the details of her life. He was already thinking of his next book, and that was enough. And nothing in her college life had thus far been worthy of his attention. This was easy to understand. It didn't fascinate her either. In contrast to the life she led with him, everything else was so flat.

She did feel secretly that the normalcy of her college life was refreshing, but it seemed somewhat remote to her. She always felt like an observer. She never joined in. Too many people had already figured out who she was. It made her a curiosity, and an object of stares and fascination. But she didn't feel worthy of their interest. She wasn't the writer. She was only his child.

The door closed softly behind her as she went off to school, mentally running over the notes she had made for herself to prepare for the exam. It was difficult to feel lively about it on two-and-a-half hours' sleep. But she'd come out all right, she always did. Her grades were quite high, which was another thing that frequently set her apart from the others. She wasn't even sure now why she had let her father talk her into going on with school. All she wanted to do was find a corner somewhere to write her play. That was all. Just that. . . . And then she grinned to herself as the elevator reached the ground floor. There was more to the fantasy after all. She wanted to write a *hit* play. That would take more time . . . like twenty or thirty years.

"Morning, miss." She smiled at the doorman as he tipped his hat, and for a moment she almost ran back into the building. It was one of those stunningly cold days when the first breath of air feels like nails being inhaled. She hailed a cab and climbed in. Today was not a day to prove anything by taking the bus. To hell with it. She would rather stay warm. She settled back against the seat and looked long and hard at her notes.

"Bettina couldn't come?" Ivo looked up in surprise as Justin joined him at the huge bar that was always their meeting spot at 21.

"Apparently not. I forgot to ask her last night, so she left me a note this morning. Something about exams. I hope that's all it is."

"What's that supposed to mean?"

"It means I hope she's not involved with some little fool at college." Both of them knew that up until now there had been no man in her life. Justin didn't give her time.

"You expect her to stay unattached for the rest of her life?" Ivo looked at him dubiously over his martini.

"Hardly. But I expect her to make an intelligent choice."

"What makes you think she won't?" Ivo watched his friend with interest and he could see the tired look about his eyes that

Bettina had mentioned the night before.

"Women don't always make wise choices, Ivo."

"And we do?" He said it with amusement. "Do you have any reason to suspect she's met someone?"

Justin Daniels shook his head. "No, but you never know. I abhor those little bastards who go to college just to screw girls."

"Like you, you mean." Ivo was now grinning broadly as Justin shot him an evil look and ordered a Scotch.

"Never mind that. I feel like hell today."

"Hung over?" Ivo didn't look impressed.

"I don't know. Maybe. I've had indigestion since last night."

"It's obviously old age."

"Aren't you the smart one today?" Justin gave him a look that Ivo knew meant he'd had enough and then they both laughed. Despite their diverging views about Bettina, the two men never failed to get along. She was the only subject on which they almost never agreed and the only bone of contention between them. "By the way, can I interest you in a brief trip to London next weekend?"

"For what?"

"What do I know? Chasing girls, spending money, going to the theater. The usual."

"I thought you were already working on the new book."

"I am, but I'm stuck and I want to play."

"I'll have to see. You may not have noticed, but there are several minor wars, not to mention political coups, breaking out all over the world. The paper may want me here."

"It won't change a damn thing if you're gone for the weekend. Besides, you *are* the paper, you can call your own shots."

"Thank you, sir. I'll keep that in mind. Who's joining us for lunch by the way?"

"Judith Abbott, the playwright. Bettina's going to have a fit that she missed her." He looked somberly at Ivo then and ordered another Scotch. But Ivo had not missed the frightened look in his eyes.

For a moment Ivo wondered, and then he gently touched his friend's arm and spoke barely above a whisper. "Justin . . . is something really wrong?"

There was a pause for a moment. "I don't know. I feel strange all of a sudden. . . ."

"Do you want to sit down?" But it was already too late; a moment later he slumped to the floor and two women looked down and screamed. His face was hideously contorted, as he seemed to wrestle with intolerable pain. Frantically Ivo issued orders, and it was only moments before the paramedics arrived, moments when Ivo held his friend in his arms and prayed that it wasn't too late. But it was. Justin Daniels's hand fell limply to the floor the moment Ivo let it go, as police on the scene pushed the curious away and the paramedics fought on for almost half an hour. But it was useless. Justin Daniels was dead.

Ivo watched helplessly as they pounded his heart, gave him artificial respiration, oxygen, everything, while Ivo gave him prayers. But it made no difference. At last they covered his face as tears rolled down Ivo's cheeks. They asked him if he wanted to come with the body to the hospital morgue. The morgue? Justin? It was unthinkable. But it wasn't. And they went.

Ivo felt gray and trembling as he walked out of the hospital an hour later. There was nothing more to be done except tell Bettina. He felt sick when he thought of it. Jesus . . . how was he going to tell her? What could he say? What did this leave her? And who? She had no one in the world except Justin. No one. She had the best guest list in New York and knew more celebrities than the Society writer at the *Times,* but that was all she had. Other than that she had nothing. Except Justin. And now he was gone.

3

The clock on the mantelpiece ticked interminably as Ivo sat in the den, staring bleakly out over the park. It was already late in the afternoon and the light was slowly failing. In the street below, the usual angry snarl of traffic crawled south along Fifth Avenue. It was rush hour and there was snow on the ground, to add an extra impediment to Bettina's getting home at the end of the day. The cars barely moved as drivers honked angrily. In the Danielses' apartment the distant honking was a muted sound. Ivo didn't even hear it as he sat there, waiting to hear Bettina's footstep in the hall, her voice calling out, her laughter as she came home from school. He found himself looking around the room, at the trophies, the artifacts handsomely displayed on shelves in the bookcase along with the leather-bound volumes Justin had treasured. Many of them had been bought at auction in London when Ivo had been with him on occasional trips over the years. Just like their trips to Munich and Paris and Vienna. There had been so many years, so many moments, so many good times they had shared. It was Justin who had celebrated and cried and cavorted with him for the thirty-two years of their friendship, over love affairs and divorces and victories of all kinds . . . Justin who had asked Ivo to sit with him at Doctor's Hospital the night Bettina was born, as they both got blind drunk on champagne, and then went on to celebrate afterward on the town . . . Justin . . . who was suddenly no more. So swiftly gone. Ivo's thoughts wandered soberly back to the moments in the hospital that afternoon. It all seemed so unreal. And then Ivo realized that it was Justin he was waiting for, not Bettina . . . Justin's voice in the long empty hall . . . his elegant frame in the doorway with a smile in his eyes and laughter on his lips. It was Justin, not Bettina, whom Ivo expected to see as he sat in the quiet, wood-paneled room staring at the cold cup of coffee the butler had brought him an hour before. They knew. They all knew. Ivo had told the servants shortly after he arrived at the house. He had also called Justin's lawyer and his agent. But no one else. He didn't want anything in the press or on the radio before Bettina knew. The servants knew also that they were to say nothing to her when she arrived. They were only to direct her to Ivo in the den . . . where he waited . . . in the stillness . . . for one of them to come home. . . . If only Justin would come home, then it would all be a lie after all and he wouldn't have to tell her . . . he wouldn't have to . . . it wouldn't be. . . . He felt tears sting his eyes again as he fingered the delicate blue and gold Limoges cup set before him.

Absently Ivo touched the lace on the edge of his napkin as he suddenly heard the front door open. There was a hushed voice, the butler's, and then her brighter one. Ivo could almost see her, smiling, open, shrugging out of the heavy red coat, saying something to the butler, who smiled for no one else except "Miss." For "Miss," everyone smiled. Except Ivo; this afternoon he couldn't smile. He stood and walked slowly to the door, feeling his heart pound as he waited for her. Oh God, what would he say?

"Ivo?" She looked surprised as she came toward him across the hall. They had just told her that he was waiting for her in the den. "Is something wrong?" She looked instantly sympathetic and reached out both hands. It was too early for him to leave the office and she knew it. He rarely left his desk before seven or eight. It made him difficult to have as a dinner guest sometimes, but it was a foible everyone easily forgave. The publisher of the *New York Mail* had a right to keep long hours, and he was still sought out by every hostess in town. "You look tired." She looked at him reproachfully and held his hand as they sat down. "Isn't Daddy home?"

He shook his head dumbly, and his eyes filled with tears as she kissed his cheek. "No. Bettina. . . ." And then, hating himself, he heard himself add, "Not yet."

"Would you like a drink, instead of that miserable-looking cup of coffee?" Her smile was so warm and gentle that it tore at his heart, as her eyes took in every detail. She was worried about him and that made him smile. She looked so incredibly young and lovely and innocent that he wanted to tell her anything but the truth. Her auburn hair looked like a halo of curls as it floated around her head. Her eyes were bright and her cheeks pink from the cold, and she looked tinier than ever. But her smile faded as she watched him. Suddenly she knew that something was terribly wrong. "Ivo, what is it? You've hardly said a word since I came in." Her eyes never left his, and then slowly he reached for her hand. "Ivo?" She grew pale as she watched him, and in spite of himself tears filled his eyes as he pulled her gently into his arms. She didn't resist him. It was as though she knew that she would need him, and he her. She found herself holding tightly to Ivo as she waited for the news.

"Bettina . . . it's Justin. . . ." He felt a sob rise in his throat, and he fought it. He had to be strong. For Justin. For her. But she had gone tense in his arms now, and suddenly she pulled away.

"What do you mean? . . . Ivo. . . ." Her eyes were frantic, her hands like frightened little birds. "An accident?" But Ivo only shook his head. And then slowly he looked at her, and in his eyes she saw the full force of her fear.

"No, darling. He's gone." For an instant nothing moved in the room as the shock washed over her like a wave, and her eyes stared into his, not fully understanding, and not wanting to know.

"I — I don't understand. . . ." Her hands fluttered nervously, and her eyes seemed to dart from his face to her hands. "What do you mean, Ivo? . . . I —" And then, in anguish and horror, she jumped to her feet and crossed the room, as though to get away from him, as though by fleeing him, she could flee the truth. "What the hell do you mean?" She was shouting at him now, her voice tremulous and angry, her eyes filled with tears. But she looked so fragile, so frail, that he wanted to take her in his arms again.

"Bettina . . . darling. . . ." He went to her, but she fought him off, unthinking, unknowing, and then suddenly she reached out to him and clung to him as her whole body was wracked by sobs.

"Oh, God . . . oh, no . . . Daddy. . . ." It was a long, slow, childlike wail. Ivo held her tightly in his arms. He was all she had.

"What happened? Oh, Ivo . . . what happened?" But she didn't really want to know. All she wanted to know was that it wasn't true. But it was. Ivo's face told her again and again that it was.

"It was a heart attack. At lunch. They sent an ambulance immediately, but it was too late." He sounded anguished as he said it.

"Didn't they do anything? For God's sake. . . ." She was sobbing now, her narrow frame shaking, as he kept an arm around her shoulders. It was impossible to believe. Only the night before they had danced in this room.

"Bettina, they did everything. Absolutely

everything. It was just —" God, what an agony it was to tell her all of it. It was almost unbearable for him. "It happened very quickly. It was all over in a matter of moments. And I promise you, they did everything they could. But there wasn't much they could do." She closed her eyes and nodded, and then slowly she left the comfort of his arms and crossed the room. She stood with her back to him, looking down at the snow and the gnarled, naked trees across the street in Central Park. How ugly it looked to her now, how lonely, how bare, when only the night before it had looked beautiful and fairylike as she stood at her bedroom window, dressing for the party and waiting for the first guests to arrive. She hated them now, all of them, for having robbed her of her last night alone with him . . . her last night . . . he was gone now. She closed her eyes again tightly and braced herself for the question she had to ask.

"Did he — did he say anything, Ivo. . . . I mean . . . for me?" Her voice was a tiny mouse sound from her vigil at the window, and she didn't see Ivo shake his head.

"There wasn't time."

She nodded silently, and a moment later took a deep breath. Ivo didn't know whether to go to her, or let her stand there alone.

He felt he might break her in half with the merest touch of his hand, so taut and brittle and fragile she seemed as she stood there, aching and alone. She was alone now, and she knew it. For the first time in her life. "Where is he now?"

"At the hospital." Ivo hated to say it. "I wanted to speak to you before making any arrangements. Do you have any idea what you'd like to do?" He approached her slowly and turned her around to face him. He looked down at her. Her eyes seemed suddenly a thousand years old, and it was the face of a woman she turned up to him, not the face of a child. "Bettina, I — I'm sorry to press you about this, but . . . do you have any idea what your father would have wanted?"

She sat down again, softly shaking the halo of auburn curls. "We never talked about — about things like that. And he wasn't religious." She closed her eyes and two huge tears rolled somberly down her face. "I suppose we ought to do something private. I don't want" — she could barely go on speaking — "a lot of strangers there to stare at him and —" But then all she could do was bow her head as her shoulders shook pathetically, and Ivo took her once again in his arms. It took her fully five minutes to compose herself, and then she looked up at Ivo with a bleak look in her eyes. "I want to see him now, Ivo." He nodded, and she stood up and walked silently to the door.

She was terrifyingly quiet on the way to the hospital and she was dry-eyed and poised as she sat in the backseat of Ivo's limousine. She seemed to shrink as she sat there, huddled into a silver fox coat, her eyes huge and childlike beneath a matching fur hat.

She stepped out of the car ahead of him at the hospital, and she was instantly through the door, waiting impatiently for Ivo, wanting to be taken to her father's side. In her heart she had not yet understood the reality, and somehow she expected to find him anxious to see her and very much alive. It was only when they came to the final doorway that she seemed to slow down, the staccato of the heels of her black kid boots silenced on the hospital floor, the light beyond the doorway dim, and her eyes suddenly huge as she stepped slowly inside the morgue. He was there, covered with a sheet, and on tiptoe she went to him, and stood there, trying to get up the courage to pull the sheet down so she could see his face. Ivo watched her for a moment, and then walked softly to her side.

He whispered to her and gently took her arm. "Do you want to go now?" But she only shook her head. She had to see him. Had to. She had to say good-bye. She wanted to tell Ivo that she wanted to be alone with her father, but she didn't know how, and in the end she was just as glad.

With a trembling hand she reached out and touched the corner of the sheet, and slowly, slowly, pulled it back until she could see the top of his head. For an instant it seemed as though he was playing with her, as though she were a child again and they were playing peekaboo. More quickly now she pulled the sheet down until she dropped it on his chest. The eyes were closed, the face peaceful and eerily pale as she looked down at him, her eyes wide and filled with pain, but she understood now. It was as Ivo had said — her father was gone. The tears poured steadily down her face as she bent to kiss him and then took a step back, as firmly Ivo put an arm around her again and led her out of the room.

4

But the truth of it didn't hit Bettina until after the funeral. Between her father's death and his final ritual were two days of frantic surrealism, picking out something for him to wear, checking constantly with the secretary she had hired to help with the arrangements, talking to Ivo about who had been called and who must be, organizing servants, and reassuring friends. There was something wonderfully comforting about "arrangements." They were a place to flee from her emotions, from the truth. She hurried between the apartment and the funeral home, and finally stood in the cemetery, a fragile figure in black, carrying one long, white rose, which she lay silently on her father's coffin as the rest of the group stood apart from her. Only Ivo hovered somewhere near her. She could see his shadow falling across the snow near her own. Only Ivo had bridged the gap again and again in the painful days after her father's death. Only Ivo had been able to reach out and touch her. Only Ivo was there to let her know that someone still cared, that she was not totally unprotected in the world now, frightened and alone.

He took her hand silently and led her back to his car. Half an hour later she was secure in her apartment again, locked in the safe little world she had always known. She and Ivo were drinking coffee, and outside a bright November sun shone on the fresh snow. The winter snow had come early, and the only place it looked lovely was in the park. The rest of the city had lain beneath a blanket of slush for three days. Bettina sighed to herself, sipped her coffee, and looked absently at the brightly burning fire. It was an odd comparison, but she felt the way her father used to when he finished a book. Suddenly she had lost her "people" and she was out of a job. There was no one to care for and fuss over, to order cracked crab for, to make sure his cigars were at hand, the guest list was to his liking, and the plane reservations to Madrid were exactly as he wanted. There was no one to take care of now except herself. And she wasn't quite sure how to do that. She had always been so busy taking care of him.

"Bettina." There was a long pause as Ivo set down his cup and slowly ran a hand through his white hair. He only did that when he felt very awkward, and she wondered why he should feel that way now. "It's a bit early to bring it up to you, darling, but we ought to meet with the lawyers this week." He felt his heart sink as she turned her wide green eyes to his.

"Why?"

"To discuss the will, and . . . there are several other points of business that we ought to talk to them about." Justin had left him as executor, and the lawyers had already been clawing at him for two days.

"Why now? Isn't it too soon?" She looked puzzled as she stood and walked to the fire. She was feeling tired and restless all at the same time. She wasn't sure whether to run around the block a hundred fifty times or just go to bed and cry. But Ivo was looking distressingly businesslike as his eyes followed her to the fire.

"No, it's not too soon. There are some things you'll have to know, some decisions to be made. Some of it should get rolling now."

She sighed in answer and nodded as she went back to the couch. "All right. We'll see them, but I don't understand the rush." She looked at Ivo with a quiet smile and he nodded and reached out a hand. Even Ivo didn't know the full extent of what the lawyers had on their minds. But twelve hours later they did.

Ivo and Bettina looked at each other in shock. The lawyers looked at her gravely. No stock. No investments. No capital. In brief, there was no money. According to his attorneys, Justin hadn't been upset about it because he always expected things to "come around," but the turnaround had not yet come. In fact it hadn't come in several years, and he had been living on credit for too long. Everything he owned was heavily mortgaged or had been put up as collateral and it turned out that he had fabulous loans to repay. His last advances had all been spent, on cars — like the new Bentley, and then shortly afterward the 1934 Rolls — antiques, racehorses, women, trips, houses, furs, Bettina, himself. The winter before he had bought the country's most extravagant Thoroughbred from a friend. Two point seven million he had paid for it, the papers had said. In fact it had been slightly more, and the friend had allowed him to defer payment for a year. The year wasn't yet over, and the debt was still unpaid. He knew he would cover it, there would be more advances, and he had his royalties, which never failed to come in, in six-figure checks. What Ivo and Bettina then learned as they sat there was that even his future royalties had been borrowed against, from some of his wealthier friends. He had borrowed to the hilt from everyone, bankers, as well as friends, against real property, future income, and dreams. What had happened to his investments, to the snatches of conversations she had heard about "sure things"? As the hours with the attorneys wore on, it became clear that there were no sure things, except his astronomical debts, they were sure. He had kept much of his borrowing private. He had dispensed with his investment advisers years ago, calling them fools. It became increasingly confusing and Bettina sat baffled and stunned. It was impossible to make heads or tails out of what they were saying except that it would take months to sort it all out and that the vast estate of the illustrious, charming, celebrated, much adored Justin Daniels amounted not to a king's ransom, but to a mountain of debt.

Bettina looked at Ivo in confusion, and he looked at her in despair. He felt as though he had just aged another ten years.

"And the houses?" Ivo looked at the senior attorney with fear.

"We'll have to look into that, but I assume that they'll all have to be sold. We've been recommending that course of action to Mister Daniels for almost two years now. As a matter of fact it's quite possible that once we sell the houses, and . . . er" — there was an embarassed cough — "several of the antiques and artifacts in Mister Daniels's New York apartment, it's possible that we will have brought matters back into the black."

"Will there be anything left?"

"That's difficult to say at the moment." But the look on his face told its own tale.

"What you're saying then" — Ivo's voice was tense and angry, and he wasn't sure if he was angrier at Justin or his lawyers — "is that after all is said and done, there won't be anything left except the apartment here in New York. No stocks, no bonds, no investments, nothing?"

"I believe that will prove to be correct." The elderly man fingered his glasses uncomfortably, while his junior partner cleared his throat and tried not to look at the slender young girl.

"Was there no provision made for Miss Daniels?" Ivo couldn't believe it.

But the lawyer spoke one word. "None."

"I see."

"Of course there was" — the senior partner checked some papers on his desk — "a sum of eighteen thousand dollars in Mister Daniels's checking account on the day he died. We have to clear probate of course, but we would be happy to advance a small sum of money to Miss Daniels in the interim, to enable her to pay whatever living expenses —" But Ivo was steaming by now.

"That won't be necessary." Ivo snapped closed his briefcase and picked up his coat. "Just how long do you think it will take to let us know where things stand?"

The two lawyers exchanged a glance. "About three months?"

"How about one?" Ivo's look was not one to quibble with, and unhappily the elder attorney nodded.

"We'll try. We do understand that the circumstances are somewhat trying for Miss Daniels. We'll do our very best."

"Thank you." Bettina shook hands with them and quickly left the office. Ivo said almost nothing on the way to the car, he only glanced anxiously again and again at her face. She was ivory-pale, but she seemed quiet and very much in control. Once they were in his car again, he raised the window between them and his driver and turned to her with a look of sorrow in his eyes. "Bettina, do you understand what just happened?"

"I think so." As he watched her he saw that even her lips were frighteningly pale. "It looks like I'm about to learn a few things about life."

As they drove up in front of her elaborate building he asked.

"Will you let me help you?"

She shook her head, kissed his cheek, and got out of the car.

He sat watching her until she had disappeared into the building, wondering what would happen to her now.

5

The doorbell rang just as Bettina looked at her watch. His timing was perfect and she smiled as she ran to the door. She greeted him with a kiss and Ivo entered and bowed, looking very debonair in a black coat and a homburg. Bettina, on the other hand, was wearing a red flannel shirt and jeans.

"You're looking very lively this evening, Miss Daniels. How was your day?"

"Interesting. I spent the day with the man from Parke-Bernet." She smiled tiredly, and he thought for a moment how he missed seeing her in her usual elegant clothes. She seemed to have abandoned her other wardrobe in the month since Justin had died. But she also hadn't gone anywhere, except to the lawyers, to hear more bad news. Now all she wanted was to get the hell out of the mess. She was about to start meeting with art dealers, real estate agents, antiquaries, jewelers, anyone and everyone who could take the goods off her hands and leave her with something with which to whittle away the debts.

"They're taking all of this stuff off my hands" — she waved vaguely at the antiques — "as well as everything out of the house in South Hampton and the one in Palm Beach. They've already had someone to look it all over. The furniture in the South of France I'm getting rid of over there, and" — she sighed absent-mindedly as she hung up his coat — "I think the house in Beverly Hills will sell with everything in it. Some Arab is buying the place, and he left everything he had in the Middle East. So it should work out well for both of us."

"Aren't you keeping anything?" Ivo looked appalled, but he was getting used to the feeling and she was getting used to the look on his face.

She shook her head with a small smile. "I can't afford to. I'm dealing with the national debt, Ivo. Four and a half million dollars is not exactly easy to wipe out. But I will." She smiled again, and something turned over near his heart. How could Justin do this to her? How could he not have known that something like this might happen, that she would be left to clean up his mess? The unfairness of it tore at Ivo's soul. "Don't look so worried, love." She was smiling at him now. "It'll all be sorted out one of these days."

"Yes, and in the meantime I sit here helplessly and watch you tear your life apart." It was hard to remember now that she was only nineteen. She looked and sounded so much older. But there was still an occasional look of mischief in her eyes.

"And what would you like to do, Ivo? Help me pack?"

"No, I wouldn't." He snapped at her, and then apologized with his eyes. But it was she who spoke first.

"I'm sorry. I know you want to help. I don't know. I guess I'm just tired. I feel like this is never going to end."

"And when it does end, what then? I don't like your having given up school."

"Why? I'm getting an education right here. Besides, tuition is expensive."

"Bettina, stop that!" She sounded so bitter and there was suddenly something so jaded in her eyes. "I want you to promise me something."

"What's that?"

"I want you to promise me that when the worst of this is over, when you've taken care of the apartment, the furniture, whatever you have to do, you'll go away for a while, just to restore yourself and get some rest."

"You make it sound like I'm a hundred years old." And she didn't ask him how he thought she was going to pay for the trip. There was almost nothing anymore. She was cooking for herself in the vast kitchen, and she was not doing much else. She wasn't buying anything, going anywhere. In fact, just that morning, she had been thinking of selling her clothes. The evening clothes at least. She had two closets of them. But she knew that if she told Ivo, he'd have a fit.

"I mean it, I want you to go away somewhere. You need it. This has been an enormous strain. We both know that. If I could, I'd send you away right now, but I know that you have to be here. Will you promise me to think about it?"

"I'll see." She had survived Christmas by forgetting it entirely, and spent the holidays packing up her father's books. Somehow now she couldn't think of much else. The rare books were going to London, to auction, back whence they had come, and hopefully they would bring a good price. The appraiser said they were worth several hundred thousand dollars. She hoped he was right.

"What did Parke-Bernet tell you?" Now

Ivo looked tired too. He came by to see her almost every day, but he hated her news. Selling, packing, getting rid of, it was like watching her unravel her whole life.

"The sale will be in two months. They'll make space for it in the schedule. And they are very pleased with our things." She handed Ivo his usual Scotch and soda and sat down. "Can I interest you in some dinner?"

"You know, I'm very impressed with your cooking. I never knew you could cook."

"Neither did I. I'm discovering that there are a lot of things I can do. Speaking of which" — she smiled at him as he took a long swallow of his Scotch — "I've been wanting to ask you about something."

He smiled as he sat back against the couch. "What's that?"

"I need a job." The matter-of-fact way she said it almost made him wince.

"Now?"

"No, not this minute, but when I finish all this. What do you think?"

"At the *Mail*? Bettina, you don't want that." And then, after a moment, he nodded. At least he could do that much for her. "As my assistant?"

She laughed and shook her head, "No nepotism, Ivo. I mean a real job that I'm qualified for. Maybe a copy girl."

"Don't be ridiculous. I won't let you do that."

"Then I won't ask you for a job." She looked determined. And the agony of it struck him again and again. But the truth of it was that she would need a job. She had faced it, and he was going to have to face it too. "We'll see. Let me give it some thought. Maybe I can come up with a better idea than something at the *Mail.*"

"What? Marry a rich old man?" She said it in jest and they both laughed.

"Not unless you audition me first."

"You're not old enough. Now, how about dinner?"

"You're on."

They exchanged another smile, and she disappeared into the kitchen to put on some steaks. She quickly set the long refectory table that her father had brought back from Spain, and she set a vase of yellow flowers down on the deep-blue cloth. When Ivo wandered into the kitchen a few minutes later, everything was underway.

"You know, Bettina, you're going to spoil me. I'm getting used to stopping here every night on my way home. It beats the hell out of frozen dinners or sandwiches on stale bread."

She turned to laugh at him as he said it, pushing back her rich coppery locks with the back of one hand. "Ha! When did you ever eat a frozen dinner, Ivo Stewart? I'll bet you haven't eaten dinner at home once in ten years! Speaking of which, what's happened to your social life since you started to baby-sit for me? You never go out anymore, do you?"

He looked vague as he touched the bright flowers on the table. "I haven't had time. Things have been awfully busy at the office." And then, after a moment, he looked at her again. "And what about you? You haven't been out in a long time either." His voice was very gentle, and she turned away with a soft shake of her head.

"That's different. I couldn't . . . I can't. . . ." The only invitations were from her father's friends and she couldn't face them now. "I just can't."

"Why? Justin wasn't the kind of man to expect you to go into mourning, Bettina." Or was it something else? Was she embarrassed to face people now that the truth had come out in the papers? Was it that? They had been unable to hide the truth of Justin's finances from the press.

"I just don't want to, Ivo. I'd feel strange."

"Why?"

"I don't belong in that world anymore." She said it so forlornly that he walked to her side.

"What in hell do you mean?"

Her eyes filled with tears as she looked at him, and suddenly she looked young again.

"I'd feel like a fraud, Ivo. I . . . oh, Christ, Daddy's life was such a lie. And now everyone knows it. I know it. I don't have anything. I have no right to flounce around at fancy parties anymore or hang out with the illustrious and the elite. I just want to sell all this stuff, get out of here, and go to work."

"That's ridiculous, Bettina. Why? Because Justin ran into debt you're going to deprive yourself of the world you've lived in all your life? That's crazy, don't you know that?"

But she shook her head as she wiped her eyes with the tail of her shirt. "No, it's not crazy. Daddy didn't belong in that world either if he had to run into debt for four million dollars to stay there. He should have led a very different life." All the pain and disillusionment of the past weeks suddenly came out in her voice, but Ivo pulled her gently toward him and held her in the crook of one arm. It was like being a little girl again. For a moment, she almost wanted to crawl onto his lap.

"Now wait a minute, Justin Daniels was a brilliant author, Bettina. No one can ever take that away from him. He was one of the greatest minds of his time. And he had a right to be in all the places he was, with all the people he was. What he shouldn't have done was let his judgment get so insanely out of hand, but that is entirely another matter. He was a star, Bettina. A rare and special star, just as you are. Nothing will ever change that. No debt, no sin, no failure, no mistake. Nothing will change what he was, or what you are. Nothing. Do you understand?" She wasn't sure that she did, but she looked at him now with a look that blended confusion and pain.

"Why do you say I'm special too? Because I'm his daughter? Is that why? Because that's another thing that makes me feel I don't belong in that world anymore, Ivo. My father is gone. What right have I to go back to those people? Especially now, with absolutely nothing. I can't give them fabulous parties anymore, or wonderful introductions over lunch to the people they want to meet. I can't do anything, or give them anything . . . I have nothing. . . ." And then her voice caught on a sob. "I *am* nothing now."

Ivo's voice was sharp in her ears, and his

arm tight around her. "No, Bettina! You're wrong. You *are* something. You always will be, absolutely nothing will change that. And not because you're Justin's daughter, because you're *you.* Don't you realize how many people came here for you? To meet *you?* Not just him? You're something of a legend; you have been since you were a little girl, and you've never even realized it, which was part of your charm. But it's important that now you understand that *you* are Someone. *You.* Bettina Daniels. As a matter of fact I'm not going to accept this recluse act of yours anymore." He looked purposeful as he suddenly strode across the room and picked up a bottle of wine. He helped himself to two glasses, opened the bottle, poured the deep garnet-colored Bordeaux wine, and handed her a full glass. "I have just made a decision, Miss Daniels, and that's that. You are coming with me to dinner and the opera tomorrow night."

"I am? Oh, Ivo, no. . . ." She looked horrified. "I can't. Maybe later . . . some other time. . . ."

"No. Tomorrow." And then he smiled gently at her. "Child of mine, don't you realize what day tomorrow is?" She shook her head blankly as she took their steaks off the grill. "It's New Year's Eve. And no matter what else is happening, we are going to celebrate, you and I."

He held up his glass of wine. "The year of Bettina Daniels. It's time we realized that your life isn't over. Darling, it has just begun." She smiled slowly at him as she took the first sip of her wine.

6

Bettina stood in the darkened living room, watching the traffic honk its way impatiently down Fifth Avenue. Cars were crammed side by side and bumper to bumper as the festivities began. Horns blared, sirens whirred, people shouted, and somewhere in the night there was laughing too. But Bettina stood immeasurably still as she waited. It was a strange electrifying feeling, as though her whole life were about to begin again. Ivo was right. She shouldn't have stayed in by herself so much.

Perhaps her strange feelings were due to all the changes going on in her life. She was no longer a child. She was on her own. And she felt oddly grown-up in a way she never had before. Her adulthood was no longer borrowed; it was real.

The bell rang a few moments later, and suddenly all her grown-up feelings seemed silly. It was only Ivo after all, and what was so different about going to the opera with him? She ran to the door and let him in. He stood smiling on the doorstep, tall and handsome, and long and lean, the white mane dusted with snowflakes, and around his neck a rich, creamy silk scarf, which was in sharp contrast to the black cashmere coat he wore over tails. She stood back for a moment, smiling at him, and then clapped her hands together like a child as he stepped inside.

"Ivo, you look lovely!"

"Thank you, my dear, so do you." He smiled gently down at her as she bent her head gracefully in the monklike velvet hood of her midnight-blue coat.

"Are you ready?" She nodded in answer, and he crooked his arm. With a tiny smile she slipped her white-gloved hand into it and followed him back to the door. The house was eerily quiet. Gone the servants who would have held the door or taken Ivo's coat. Gone the polite bows, the instant service, the protection . . . from reality . . . from the world. For an instant Bettina stood very quietly as she hunted in her small navy silk evening bag for the key. And then she smiled up at Ivo as she found it and locked the door.

"Things have changed, haven't they?" She

looked wistful despite the bright smile. He only nodded, feeling her pain.

But she seemed more herself as they chatted, going down in the elevator, and then in his car. The driver urged the car patiently through the endless holiday traffic, and in the backseat Bettina made Ivo laugh with tales of the people she had met a few months before in school.

"And you mean you don't miss it?" He looked at her searchingly, his eyes growing sober. "How could you not?"

"Very easily." This time her eyes were serious too. "In fact not going there anymore is a relief." The look on his face said that he didn't understand her as she looked at him and then turned away. "The truth of it is, Ivo, that my father saw to it that I never saw people my own age. They're strangers to me now. I don't know what they talk about, what to say. They talk of things I don't even understand. I'm an outsider."

Listening to her, Ivo realized once again the high price she had paid for being Justin Daniels's daughter.

"But what does that leave you?" He looked troubled, but she laughed a silvery laugh in the darkened limousine. "I'm serious, Bettina, if you don't belong with people your own age, then whom do you belong with?"

She smiled gently up at him and whispered softly. "You." And then she looked away again and patted his hand. And for a moment an odd sensation ran through his entire body. He wasn't sure if it was excitement or fear. But it wasn't pity or regret. Certainly neither of those, and it should have been, he reproached himself. It should have been either, or both. He should have felt sorry for her, worried, concerned, not excited by her, as suddenly he undeniably was. But that was insanity. And worse than that, it was terribly wrong. He fought back what he was feeling and smiled at her while gently patting the gloved hand. There was a twinkle of mischief in his eyes when he spoke.

"You should be out playing with children your own age."

"I'll keep it in mind." And then after another pause, which brought them almost to the door of the Metropolitan Opera, she turned to him with a small smile. "Do you know, Ivo, this will be the first uninterrupted opera I'll have seen in years?"

"Are you serious?" He seemed surprised.

She nodded as she smoothed her gloves over her hands. "I used to dash out to the

Belmont Room to make sure they had everything ready for Daddy and his party. Then, invariably, there were messages. I had to check the supper reservations and make sure everything was right there. That usually wiped out the second half of the first act. During the second act he'd think of thirty-seven things he'd forgotten to tell me during the first act, which meant more calls, more messages. And then I never got to see the end of the third act because he wanted to leave early to avoid the crowd."

For a moment Ivo looked at her strangely. "Why did you do it?" Had she loved him that much?

"I did it because it was my life. Because it wasn't all organizing and arranging and servitude, as you seem to think now. It was special and exciting and glamorous, and —" Then she looked embarrassed. "It made me feel important, as though I mattered, as though without me he couldn't go on —" And then she faltered and looked away as Ivo's voice grew soft.

"That's probably true, you know, without you he couldn't have gone on. Certainly not as happily and comfortably and smoothly. But no human being deserves to be spoiled like that, Bettina. Certainly not at the expense of someone else."

The deep green eyes flashed emerald fire now. "It wasn't at my expense." And then in irritation as she reached for the door, she snapped at him. "You don't understand." But he did. He understood much more than he told her. Much more than she wanted him to know. He understood the loneliness and the pain of the life with her father. It hadn't been all glamor and Arabian nights. For her it had been sorrow and solitude as well.

"May I help you?" He reached out to assist her with the door handle and she turned to him with smoldering eyes, ready to say no, to push his hand away, to insist on doing it herself. It was a symbolic gesture, and he had to fight to keep the smile from his eyes. And then he couldn't resist laughing and reaching out a hand to rumple the soft caramel curls peeking out from her hood. "It might help if you unlock it, Miss Independence. Or would you rather just break out the window with your shoe and crawl through?"

And then suddenly she was laughing too as she pulled up the door lock and tried to glare at him, but the moment of anger was already gone. The chauffeur was waiting outside to assist them, and she sprang from the car to the street, smoothing her coat and pulling her hood up against the sharp wind.

Ivo held open the door of his box as they reached it and Bettina slipped inside. For a moment she was reminded of the evenings she had spent there with her father, but she forcefully swept aside the memories and looked into Ivo's blue eyes. He looked wonderful and alive and electric, and it felt good just to be looking into those blue eyes. She looked up at him candidly and patted his cheek gently, while he felt something tender inside him stir.

"I'm glad I came with you tonight, Ivo."

Everything stopped for a moment as he looked at her, and slowly he smiled. "So am I, little one. So am I." And then with chivalry and decorum he assisted her with her coat, and this time it was Bettina who smiled. She could still remember the first time he had done that for her, when she had come to the opera with him and her father more than ten years before. She had been wearing a burgundy-colored coat with a little velvet collar, and a hat to match, white gloves, and Mary Jane shoes. The opera bad been *Der Rosenkavalier,* and she had been horrified to see a woman dressed as a man. Ivo had explained it all to her, but she had still been greatly chagrined.

Suddenly, as she thought of it, she found herself laughing, while she slipped out of her dark-blue velvet evening coat and turned once again to face Ivo's eyes. "And may I ask what's so funny?" He looked warm and already amused.

"I was thinking of that first time I came here with you. Remember the woman 'trying to fake that she was a man'?" And suddenly at the memory Ivo was laughing with her, and then as the memory faded she saw something very different in his eyes. He was looking at the dress she was wearing, and as he did so the night of *Der Rosenkavalier* seemed to die in his mind. The dress that she had worn beneath the midnight-blue evening coat was of the same deep, deep blue, but it seemed to float about her in a cloud of chiffon; the long full sleeves cast a kind of dreamlike spell about her arms, and the tiny waist exploded into billows of soft flowing fabric that fell to her feet. She looked infinitely delicate and startlingly beautiful as she stood before him, her eyes as bright as the sapphires and diamonds in her ears. "Don't you like the dress?" She looked up at him innocently in barely concealed disappointment, and suddenly the laughter came back to his eyes as he reached out both arms. How young she still was in some ways. It always surprised him. It was difficult to understand how she had maintained a core of innocence beneath such a knowing veneer, and in spite of her constant exposure to men who couldn't possibly have escaped the kind of thoughts he was having now.

"I love the dress, darling. It's beautiful. I was just . . . a little taken aback."

"Were you?" She twinkled at him. "And think, you haven't even seen the half." And with that she pivoted neatly on one heel to turn her back to him, and in sharp contrast to the long sleeves, high neck, and full skirt, the back of the dress was cut away, and all that Ivo seemed to see dancing before him was the most devastatingly perfect expanse of creamy flesh.

"Good God, Bettina, that's not decent."

"Of course it is, don't be stupid. Let's go sit down. The music is starting."

Ivo sighed to himself as he sat there. He wasn't sure which image of her he should be addressing, which he should be holding to in his mind. The child he remembered or the woman sitting there. There were several things he could offer the child. He could make room for her in his home. But as a woman, the problem was a good deal more complicated. . . . What then? A job at the paper? An evening at the opera, as her friend? He could help her find an apartment . . . but then what? How would she pay? The problem was truly intolerable. When the first act came to an end, he realized how little of it he had heard.

"Ivo, isn't it marvelous?" Her eyes were still dreamy as the curtain fell.

"Yes, it's lovely." But he wasn't thinking of the opera, only of her. "Would you like something from the bar?" The others were already standing and forming a line at the exits. A trip to the bar was a must for all serious operagoers, not so much for what they drank, but whom they saw. But Ivo saw that she seemed to hesitate. "Would you rather stay here?" Gratefully she nodded, and they both sat back down.

"Do you mind terribly?" She was instantly apologetic, but Ivo waved a nonchalant hand.

"Of course not. Don't be silly. Would you like me to bring you something here?" But she only shook her head again and laughed.

"You're going to have me as spoiled as I had my father, Ivo. Watch out! It becomes damn hard to live with." They spoke of Justin briefly and then Ivo remembered the stories Justin had shown him. The stories Bettina had written.

"One day, if you want to, you can be an even greater writer than Justin."

"Do you mean that?" She stared at him, as though too terrified to breathe, waiting, wanting to hear his answer, and yet much too afraid. But he was nodding, and she let out a very small sigh.

"I do. Your last four or five stories. You know, the ones you wrote last summer in Greece . . . they're extraordinary, Bettina. You could publish them if you wanted to, in fact I was going to ask you sometime if that was what you had in mind." He looked at her seriously, and she gazed at him, stunned.

"Of course not. I just wrote them to — to write them. For no reason. Did Daddy show them to you?"

"Yes."

"Did he think they were good?" Her voice was dreamy and wistful now, and she seemed to have almost forgotten that Ivo was there. But he stared at her in astonishment.

"Didn't he tell you?" Gently she shook her head. "That's criminal, Bettina. He loved them. Didn't he ever say?"

"No." And then she looked at Ivo squarely. "But he wouldn't have actually. That kind of praise wasn't really his style." No, but hearing it was. Oh, yes, how he loved that,

Ivo thought.

Ivo was annoyed again as he thought of it. "Suffice it to say that he truly loved them."

She smiled carefully at Ivo again. "I'm glad."

Perhaps here was a way he could help her. "Are you going to try to publish them?"

"I don't know." She shrugged, suddenly childlike again. "I told you, I dream about writing a play. But that doesn't mean I will."

"It could if you wanted it to. One good strong dream is enough. If you hold it, and cherish it, and build on it. If you never give up that dream. No matter what." For a long time Bettina said nothing, and she averted her eyes. He moved a little closer, and she could feel him next to her, his hand just near hers where they sat. "Don't give up your dreams, Bettina . . . don't ever, ever do that."

When she looked up at him at last, it was with wise, tired eyes. "My dreams are already over, Ivo."

But he shook his head firmly, with the smallest of smiles. "No, little one, they've only just begun." And with that, he leaned forward and kissed her softly on the mouth.

7

It had been a strange and wonderful evening with Ivo. After the opera they had gone to dinner at La Côte Basque, and then they had gone dancing at Le Club. Ivo and her father had been members there since it had opened, but years later it was still a nice club and it was the perfect place to spend New Year's Eve. They had reverted to their old easy ways of friendship, only his kiss had confused her for a moment, but she pushed it from her mind. He was a very dear friend. For the most part it had been like old times. They talked and laughed and danced. They drank champagne and stayed on until three, when at last Ivo professed exhaustion and announced that he was taking her home. They were both oddly quiet in the limousine driving back to her apartment, Bettina thinking of her father and how odd it was not to have been with him, or at least called him to wish him a happy new year. They rode slowly up the East Side, until at last they reached her door.

"Do you want to come up for a cognac?" She said it almost by rote, between yawns, but it was very close to four in the morning, and Ivo laughed.

"You make it sound very tempting. Do you suppose you can stay awake long enough to get upstairs?" He helped her from the car and followed her inside.

"I'm not sure . . . mmm . . . all of a sudden I'm so sleepy. . . ." But she was smiling as they rode up in the elevator. "Sure you don't want another drink?"

"Positive."

And then she grinned at him. "Good. I want to go to bed." And as she said it she looked twelve years old again, and they both laughed.

The house was eerily empty as she turned her key and flicked on the light as she opened the door.

"Aren't you afraid to be alone here, Bettina?"

She looked at him honestly and nodded. "Sometimes."

His heart ached again as he looked at her. "Will you make me a promise? If you ever, ever have a problem, you'll call. And I mean immediately. I'd come right over."

"I know you would. It's a nice feeling." She yawned again, sat down on a Louis XV chair in the hall, and kicked off her elegant navy-blue satin shoes. He sat down on a chair facing her, and they both smiled.

"You look beautiful tonight, Bettina. And terribly, terribly grown up."

She shrugged, looking much like the young girl she was. "I suppose I am grown-up now." And then with a chortle she tossed one of the navy satin shoes in the air. She caught it again, barely missing a priceless vase that sat on a little marble ledge. "You know the weirdest thing of all, Ivo?"

"What?"

"I mean aside from the loneliness, it's being responsible for me. There is no one, absolutely no one, to tell me what to do, to give me hell, to give me praise, to figure things out for me . . . none of it. . . . If I had just broken that vase, it would have been my problem, no one else's. That's a lonely feeling sometimes too. Like no one gives a damn." She looked pensively at her shoe, and then dropped it to the floor again, but Ivo was watching her intently.

"I give a damn."

"I know you do. And I care about you too."

He said nothing in answer for a moment. He just watched her. "I'm glad." Then he stood up and wandered slowly over to where she sat. "And now, contrary to your theory, I'm going to tell you to go to bed, like a good girl. Shall I walk you upstairs to your room?" She hesitated for a long moment, and then she smiled.

"You wouldn't mind?"

He looked oddly serious when he shook his head. She walked toward the stairs in bare feet, her shoes lying forgotten on the foyer floor, and threw her blue velvet coat over her arm, as Ivo followed the naked oval of her back up to her bedroom. But he was in control now. In the course of the evening he had decided what he was going to do. She turned to look over her shoulder at him when they reached the top of the stairs.

"Are you going to tuck me into bed?" She was half teasing and half serious, and he wasn't quite sure what else he saw in her big green eyes. But he wasn't going to ask questions.

She ran a hand tiredly over her eyes, and she suddenly seemed very old. "There's so much I have to do, Ivo. Sometimes I'm not sure how I'm going to do it all." But as she said it he patted her shoulder, and she looked up at him, smiling.

"You will, darling. You will. But what you need first, mademoiselle, is a good night's sleep. So good night, little one. I'll let myself out." She heard him walk softly down the carpeted hall, and then there was silence as she knew he had reached the stairs, and at last she heard his heels click on the marble floor below, and he called out "Good night" for the last time before he closed the front door.

8

Bettina followed the woman upstairs and down, smiling pleasantly, opening closet doors, and standing by as the real estate agent extolled the apartment's virtues and then unabashedly indicated its flaws. Bettina didn't have to be there for the performance, but she wanted to be. She wanted to know what they were saying about her home.

At last it was over, after almost an hour, and Naomi Liebson, who had been there three times that month, prepared to leave. There had been other visitors as well, with other realtors, but so far this was the most definite bite.

"Aahh just don't know, honey. Aahhm not really, really sure." Bettina tried to smile again as she watched her, but the charm of showing the apartment was beginning to wear thin. It was exhausting escorting this army of would-be buyers through the place every day. And there was no one to relieve the tension for her. Ivo had been in Europe on business for three weeks. There had been an international conference in China, and as it had been the first of its kind, he had to go. After which he had business appointments in Europe: Brussels, Amsterdam, Rome, Milan, London, Glasgow, Berlin, and Paris. It was going to be a long trip. And it already felt as though he had been gone for years.

"Miss Daniels?" The real estate agent dragged her back from her reverie with a touch on the arm.

"I'm sorry. . . . I was dreaming. . . . Was there something else?" Naomi Liebson had apparently disappeared into the kitchen again. She wanted to look again, to try to envision how it would look if they broke through two walls. From the sound of what she'd been saying, she was going to gut the place anyway, upstairs and down. It made Bettina wonder why she didn't buy something more to her liking, but apparently this was what she did for fun. She had performed similar mutilation on five co-ops in as many years. But then she sold them again at enormous profits, so maybe she wasn't so crazy after all. Bettina looked curiously at the realtor, and then smiled. "Think she'll buy it?"

The realtor shrugged. "I don't know. I'm bringing two more people by later today. I don't think they're right for it though. It's too big for them, and one couple is elderly, and you've got too many stairs."

"Then why bring them?" Bettina looked at her with fatigue beginning to pull down the corners of her delicate mouth. But she hadn't been able to resist asking. Why did they all come? There were people who wanted more bedrooms, older people who didn't want stairs, large families who needed more servants' rooms than even she had; there had been people for whom the apartment could never have been right, yet the realtors continued to come in droves, showing the place off to only a handful for whom the place made some sense. It seemed like a monstrous waste of time, but it was all part of the game.

And then of course it was Justin Daniels's apartment, and that was always worth a thrill. . . . "Why are they selling? . . ." Again and again Bettina had heard the whispers. And then the answer, "He died and left the daughter flat broke. . . ." The first time she had cringed when she heard it, and angry tears of indignation had stung her eyes. . . . *How dare they! How could they?* But they dared and they could. And it didn't matter anymore. She just wanted to sell the place and get out. Ivo was right, it was too big and too lonely, and now and then she had been scared. But the worst of it was that she couldn't afford it, and each month when the gargantuan maintenance was due, she trembled as she depleted her dwindling funds still more. It was high time that someone bought it. Naomi Liebson or whoever else.

The other houses had all sold after the first of the year. The one in Beverly Hills brought a windfall a few weeks before. The young man from the Middle East had bought it, lock, stock, and barrel, with carpets, dressers, eighteenth-century mirrors, modern paintings, and all. The place had always been an odd mélange of the extremely showy and the very refined and Bettina had never liked it as much as the apartment in New York. It barely hurt at all to sign the papers. Now all that remained abroad was the flat in London, but according to Ivo that was almost empty now. He had called from over there. Her father's London solicitor had also assured her that he had someone to buy the place. He would let her know at the end of the week. Which left only the co-operative apartment on Fifth Avenue in New York. Even that wasn't going to look the same in another two weeks. She sighed to herself again as she thought of the auction. They had moved the date up, as a favor. And in ten days Parke-Bernet was arriving to take it all. Literally everything. She had spent the three weeks of Ivo's absence going over each table, each bookcase, each chair. In the end she knew she could hang on to nothing, only a few mementos, some small objects that had no value, but meant something to her.

But other than that there would be nothing left that was hers after the auction, and she hoped to have sold the apartment by then. Camping out in the empty apartment would be more than she could bear.

The agent looked at her curiously as they both stood patiently, waiting for Mrs. Liebson to return. It was unusual for a seller to help show the apartment, but then again Bettina was an unusual girl.

"Have you found anything else yet?" She eyed Bettina with interest. Hell, Naomi thought, even if Bettina were broke, after they sold this palazzo, she could buy herself something small and pretty, maybe a studio, or a little one-bedroom penthouse overlooking the park. That wouldn't cost her more than 100 thou. The woman didn't realize that it was going to take every dime from the sale of the large apartment, as well as all the profits from the auction, to put her father's estate in the black.

Bettina only shook her head. "I'm not looking yet. I don't want to start until I sell this."

"That's all wrong. You know how it is when you sell. The buyer drags his feet for three weeks, and then suddenly bango, they buy it, and they want you out overnight."

Bettina attempted a smile, but it was bleak. She was planning on moving to the Barbizon Hotel for Women at Lexington Avenue and Sixty-third, read *The New York Times* every day and of course the *Mail,* and hoped to find herself an apartment to rent in a matter of days, or maybe even weeks. She was even willing to share, if she had to. And then after that she would look for a job. She had decided not to discuss it with Ivo again. He would just set her up in a fancy office for a salary she didn't deserve and she didn't want that. She wanted to earn her living. She had to find a real job. The prospect of it almost crushed her with exhaustion as Mrs. Liebson returned.

"Aahh just don't know what I'm goin' to do with that kitchen. Honey, it's a mess." She looked reproachfully at Bettina, while still managing a broad smile. She looked at the realtor then and nodded, and with barely a good-bye they left. Bettina stood there for a moment, hating them both, as she softly closed the door. She didn't give a damn if the woman bought the apartment. She didn't want her to have it anyway. She didn't want her touching the kitchen, or anything else. It was *her* home, and her father's, theirs; it didn't belong to anyone else.

She sat down slowly in the winter twilight and stared around her and then down at the richly inlaid floor. How could he do this to her? How could he have left her in this god-awful mess? Didn't he understand what he was doing? Couldn't he have known? The resentment for her father rose up slowly in her throat like bile, and she let the tears start to flow. They were tears of anger and exhaustion, and her shoulders began to shake as she dropped her face in her hands and started to sob. It seemed hours later when she finally heard the phone. She let it ring for a while, but it was persistent, so at last she stood up and crossed the hall to the discreet closet in the entry where it was concealed. She was just getting used to having to answer the phone herself no matter how rotten she felt. Gone were the days of glory, she thought as she wiped her eyes with a handkerchief and sniffed.

"Hello?"

"Bettina?"

"Yes?" She could barely hear the muffled male voice.

"Are you all right, darling? It's Ivo. Is this a good time to call?" Her face lit up as she heard him and she suddenly had to brush away fresh tears.

"Oh, is it!"

"What? I can't hear you, darling, speak up! Are you all right?"

"I'm fine." And then suddenly she wanted to tell him the truth, all of it. . . . *No, I'm lonely, I'm miserable. . . . In a few weeks I won't have a home.*

"What's happening with the apartment? Have you sold it?"

"Not yet."

"All right. Well, we've sold London. The deal closed tonight." He quoted a figure. It was enough to make a healthy inroad in her debts.

"That ought to help. How's your trip going?"

"It seems endless." She smiled into the phone.

"It certainly does. When are you coming home?" She hadn't realized how anxious she was to see him.

"I don't know. I should really have come back days ago, but I got involved in some special meetings over here. I may have to delay it a bit." She felt herself pouting and didn't give a damn if she sounded like a little girl. She could do that with him. He understood.

"How long?"

"Well" — he seemed to hesitate — "I've just arranged to stay for another two weeks."

"Oh, Ivo!" He had been gone since two days after their New Year's Eve date. "That's awful!"

"I know, I know. I'm sorry. I'll make it up to you when I get back, I promise."

"Will you be back in time for the sale?"

"What sale?"

"The auction."

"When is it? I thought it wasn't for a while."

"They moved it up for me. It's two weeks from tomorrow. Friday and Saturday. And it's only Daddy's stuff. It's all of it."

"And what about you, for God's sake? You go off into the world with one suitcase and your name?"

"Hardly. You haven't seen my closets. It'll take more than one suitcase." At last she smiled.

"You can't give everything up. What the

hell are you going to do? Sleep on the floor?"

"I checked into it and I can rent a bed. It's either that or wait another year for Parke-Bernet to have another date to schedule the sale. And then what? What if this place sells? I'd have to pay storage for the furniture. . . . Never mind, Ivo, it's too complicated. It has to be like this."

"For God's sake, Bettina, I wish you'd waited for me to come back before you got into all this." He sounded distraught and he was looking around his hotel room with dismay. There wasn't a great deal he could do to stop her from three thousand miles away, and the fact was that she was right to do what she was doing. He just hated to have her face it all alone. But she was good at it. All her life, in a way, Bettina had faced the difficult moments alone.

"Anyway, don't worry about it, Ivo, it's all under control. I just miss you like crazy."

"I'll be back soon." He checked his calendar and gave her the exact date of his return.

"What time are you coming in?"

"I'm taking a seven A.M. flight out of Paris, which should get me into New York at nine in the morning, New York time. I'll be in the city by about ten." She had wanted to surprise him by being at the airport, but she suddenly realized that there was no way she could. "Why?"

"Never mind. That's the day of the Parke-Bernet sale."

"What time does it start?"

"Ten o'clock in the morning."

He made a note on his calendar. "I'll meet you there."

Suddenly Bettina was smiling. Unlike her father, Ivo never let her down. "Are you sure you can do that? Don't you have to go to work?"

This time he smiled at her as he held the phone. "After five weeks, one day can hardly make that much difference. I'll be there as early as I can. And I'll call you long before that, little one. Now you're sure you're all right?" But how all right could she be with realtors crawling all over her apartment and all her belongings about to be sold at auction by Parke-Bernet?

"I'm fine. Honest."

"I don't like your being there all alone."

"I told you. I'm all right."

They spoke a few minutes more. Then it was time for him to go.

"I'll call you. Bettina —" There was a strange, empty pause as he hesitated, and she held her breath.

"Yes?"

"Never mind, little one. Take care."

9

The phone rang the next morning before Bettina had gotten out of bed. It was the real estate agent. Five minutes later Bettina sat up in her bed with a look of dismay.

"For God's sake, this is very good news!" The real estate woman spoke to her in obvious irritation, and Bettina nodded. It was good news. But it still came as a shock. She had just lost her home. For a handsome price. But still, it was gone. The moment had come.

"I suppose it is. I just . . . I hadn't . . . I didn't expect it to happen so quickly. When will she . . . how soon —" She couldn't find her words and suddenly she hated the woman from Texas. She was buying the co-op. And for a sum that should have made Bettina squeal with delight. But she didn't feel like squealing. The agent talked on while Bettina's eyes filled with tears.

"Shall we say we'll close two weeks from

tomorrow? That will give you both two full weeks to get organized."

The arrangements made, Bettina hung up, sitting in silence in her bedroom, looking around her as though for the last time.

She spent the next week alternately packing and stopping to dry her tears. And at last on Wednesday they arrived to remove the countless priceless pieces to the hallowed halls of Parke-Bernet. It was the same day she went to her attorney to finalize the sale of the apartment. She didn't even bother calling to rent a bed. She uncovered an old sleeping bag she had bought years before and slept on the floor of her room. It was only for three nights; she could have moved to the hotel early, but she didn't want to. She wanted to stay there until the end.

The day of the sale at Parke-Bernet she woke up early. She began to stir as the first light of dawn crept across the floor. She didn't even bother to close the curtains anymore. She liked waking up early and sitting cross-legged with her coffee on the thick carpeting in her room.

But this morning she was even too nervous for coffee, and she paced catlike about the house in her nightgown and bare feet. If she closed her eyes, she could still see the apartment as it had been only last week. With her eyes open, it was strangely barren, and the parquet floors cold beneath her feet. She went hastily back to her room shortly after seven and tore through her closet for almost an hour. This wasn't a day for blue jeans. She wasn't going to wear work clothes or hide in a back row. She was going to walk in proudly and hold her head high. For this one last time she was going on view as Justin Daniels's daughter, and she was going to look fabulous. As though nothing had changed.

She emerged at last with a striking black wool Dior suit with padded shoulders, a cinched waist, and a long narrow skirt. Her hair would look like flame atop a black candle. And the jacket buttoned high in a mandarin collar. She didn't need a blouse. She would wear her mink over it, and on her feet, high-heeled black kid Dior shoes.

She bathed in the pink marble bathroom for the last time and emerged smelling faintly of gardenias and roses. She brushed her hair until it shone like dark honey, put on her makeup, and slowly got dressed. When she stood in front of the mirror, she was proud of what she saw. No one would have guessed that she was only a nineteen-year-old girl who had just lost everything she owned.

The auction room was already crowded with row after row of dealers, collectors, gawkers, buyers, and old friends. All conversation stopped as she entered the room. Two men jumped forward and snapped her picture, but Bettina didn't even flinch. She walked regally to one of the first rows, almost in front of a spotter, and threw her mink coat easily over the back of her chair. Her eyes weren't smiling, and she acknowledged none of those who tried to get her attention. She was a startling vision in black, with her copper hair, and her only jewelry was a long strand of her mother's large, perfect pearls. In her ears she wore matching earrings, and on her hands, a single onyx and pearl ring. The only thing she hadn't sold in the three months since her father had died were her jewels. Ivo had assured her that she would be able to hang on to them and still clean up the debts, and he was right.

The stage was directly in front of her where she knew she would be able to see the old familiar items appear as they were auctioned. Paintings, couches, end tables, lamps. And in the corners and along the sides of the room she could already see a few pieces, the pieces that would have been too large to carry on and off the stage, highboys, enormous sideboards, his bookcase, and two very large standing clocks. Most of it Louis XV, some Louis XVI, some English, all rare, many signed, it was going to be what the catalog called an "important" sale, but that was only fitting, Bettina thought to herself, Justin Daniels had been an important man. And she felt important again now, as she sat there, because this one last time she was there as his daughter, not simply herself.

The bidding began at exactly seven minutes past ten, and Ivo had not yet arrived. Bettina looked at the plain Cartier watch on her left wrist, and then let her eyes wander back to the man at the podium, the spotters, and the huge inlaid Louis XV chest with the marble slab on top of it, which they had just auctioned off for twenty-two thousand five. The circular platform on the stage slowly turned lazy-Susan style and another familiar item was revealed. It was the large ornate seventeenth-century mirror from their front hall.

"The bidding is open at two thousand five . . . two thousand five . . . three, I have three . . . four . . . five . . . six . . . seven . . . seven five on the left . . . eight! . . . Nine at the front of the room . . . nine five . . . ten in the rear! . . . Ten . . . ten . . . do I have . . . eleven! . . . Eleven five . . . and twelve . . . twelve at the front of the room." And with that he clicked the hammer down. It was all over in less than a minute. It went with lightning speed, and the action was all but invisible. Fingers barely moved, hands were barely raised, there were nods, signals of the eye, the slightest gesture of a pen, a hand, and the spotters were trained to see it all and report it rapidly to the auctioneer, but it was rare that the spectators could see who was doing the bidding. Bettina had no idea at all who had just bought the large antique mirror. She made a notation in her catalog and settled back in her chair to watch the next item.

There were two beautiful French bergère chairs, upholstered in delicate café-au-lait silks, that had been in her father's bedroom. There was also a matching chaise longue similarly upholstered, which was the next item in the catalog. Bettina, with pen poised and waiting for the bidding to begin, felt someone slide into the empty seat beside her. Then she heard a familiar voice in her ear.

"Do you want those?" His eyes looked tired and his voice sounded grim. As she turned to see Ivo the funereal air of intensity of the hour before momentarily fled.

She put her arms around his neck for a moment and held him close. Slowly his face broke into a smile. She pulled away from him briefly and whispered in his ear. "Welcome home, stranger. I'm so glad you could come."

He nodded and then, sobering, repeated his first question. The bidding was already at nine thousand five. "Do you want them?" But she only shook her head. And then, leaning closer to her again, he gently took her hand. "I want you to tell me what you want from all this. Anything that means something to you, tell me. I'll buy it and keep it for you at my place. You can pay me later if you want to and I don't give a damn if that means in twenty years. . . ." And then he smiled and leaned toward her again. "If I'm still around to collect it, which I doubt." He knew how proud she was and that he had to make the offer as he did.

She whispered again as they closed the bidding at thirteen and a half for the two chairs. "You damn well better be around, Ivo."

"At eighty-two? For God's sake, Bettina, give me a break." They looked at each other as though they had seen each other every day for the past month. It was difficult to believe, suddenly, that he'd been gone for five weeks. "Are you all right?"

She nodded slowly. "I'm fine. Are you exhausted from the flight?" A couple in front of them shushed them, and Ivo glared malevolently at the pair. And then he turned to Bettina with a tired smile.

"It was a long flight. But I didn't want you to be here alone. How long will this go on today? All day?" He prayed that it wouldn't, he needed a few hours sleep.

"Just till lunch. And tomorrow morning and afternoon." He nodded and turned his attention to what was being shown on the stage. Bettina had grown strangely quiet, and Ivo squeezed her hand. It was Justin's desk.

Ivo leaned quietly toward her and spoke once again in her ear. "Bettina?" But she shook her head and looked away.

"Seven thousand . . . seven . . . eight? Seven five! . . . Eight! . . . Eight . . . Nine! . . ." It went for nine thousand dollars, and Bettina supposed that to an antique dealer it was worth the price. It was worth more than that to her though. It had been the desk where her father worked, where he had written his last two books, where she had seen him again and again, poring over manuscripts. . . . Her mind drifted painfully into the past, but Ivo was watching her and still holding tightly to her hand.

"Relax, little one. . . . It's still yours." He spoke infinitely gently, and she looked up at him in confusion.

"I don't understand."

"You don't have to. We can discuss it later."

"Did you buy it?" She looked at him, stunned, and wanting to laugh for a moment, he nodded.

"Don't look so surprised."

"For nine thousand dollars?" She looked horrified, and someone behind them told her to lower her voice. Thousands of dollars were being bandied about between bidders, this was no time for distractions from the audience. This was a serious crowd. Like gamblers, they paid attention to what they were doing and little else. But Bettina was still staring at Ivo in astonishment. "Ivo, you didn't!" This time she whispered more softly, and he smiled.

"I did." And then he cast an eye toward the stage again and raised an eyebrow questioningly. It was another desk. He leaned toward her again. "Where was that?"

"In the guest room, but it's not a good one. Don't buy it." She looked at him seriously, wondering just how many pieces he was planning to buy, and he watched her, amused.

"Thanks for the advice." Apparently the dealers and collectors shared her sentiments about the piece. It went for only eighteen hundred dollars. By that day's standards it was cheap.

The proceedings seemed to go on for hours, but Bettina didn't let him buy anything more. At last it was over. At least for the day. It was five minutes to twelve. They stood up as the rest of the crowd got up to leave, clutching their catalogs and discussing the bidding with friends. She realized Ivo was staring at her. It made her feel warm inside, though slightly uncomfortable.

"What are you looking at?"

"I'm looking at you, little one. Because it's so good to see you." His voice was like velvet on the words. And she wanted to tell him that she missed him, but instead, with a faint blush on her cheeks, she bowed her head.

As he watched, a shadow darted into her eyes. Now what was wrong? There was something different about her already. Once again something had changed since he had been gone. But he wasn't sure what this time and he wasn't sure he liked what it was.

He looked at her very seriously. "Will you come home with me, Bettina, for lunch?" She hesitated for a long moment, and then she nodded.

"That would be nice."

He beckoned to his driver, who was waiting, and a moment later they sped away toward his apartment, twelve blocks south of hers, on Park Avenue. It was comfortable there. It was far less grandiose, but filled with lovely things that looked inviting and warm. There were big leather chairs and soft couches, paintings of hunting scenes, and bookcases filled with rare books; there was lots of brass around the fireplace, and the windows were large and inundated with sun. It was clearly a man's apartment, yet it was friendly and cozy and would have been large enough for more than just him. Downstairs he had a living room, dining room, and library. Upstairs he had two bedrooms and his private den. There was also a spacious wood-paneled country kitchen. Behind it there would have been room for two maids, but he only kept one. His driver lived elsewhere and was actually employed by the *Mail.* Bettina had always liked coming to his apartment. It was like going to someone's house in the country, or like visiting a favorite uncle in his lair. Everything smelled of tobacco and cologne and fine leather. She liked the feel of his things, their texture, and their smell.

Bettina looked around her with a feeling of homecoming as they walked into the sunny living room and he checked back over his shoulder. She looked better again, and for a moment the look of terror seemed to have fled. "It's nice to be back here, Ivo. I always forget how pretty it is."

"That's because you don't come here often enough."

"That's only because you don't ask me." She was teasing now, and happy, as she plunked herself down on the couch.

"If that's all that keeps you away from here, I will ask! And often!" He smiled and tried not to glance at the mountain of mail. "Oh, God, will you look at that, Bettina. . . ."

"I was trying not to. It reminds me of my father's after he'd been away for a few days."

"And this is nothing. I'm sure it's worse at the office." He ran a hand across his eyes and then walked into the kitchen. Mathilde seemed to have mysteriously disappeared. He had expected her to be waiting.

"Where's Mattie?" Bettina reflected his

thought. She had called her that since she was a very small child.

"I don't know. Can I offer you a sandwich? I'm starved."

She looked at him sheepishly. "So am I. I was so nervous during the bidding, and now suddenly I'm ravenous." And then she remembered. "Speaking of which, Ivo . . . what about that desk?" She looked at him pointedly, but there was something far softer in her eyes.

"What desk?" He looked nonchalant as he headed for the kitchen. "I hope there's at least something to eat."

"Knowing Mattie, enough for an army. But you didn't answer my question, Ivo. What about the desk?"

"What about it? It's yours."

"No, it was Daddy's. Now it's yours. Why don't you keep it? He'd like you to have it, you know." She looked at him gently once they arrived in the kitchen, and he reached into the fridge and turned his back.

"Never mind that, you can write your play on that desk. Let's not discuss it." It was still too soon to talk to her about what he had in mind.

She sighed. They would have to discuss it another time. "Why don't you let me make the lunch?"

He couldn't resist stretching out a hand to rumple her hair. His voice was hoarse but gentle when he spoke again. "You look very pretty today, little one . . . in your black suit."

She said nothing for a long moment, and then she walked past him, preparing to make lunch. His eyes never left her, and when her back was turned, he finally asked. "What is it that you're not telling me, Bettina? I get the feeling there's something you have on your mind." He felt stupid once he had said it. Every stick of furniture her father had owned was being sold at auction, it was natural that she should be disturbed. Yet he had the feeling that there was more than that. He had seen something even more painful in her eyes. "Is there something you're not telling me?"

"I've sold the apartment."

"What? Already?" Bettina nodded mutely. "And when does the new owner take possession?"

Bettina looked away and tried to catch her breath. "Tomorrow. I said I'd be out by tomorrow afternoon. As a matter of fact it's in the contract."

"And who was the fool who let you do that?" Ivo looked at her ominously and then held out his arms. "Never mind who, I can guess. It was your father's idiot lawyer. Oh, Christ." And then all she knew was that he was holding her and it didn't quite feel as though the world had come to an end. "Oh, baby . . . poor baby . . . all the furniture and now the whole place. Oh, God, it must feel awful." He held her and swayed softly, and in his arms she felt suddenly safe.

"It does, Ivo . . . it does . . . I feel. . . ." And then the tears suddenly crowded into her eyes. "I feel as though . . . they're taking away . . . everything . . . as though there's . . . nothing left. Just me, alone in the apartment . . . it's already over . . . there is no more past . . . and I have nothing, Ivo . . . nothing at all. . . ." She was sobbing in his arms as she said it, and he only held her tight.

"It'll be different one day, Bettina. One day, you'll look back at all this and it will seem like a dream. A dream that happened to somebody else. It will fade, darling . . . it will fade." But how he wished he could make it fade quickly and make her pain disappear. He had already made a decision before he left for London, but he wondered if this was the right time. He waited until she was quieter before he asked her any questions, but then he brought her into the living room and sat her down next to him on the couch. "What are you going to do tomorrow, Bettina, when you move out?"

She took a deep breath and looked at him. "Go to a hotel."

"What about tonight?"

"I want to sleep there."

"Why?"

She started to say Because it's my home, but it sounded ridiculous, it was only an empty apartment. It wasn't anyone's home anymore. "I don't know. Maybe because it's my last chance."

He looked at her kindly. "But that doesn't make much sense, does it? You've lived there, you've collected all the good memories it had to give. And now it's all gone, it's empty, like an empty tube of toothpaste, all squeezed out. There's no point keeping it a moment longer, is there?" And then, after only an instant, he looked at her more deeply. "I think it would make a lot of sense if you moved out today."

"Now?" She looked startled, and once again like a frightened child. "Tonight?" She stared at him blankly and he nodded.

"Yes. Tonight."

"Why?"

"Trust me."

"But I don't have a reservation. . . ." She was clutching at straws.

"Bettina, I've been waiting to ask you this, but I'd like you to stay here."

"With you?" She looked startled, and he laughed.

"Not exactly. I'm not a masher after all, darling. In the guest room. How does that sound?" But nothing had really registered. Suddenly she felt very confused.

"I don't know . . . I suppose I could . . . just for tonight."

"No, that wasn't what I had in mind. I'd like you to stay until you get settled, till you find a nice place of your own. Something decent," he admonished gently, "and the right job. Mattie could take care of you. And I'd feel a lot better if I knew you were safe here. I don't think your father would have objected. In fact I'd say it was what he'd have liked best. Now" — he watched her eyes carefully — "what about you?"

But her eyes were filling slowly with tears. "I can't, Ivo." She shook her head and looked away. "You've been too good to me already, and I could never pay you back. Just today . . . the desk . . . I can't ever —"

"Shh . . . never mind. . . ." He took her in his arms again and gently stroked her hair. "It's all right." And then he pulled away to look at her and tried to coax her to smile. "Besides, if you're going to cry all the time, you can't stay at a hotel. They'd throw you out for making too much noise."

"I don't cry all the time!" She sniffed and accepted his handkerchief to blow her nose.

"I know that. In fact you've been unbelievably brave. But what I don't want you to be is foolish. Going to a hotel would be foolish." And then more firmly he added, "Bettina, I want you to stay here. Is that so awful? Would you really hate it, being here with me?" But all she could do was shake her head. She wouldn't hate it. In fact that was one of the things that frightened her most. She wanted to be there with him. Maybe even a little too much.

For a moment she wavered, and then sighed again as she blew her nose. And then at last she let her eyes find his. He was right. It did make more sense than going to a hotel. If she just didn't feel like that . . . if he weren't so damn good-looking in spite of his age. She had to keep reminding herself that he wasn't forty-seven or even fifty-two . . . he was sixty-two . . . sixty-two . . . and her father's very dearest friend . . . it was almost like incest . . . she couldn't let herself feel that way.

"Well?" He turned to look at her from where he stood at the bar while he was reproaching himself for thoughts similar to hers.

She sounded almost breathless as she answered. "I'll do it. I'll stay."

Their eyes met and they smiled. It was an end and a beginning, and a promise, and the birth of hope. For them both.

By Saturday it was over. They had to go back to the apartment, to pick up the last of her stuff. She had spent the night before in Ivo's guest room, catered to and pampered by the jovial and warmhearted Mathilde, who had prepared their dinner and in the morning brought Bettina a tray. Ivo was glad to be able to restore her to comfort again. It had to be a relief from the emptiness of the apartment she had hung on to almost till the end.

"I told Mrs. Liebson I'd be out by six." Bettina looked at her watch nervously, and Ivo took her arm.

"Don't worry, we have time." He knew how little she had left there. He had gone over with her the night before to pick up one of her bags. And his heart had ached for her when he saw the sleeping bag stretched out on the floor. Now it was a question of a dozen suitcases, two or three boxes, and that was all. He had assured her that there was room in his storeroom and Mathilde had already cleared two closets for her. It would be more than enough.

As usual Ivo's driver was waiting, and he sped them quickly over to Fifth and was rapidly at Bettina's door. She clambered out quickly, and Ivo was hard on her heels. She looked up at him questioningly. "Do you really want to come up?"

He realized with a flash of understanding what was on her mind. "Do you want to be alone?"

Her eyes wavered as she answered. "I'm not sure."

He nodded softly. "Then I'll come." And she looked somehow relieved.

Two porters were summoned, and a few moments later they all stood in the empty front hall. There were no lights lit and it was dark outside. Ivo watched her as she stared bleakly past the front hall.

She glanced hurriedly over her shoulder at Ivo, and then at the two men. "Everything is upstairs in the front bedroom. I'll be right back, I want to check around." But this time Ivo didn't follow her. He knew she wanted to be alone. The two men scurried off to get her things, and he lingered in the hallway, listening to her footsteps as she wandered from room to room, pretending that she was checking to see if anything had been forgotten or mislaid. But it was memories she was collecting, moments with her father that she wanted to touch for one last time.

"Bettina?" Ivo called out softly. He hadn't heard her heels in a long time. But at last he found her, standing tiny and forgotten in her father's bedroom, with tears streaming from her eyes.

He went to her, and she held him, whispering softly into his arms. "I will never be back here again." It seemed hard to believe. It was over. But it had been for a while.

Ivo held her gently. "No, little one, you won't. But there will be other places, other people, who may one day mean almost as much to you as this."

She shook her head slowly. "Nothing ever will."

"I hope you're wrong. I hope that — that there are other men you love at least as much as him." And then he smiled down at her very gently. "At least one." Bettina didn't respond.

"He didn't leave you, little one. I hope you know that. He simply moved on."

That seemed to reach her, and suddenly she turned around and walked solemnly from the room. She paused in the doorway and held out her hand. He put an arm around her shoulders and walked her to the front door, which she locked for the last time, and slipped her key under the door.

10

The sun was streaming in the dining room windows as Mathilde poured Bettina a second cup of coffee. She had been intently studying the newspaper, and suddenly she looked up with a smile.

"Thank you, Mattie." The month of living at Ivo's had been restful for her. It had helped heal the wounds. Ivo had made everything easy. She had a beautiful little room, three meals a day of Mathilde's excellent cooking. She had all the books she wanted to read. She joined him in the evening to go to operas, or concerts, or plays. It was not unlike living with her father, yet in many ways it was a far more peaceful way of life. Ivo was a good deal less erratic, and his every thought seemed to center around her. He had spent the last month with her, almost every evening, going out to interesting places or sitting home by the fire and talking for hours. On Sundays they did the *Times* crossword puzzle together and went for walks in the park. It was March and the city was still cold and gray, but now and then the air smelled of spring.

He looked over his paper at her now with a smile. "You look embarrassingly cheerful this morning, Bettina. Any reason for it, or were you still thinking about last night?" They had gone to the opening of a new play and they had both loved it. Bettina had talked passionately of it all the way home. Ivo assured her that one day she would write something even better than that. And now she was smiling at him, with her head tilted to one side. She had been reading *Backstage,* the little weekly theatrical paper she had to travel halfway across town to buy.

"There's an ad in here, Ivo." Her eyes were full of meaning and he gave her his full attention.

"Is there? What kind of ad?"

"There's a new repertory group forming, off Broadway."

"How far off Broadway?" He was instantly suspicious. And when she gave him the address, he was more so. "Isn't that a little remote?" It was a grim neighborhood near the Bowery. One which Bettina had never even seen.

"What difference does that make? They're looking for people, actors, actresses, and technical people, all nonequity. Maybe they'd give me a chance."

"At doing what?" He felt dread crawl up his spine. He had been afraid of something like this. Twice he had reiterated his offer of a job at the paper, something nice, decent, and slightly overpaid. And both times she had refused. The last time with such vehemence that he no longer dared to mention the offer.

"Maybe I could get some kind of technical job, helping set up the scenery, working the curtain. Anything. I don't know. It would be a terrific opportunity to see how the inside of a theater works . . . you know, for when I write my play."

For an instant he almost smiled. She was so incredibly childish at times. "Don't you think you'd learn more just going to see the successful shows on Broadway, like last night?"

"That's different. It doesn't show me how everything gets put together behind the scenes."

"And you feel you have to know that?" He was stalling and she knew it. She laughed gently.

"Yes, Ivo, I do." And then, without saying

more, she went to the phone in his study across the hall, the paper still clutched in her hand. She was back five minutes later, beaming at him. "They said to come down today, around three."

Ivo sat back in his chair with a discouraged sigh. "I'll be back from lunch then. You can take the car."

"To this theater? Are you crazy? They'll never hire me if I show up in a limousine."

"That wouldn't be the worst news I'd heard all day, Bettina."

"Don't be silly." She leaned down to kiss his forehead and lightly touched his hair. "You worry too much. It'll be fine. And think, maybe I'll get a job out of it."

"Then what? You work in that horrendous neighborhood? How do you propose to get there every day?"

"On the subway, like the rest of the people who work in this town."

"Bettina —" He looked almost menacing, except that behind the menace was fear. Fear of what she was doing, where she was going, and of what it might mean for him.

"Now, Ivo. . . ." She waggled a finger at him, blew a kiss, and disappeared into the kitchen to say something to Mathilde. Feeling very elderly, Ivo folded his newspaper, called out his good-byes, and left for work.

At two thirty that afternoon Bettina made her way to the subway, disappeared into its bowels, and stood waiting in the dank chill for a train to arrive. When it did, it was smelly, graffiti-covered, and half empty; the only other passengers seemed to be old women with curling hairs on their chins, thick elastic stockings, and shopping bags, filled with mysterious items, that seemed to pull at their frail shoulders like rocks. There were a few teen-aged boys wandering by, and here and there a man nodding off to sleep with his face buried in the collar of his coat. Bettina smiled to herself, thinking of what Ivo would say to all this. But he would have said a great deal more had he seen the theater at the address given in the ad. It was an old ramshackle building that had been a movie theater some twenty years before. In the interim it had often stood empty, housed some unsuccessful porno ventures, and at one time been turned into a church. Now it was being reinstated as a theater, but not in any grand style. The repertory group would do nothing to revive the exterior of the building, they needed the few pennies they had to put on their plays.

As Bettina entered the building with mixed emotions of awe, excitement, and fear, she looked around her. There seemed to be no one around but she heard her footsteps echoing on the bare wooden floors. Everything seemed to be intensely dusty and there was an odd smell that reminded her of an attic.

"Yeah?" A man in blue jeans and a T-shirt was looking her over, with cynical blue eyes and a full, sensual mouth. His hair sprang from his head in a profusion of tight blond curls and gave his face a softness belied by the toughness of his eyes. "What is it?"

"I — I came . . . actually I called this morning . . . I . . . there was an ad in the paper. . . ." She was so nervous, she could hardly speak, but she took a deep breath and went on. "My name is Bettina Daniels. I'm looking for a job." She held out a hand, almost as an offering, but he didn't shake it, he just kept his hands shoved into his jeans.

"I don't know who you talked to. It wasn't me, or I'd have told you not to bother coming down. We're full up. We cast the last female role this morning."

"I'm not an actress." She said it with radiant cheer, and for a minute the man with the blond curls almost laughed.

"At least you're the first one who's honest. Maybe we should have cast you. Anyway, kiddo, sorry." He shrugged and started to move away.

"No, wait . . . really . . . I wanted a job doing something else."

"Like what?" He looked her over unabashedly, and had Bettina been less anxious, she would have wanted to slap his face.

"Anything . . . lights . . . the curtain . . . whatever you've got."

"You got any experience?"

Her chin went up just a fraction. "No. I don't. But I'm willing. I'd like to learn."

"Why?"

"I need the job."

"So how come you don't go to work as a secretary somewhere?"

"I don't want to do that. I want to work in the theater."

"Because it's glamorous?" The cynical eyes were laughing at her now and she was slowly getting angry.

"No, because I want to write a play."

"Oh, Jesus. So you're one of those. I suppose you went to Radcliffe, and now you think you're going to win a Tony in one year."

"No, I'm a dropout, and I just want a chance to work in a real theater. That's all." But she felt beaten. She knew that she had already lost. The guy hated her. She could tell.

He stood there watching her for a long time, then slowly he took a step closer to where she stood. "You know anything about lights?"

"A little." It was a lie but she was desperate now. She felt like it was her last chance.

"How little?" The eyes were boring into her own.

"Very little."

"In other words you don't know shit." He sighed and slumped hopelessly. "All right, so we'll train you. If you don't make a pain in the ass of yourself, I'll train you myself." And then in a sudden, unexpected motion he stuck out his hand. "I'm the stage manager. My name's Steve." She nodded her head, not sure of what he was saying to her. "Jesus, relax for chrissake, will you? You got the job."

"I did? Doing lights?"

"Working the dimmer board. You'll love it." She was to learn later that it was hot, boring, claustrophobic work, but at that moment in time it was the best news she had ever had.

She smiled at him radiantly. "Thank you so much."

"Don't worry about it. You just happen to be the first one who came for the job. If you're lousy, I'll fire you. No big deal."

"I won't be."

"Good. Then that's one headache I won't have. Be here tomorrow. I'll show you around. I don't have time today." As he said it he glanced at his watch. "Yeah, tomorrow. And once we go into rehearsals at the end of this week, that's it, kiddo, seven days a week."

"Seven?" She tried not to look shocked.

"You got kids?" She quickly shook her head. "Good. Then you don't have to worry. Your old man can come to see the plays at half price. And if we don't make it, you won't have to worry about working seven days a week. Right? Right." Nothing seemed to bother him. "Oh, by the way you know we don't pay you. You're lucky to have the job. We split the box office take."

Bettina was shocked again. She was going to have to be careful with the six thousand dollars she had left.

"So you'll be here tomorrow. Right, kid?" She nodded obediently. "Good. If you're not, I'll give someone else the job."

"Thank you."

"You're welcome." He was making fun of her, but now there was something softer in his eyes. "I shouldn't tell you this, but I got started just like you. It's a bitch. Only at first I wanted to be an actor, and that's worse."

"And now?"

"I want to be a director." The camaraderie of the theater had already taken hold; they were making friends.

Bettina smiled at him with a burst of her old spirit. "If you're very nice to me, maybe I'll let you direct my play."

"Never mind the bullshit, kiddo. Get lost, I'll see you tomorrow." And then, as the heels of her boots clattered across the barren floor toward the door, he called out to her, "Hey, what did you say your name was?"

"Bettina."

"Right." He waved, turned away distractedly, and walked quickly through the theater toward the stage. For only an instant Bettina watched him, and then rushing back into the sunshine, she let out a whoop of delight. She had a job!

11

"I keep forgetting that I don't have to look at the want ads anymore." Bettina looked at Ivo over the Sunday paper with a smile. It was the first time she had been able to sit down and relax in three weeks. It was Sunday morning and they had just taken their favorite seats, near a roaring fire. The play was "up," and Bettina had until the evening before she had to go downtown.

"Do you really like it?" He was still troubled. He hated the neighborhood, the idea, and the hours. And he didn't like the circles under her eyes. But that was mainly from the excitement. She had come home every night and been too wound up to go to bed much before three.

But she looked at him earnestly now, and he could see that she meant what she said. "Ivo, I love it. Last night I almost felt" — she seemed to hesitate — "like Daddy with his books. If I'm going to write for the theater and put together a decent play, I have to know everything about the theater. This is the only way that makes sense."

"I suppose so. But couldn't you just write novels like your father?" He sighed with a small wintry smile. "I worry about you coming home from the theater at night, in that stinking neighborhood, at that appalling hour."

"It's busy, and I'm safe. It never takes me more than a minute to find a cab." She didn't dare take the subway at those hours.

"I know, but —" He shook his head dubiously, and then threw up both hands. "What can I say?"

"Nothing. Just let me enjoy it. Because I am."

"How can I argue with anything that makes you that happy?" It was written all over her face. Even he had to admit it. And it had been that way for weeks.

"You can't, Ivo." And then she looked back at the paper again, but this time more pensively. "Now all I have to do is to find my own place."

"Already?" Ivo sounded shocked. "What's your rush?"

She looked up at him slowly. There was something very quiet in her eyes. She didn't want to leave either, but she knew it was time. "Aren't you getting a little tired of having me hang around?"

But Ivo shook his head sadly as she asked. "Never, Bettina. You know better than that." The very thought of her leaving weighed down his soul. But he had no right to hold on to her.

She didn't dare tell him that there were two apartments she thought she should see. She'd have to take a chance and let them wait until Monday. She at least owed him that. And it was obvious that her going out on her own upset him. Maybe he still felt he owed something more to her father. But he couldn't play nursemaid to her forever. She had gotten too comfortable living there. It was definitely time she moved on. It would be better that way really. It was too easy like this. She had even learned to control what she had at first felt for him. They were friends now, companions, but nothing more. She had understood that those odd stirrings of hers had had to be squelched.

They went for their usual Sunday walk, putting the conversation about her leaving behind them.

They stopped for a time, watching New Yorkers whirl around them, skating, bicycling, jogging in Central Park. She sat down on the grass and patted a spot next to her. "Sit down, Ivo." And then, after a time, "Something's bothering you. Can I ask what?"

But it was nothing he could tell her. That was the bitch of it. He avoided her eyes. "Business."

"You're lying. Now tell me the truth."

"Oh, Bettina. . . ." He closed his eyes and sighed. "I'm just tired. And once in a while" — he opened his eyes and smiled at her — "I feel very, very old." And then, not sure why he let himself tell her, he went on. "Some things are reserved to special ages. Having babies, getting married, getting gray hair, falling in love. And no matter how smoothly our lives run, now and then we find ourselves in the wrong time slot, the wrong age. . . ."

She looked puzzled as she watched him. And then the light of teasing came gently to her eyes. "All right, Ivo. You're pregnant? Now tell me the truth." He had to laugh at her as she tenderly patted his hand.

And then, throwing caution to the wind, he told her as he watched her eyes. "All right. It's your moving out. Suddenly I can't imagine a life without you." And then he smiled at her. "Doesn't that sound strange? But you've spoiled me. I can't even remember how it was before."

"Neither can I." She played with the grass and spoke barely above a whisper before at last she looked back into his eyes. "I hate to leave you, but I have to."

And then he asked the question they both wondered about. "Why?"

"Because I should be independent, because now I have to grow up. Because I have to support myself. I can't just live in your house forever. That wouldn't be right. And it isn't very proper either, I suppose."

"What would make it right?" He was pushing. He wanted her to say it — but for the first time in years he was afraid.

"You could adopt me." They both smiled at that. And then he looked at her seriously again.

"You're going to think I'm crazy, and I probably shouldn't tell you, but when I was in Europe, I came up with what I thought was a splendid plan. In the meantime, of course, I've come to realize that I was out of my mind." He smiled down at her tensely, and then looked away. "Do you know what I was going to do, Bettina?" He said it almost to himself as he lay full length on the grass, leaning on his elbows and squinting at the sky. "I was going to ask you to marry me. In fact I was going to insist. But you were living in Justin's apartment then, and things were different. Suddenly you moved into my place, and I felt as though you were at my mercy. I didn't want to take advantage of you. I didn't —" He stopped as he heard her sniff and he turned to see her looking at him in stupefaction, with tears running down her face. He smiled gently as he saw her and with one hand touched her wet cheek. "Don't be so horrified, Bettina. I didn't do it, did I, you big silly? Now stop crying."

"Why not?"

"Why not what?" He handed her his handkerchief and she dabbed at her eyes.

"Why didn't you ask me?"

"Are you serious? Because you're not quite twenty and I'm sixty-two. Isn't that enough reason? I shouldn't even be telling you this, but it's strange now, with you planning to leave suddenly. I suppose I want to hang on to you. I want to be able to tell you everything I think and feel, as I have in these last weeks, and I want you to be able to do the same."

"Why the hell didn't you ask me?" She jumped up then and stared down at him as he lay there, somewhat stunned.

"To marry me?" He was astonished. "Are you crazy? I told you. I'm too goddamn old." Ivo looked suddenly angry as he pulled his legs toward him and sat up straight.

She sank back down onto the grass next to him, staring at him with flashing eyes. "Couldn't you at least have given me a chance? Couldn't you have asked me how *I* felt? No, you're so busy treating me like a baby that you have to make all the decisions yourself. Well, I'm not a baby, you moron, I'm a woman and I have feelings too. And I've been in love with you since — since — goddamn it, forever. And do you ask me? No. Do you say anything? No! Ivo —" But he was grinning at her as they sat there, and he silenced her quickly with a long, powerful kiss.

"Are you crazy, Bettina?"

But now she was smiling too. "Yes, I am. I'm crazy about you. Jesus, didn't you know it? Didn't you guess? New Year's Eve when you kissed me, everything fell into place. But then, well, you seemed to withdraw — that way."

"Do you mean to tell me, Bettina, that you love me? I mean really love me, not just as your father's old friend?"

"That is exactly what I mean. I love you. I love you. . . ." And then she leaped to her feet and shouted it to the trees. "I LOVE YOU!"

"You're crazy!" He said it laughingly and tackled her to the ground. But she was lying next to him now and his eyes found her, and slowly his hands. "I love you . . . oh, darling, I love you. . . ." And then, gently, his mouth came down slowly on hers.

12

They tiptoed back into the apartment like two thieves, but Bettina was giggling hopelessly as Ivo tried to help her off with her coat. And then he whispered at her hoarsely as they tiptoed up the stairs, “Mattie said she was going to visit her sister in Connecticut. I know she won’t be back until tonight.”

“What difference does it make?” She looked up at him teasingly with those green eyes, and he suddenly didn’t give a damn who knew what he was feeling for her. He didn’t even feel guilty. All he knew was that he wanted her, desperately, with every part of his body and soul. It was only when they stood in his bedroom that he came to his senses, and there was suddenly a gentler light in his eyes. She stood near the door, watching him, childlike, barefoot, in her blue jeans and red sweater. Carefully he walked toward her and took her by the hand. He led her back to a big deep red easy chair, where he sat down, and pulled her down slowly onto one of his knees. Fleetingly he thought it was not unlike the many times she had sat on his lap when she was a child.

"Bettina . . . darling. . . ." His voice was a caress as his hand touched her neck and his lips rapidly followed suit. But he pulled away from her quickly and looked into her eyes. "I want you to tell me something — and you have to be honest. Has there ever been a man?" She shook her head slowly, wearing a small smile.

"No. But that's all right, Ivo." She wanted to tell him that she wasn't afraid. That she had wanted him for so long, that every moment of pain would be worth it, and after the first time she would give him pleasure for the rest of his life. That was all she could think of. What she would do for him.

"Are you afraid?" His arms were gentle around her, and she slowly shook her head. And then he laughed softly. "I am, silly girl."

She looked at him with those big lovely green eyes and smiled. "Why?"

"I don't want to hurt you."

"You won't. You never have." And then he nodded and took her gently by the hand, and after a moment she looked at him again with a thought. "Will I get pregnant?" She wasn't afraid of it, she just wondered. She had heard of girls who had gotten pregnant the very first time. But he was shaking his head and smiling and she was surprised.

"No, darling. Never. I can't have children. Or at least not anymore. I had that taken care of a long time ago." She nodded, accepting, not wanting to know why. He stood up next to her then and scooped her up, doll-like in his arms, and she let him carry her carefully to his bed, where he lay her down and began to undress her slowly. The room darkened and night fell. His eyes and his lips and his fingers caressed her as slowly he bared each inch of her flesh, and at last she lay naked, tiny, perfect. He longed to press against her and feel the satin of her flesh. But instead he covered her gently with the covers and turned to undress himself in the room that was finally dark.

"Ivo?" Her voice was very young and small.

"Yes?" Even in the dark she could hear him smile.

"I love you." It thrilled him just to hear it, and he slipped into the sheets just behind her back.

"I love you too." Gently he touched her, his hands covering her body, slowly, achingly, softly, as he could feel his whole body throb. Then gently he turned her to face him, and he kissed her long and hard on the mouth. He wanted her to want him as much, if not more, as he needed her. And at last she was pressed against him, moving, grinding, touching, almost begging, as firmly he held her and then pressed within her, quickly, jabbing, feeling her wrench upward and tense, clutching at his back, as he pressed into her more. He knew it would be painful but he wanted her to know how much he loved her, and as he held her he told her again and again until at last they both lay still. He could feel her warm blood on the sheets, but he didn't care. He only held her very tightly, feeling her tremble and holding her close to him in his arms. "I love you, darling . . . oh, Bettina, how I love you . . . with all of my heart." Even in the darkness she turned her eyes up to his in answer, and slowly he kissed her, sharing the moment and wanting to end her pain. "Are you all right?" She nodded slowly, and then at last she seemed to catch her breath.

"Oh, Ivo. . . ." And then, as she smiled at him, tears spilled down her face to her chin.

"Why are you crying, little one?" It had been so many years since he had done something like that, he was suddenly afraid he had hurt her. He looked into her eyes almost with grief. But she was smiling and laughing through her tears.

"Just think what we've been missing all month!" And then suddenly he laughed too.

"You're silly and I love you." But there was something he wanted to ask her and it was too soon. Yet he wanted to talk to her, to tell her, to ask her What now? And then he smiled down at her again as he turned onto his side and propped himself up on one elbow. As he did Bettina thought to herself that he looked incredibly young. "Does this mean you won't be moving out, mademoiselle?"

She looked at him impishly, shrugged her shoulders, and smiled at him. "Is that what you want, Ivo? For me to stay here?"

He nodded, feeling young again. "What about you? Do you want to stay?"

She lay back among his pillows feeling happier than she ever had before. "Yes, I want to stay."

"But have you really thought about it? Bettina, I'm a very old man!"

But at that she laughed at him and stretched out comfortably on the bed. It was extraordinary. She wasn't even embarrassed with him. Exposing her body to him was like opening up to the other half of her soul. "You know something, Ivo, I think you lie about your age. I think you're really all of about thirty-five and you dye your hair white . . . because no one can tell me after today, least of all you, that you are a very old man."

He looked at her seriously. "But I am. Do you care?"

"I don't give a damn."

But he knew better. "Now you don't. But one day you will. And when that day comes, when I seem too old to you, when you want a young man, I'll step aside. I want you to remember that, darling. Because I mean it, with all my heart. When your time with me is over, when it is no longer right for you, when you want a younger man, and a different life, and babies, I'll go. And I'll understand, and I'll love you, but I will go."

Her eyes were filled with tears as she listened. "No, you won't." But he only nodded and took her gently back into his arms again.

He whispered softly in her ear. "Are you terribly sore, my darling?" She shook her head. Gently he took her, and this time she moaned softly and there was pleasure in her eyes. And at last as they lay together, happy and spent, he remembered something and looked at her with a soft smile. "I assume that you understand, Bettina, that I want to marry you." She looked up at him this time in surprise. She had hoped, but she hadn't been sure.

Her copper hair was tousled and she looked wonderfully sleepy but there was something very soft and lovely in her eyes. She hugged him. "I'm glad. Because I want to marry you too."

"Mrs. Stewart."

And then, laughing softly, she kissed him and muttered, "The Third." He looked at her in surprise then and pulled her to him.

"Are you ready?" He knocked softly on the door and waited on the other side, but Bettina was flying about in a panic, still in her slip, her eyes frantic, her arms flapping wide.

"No, no, wait!" Mathilde went hurriedly to the closet to get the dress and slipped it carefully over Bettina's hair, and then she smoothed it over the narrow shoulders, closing hooks, buttons, snaps, and a zipper that ran imperceptibly up one side. It was a dress Bettina had bought in Paris with her father, but she had never worn it and it was perfect now.

She stood back to look at herself in the mirror, and over her left shoulder the reflection of the elderly Mathilde smiled benevolently too. Bettina looked beautiful in the simple cream satin dress. It was a mid-calf length, high-necked and short-sleeved with perfectly belled cap sleeves, and a jacket with much the same lines. She pulled on little white kid gloves and felt for the pearls in her ears, and then she stared down at her ivory-colored stockings and the virginal satin shoes. Everything was perfect, and she looked up at Mathilde now with a soft smile.

"You look beautiful, mademoiselle."

"Thank you, Mattie." She reached out to kiss the old woman then and after that walked slowly to the door. She hesitated for a long moment, wondering if he was still waiting on the other side. "Ivo?" She almost whispered it, but he heard her from behind the still closed door.

"Yes. Are you ready?"

She nodded, and then giggled. "I am. But aren't you supposed to wait to see me until we get there?"

"How do you propose to do that? Blindfold me in the car?" He was amused by her insistence on tradition, considering the circumstances. He was amused by everything she did these days. She was suddenly once again like a very enchanting child. She was free of worry, and the disastrous winter of tragedy had finally come to an end. She was his now, and she had a new life ahead of her, as his much pampered wife. "Come on, darling. We don't want to be late for Judge Isaacs. How about if I just close my eyes?"

"Okay. Are they closed?"

"Yes." He smiled, and feeling slightly foolish, he closed his eyes. He heard the door open, and a moment later he was aware of her perfume nearby. "Can I open them yet?"

She looked at him for a long moment, and then nodded slowly. "Yes." And he did, sighing softly as he saw her, wondering why the winter of his life should be so blessed, by what right?

"My God, you look lovely."

"Do you like it?"

"Are you serious? You look exquisite."

"Do I look like a bride?" He nodded gently, and then took her once more in his arms.

"Do you realize that an hour from now you'll be Mrs. Ivo Stewart?" And then he smiled down at her, dwarfed beside him. "How does that sound?"

"Lovely." She kissed him again, and then left his arms.

"Oh, that reminds me . . ." He reached suddenly behind him to something enveloped in pale-green tissue on the hall chair. He held it out to her with a look of tenderness. "For you."

She took it from him carefully, tearing the paper, and the smell of lilies of the valley suddenly filled the hall. "Oh, Ivo, where did you get them?" It was a beautiful little bouquet made of white roses and the tiny delicate white flowers from France.

"I had them sent over from Paris. Do you like the bouquet?"

She nodded happily and reached up to kiss him once more. But he stopped her and presented with a flourish a smaller package. She opened it up. There weren't words big enough to describe the nine-carat diamond ring gleaming brilliantly on a bed of midnight-blue velvet.

"Oh, Ivo, I don't know what to say."

"Say nothing, my love, just wear this ring and be happy and safe and secure forever."

The ceremony was over in minutes. The words had been said, the rings exchanged. Bettina was now Ivo's wife. She hadn't even wanted a party. She was still, after all, grieving for her father. They had dinner at Lutèce, at a quiet table in the rear, and afterward they went dancing, and Bettina stood on tiptoe to whisper in his ear.

"I love you, Ivo." She looked so tiny, so fragile, and so much like a little girl. But she wasn't, she was his woman. Now. Entirely his. Forever.

13

Nervously Bettina fastened diamond clips to her ears and ran a brush through her hair. She swirled it around her hand deftly and wound it into a smooth, ladylike knot. The deep auburn lights shone as she smoothed it, and when she had put the last of the pins in her hair, she stood up. Her body seemed tighter and thinner, and as she stood in a black lace dress, which reached to her ankles and black satin shoes, she could see her reflection across her dressing room in the long mirrored wall. Ivo had had the room put in especially for her, in the new apartment they'd bought on their first anniversary five months before. It was perfect for their life-style, a duplex with a beautiful view of Central Park. Their bedroom had a large handsome terrace, they each had a dressing room, and there was a small den for Ivo upstairs. Downstairs there was a living room, a wood-paneled dining room, and a kitchen, and behind it a nice-sized room for Mathilde. It was perfect. Not too grandiose, and yet it was far from small. Bettina had done it precisely as she wanted, except for the few touches Ivo had added for her, the little room of closets, the funny little gazebo on the large terrace, and a wonderful old-fashioned swing that he had hooked to the thin lip of overhanging roof. He had teased her that they would sit out there on summer evenings, dreaming and "necking on their back porch."

But it was rare for them to spend a night in the city during the summer. The repertory group for which she was now assistant manager and which had become more legitimate and moved uptown, had no performances in July and August and she and Ivo summered in South Hampton now. They had bought their own house. Her life was once more as it had been with her father, with the exception that she was happier than she had ever been before. She only worked five nights a week now, and on Sundays and Mondays, they gave elegant dinners for twelve or fourteen or showed films at home. Ivo had access to all the new movies, and once in a while she was able to sneak away for a ballet, a gala, an opening, or just an evening at Lutèce or Côte Basque.

And in spite of it all they managed to spend quite a bit of time alone, after the theater or in the daytime if Ivo could get away. He never had enough of her, and there were times when he wanted to share her with no one at all. He was lavish with his time, his attention, his affection, and his praise. Bettina was secure in his love. It was like the culmination of a long, happy dream.

She smiled at herself in the delicate black lace dress. It seemed to drift around her like a soft cloud, and she arranged the folds of her skirt before she zipped what little fabric there was in the back. It left her shoulders and arms and back bare, dwindled her waist to almost nothing, and floated up toward her throat, where it clasped with one hook around her neck. It looked like the sort of dress for which only one or two severed threads could have been disastrous, but there was no danger of that, the dress was exquisitely made. Checking the diamond earrings again and glancing at the smooth knot of hair, she squinted at her reflection with a small smile of excitement. "Not bad for an old broad," she whispered softly and grinned.

"Hardly that, my love." She turned in surprise. She hadn't seen her husband smiling at her from the doorway.

"Sneaky. I didn't hear you come in."

"I didn't intend you to. I just wanted to see how you look. And you look" — he smiled appreciatively and bent to kiss her softly on the mouth — "ravishing." He stepped back again and looked at her. She was even more beautiful than she had been a year and a half before. And then his smile deepened. "Excited, Bettina?" She was about to say no, but then, laughing, she nodded her head.

"Maybe a little."

"You should be, my darling." And then he himself had to laugh. Was it possible that was all she was? Twenty-one? Tonight was her twenty-first birthday. And then, as he watched her, he slipped a hand into his pocket and came out with a dark-blue velvet box. There had been so much of that since they had married. He had showered her with presents and spoiled her since the day they'd got home from their precious honeymoon in East Hampton.

"Oh, Ivo. . . ." She looked at him as he handed her the dark blue box. "What more can you give me? You've already given me so much."

"Go ahead, open it." And when at last she did, he smiled at her small gasp.

"Oh, Ivo! No!"

"Oh, yes." It was a magnificent pearl and diamond choker she had seen and admired at Van Cleef's. She had told him about it after they first married, in a funny, half-joking confidence, when she told him that one knew one had really grown up when one had a choker of pearls. He had been amused by her theory, and she had gone on to describe the elegant women who had worn chokers at her father's parties, sapphires, diamonds, rubies . . . but only the truly "grown-up" women had had the good taste to wear chokers made of pearls. He had enjoyed the story and, like everything else she told him, he never forgot. He had been waiting impatiently for her twenty-first birthday to give her the choker of pearls. The one he had chosen was also enhanced by diamonds that hung together in a handsome oval clasp, which could be worn in the back or front. As she fumbled to put it on and he watched her, he could see bright tears standing out in her eyes, and then suddenly she was crushed against him, holding tightly to him, as she bowed her head against his chest. "It's all right, darling. . . . Happy birthday, my beloved. . . ." He tilted her face toward him then and kissed her ever so softly on the lips.

But there was something more than just

gratitude in her face when she kissed him. "Don't ever leave me, Ivo . . . never . . . I couldn't bear it. . . ." It wasn't the diamonds and the pearls that he gave her, it was that he always understood, he always knew, he was always there. She knew that she could always count on him. But the terrifying thing was — what if one day he wasn't there? She couldn't bear to think of it. What if he stopped loving her one day? Or what if he left her helpless and gasping as her father had. . . . But as he looked at her Ivo understood the horror he could see hiding in her eyes.

"As long as I can help it, darling, I'll never leave you. Never."

And then they wandered downstairs, his arm firmly around her shoulders. It was only a few moments later when the doorbell rang with the first guests. Mathilde was being assisted by a bartender and two rented butlers, and a caterer had been arranged for the food. For once Bettina had to do absolutely nothing. Everything had been organized by Ivo. All she had to do was relax, have a good time, and be one of the guests.

"But shouldn't I just take a look in the kitchen?" She whispered it to him softly as they wandered away from a group of guests, but he held on to her firmly with a long, tender smile.

"No, you should not. Tonight I want you out here, with me."

"As you wish, sire." She swept a low curtsy and he patted her gently on the fanny as she rose. "Fresh!"

"Absolutely!" Their love life hadn't dwindled either in the past year. She still found him exciting and appealing, and they spent a remarkable amount of their time in bed.

She stood in tiny, regal splendor, Ivo at her side, a champagne glass in one hand, the other on her choker, surveying her domain. She felt like she had turned a corner. She was a woman, a lover, a wife.

14

"Ready to call it a night, little one?" Ivo looked down at her with a gentle smile as they circled the dance floor for a last time. She nodded as she looked up at him. For once the emeralds in her ears shone more than her eyes. She looked tired and troubled, despite the brilliantly beautiful green and gold sari dress she was wearing, and the new emerald earrings, which were an almost perfect match for her mother's ring. Ivo had just bought her the earrings the previous Christmas and she loved them.

As they turned to go back to their table, all of the guests stood and applauded. She was so used to the sound of applause, that she was comforted by it. But tonight the applause wasn't for the repertory group but for Ivo, who was retiring, finally, after thirty-six years at the paper, twenty-one years as its chief. He had decided, after much agony, to end his career at sixty-eight rather than push it all the way to mandatory retirement in two years. Bettina had not yet quite adjusted to what was happening, and he knew that it troubled her more than she would admit. Together they had shared six untroubled, endlessly happy years of winters in the city, summers in the country, trips to Europe, and moments that they shared. And at twenty-five she enjoyed it, and he indulged her, although now when she worked, he had his chauffeur pick her up around the corner from work. He no longer bowed to all of her ideas about her independence, and having proven herself with the rep group, she was less fierce about the little things. Yet it was comfortable to depend on Ivo. He made life so easy and so happy.

"Come on, my darling." He took her gently by the hand and led her through the crowd of well-wishing friends in evening dresses and tuxedos. In fact as he looked at them he was grateful for the touch of her hand. There was so much that he was leaving, and suddenly he wondered if he had been wrong. But it was too late to reverse his decision. The announcement of the new publisher had already been made. And Ivo was becoming the chief adviser to the chairman of the board. It was an illustrious title, which in fact held very little power. He would simply become now a respected elder, and as he rode home in the limousine with Bettina, he found himself close to tears.

But they had already done some careful planning. She had taken three months off from the rep group and they were leaving the next day for the South of France. He had arranged their passage by ship, since suddenly they had so much spare time.

They drove down in leisurely fashion from Paris to St.-Jean-Cap-Ferrat, after a two-week stay at the Ritz, where Bettina teasingly said they did nothing but eat. Cap-Ferrat was heavenly in September, and in October they went on to Rome. And at last, in November, they regretfully returned to the States. Ivo called a vast number of his cronies and arranged to have lunch with everyone at their assorted favorite hangouts and clubs. And Bettina went back to The Players. Things were on the upswing for them, the previews good, the audiences plentiful, and Bettina was happy with her job. Steve was finally directing, and she had his old job as theater manager, for which she had gotten her equity card at last. The play they were doing was an original work, by an unknown playwright, but it had seemed different to her right from the beginning. There was a tension, an excitement, a kind of tangible magic one could feel in the air.

"All right, I believe you." Ivo had said it teasingly as she told him about it with excited, emphatic eyes.

"Will you come and see it?"

"Sure." He went back to his paper and his breakfast with a smile. It was rare, but the night before, he hadn't waited up for her. He had had a long day himself. Now and then his age peeked at him around corners, but most of the time nothing much had changed.

"When will you come and see it?"

He looked up at her again with a rueful smile. "Will you please stop pushing, Mrs. Stewart?"

But she grinned at him and firmly shook her head. "No. I won't. This is the best play I've ever worked on. It's brilliant, Ivo, and it's exactly the kind of play I want to write."

"All right, all right, I'll see it."

"You promise?"

"I promise. Now can I read my paper?"

She looked at him sheepishly. "Yes."

But by noon she was already anxious to get back to the theater. She watched Ivo dress for a luncheon at the Press Club, and then she showered and climbed into jeans. She left him a note that she had left early, and she'd see him late that night. She suspected he wouldn't mind it. Since they'd gotten back from Europe, he'd been very tired, and it would probably do him good to take it easy for the rest of the day. Besides, he was used to her crazy theater schedule.

She jumped out of the cab hastily and walked the rest of the way, humming to herself and feeling the bitter winter wind in her hair. She still wore it long to please Ivo, and today it flew out past her shoulders, like fine copper thread.

"What's your hurry, lover? You can't be late for work." As she crossed the street near the theater she looked over her shoulder in surprise. The voice was British and familiar, and when she saw him, he was wearing a warm tweed coat and a red cap. He was the star of their new play.

"Hi, Anthony. I just thought I'd tie up some loose ends."

"Me too. And we have a quick rehearsal at four thirty. They're going to change the opening of the second act."

"Why?" She looked at him with interest, and as they reached the theater he held open the door.

"Don't ask me." He shrugged boyishly. "I just work here. I never understand why playwrights do all that scribbling and switching. Paranoia, if you ask me. But that's the theater, love." He stood for a moment in front of his dressing room and eyed her with a long, friendly smile. He was more than a head taller than she and he had enormous blue eyes and soft brown hair. There was something enchanting and innocent about him, probably due to his very British intonations and the light in his eyes. "Are you doing anything for dinner tonight?"

She looked pensive, and then shook her head. "Probably not. I'll just eat a sandwich here."

"Me too." He made a face and they both grinned. "Care to join me?" He waved behind him into the dressing room, and she hesitated for a moment, and then slowly nodded.

"Sure."

"And then what?" He was looking at her with fascination over the pastrami. They had been chatting, sitting on two canvas chairs in his dressing room for half an hour.

"Then I worked on *Fox in the Hen House, Little City,* let's see . . ." She hesitated pensively, and then grinned. "Oh, and *Clavello.*"

"You worked on that?" He looked impressed. "Christ, Bett, you've had more work than I've had, and I've been at it for ten years."

She looked surprised as she surveyed him, nibbling at the remains of her pickle. "You don't look old enough to have been at it for that long. How old are you?" She wasn't embarrassed to ask him questions. In the past half hour they had somehow become friends. He was easy to be with and fun to talk to, unlike the others she had met in the theatrical world. Despite the camaraderie, jealousy was always thick in the air. But it rarely touched her. She was only the stage manager, after all. Yet she never tired of what she saw in the theater, and the magic was there for her, every night.

"I'm twenty-six." He looked at her enchantingly. A small boy in a man's clothes, pretending to be in a play.

"How long have you been in the States?"

"Just since rehearsals. Four months."

"You like it?" She finished the last of the pastrami and the pickle and cast a jeans-clad leg over the arm of her chair.

"I love it. I'd give my ears to stay."

"Can't you?"

"Sure, on temporary visas. But, Christ, that's all such a mess. I take it you don't know about the never-ending search for the almighty green card."

She shook her head. "What's that?"

"Permanent resident's card, working permit, et cetera. They'd be worth a fortune if you could buy them on the black market. But you can't."

"What do you have to do to get one?"

"Work a minor miracle, I think. I don't know, it's too bloody complicated. Don't ask. And what about you?" He stirred his coffee and looked at her seriously for a moment. She was startled, she felt almost caressed by the blue eyes.

"What do you mean?"

"Oh, you know," he shrugged, smiling. "Vital statistics, age, rank, shoe size, do you wear a bra?"

She grinned back at him, startled, and then shrugged. "All right, let's see. I'm twenty-five, I wear a size five-and-a-half shoe, and the rest of it is none of your business."

"Married?" He looked casually intrigued.

"Yes."

"Damn." He snapped his fingers regretfully and they both laughed. "Been married long?"

"Six and a half years."

"Kids?" But this time she shook her head. "That's smart."

"Don't you like children?" She looked surprised, but he was noncommittal.

"They're not the greatest thing ever to happen to a career. Distracting little bastards at best." It reminded her of the egocentricity of most actors and made her think of her father too. And then he smiled at her again. "Well, Bettina, I'm damn sorry to hear you're married. But" — he looked up at her cheerfully — "don't forget to give me a call when you get divorced." But as he said it she stood up with a broad grin.

"Anthony Pearce, my friend, don't hold your breath while you're waiting." And then with a wave and a smile she walked to the door and saluted. "See you later, kid."

She saw Anthony again that night as she left the theater, and they both pulled their collars up against the cold.

"Jesus, it's freezing. God knows why you want to stay in the States."

"Sometimes I ask myself that too."

And then she smiled at him again as they walked toward the corner, trying to avoid the patches of ice. "Nice performance tonight."

"Thank you." He turned to her questioningly. "Want a lift?" He was about to hail a cab.

But she shook her head at him. "No,

thanks."

He shrugged and walked on as she turned left at the corner. And she saw Ivo's car waiting for her, with the driver, the motor running, and inside she knew it would be warm. She looked over her shoulder quickly to see if anyone was watching, and then she pulled open the door and slipped inside. But as he crossed the street, seemingly oblivious, Anthony had turned one last time to wave good night. All he saw was Bettina, disappearing into a long black limousine. He dug his hands deeper into his pockets, raised an eyebrow, and walked on with a smile.

15

"Hi, darling." It was bright and sunny the next morning at breakfast. Again Ivo had been asleep the night before when she came in. It was unlike him. And they hadn't made love in a week. She felt guilty keeping track of it, but he had spoiled her so much for so long that now she was suddenly aware of any change.

"Missed you last night."

"Think I'm over the hill, little one?" He said it softly with a kindly light in his eyes. It was clear that he didn't think so, and Bettina rapidly shook her head.

"Not a chance, so don't start counting on using that as an excuse."

He went back to his paper, and Bettina went upstairs to get dressed. She had wanted to tell him about her dinner with Anthony, but suddenly it didn't seem quite right. She was always careful not to make him feel jealous, even though they both knew he had no reason to be.

Three quarters of an hour later Bettina was wearing gray slacks and a beige cashmere sweater, brown suede boots, and a silk scarf the same color as her hair. Ivo had just come upstairs in his robe.

"What are you doing today, darling?" She had the urge to slip her hands under his robe. But he was looking at his watch and hadn't noticed the look in her eye.

"Oh, God, I have a board meeting at the paper in half an hour. And I'm going to be late." That took care of the morning.

"And after that?" She looked hopeful.

"Lunch with my fellow board members. Another meeting. And then home."

"Damn. By then I'll have left for the theater."

His eyes were both wistful and tender. "Want to quit the play?" But she shook her head emphatically.

"No!" And then in a childlike voice she explained, "It's just that I miss you so much now that we're back in the States and I'm working. In Europe we were together all the time, and now suddenly it feels like we never see each other anymore." He was touched by the remorseful tone in her voice and he reached out to hold her.

"I know." And then after stroking her hair

for a few minutes, he lifted her face up toward his and kissed her lips. "I'll see what I can do about not scheduling so many lunches. Want to take another trip?"

"I can't, Ivo . . . the play."

"Oh, for —" There was fire for a moment, and then it subsided with the wave of a hand. "All right, all right." But then he turned to her more seriously. "Don't you think after all these years you've absorbed enough to write something of your own? Really, darling, I have visions of you turning eighty-seven and still hobbling down to work the curtain for some off-off-Broadway play."

"I don't work off-off-Broadway." She looked insulted, and he laughed.

"No, you don't. But don't you think you've done it for long enough? Think of it, we could go away now for six months and you could write your play."

"I'm not ready." She seemed terrified at the thought, and he wondered why.

"Yes, you are. You're just afraid, darling. But there's no reason to be. You're going to write something marvelous when you finally do it."

"Yes, but I'm just not ready, Ivo."

"All right. Then don't complain that you never see me. You're down at that damn theater all the time." It was the first time that he had complained of it, and Bettina was surprised by the quick anger in his tone.

"Darling, don't say that." She kissed him, and his voice was gentler when he spoke again.

"Silly girl. I love you, you know."

"I love you too." They held each other for a moment, but then he had to leave.

At the theater everything was already bustling, people were hurrying everywhere, and the stars of the show had begun to arrive. Bettina saw Anthony walking around backstage in jeans, a black turtleneck sweater, and his red cap.

"Hi, Bett." He was the only member of cast or crew who insisted on shortening her name.

"Hello, Anthony. How's everything?"

"Insane. They want to make more changes." It was a new play and last-minute rewrites were to be expected. He didn't look especially perturbed. "I wanted to ask you to dinner again, but I couldn't find you."

She smiled easily. "I brought a sandwich from home."

"Made by your mother?" Bettina laughed but she couldn't very well tell him No, made by our maid. Instead she only shook her head. "Any chance I can induce you to join me for coffee a little later?"

"Sorry, not tonight." She had to get home to Ivo. She didn't want to stay out too late. Only once or twice in years of working in the theater had she gone out after hours with the crew. Last night was enough.

He shot her a disappointed look and disappeared.

She didn't see him again until after the show. He found her setting lights and overseeing the routine house cleanup before she went home.

"What did you think of the changes, Bettina?" He looked at her with interest and sat down on a stool, and she paused for a moment before answering, her eyes narrowed, reliving the scenes in her head.

"I'm not sure I like them. I don't think they were necessary."

"That's what I thought. Weak. I told you, writers are fucking paranoids."

She smiled at him again. "Yeah. Maybe so."

"Can I lure you out now for that cup of coffee?" But she shook her head.

"Maybe another time, Anthony. I'm sorry. I can't."

"Hubby waiting?" He sounded flip as he said it, and she squarely met his eyes.

"I hope so." He looked irritated, and as Bettina put her coat on she was irritated too. He had no right to be annoyed that she wouldn't go out with him. No right at all. It bothered her that he had looked aggravated, but she was strangely afraid that he wouldn't ask again. She picked up her handbag, jammed on her hat, and walked out the door. Screw Anthony Pearce. He didn't mean anything to her.

She walked briskly down the street toward the corner, feeling the wind whistle past her ears. She hastened toward the waiting limousine, grabbed the door handle, and put one foot inside, only to hear a voice behind her. She turned in astonishment. It was Anthony standing behind her, his collar turned up, the red cap on his head.

"Can you give me a lift?"

Despite the cold, she felt herself flush with embarrassment. He was the first person in six years who had discovered her getting into the car. And all she could think of to say was "Oh."

"Come on, love, I'm freezing me arse off. And there aren't any cabs." There was a fine mist of snow starting to filter into the air. And he had seen her now, so what did it matter? She looked at him for a moment, and then answered tersely.

"All right." She climbed in and he got in beside her, and she turned to him, annoyed at his pushiness. "Where do you want me to drop you off?" He seemed unperturbed by the embarrassment he had caused her. The address he gave her was in SoHo.

"I have a loft. Want to come up and see it?" She grew angry again at how persistent he was.

"No, thank you, I don't."

"Why so angry?" And then with a smile he looked at her admiringly. "But I must say, love, it becomes you."

In rapid irritation she raised the window between the driver and them. And then she looked at him hotly. "May I remind you that I'm a married woman?"

"What difference does that make? I didn't say anything out of line. I didn't tear off your clothes. I didn't kiss you in front of the chauffeur. All I did was ask for a ride. Why so touchy? Your old man must be jealous as hell."

"No, he's not, and that's none of your damn business either. I just . . . it's just that . . . oh, never mind." She sat in steaming silence as they drove south toward his loft. When at last they reached it, he held out a friendly hand.

"I'm sorry to have upset you, Bettina."

His voice was gentle and boyish as he spoke. "I really didn't mean to." And then hanging his head, "I'd like to be your friend."

As she looked at him something about him cut straight to her soul. "I'm sorry, Anthony . . . I didn't mean to be rude. It's just that no one has ever . . . I felt so awkward about the car . . . I'm really so sorry. It isn't your fault."

He kissed her cheek gently — a friendly kiss. "Thanks for that." And then hesitantly, "Will you slap me if I offer you a cup of coffee just one more time?" He looked so earnest, so anxious, that she didn't dare refuse. But she wanted so much to get home to Ivo. Still . . . she had been very sharp with the young English actor.

She sighed and nodded. "Okay. But I can't stay long." She followed him up an endless narrow staircase as her car waited downstairs, and at last when she thought they must have walked to heaven, he unlocked a heavy steel door, and on the other side was revealed to her an apartment filled with charm. He had painted clouds on the ceiling, filled corners with wonderful tall, leafy trees; there were campaign chests and Oriental objects, straw mats and small rugs, and huge comfortable chairs upholstered in a soft blue. It was more than an apartment, it was a haven, a piece of country, a garden in an apartment, a cloud riding in a pale-blue summer sky. "Oh, Anthony, it's wonderful." Her eyes widened with pleasure as she looked around.

"Do you like it?" Her looked at her innocently again, and they both smiled.

"I adore it. How did you put all this together? Did you bring it from London?"

"Some of it, and some of it I just threw together here." But nothing about it looked thrown together. It was a beautiful place. "Now, cream or sugar?"

"Neither, thank you. Black."

"That must be how you stay so thin." He glanced appreciatively at her narrow and dancer-graceful body as she let herself down in one of the blue chairs.

He was back in a few minutes with two steaming cups and a plate of cheese and fruit.

It was one thirty when she finally ran panic-stricken down the stairs to her car. What would Ivo say? And suddenly, this time, she was praying that he was asleep. As it turned out, her prayers were answered. He had waited till midnight, and then fallen asleep in their bed. Bettina felt a wild pang of guilt as she watched him, and then wondered why. All she had done was have coffee with a member of the cast. What harm could there be in that?

16

"Did he beat you?" Anthony teased.

"Of course not. He's wonderful and understanding. He doesn't do things like that."

"Good. Then let's have coffee again sometime. As a matter of fact how about dinner tonight before the show?"

"We'll see." She was purposely vague. She wanted to call Ivo. Maybe they could have dinner quickly somewhere nearby. She hadn't even seen him this morning. When she'd woken up, he was gone. He had left her a note that he had an early appointment. She was beginning to feel that they never saw each other and she didn't like it at all.

But when she called Ivo, he wasn't home. Mattie said he had called to say he'd be out for dinner, and Anthony seemed to be waiting behind her to use the pay phone. He heard the entire conversation despite her best efforts to be discreet, and when she hung up, he smiled disarmingly.

"Can I stand in for dinner, Bettina?"

She was going to say no, but in the face of those blue eyes she found herself saying "Sure." They wound up going somewhere for soup and a sandwich, and talking more about the play. And then almost imperceptibly he switched the conversation to her. He wanted to know everything about her, where she came from, where she lived, even where she'd gone to school as a girl. She told him about her father, whose work he knew. He seemed fascinated by every detail she told him. At last they walked back to the theater, and they went their separate ways. But he found her quickly after the performance as she was preparing to leave. She had a feeling he was going to ask her for a lift again, so she hurried out to the car.

At home she found Ivo waiting up. They chatted for half an hour about their respective days, and at last went upstairs. Bettina undressed slowly as they talked.

"I feel as though I've hardly seen you lately." He looked at her with regret, but no reproach.

"I know." She looked mournful, but he was quick to walk to her side. And a moment later he was helping her to undress, and then quickly he followed her to the bed. Their lovemaking was slow and gentle and fulfilling, but as they lay quietly afterward Bettina found herself longing for their first fire. She turned to Ivo slowly, wanting to see a look of fresh passion lingering in his eyes. And instead she found him sleeping, his face turned to her and a small smile on his mouth. She lay on one elbow for a long time, watching him, and gently she kissed him on both eyes, but as she did so she realized her mind had strayed to Anthony, and relentlessly she dragged it back to the man at her side.

The friendship with Anthony continued to flourish as the success of the play went on. They had sandwiches together now and then backstage, and occasionally she had coffee with him in his loft. Several times a week he brought her small bouquets of flowers, but they were always presented to her casually, as though they meant nothing more than that he was her friend. Once or twice she tried to bring it up casually with Ivo, but it somehow never sounded quite right.

It was in the dead of winter when Ivo went back to see the play, as though he also needed to be there, to see, to try to reach out and grasp something that was nagging at the back of his mind. He had timed his entrance into the darkened theater perfectly, sitting anonymously in the next-to-last row. And then, as the curtain rose and he watched him, he thought he knew. Anthony had the grace of a long sleek black leopard, moving hypnotically through the motions of his part. Ivo barely heard the words he was speaking. He only watched him, and then, with a terrible sensation of betrayal and aching, he understood. The betrayal was not Bettina's, but that of the hands of time he had fought for so long.

It wasn't until spring that Bettina looked troubled. She had come home late one night, looking disturbed, and Ivo watched her, not sure whether to ask questions or leave her alone. Something was obviously bothering her, but for the first time in their marriage she didn't want to talk. She stared at Ivo absently, and eventually wandered upstairs alone. He found her staring out at the city from the terrace, frowning, with her hairbrush hanging useless in her hand.

"Something wrong, darling?"

But Bettina shook her head vaguely. "No." And then suddenly she turned to him, with a look of terror in her eyes. "Yes."

"What's the matter?"

"Oh, Ivo. . . ." She sat down on a garden chair and stared at him, her eyes huge and luminous in the dark. Behind her was the soft light of the apartment, which caught the rich auburn glow of her hair. He thought that she had never looked more lovely, and he dreaded what she might have to say. All winter he had had a feeling of foreboding, and all winter he had been so dreadfully tired. It made him wonder sometimes if retiring had been a mistake. He had never felt that way while he had still worked.

"Darling, what is it?" He went to her, took her hand, and sat down. "Whatever it is, you can tell me. Above all, Bettina, we're friends."

"I know." She looked at him gratefully with her huge green eyes, and slowly they filled with tears. "They've asked me to tour."

"What?" He looked at her with relief and amusement. "Is that all?" Dumbly she nodded yes. "What's so awful about that?"

"But, Ivo, I'd be gone for four months! And what about you? I don't know . . . I can't do it . . . but —"

"But you want to?" His eyes never left hers, and with one hand she began to play with her hair.

"I'm not sure. They've . . . oh, Jesus, it's crazy. . . ." And then she looked at him, so unhappy, so obviously torn. "They've asked me to be the assistant director. Me, Ivo, the errand girl, the pusher of scenery, the nothing, after all these years."

"They're very smart. They know how much you've learned over the years. I'm proud of you, darling." He looked at her with a warm glow in his eyes. "Do you want to do it?"

"Oh, Ivo, I don't know . . . what about you?"

"Never mind about me. We've been together for almost seven years. Don't you think we could weather four months? Besides, I could fly out to see you now and then. After all there are advantages to being married to a man who's retired."

She smiled bittersweetly and took a tight hold of his hand. "I don't want to leave you."

But he eyed her honestly. "Yes, you do, darling. And it's all right. I've had my life, you know, a full one. I have no right to expect you to spend all of yours sitting here with me."

"Would you miss me?" She looked up at him again with the face of a little girl.

"Outrageously. But if it's what you really need to do, Bettina" — there was a long pause as he looked at her — "then I understand. Why don't you think about it for a while? How soon do they want an answer?"

She gulped almost audibly. "Tomorrow."

"Anxious, aren't they?" He tried to sound lighthearted. "And how soon would you go?"

"In a month."

"With the original cast?"

"Partly. Anthony Pearce is going, and the female lead." She rambled on for a minute, but he didn't hear her, she had already told him all he wanted to know. He looked at her gently and shrugged softly in the warm night air. "Why don't you sleep on it and see how you feel in the morning. Is Steve going to be the director by the way?"

She shook her head slowly. "No. He got a job with a Broadway play." She sat there for a while, saying nothing, and at last she got up and went inside. It was as though they both knew what was happening, but neither could speak. She left him there, on the terrace, drifting in his thoughts. Something had changed between them — without any warning, but it had. Suddenly she seemed so much younger, and he felt so old. Even their lovemaking had slowly changed over the past year. For a moment he wanted to rail at the fates for what was happening, it wasn't fair . . . but then he knew. He had had seven years with her. It was more than he had a right to.

He wandered inside. He made no move to make love to her that evening. He didn't want to confuse her even more. On her side of the bed Bettina lay wondering if she should stay with Ivo, or go. At last she heard his soft breathing and turned to look at him, so gentle, so loving, asleep on his side. She touched his arm as she watched him, and then she turned away and wiped the tears from her eyes. In the morning she would have to tell him. She had to do it. Had to. She needed to do it. She had no choice.

17

"Ivo . . . you'll call me . . . promise?" She looked at him in the airport, her huge green eyes filling with tears. "And I'll call you too. I swear . . . every day . . . and when you come for the weekend —" But suddenly she couldn't go on. All she could do was reach out to him, blindly, barely seeing through her veil of tears. "Oh, Ivo . . . I'm so sorry. . . ." She hated to go. But Ivo was there, holding her, comforting as always, his voice gentle in her ear.

"No, stop it, darling. I'll see you in a few weeks. Everything is going to be fine. And you'll write a beautiful play after this. I'll be so proud of you. You'll see." His voice was gentle and soothing as he held her in his arms.

"Do you really think so?" She looked at him, sniffing loudly, and then fresh tears came to her eyes. "But what about you?"

"We already discussed that. I'll be fine.

Remember me? I lived a hell of a long time before I was lucky enough to have you. Now just be a good girl and enjoy it. Hell, this is your big chance, Madam Assistant Director." He was teasing now and she finally smiled. He pulled her into his arms and kissed her.

"Now, my little love, you have to go, or you'll miss your plane, and that is not the way to start a new job." They were starting in St. Louis, and the rest of the cast was already there. They had left that morning, but Bettina had wanted the last hours she could spare with Ivo in New York.

She glanced back at him as she ran toward the gate, feeling like a runaway child. Yet he was firm and kind and as loving as ever as he waved to her, and he stayed until he could see no more of the plane. As he left the airport Ivo Stewart walked slowly, thinking back to that morning, that summer, last year, and then the last twenty-five. A sudden tremor of panic ran through him as he wondered if this had just been good-bye.

Bettina landed in St. Louis at 4:03 that afternoon. It was cutting it a little close for their first performance, but they had rehearsed so often that the cast was as tight as could be, and the director had flown out from New York with them, so Bettina felt safe coming in as late as she did. As the plane touched down she sighed to herself, thinking of Ivo, and slowly she forced her mind back to work. She left the plane hurriedly, anxious to pick up her bags, drop them at the hotel, and get to the theater. She wanted to reconnoiter and make sure that everything was all right. She was already busy and distracted as she hurried past the other passengers on the way to her bags.

"Good God, lover, what's the rush? You're going to knock down an old lady if you don't slow down and watch out!" She started to turn in annoyance, and then suddenly she laughed.

"What are you doing here?" She grinned at Anthony in astonishment as she stopped in her tracks.

"Oh, let's see, I came out here to pick up a friend," he grinned at her, "who just happens to be the A.D. of our show. Anyone you know, green eyes?"

"Okay, smartass. Thanks." But despite the teasing and the exchanges she was immensely glad to see him. She had felt suddenly very lost and alone as she got off the plane. "How's everything going at the theater?"

"Who knows? I've been hanging out at the hotel all afternoon."

"Is everyone all right?" She looked genuinely concerned and he laughed.

"Yes, little mother, they're fine." As they picked up her valises, his gaiety was contagious, and by the time they caught a taxi into the city, they were both laughing like two kids. He was teasing and playing and being silly. It was the closest she'd ever come to acting like a child. He brought that out in her, and she enjoyed it. It was a salute to all the moments that had passed her by as a little girl.

"This is it?" She looked at the hotel as they disembarked. The road show had put them in what had to be the oldest, and certainly the ugliest, hotel in town.

"Didn't I tell you, love? They had San Quentin moved all the way to Saint Louis just for us." He looked delighted as he said it and Bettina cracked up.

"God, it's awful. Is it as bad inside?"

"No. Worse. Cockroaches as big as dogs. But not to worry, darlin', I bought a leash!"

"Anthony . . . please . . . it can't be that bad."

"Yes, it is." He reassured her with pleasure, and when she checked into her room, she realized that he was right. The walls were cracked, the paint was peeling, the bed was hard, the bedspreads looked dingy and gray. Even the water glasses in the bathroom were dirty. "Was I right?" He looked at her cheerfully as she dropped her suitcase on the floor.

"Well, you don't have to sound so cheerful about it." She smiled at him ruefully and sat down, but his spirits couldn't be dampened. He was a little boy on holiday as he jumped up and down next to her on the bed. "Stop it, Anthony! Don't you ever get tired for chrissake?" She was suddenly hot and tired and fed up and she couldn't remember why she had left Ivo in New York. Surely not to travel around the country with this madman and to stay in fleabag hotels.

"Of course I never get tired. Why should I? I'm young! But I'm also not as spoiled as you are, Bettina." His voice was caressing, and she turned to look at him.

"What do you mean 'spoiled'?"

"I don't have a chauffeur or live in a penthouse. I've spent most of my life in dumps like this."

She wasn't sure if she should be sorry or angry, and she didn't know what to say. "So? Do you resent me for being married to a somewhat" — she hesitated — "comfortable man?"

Anthony's eyes stared straight into hers. "No. But I resent you like hell for being married to a man almost three times your age."

This time her eyes flashed. "It's none of your business."

"Maybe I think it is."

Her heart pounded, and then she turned away. "I love him very much."

"Maybe you just love his money." His voice was insinuating, and she turned in fury at what he had just said.

"Don't you ever say that again. Ivo saved me, and he's the only human being who ever gave a damn about me." She had told Anthony the whole story about her father's debts one night as they shared coffee in the loft.

"That's no reason to have married him, for chrissake." Anthony actually looked irate.

"I told you, I love him. Do you understand?" Bettina was livid. "He's my husband and he's a wonderful man."

But suddenly Anthony's voice grew softer, almost caressing her with his words. "When I think of you married to a man forty-three years older than you are, it bloody breaks my heart." He looked at her mournfully and she stared.

"Why?" Despite the throbbing in her temples, she tried desperately to calm down.

"It's not natural. You should be married to someone younger. You should be young and silly. You should have kids."

She shrugged, and then sighed deeply, sinking into the uncomfortable bed. "Anthony, I've never been young and silly. And I've known Ivo all my life. He's the best thing that could have happened to me." But why was she doing this? Why was she justifying Ivo to him?

He looked at her sadly. "I wish someone would say that about me."

She smiled then, for the first time since they had started the discussion; her anger had begun to fade. "Maybe someday someone will. Now, can we make a deal please?"

"What's that?"

"No more nonsense about Ivo, no more harping on me because he's more than twice my age."

"All right, all right, it's a deal," he said begrudgingly, "but don't expect me to understand."

"I won't." But she did expect him to if he was her friend.

"Okay, now let's get the hell to the theater before we both get fired." And a few minutes later the bad feelings were gone. They had to be together too much to allow themselves the luxury of a fight.

They arrived together, they left together, they ate together, they talked together, they watched television in hotel rooms together, they fell asleep side by side in airports and ugly hotels waiting for rooms. They were inseparable. A tiny nucleus within a larger one. The entire cast and crew hung together as though they had been grafted, but within the group cliques and couples inevitably formed. Among them were Anthony and Bettina. No one quite understood, no one dared to ask questions, but after the first couple of weeks everyone knew that if you were looking for one, you'd find the other one too.

"Bettina?" He was pounding on her door early one morning. Usually now she let him have the spare key and he pounded her on the ass to wake her up, wherever they were. She was so exhausted that it almost took brutality to waken her. But the night before, in the hotel in Portland, she had forgotten to give him the key. "Bettina! Dammit! Bettina!"

"Kick it in!" One of the understudies smiled and walked by as Anthony muttered.

"For chrissake, woman, wake up!" Finally she staggered to the door with a yawn.

"Thanks. Did it take long?"

"Jesus." He rolled his eyes and sauntered in.

"Did you bring me coffee?"

"Would you believe they don't have any in this flophouse. We have to go two blocks down the street to the nearest coffee shop."

Bettina looked at him blearily. "My heart may stop before that."

"That's what I thought." He smiled at her mysteriously and returned to the hall. He was back a moment later with a small plastic tray with two cups of coffee and a stack of fresh Danish. "Oh, God, you're wonderful. Where did you get that?"

"I stole it."

"I don't give a damn if you did. I'm starving. What time do we leave, by the way? They hadn't decided when I went to sleep last night."

"I wondered where the hell you snuck off to."

"Are you kidding? If I hadn't gotten some sleep, I'd have dropped dead in my tracks." No one had told them that they'd be performing every day. It was one of those little details that hadn't been mentioned. It was also why Ivo had not come out to see her yet, although she had already been gone for a month. But there was no point flying out to meet her if she would be working every day of the week. They called each other every day though, but she was getting increasingly vague with her news. Her whole existence centered around the tour. It was like being in Marine boot camp. It was becoming harder and harder to relate to anyone not living it with her. "So what time are we leaving?"

He looked at his watch with a smile. "In an hour. But, hell, look at it this way, Bett, we'll be in San Francisco by this afternoon."

"So who gives a damn? Do you think we'll see it? No. We'll be stuck in some rotten hotel. And three days from now we fly out of there." The charm of the road show was definitely wearing thin, but it was also a valuable experience. She told Ivo that every day.

"Not three days later, lover. A week. A whole week!" For a moment her face lit up and she wondered if she should tell Ivo and ask him to come out.

"Do we get a day off?"

"Not that I know of, but who knows? Come on, get yourself ready. I'll keep you company while you pack." She smiled at him as she climbed off the bed in her nightgown. By now it was almost like being married, and she had to remind herself to put on a robe.

"Did you get through to your agent today?" She called out to him from the shower and he shouted back.

"Yeah."

"What did he say?"

"Nothing good. I've had my last bloody extension from immigration, and as soon as I leave the show, I have to get out."

"Of the country?"

"Obviously."

"Oh, shit."

"Precisely. That was more or less what I said, give or take a few pungent expressions." He smiled at the half-open door, and a few minutes later she turned off the shower and returned, wrapped in a towel, with another around her auburn hair.

"What are you going to do about that?" She looked concerned for him. She knew how much he wanted to stay.

"There's nothing I can do, love. I'll go." He shrugged and looked into his coffee with a wistful look in his eyes.

"I wish there were something I could do for you, Anthony."

But this time he only grinned lopsidedly. " 'Fraid not, love, you're already married."

"Would that do it?" She looked surprised.

"Sure. If I marry an American, I'm home free."

"So marry someone just for the hell of it. You can always get a quickie Dominican divorce right afterward. Hell, that's a terrific idea."

"Not really. I'd have to live with her for six months."

"So? There must be someone."

But he shook his head. "I'm afraid not."

"Then we'll have to drum up someone for you." But this time they both laughed, and she disappeared into the bathroom again. When she emerged, she was wearing a turquoise silk blouse and a white linen skirt. There was a matching jacket over her arm, and she was wearing high-heeled black patent leather sandals. She looked wonderfully crisp and summery, and Anthony smiled as he looked at her.

"You look lovely, Bettina." He said it gently, with a mixture of affection, awe, and respect. And then later, as they were riding to the airport, "How's your husband, by the way? Isn't he ever coming out?"

But Bettina shook her head slowly. "He says there's not much point if we don't get a day off. I guess he's right." She didn't seem anxious to pursue the subject, and after that there was chaos getting them all onto the plane. At last they were seated side by side on the aircraft. He read a magazine, and she read a book. From time to time he said something to her sotto voce, and she laughed, and then she shared something amusing with him from the book. To anyone who didn't know them, they looked as though they had been married for years.

The San Francisco airport looked like all the others, large, spread out, crowded, and chaotic. And at last they got everyone into the appropriate bus to the city, and then finally into cabs to the hotel. Bettina gritted her teeth to see one more ugly hotel room, and when the taxi stopped, she looked up in surprise. It wasn't the usual plastic commercial hotel she had expected. Instead it looked small and French, and it was perched on a hill with a breathtaking view of the bay. It looked in fact more like someone's home than a hotel where the road show would stay.

"Anthony?" She looked at him in astonishment. "Do you suppose they made a mistake?" She got out slowly and looked around with a mixture of pleasure and dismay. "Wait till the others see this." And then she grinned at him as he paid the driver. She was suddenly very amused. But there was something in Anthony's eyes that she did not quite understand.

"The others aren't staying here, Bettina." He said it to her very softly as they stood on the street.

"What do you mean?" She looked at him in confusion, not able or willing to understand. "Where are they?"

"At the usual fleabag hotel downtown." And then with a gentle look in his eyes, "I thought you'd like it better here."

"But why?" She looked suddenly frightened. "Why should we stay here?"

"Because you're used to this kind of thing, and it's beautiful. You'll love it, and we're both sick to death of lousy hotels." It was true. But why here? And why did he always talk about what she was used to? Why should they stay in a separate hotel, just the two of them? "Will you trust me?" And then he turned to her with a look of challenge. "Or do you want to go?" She hesitated for a long moment, sighed, and then shook her head.

"No, I'll stay. But I don't know why you did it. Why didn't you say something to me first?" She was tired and suspicious and she was suddenly unsure of what she saw in his eyes.

"I wanted to surprise you."

"But what will the others say?"

"Who cares?" But she was hanging back again and he dropped the bags and reached for her hands. "Bettina, are we friends or not?"

She nodded slowly. "We are."

"Then trust me. Just this once. It's all I ask." And she did. He had already asked for adjoining rooms, and when she saw them, she had to admit that they were so pretty that suddenly she wanted to throw her arms around his neck and laugh.

"Oh, screw it, Anthony, you're right. God, it's lovely!"

"Isn't it?" He looked victorious as they stood on her terrace and enjoyed the view.

And then she looked at him sheepishly. "I'm sorry I made such a fuss. I'm just so damn tired, and I . . . oh, I don't know . . . it's been so long since I've seen Ivo, and I worry about things, and. . . ."

But he spoke softly with an arm around her shoulders, "Never mind, love. Never mind."

She smiled at him and walked slowly back inside to relax luxuriously on a pale-blue-velvet chaise longue. There was fabric on the walls, and lovely French furniture, a little marble fireplace, and a four-poster bed. When he walked back into the room, she smiled at him again. "How did you ever find this place?"

"Luck, I guess. The first time I came to the States. And I always promised myself" — he looked down at his hands as he spoke — "that I'd come back here with someone I care about a great deal." And then his eyes rose to hers again. "And I care very much about you." He was barely able to say the words, and as he did Bettina felt her whole body grow warm. She didn't know what to answer, but she knew that she cared about him too.

"Anthony, I — I shouldn't. . . ." She stood up, feeling awkward, and turned her back to him as she stood in the middle of the room. And then she heard him, next to her, and she felt him touching her shoulders gently until he had turned her to face him, and without saying anything more, he kissed her, with body and soul and fire and ecstasy, full on the lips.

18

At first Bettina didn't understand how it happened, or even what led her to do a thing like that, except that it had been five weeks since she had seen Ivo, and being on the road with the show, she felt as though she were existing in a whole other world. And now she realized for how long she had been attracted to Anthony, and much as she hated to admit it, how exquisite it was to be joined with a youthful body and young flesh. They drank of each other endlessly, until it was almost time to go to the theater. And Bettina left her bed almost in a daze, not knowing what to say to him, or what to think of herself. But Anthony was quick to see her expression and he sat her back down on the bed.

"Bettina, look at me. . . ." But she wouldn't. "Darling, please."

"I don't know what to think. I don't understand. . . ." And then she looked at him, agonized. "Why did we —"

"Because we wanted to. Because we need each other and we understand each other." And then he looked at her very hard. "I love you, Bettina. That was part of it too. Don't overlook that. Don't tell yourself it was just bodies here in this bed. It wasn't. It was much, much more than that. And if you deny that, then you're lying to yourself." And then, firmly, he brought her face up to his. "Look at me, Bettina." And slowly, agonizingly, she did. "Do you love me? Answer me honestly. Because I know I love you. Do you love me?"

Her voice was barely a whisper. "I don't know."

"Yes, you do. You'd never have made love to me if you didn't love me. You're not that kind of woman. Are you, Bett?" And then more softly, "Are you?" And this time she nodded, and then quickly shook her head. "Do you love me? Answer me . . . say it . . . say it please. . . ." She could feel his words begin to caress her body again and as she looked at him she heard herself speaking.

"I love you." And then he put his arms around her and held her.

"I know that you do." He looked down at her tenderly. "Now we'll go to the theater, and afterward we'll come back here." But just to remind her of what would happen, he made love to her again quickly, there on the bed. She was breathless and panting when he left her, and astonished at her own passion, her hunger. She was like an alcoholic guzzling wine. She couldn't get enough of him, of his body, so satiny smooth beneath her hand. But on the way to the theater thoughts of Ivo began to press into her head. What if he called her? If he knew? What if he asked where they were staying? What if he came out to California as a surprise? What in hell was she doing? But each time she tried to tell herself it was madness, she thought of their lovemaking and knew she didn't want it to end. She could barely get through her work at the theater that evening, and when they got back to the hotel, they made love all night. It made her wonder how long they had kept the friendship so platonic, and for so long.

"Happy?" He smiled down at her, in the crook of his arm.

"I don't know." She looked up at him honestly, and then smiled. "Yes, of course." But in her heart was a terrible aching for Ivo. She felt pierced by a knife edge of guilt.

But Anthony knew. "I understand, Bettina. It's all right."

But she wondered if he did. She wondered

if he had Ivo's genius for loving. He didn't have Ivo's experience or his years. There were benefits in loving a man that much older. He had used up his unkindness, learned his lessons long before. All he had left for her now was kindness and gentleness and loving. She grew very pensive as she thought of that. And then Anthony seemed to know what she was thinking. "What are you going to tell him?"

"Nothing." And then she turned to look at Anthony. He looked suddenly hurt. "I couldn't, Anthony. It's not the same. If he were younger, it would be different. This way it just becomes an issue of his age."

"But isn't that the issue? Partly?" Jesus, she was tough to convince. He suddenly realized what kind of fight he had in store.

"I don't know." He didn't press the point that night. They had better things to do. But again and again Bettina found herself thinking first of Anthony, then of Ivo, then of Anthony again. It was a maddening circle, and her only escape from it was in Anthony's arms. In the course of the week she found herself not calling Ivo. Her guilt would have weighed on her too much. She couldn't pretend to him. She didn't want to lie. And she didn't want to tell him. So she simply fled. He called often, he left messages, and at last he reached her, in Los Angeles late one night. They hadn't spoken in nine days. And now there was no longer any pretense. She and Anthony were sharing a room.

"Darling? Are you all right?" There was a faint hint of desperation in his voice, and as Bettina heard him her eyes filled with tears.

"Ivo . . . I'm fine . . . oh, darling —" And then suddenly she couldn't speak. But she had to . . . had to . . . or he would know. She was suddenly grateful that Anthony was already asleep. "It's been so crazy, so much work . . . I haven't stopped. And I didn't want to call until I could tell you when to come out."

"Is it still just as crazy?" His voice sounded oddly tense, and next to her in the bed Anthony stirred. She hesitated for a moment, and then nodded, squeezing the tears from her eyes.

"Yes, it is." It was barely a whisper, but at his end Ivo understood.

"Then we'll wait, darling. I'll see you when you get home. You don't need to feel pressed. We have the rest of our lives." But did they? He was no longer sure. Bettina felt as though she were being torn from him by hands stronger than hers.

"Oh, Ivo, I miss you so much. . . ." She

sounded like a desperately unhappy child, and at his end Ivo closed his eyes. But he had to tell her. Had to. It was only fair.

"Bettina . . . little one. . . ." He took a deep breath. "This is all part of your growing up, little one. You have to do it. No matter what."

"What do you mean 'no matter what'?" She sat up in bed, straining to hear. Did he know? Had he guessed then? What was he saying or was he talking about the show?

"I mean that no matter what it costs you, if it's what you want, Bettina, it's right. Don't ever be afraid to pay the price. Sometimes we have to pay some pretty high prices . . . even if that means our not seeing each other for you to be with this play, even if that means —" He couldn't go on. But he didn't have to. "Just be a big girl, Bettina. You have to, darling. It's time." But she didn't want to be a big girl. Suddenly all she wanted to be was a very little girl with him. "Go to sleep now, Bettina, it's late."

And then she realized. "It's even later for you." Back East it was three hours later, and it was two thirty in the morning in L.A. "Good Lord, what are you even doing up at this hour?"

"I wanted to be sure I got hold of you."

"Oh, darling, I'm sorry." Once again she

was overcome with remorse.

"Don't be. Now be young, and have fun, and —" He had been about to say And remember that you're mine, but he didn't want to say that. He wanted to let her fly free if that was what she wanted. Whatever it cost him. "I love you, little one."

"I love you, Ivo."

"Good night."

When she hung up, there were tears streaming down her face and Anthony was snoring softly. For a brief moment she hated him.

But three days later she wasn't sure if she didn't hate Ivo more. There was an article in an L.A. paper about the well-known star of the Hollywood screen, Margot Banks, spending the weekend in New York, visiting a very dear old friend, whose name she had refused to disclose to the press. The piece went on to mention however that she had been seen dining at 21 with the retired publisher of the *New York Mail,* Ivo Stewart. Bettina knew full well that Margot had been one of her father's paramours, and later one of Ivo's, while Bettina was still growing up. Was that why he was being so understanding? Was that why he hadn't come out? Jesus, here she was crucifying herself every night for making love with Anthony when he had revived his old affair with Margot Banks. Was that what was happening? Was it he who felt like roving after their seven years? As she thought of it Bettina felt a wave of white-hot fury rise in her. The next time Ivo called her, she had one of the gophers tell him that she was out. And from where he sat, drinking coffee in his chair, Mr. Anthony Pearce looked enormously pleased.

19

For three more months it went on, until the road show closed. Anthony and Bettina passionately made their way from town to town, hotel to hotel, and bed to bed. They never saw anything of the cities they worked in. They spent their time rehearsing, performing, and making love. And more and more often now Bettina was seeing Ivo's name in the papers linked with one or the other of the women who had long ago populated his life. But mainly with Margot, the old bitch. Bettina almost snarled each time she saw her name. It only made Anthony laugh at her. She was hardly in a position to make jealous scenes. And she never mentioned the gossip to Ivo, but there was a definite strain between them now when they spoke on the phone. The four months away from each other hadn't done much good.

"So?" Anthony looked at her questioningly

on their last day on the road. "Now what?"

"What the hell does that mean?" She was exhausted and it was broiling out, on a summer day in Nashville, Tennessee.

"Don't get nasty, Bettina. But I think I have a right to ask you what I can look forward to now. Is it over? Is this it? Now you go home to your penthouse and your old man?" He looked at her bitterly. He was equally tired, and the heat was getting to him too.

Bettina seemed to wilt as she looked at him and slowly she sat down on the creaking bed. As it turned out the accommodations Anthony had made for them in San Francisco had been their only decent hotel rooms in four months. If for no other reason it was going to be good to get home, just so she could climb into her own bed. But the fact of it was that despite the gossip she was longing to see Ivo. So they had both been foolish. That was no reason to end what they had. And she had learned a lesson. She would never go on the road again. As much as she had enjoyed the affair with Anthony, it was time to go home.

"I don't know, Anthony. I can't give you any answers."

"I see." And then after a moment, "I suspect that means you're staying with him."

"I told you" — her voice rose ominously — "I don't know. What do you want from me? A contract?"

"Maybe, love. Maybe that. Has it occurred to you that while you go home to your darling little elderly husband, I am out of a job, out of a romance, and possibly out of a country? I'd say I have good reason to be concerned."

Suddenly she felt for him. He was right. She did have Ivo. And what did he have? From the sound of it he had nothing left. "I'm sorry, Anthony." She went to him and touched his face with her hand. "I'll let you know what's happening as soon as I know myself."

"Wonderful. This is beginning to sound like a job interview. Well, let me tell you one thing, Miss Assistant Director, whatever you may think, whatever I may or may not mean to you, I want to make one thing very clear before we go. And that is that I love you." His voice quavered on the words. "And that if you'll be so kind as to leave your husband, I want to marry you. Immediately. Do you understand?"

She looked at him, stupefied. "Are you serious? But why?"

He couldn't keep from smiling at her words, and then softly he ran a finger around her face, down her neck, and slowly toward her breasts. "Because you're beautiful, and you're intelligent, and wonderful, and" — he looked at her seriously for a moment — "you're not the sort of girl one just plays around with. You're the sort of girl one marries, Bett." She looked at him in amazement and he smiled. "So, my darling, if I can pry you out of your existing situation" — he went down on one knee next to her and kissed her hand — "I would like to make you Mrs. Anthony Pearce."

"I don't know what to say."

"Just call me the day after we get to New York and say yes."

But she knew that she wouldn't do that. She couldn't have done that to Ivo. What she hadn't counted on was Ivo doing it to her.

20

"Ivo, you don't mean it." As she stared at him her face turned an ashen gray. "But why?"

"Because it's time. For both of us." What was he saying? Oh, God, what did he mean? "I think it may be time for both of us to start with lovers our own age."

"But I don't want that!" And then with horror, "Do you?" He didn't answer. But only because his guts were being torn apart. He was certain of what had happened. And he had availed himself of certain reports. She was involved with the actor. And she had been involved with him for months. Perhaps even before they left New York. Ivo wasn't going to stand in the way of that. She had a right to something more. She was so young. "But I don't *want* to leave you!" She almost shrieked it at him as he sat calmly in his den.

"I think you do."

"Is it because of the other women I've been reading that you're going out with? Is it because of them? Ivo, tell me!" She was suddenly frantic and frighteningly pale, but he held firm.

"I told you, this will be better for both of us. And you should be free."

"But I don't want to be free."

"But you are free now. I'm not even going to drag this thing out unbearably for both of us, I'm going to fly to the Dominican Republic next weekend and it'll all be over. Finished. You will be legally free."

"But I don't want to be legally free, Ivo!!" She was shouting so loud, he was sure that Mathilde could hear everything through the door. Gently he reached out to Bettina and held her close to him.

"I will always be here for you, Bettina. I love you. But you need someone younger than I am." And then, as though explaining to a very slow child, he told her, "You can't be married to me anymore."

"But I don't want to leave you." She was wailing now and almost hysterical as she clutched at his hand. "Don't make me go . . . I'll never do it again . . . I'm sorry. . . . Oh, Ivo, I'm so sorry. . . ." Now she knew that he knew. He had to. Why else would he be doing this to her? As she clung to him she wondered how he could be so cruel.

And the tragedy of it was that inside he was dying, but he felt that it was the one thing he owed her. And yet it was the one thing she didn't want. He tried to explain to her through her hysteria that there would be a sum of money provided for her every month. He would never leave her penniless or stranded. He had also provided for her in his will. She could stay in the apartment until after he got back from the Dominican Republic, after which he suggested she move in with — er — a friend. And while she remained in residence, he himself would stay at a friend's club. Bettina listened to him in a stupor, she couldn't believe this was happening to her, this man who had rescued her, whom she had so desperately loved. But she had spoiled everything by sleeping with Anthony, and Ivo knew. Now she had to be punished.

The next days passed by her like a nightmare, and she could remember no more painful moment in her life. Not even the death of her father had left her feeling so broken, so abandoned, so desperately unable to turn the tides of what had come. She didn't even want to speak to Anthony, yet the day before Ivo returned from the

Dominican Republic, she sat in her bedroom late at night, almost hysterical, and she could think of no one to reach out to but him.

"Who? What? Oh, my God, you sound awful . . . are you all right?" And then after a pause, "Do you want to come over?" She hesitated for a moment, and then she said yes. "Do you want me to come and get you?" It was a gesture of chivalry she appreciated but didn't feel was quite right. So she climbed into blue jeans, sandals, and a shirt, and a few minutes later she got in a cab and was on her way to him.

"He *what?*" Anthony was making them coffee as they sat in his comfortable kitchen on ladder-back chairs.

"He told me he wants a divorce, and he's in the Dominican Republic this weekend getting it." She repeated it mechanically as fresh tears washed over her face.

Anthony stood there and grinned. "I told you, ducky, he's senile, but who am I to complain? You mean he's divorcing you?" She nodded. "This weekend?" She nodded again and he gave out a whoop.

"I might tell you, Anthony," she sniffed loudly, "I think your elation is in very poor taste."

"Do you?" He grinned at her. "Do you,

my love? Well, I don't. I've never been so bloody happy about anything in my life." And then with a polite bow he turned to her. "Will you do me the honor of marrying me on Monday?"

She curtsied equally politely and said, "I will not."

He was momentarily taken aback. "Why the hell not?"

She sighed and walked to the couch and sat down, blowing her nose again. "Because we hardly know each other. Because we're both young. Because . . . Jesus, Anthony . . . I've been married to someone for seven years whom I cared about a great deal, he's gone off to get a divorce, and you expect me to get married the next day? I'd have to be crazy. At least give me a chance to catch my breath." But catching her breath wasn't the point really. She didn't want to marry him. She wasn't sure of him. As a lover yes, but not as a mate.

"Fine. And you can write to me in England." He looked suddenly sour.

"What's that supposed to mean?" She looked over at him and frowned.

"Precisely that. I have to be out of the country by Friday."

"At the end of next week?"

"That's when Friday usually comes

around."

"Don't be cute, I'm serious."

"So am I. Extremely so as a matter of fact. In fact I was about to start packing when you called." And then he brightened. "But if we got married, I wouldn't have to go anywhere, would I?"

She looked at him squarely. "That's a hell of a reason to get married."

But he moved close to her as she said it, and then he sat down and took her hand. "Bett, think of our months with that damn road show. If we can stay happy and close through all of that, we can make it through anything. You know I love you. I told you I wanted to marry you, so what difference does it make if it's this week or next year?"

"Maybe a lot of difference." She looked at him nervously and shook her head, and quickly he dropped the subject. A little while later they wound up in bed, and the subject didn't come up again until the next morning, when he reminded her that she was not only about to lose her husband, but her lover as well. That dismal reality had not yet fully come home to her, and she burst into fresh tears.

"Oh, for God's sake stop crying. There's a way to solve everything, you know."

"Stop pushing for your own goddamn

interests." But he did, and he was brilliant at it. By the end of the afternoon, she was a nervous wreck. And then, checking her watch, she realized that she had to go back to Ivo's apartment. She had to finish packing the rest of her things and get them to a hotel. But when she told Anthony, he insisted that she stay with him. She wasn't absolutely sure that she ought to, but on the other hand it would be less brutally lonely for the first few days than a hotel. And as long as she had lived with him in hotel rooms all summer, there was no reason not to stay with him now. She also realized with a dull thud that she was no longer married. By that day Ivo would have gotten the divorce.

So at five o'clock she went uptown in a taxi to collect the rest of her things, and she was oddly reminded of when she had moved out of her father's empty apartment and come to stay at Ivo's. It was seven years later, and now she was moving in with another man. But only briefly, she promised herself. And then she reminded herself that she had only come to Ivo's to stay briefly too.

By Monday she was feeling more herself. On Monday evening he took her out to dinner. And on Tuesday he started to pack. By Wednesday the apartment was a shambles, and it was clear that in two days she was going to have to face another wrenching adieu. That morning she spoke to Ivo, and he was odd and cool and determined about what he had done. And when she hung up, she looked at Anthony, with fresh tears in her eyes. In two days he would be gone too. But he knew what she was thinking, and he had looked pointedly into her eyes. "Will you do it?" She looked at him blankly. "Will you marry me, Bettina? Please?"

And then she had to smile. He looked like a small boy as he asked her.

"But it doesn't make any sense. It's too soon."

"No, it's not too soon." And this time there were tears in his eyes. "It's almost too late. If we don't get a license today, we can't do it by Friday. And then I'm going to have to leave you. No matter what I feel . . . no matter what. . . ." The words had an oddly familiar ring to Bettina and she remembered Ivo saying them to her on the phone when she was in California with Anthony. She also remembered his telling her to pay the price for what she believed in, "no matter what."

"And if it doesn't work?" She looked at him steadily.

"Then we get divorced."

She spoke softly. "I've already done that, Anthony. I don't want to do that again."

He moved closer and reached out to hold her. "We won't have to. We'll be together forever and always. . . ." And then he held her tighter. "We'll have a baby . . . oh, Bettina, please. . . ." And as he held her she couldn't resist him. She wanted so desperately to cling to him, not to lose yet one more person who had meant something to her. And she wanted equally desperately to be loved. "Will you?"

She held her breath for a moment and nodded. He could barely hear her answer. "Yes."

He got to City Hall before closing on Wednesday. They got the license, the blood test, and Anthony got the ring. And on Friday morning, at City Hall again, they were married. And Bettina Daniels Stewart became Mrs. Anthony Pearce.

21

Anthony and Bettina spent the autumn months hibernating quietly after their September wedding. He hadn't gotten cast in another play and she hadn't returned to her job. She realized that she had the background she needed. And she certainly had the experience, the heartache to begin to write. Anthony didn't feel pressure to return either. Married to Bettina, he could stay in the States. And living on her alimony from Ivo, he decided that he could wait for the right part. Once or twice Bettina felt awkward about it, after all Ivo had provided the money for her. But it was obvious that Anthony felt embarrassed enough about his lack of employment, so she didn't press the point. And after all she wasn't working either. She decided she would take a break, get to know Anthony, every nook, every corner, every cranny of his mind. There were parts that she realized she didn't really know, parts of him that she knew he kept from her, however close they might seem.

So they tucked themselves into his apartment, read plays, cooked spaghetti, went for long walks, and made love. They laughed and talked and chuckled into the morning hours . . . when Anthony was at home. There were many evenings when he went to see other actors perform, and afterward he and his friends talked far into the night. Alone in the loft, she understood how Ivo must have felt when she left him to work at the theater.

In fact she thought about Ivo a lot. She wondered what he was doing, if he was still so tired, if he was all right. She found herself wanting to turn to him, to hear his gentleness, his encouragement, and his praise. And what she found instead was Anthony's nonchalance and his humor, his warmth, and his passion, which spent itself so readily in her arms.

"What are you looking so glum about, love?" He had been watching her for a while, gnawing at a pencil as she poised over some notes for her play. She looked up in surprise as she heard him. He had been out for hours and she hadn't heard him come in.

"Nothing. How was your evening?"

"Very pleasant. Yours?" he asked her casually as he unwound a long cashmere scarf from around his neck. Bettina had bought it for him at the first sign of winter. After he insisted that she sell her mink coat. They had been living on the proceeds for two months.

"It was okay." But she was looking gloomy, and she hadn't been feeling well all day.

He smiled as he looked at her and came to sit down on the edge of the bed. "Now, come on, lover. Tell me. Something's wrong."

At first she only shook her head, and then she laughed softly and took his face in her hands. "No. I was just thinking about Christmas. And I wanted to give you something wonderful. But I don't see how I can." She looked at him regretfully and he pulled her into his arms.

"That doesn't matter, silly. We have each other. That's all I want." And then he grinned mischievously. "That and a Porsche."

"Very funny." But it was odd to remember that Ivo had given her a diamond bracelet the Christmas before. And she had given him a new cashmere coat, a four-hundred-dollar briefcase, and a gold lighter. But those days were gone forever now. All she had left was the jewelry, and that was carefully stowed in the vault. She hadn't even told Anthony. She had simply told him that she'd returned it all to Ivo when she left. As a matter of fact she had offered to return to him all the pieces that he'd given her, but he had insisted that she keep them, on the condition that she told no one where they were. He wanted her to keep them, like a nest egg, and she had followed his advice. Now, for a moment, she contemplated selling something, just for Christmas. But she knew that to do so would arouse Anthony's suspicions that she was hiding something more. And she was. Now she sighed as she looked at him. "Do you realize that we can't afford to give each other anything?" She looked like a child who had just lost her most cherished toy.

But Anthony was undaunted. "Sure we can. We can give each other a turkey and a Christmas dinner. We can write each other poems. We can go for a long walk in the park." And he made it sound so lovely that she smiled and brushed away her tears.

"I wanted to give you much more than that."

And then, reaching out for her gently, he whispered. "You already have."

■ ■ ■ ■

But in the week that followed, her thoughts of Christmas were all but obscured. She became violently ill with some kind of flu that had her retching and gagging most of the day on the bathroom floor. By evening she would feel a little better. But it all started with fresh anguish in the morning. And by the end of the week she looked ghastly and wan.

"You'd better see a doctor, Bett." Anthony looked at her one afternoon as she staggered out of the bathroom.

But she was hesitant about going to Ivo's doctor. She didn't want to have to explain to him, didn't want him to report to Ivo, or to pry. So she got the name of a doctor from a friend of Anthony's, some girl they had worked with on their last show. The waiting room was tiny and crowded, the magazines dog-eared, the furniture old, and the people all downcast and poor. By the time she got in to see the doctor, she was feeling not only nauseated but faint, and it was only a few moments later that she was retching violently into a bowl. But as she looked up at him his eyes were gentle, and with kind hands he helped her smooth back her hair.

"That bad, huh?" She nodded, trying to catch her breath. "Has it been like this for long?" His eyes looked her over carefully, but they were nice eyes, and Bettina felt less frightened as she lay down on the table with a soft sigh.

"It's been almost two weeks."

"Any worse? Any better? Or has it been like this the whole time?" He pulled up a stool on casters and sat down next to her with a small smile.

"It's been pretty much like this the whole time. Sometimes it's better in the evening, but not much." He nodded slowly then and made a note on her chart.

"Has this ever happened before?"

She shook her head quickly. "Never."

And then he looked at her very gently and searched her eyes. "Have you ever been pregnant before?"

But she only shook her head as she watched him. And then it dawned on her, and she sat up quickly. "Am I pregnant now?"

"You might be." And then, "Would that be very bad?"

She shrugged pensively, and then a small smile dawned in her eyes. "I don't know."

"Is your husband an actor?" Most of his patients were. It was a world in which everything spread like wildfire, recommendations, referrals, gossip, diseases. And along with the rest, his name had been passed along. She nodded. "Is he working right now?" He knew how that was also. Sometimes he had to wait to get paid for five or six months, if at all.

"No, he's not. But I'm sure he will be shortly."

"What about you? An actress?"

She shook her head, smiling slowly. What was she? An assistant director? A budding playwright? A gopher? She was nothing now. She could no longer just say, "I'm Justin Daniels's daughter" or "I'm Ivo Stewart's wife." "I'm just Anthony Pearce's wife." She said it as though by reflex as the doctor watched her, sensing that there was a lot more to her story than that. The sweater she was wearing was expensive, as was the tweed skirt. The loafers were Gucci, and although the coat she had been wearing had been oddly cheap in contrast, he saw that she was wearing a very fancy gold watch.

"Well, let's take a look at you." And he did and he made an accurate guess. To confirm it they did a pregnancy test in his office, which showed that he had been right. "I'd say you're about two months pregnant, Bettina." He watched for her reaction and was touched by the broad smile. "You don't look too unhappy."

"I'm not." She thanked him and made another appointment, although after that he said he'd have to refer her to someone else. He couldn't give her anything for the vomiting and nausea, but suddenly they didn't seem so bad, and he assured her that in another month it would probably disappear, or at least subside. She didn't even care now. It was worth it. She was going to have a baby! She was going to have Anthony's child! Suddenly even betraying Ivo didn't seem so terrible. It was worth it now. She was going to have a *baby!* She floated all the way home and almost raced up to the loft, and then suddenly she felt stricken. Maybe she shouldn't have run . . . maybe it was bad for the baby. She came roaring into the living room like a tornado, brimming with her news, but Anthony wasn't there.

She drank bouillon, ate some crackers, got sick again, and tried to eat again. The doctor had told her that she should try it. And she had promised that she would. For the baby. And then suddenly, as she sat there, she had an idea. She wouldn't tell Anthony. Not yet. She'd wait till Christmas. That would be her gift to him. It was only another five days away. And she giggled to herself as she thought of her secret . . . she clapped her hands like a child as she thought of it . . . they were going to have a baby! She could hardly wait to hear what he'd say.

22

On Christmas Eve Anthony surprised her and came home with a tiny little tree. They set it on a table, and she tied it with ribbons. They made popcorn, which she didn't eat, and they each put one tiny package under the tree. It reminded them both of an old movie, and they laughed as they kissed. She opened hers first. It was an old-fashioned fountain pen, a lovely one, and he smiled at her pleasure. "To write your first play!" She hugged him and thanked him and he kissed her long and hard.

"Now yours." She had given him a pair of silver cuff links that he had been drooling over for weeks in a nearby antique shop.

"Bettina, you're crazy!" He was delighted and ran to change shirts so he could put them on. And with a small smile she followed him and sat down quietly on the bed.

"Anthony?" Her voice was strangely soft as she spoke to him, and not knowing why, he turned around.

"Yes, lover?" His eyes met hers.

"I have another present for you."

"Do you?" He tilted his head to one side, but neither of them moved.

She nodded. "Yes. A very special one." And then she held out her arms to him. "Come here and sit down."

Something very odd crawled up his spine. He came to her hesitating, with a look of anxiety in his eyes. "Is something wrong?" But she shook her head quickly and smiled.

"No." She kissed him then, tenderly, softly, and afterward ran her fingertips across his mouth. In a whisper that only he could have heard, "We're going to have a baby, darling." And then she waited. But what she wanted never came. Instead he looked at her, frozen. It was as bad as he had thought. The possibility had crossed his mind with all her vomiting, but he had forced it out of his head. It was more than he could cope with, and it would spoil all his plans.

"Are you kidding?" He stood up next to her and then looked down again. "No, I guess you're not." He threw the cuff links on the table and walked out of the room, and Bettina tried to fight an urge to cry and get sick all at the same time. Slowly she followed him out to the living room and watched him as he stood at the window, his back to her, and running a distracted hand through his hair.

"Anthony?" She looked at him hesitantly, and slowly he turned around.

"Yeah." He stared at her angrily, saying nothing for a time, and then the look of accusation came clear in his eyes. "Did you do that on purpose, Bettina?" With tears in her eyes she shook her head. She had wanted him to be so happy. She wanted it to mean something to him too. And then, never taking his eyes from hers, "Would you consider an abortion?" But this time she couldn't hold back the tears, and shaking her head, she fled the room. And when she emerged from the bathroom half an hour later, he was gone.

"Merry Christmas," she whispered to herself softly with one hand resting gently on her still flat stomach and the other wiping her ceaselessly crying eyes. She fell asleep at last at four in the morning. But Anthony never came home that night.

He didn't return until five o'clock the next afternoon. Christmas was almost over, and for Bettina it had been ruined. She didn't ask him where he'd been. She didn't say anything. She was packing her bags. But that had been what he had feared. And it was what had brought him home. Three months into the marriage he couldn't afford to lose her. Not yet.

"I'm sorry." He looked at her bleakly from the bedroom doorway. "You just took me by surprise."

"So I gathered." She turned her back to him and continued to pack her bags.

"Look, Bettina . . . baby, I'm sorry." He went to her and tried to hold her but she shook him off.

"Don't do that."

"Look, dammit, I love you!" He turned her around to face him, and once again there were tears in her eyes.

"Just leave me alone . . . please . . . Anthony, I. . . ." But she couldn't go on. She wanted him so badly. Wanted to share with him the joy of his child that she found herself melting into his arms and hoping that the dreams would come true after all.

"It's all right, baby. It's all right. I just couldn't imagine . . . I'm not . . ." And then at last when her tears had subsided, they sat down. "But are we ready, Bettina?"

She smiled valiantly through red eyes. "Sure. Why not?" For all those years with Ivo she had stifled that dream. She hadn't even known how much she wanted children.

Until now. Suddenly this meant everything to her.

"But how will we feed it?" He looked bleak, but she was thinking of her jewelry. She'd sell everything if she had to, just to take care of the child.

"Don't worry. We'll manage. We manage now, don't we?"

"That's not the same thing."

And then, sighing deeply, as though it caused him pain too, he looked at her regretfully. "As much as I'd hate to do it, don't you think it would make more sense this time to have an abortion and then try again later, when we've saved some money, when we're both on our feet, when I'm not out of work?" But she was shaking her head determinedly.

"No."

"Bettina . . . be reasonable!"

"Goddamn it, is that all you want? An abortion?" On and on the argument raged. In the end Bettina won. But Anthony looked grim for the next two weeks. She didn't leave him, but she thought of it often, and then suddenly one day he came home radiant and gave out a loud whoop.

She came to find him in the doorway and smiled when she saw his broad grin. "What happened to you?" But she could guess.

"I got work!"

"What kind of work? Tell me!" She was happy for him and followed him to the couch; suddenly their hostility of the past weeks seemed to dim. "Come on, Anthony . . . tell me!"

"I will, I will!" But for a moment he seemed too happy to talk. It was a beautiful part. "I got the lead in *Sonny Boy*!" He looked at her triumphantly. It was the biggest hit on Broadway.

"On Broadway?" She looked stunned. She had recently heard a rumor that the star was leaving the show after its stellar fifteen-month run. But Anthony was shaking his head.

"On the road, my love, on the road. But not shit towns this time, my darling. All the best cities in the States. This time we travel with a little class! No flophouses, no cockroaches. We can even stay in some decent hotels for a change." And then he told her how much they were paying him.

"Anthony! That's fabulous." But she realized she had to tell him something then. She had noticed his "we." Regretfully she took his hand and spoke gently. "But sweetheart, I can't . . ." She hated to say it, but she had to. "I can't go along."

"Of course you can. Don't be ridiculous.

Why can't you?" He looked at her nervously and stood up.

But Bettina looked at him firmly. "No, darling. I can't. The baby. That kind of traveling would be too much."

"Bullshit it would, Bettina. I told you, we'll be staying in decent hotels. We're going to big cities. So what the hell is your problem? Christ, it doesn't even show!" He was shouting at her, and she could see his hands shake.

"Just because it doesn't show doesn't mean it isn't there. And it doesn't matter what kind of hotels we stay in, that's a lot of traveling."

"Well, you'd better make up your mind to do it." He stalked across the room and looked back at her. "Because if you don't go with me, I'm still out of work."

"Don't be ridiculous, Anthony." But she was momentarily touched. "You mean you won't go without me?"

He paused for a long time, standing in the doorway. "I mean that they want you as assistant director, sister. They want us as a pair. And they want us together. You don't do it, they won't hire me."

"What? But that's crazy!"

"The producer saw us work together on the road and they think we make a good team. As it so happens their director on this one is kind of a figurehead, so he'll get the glory, but you'll be doing the work. It's not a great arrangement, but the money is good. Two fifty a week for you." But she didn't seem to care.

"That's not the point, Anthony. I'm pregnant. Did you tell them that?"

"Hardly." He spat the word at her.

But now she was angry too. It was starting all over again. "I won't do it, damn you!"

"In that case, madam" — he swept her a low bow — "allow me to thank you for destroying my career. I hope you realize" — he stood up very straight and faced her across the room with fury in his eyes — "I hope you realize that if I turn this down I may not work for years."

"Oh, Anthony, that's not so. . . ." There were suddenly tears in her eyes again. But she also knew that was how it sometimes worked. Turn down a good offer, and word got around. "Whose company is it?" She heard the name Voorhees and she cringed. They were one of the most hard-nosed outfits in the business. "But, darling, I can't."

He didn't answer, he simply walked out and slammed the door. Dammit. It was a ridiculous arrangement. Why did they have to insist on having her too? She had gotten all the experience she wanted in the last seven years. Now she wanted to read every play she could get her hands on, and then she would write her own. Her in-house training was over as far as she was concerned. But Anthony was a different story. If she blew it for him, he could be out of work for a very, very long time. After thinking it over for two hours, she called the doctor and discussed the matter with him.

"What do you think?"

"I think you're crazy!"

"Why? Because it would be bad for the baby?"

"No, the baby won't care. But the way you've been feeling, can you think of anything worse than traveling from hotel room to hotel room for the next five or six months?" She nodded grimly in silent answer. "How long is the tour?"

"I don't know. I forgot to ask."

"Well, let's put it this way, if you can stand it, I don't see any physical reason why you shouldn't go, as long as you get as much rest as you can, eat decently, stay off your feet whenever possible, and come back to home base in" — he looked at her chart — "no more than five months. I want you back here when you're no more than seven and a half months pregnant. Any sensible obstetrician would tell you that. And I also want you to go to prenatal clinics when you're on the road. Call the biggest hospital in every town you hit and get checked once a month. Think you can handle all that?" His voice smiled at her over the phone.

"I guess I'll have to."

"Actually" — he sounded more gentle — "once the nausea settles down, it may not be so bad. The old vaudevillians used to do things like that. You've heard the expression 'born in a trunk'? They weren't kidding. I can think of easier ways to have a baby, but if you're sensible, it won't hurt you or the baby." With a long sigh Bettina hung up the phone. She had her answer. And four hours later Anthony had his.

But the tour was even more exhausting than the last one, and she worked her ass off every day on the road. It turned out that the director had an ironclad contract with the company so they had to take him along, but he was an alcoholic who spent every day drinking in his room, which left everything on Bettina's shoulders. And by the second month on the road she thought she would collapse. The hotels were not nearly as lovely as Anthony had promised, the hours were endless, and with no director to lean on, and an inadequate staff, Bettina was hauling, yelling, working, running every hour of the day. She was losing weight instead of gaining, and she had constant pains in her legs. She hardly ever saw Anthony, who spent every day, when they weren't rehearsing, out playing with his friends. In particular, with a little blond model from Cleveland who was making her debut in the show. Her name was Jeannie, and by the time they had left New York City, Bettina hated her guts. It made working with her difficult, as assistant director, but Bettina forced herself to be professional. She owed it to the girl, to herself, to the company, and to Anthony.

The second time she went to a clinic, the doctor told her where things stood. She was overworked, overwrought, and underweight, and if she didn't take things a little easier, she would lose the baby. She was almost four months pregnant. He suggested she ask her husband to help her a little, to reduce the pressure of her job. And that night after the performance she spoke to Anthony and asked him to help.

"Why, for chrissake? You planning to go up onstage and act for me?"

"Anthony . . . be serious. . . ."

"I am serious. What do I care if you lose the baby? I never wanted it in the first place. Listen, lover, that baby is *your* kid. You don't want to lose it, find someone else to help you out." And he had walked past her then and slid a hand into Jeannie's arm. He then informed Bettina that they were going out to dinner and not to wait up. She looked at him in stupefaction. What was happening to them? Why was he doing this? Was it just because of the child? She returned to her hotel room, troubled, and for the first time in two months the urge to call Ivo was almost overwhelming. But she couldn't do that anymore. She wasn't a little girl now. And she couldn't turn to Ivo just because this was hard. But she sat alone, alternately thinking and crying. Anthony never came home. She waited in her hotel room to confront him. But at noon the next day she finally had to leave for the theater. And Jeannie was waiting for her there.

"Looking for Anthony?" she cooed at Bettina, and Bettina felt everything inside her go taut.

"No, I came here to work. Anything I can do for you?"

"Yeah. Act like a lady." Jeannie hopped up on a stool, and it took all of Bettina's self-control not to knock her off.

"I beg your pardon?" Bettina's voice was like ice.

"You heard me, Betty."

"The name's Bettina. And just exactly what do you mean?" Suddenly Bettina knew that there was something major happening here. What was this girl saying? And where was Anthony in all this? Bettina felt her guts ache, but she didn't waver as she looked at the pretty blond girl.

"All right, Betty" — she had what the French call "a face to slap" — "why don't you just let Anthony do his thing now? His six months are almost up."

"What six months?" She made it sound like a jail sentence, and Bettina looked stunned.

"Just why do you think he married you, sweetheart? Because he was so madly in love? Hell, no, he wanted his green card, or didn't he tell you that?" Suddenly Bettina was horrified. "And you were the most likely candidate around. He knew your ex-husband would support you so he wouldn't have to worry about it. And he married you in September, right?" Bettina nodded dumbly. "Well, he only has to stay with you for six months, babe, and he gets the green card. He can get rid of you after that. And if you think he won't you're crazy. He doesn't give a damn about you, and he doesn't want that kid you were dumb enough to get knocked up with. And let me tell you something else" — she hopped off the stool and swung one well-formed hip — "if you think you're going to hang on to him when we get back to New York, you're nuts."

All day she hid in the theater, trying to concentrate on her work. And when at last Anthony arrived for the performance, she slipped into his dressing room and closed the door. She was there waiting for him when he walked into it, and fortunately he was alone. He eyed her strangely, and then walked to the closet and hung up his coat.

"What do you want, Bettina?"

"To talk." Her voice was firm, and he looked vague.

"I don't have time. I have to do my makeup for the show."

"Fine. We can talk while you do it." She pulled up a chair and sat down and he looked annoyed. "I had a little talk with your friend Jeannie today."

"What about?" He suddenly looked uncomfortable.

"Oh, let's see. Oh . . . that's right, she says that you married me just to get a green card, and that when the mandatory six months of living together are up in three weeks, then you're going to split. She also told me that you're crazy about her, more or less. She's awfully cute, darling. But is she accurate? That's what I wanted to ask you."

"Don't be silly." He avoided her eyes and dug around in his makeup box, but Bettina was right behind him, watching him in the mirror when he raised his eyes.

"What does that mean, Anthony?"

"It means that she may have gotten a little carried away."

Bettina grabbed his arm. "But that was more or less the truth, is that it? Is that what you're telling me, Anthony? Are you going to leave me after this show? Because if that's what you have in mind, I'd like to get used to the idea right now. I mean, after all" — she started to lose control of her voice and she sounded panicky — "I am having a baby and it might be nice to know if I'm going to be alone."

But suddenly he stood up and faced her, and he was shouting as he did. "I told you not to have the fucking baby, dammit! Everything would have been perfectly simple if you'd done as I said!" But he suddenly seemed to regret what he was saying and sat down.

"She was telling the truth, then?" Bettina's voice was grim. "It was just for the green card?"

And then for once he looked at her honestly and nodded. "Yes." She closed her eyes as she heard him and sat back down.

"My God, and I believed you." She looked at him and started to laugh as tears filled her eyes. "What a brilliant actor you are after all."

"It wasn't like that." He hung his head sheepishly.

"Wasn't it?"

"No. I cared about you, I really did. I just couldn't see it forever . . . I don't know . . . we're very different. . . ."

"You bastard." She'd been had, then. She'd been had all along. She slammed the door to his dressing room and hurried back toward the stage. The performance went smoothly and she left the theater immediately afterward, went back to the hotel, and asked for her own room. Not that it mattered, he probably wouldn't have come back to spend the night. But she didn't want to chance it. She wanted to be alone to think.

Now she was going to go home and write her play. And in another five months she'd have the baby. . . . As she thought of it she closed her eyes tightly and tried not to cry.

But it was hopeless. Each time she thought of having the baby alone, with no father, she panicked and wanted desperately to reach out to him . . . Ivo . . . anyone . . . she couldn't do it alone . . . couldn't . . . but she had to. Now she had no choice.

After hours of crying and mulling it over, at last she fell asleep, and it was four in the morning when she awakened with a strange sensation of cramps, and when she sat up in bed and looked down at the sheets, she saw blood. Her first instinct was to panic, and then she forced herself to calm down. After all, this was Atlanta. They had good hospitals. Two days earlier she had seen a doctor; now all she had to do was call the hospital and ask for him.

When she called, the nurse in the emergency room listened to the symptoms and told her to come in right away. She assured Bettina that it was probably nothing. Sometimes bleeding occurred, and with a few days of rest everything settled down. She told her to just have her husband bring her in. It was a nice assumption, but Bettina didn't even call his room. She dressed hastily, trying to stand upright in spite of the strange cramps, and she hurried to the lobby, and then out to the street to call a cab. But just walking from her room to the lobby had increased the intensity of the pain, and she was writhing badly in the backseat of the taxi as they hurried to the hospital. The driver caught sight of her in the rearview mirror, and suddenly she gasped and then there was a small scream.

"Lady, you all right back there?"

She tried to reassure him, but just as she did so, she was caught unprepared by another searing pain. "Ohhh . . . God . . . no . . . I'm . . . oh, please . . . can you hurry. . . ." But from the mild discomfort of only half an hour ago, she was suddenly in almost unbearable pain.

"Lie down on the seat." She tried to lie there, but even lying down no longer helped. She couldn't lie still on the seat as he drove her. She kept having to turn and clutch, and suddenly she wanted to tear and scream.

"Oh, God . . . hurry . . . I can't —"

They got the information they needed about her identity and her insurance from the wallet in her handbag; Bettina was too far gone to make any sense. She could barely speak. All she could do was clutch the straps on the gurney, and every few minutes she writhed horribly and screamed. The three nurses hovering over her exchanged a look, and then nodded, and when the doctor came in she was rushed immediately to a delivery room. The baby came only half an hour later. A small fetus that shot out of her as she screamed uncontrollably. It was already dead.

23

The plane touched down gently at Kennedy Airport, and Bettina stared out the window woodenly as they rolled toward the gate. She had just spent a week in the hospital, and she had only been discharged that afternoon. The day after her miscarriage she had called the theater company and explained that she was in the hospital and the doctors had ordered her to rest for three months. It wasn't true but it got her off the hook, and a new assistant director was flown out from New York, a young man who was very sorry for her and delivered all of her things from the hotel to the hospital room. Anthony had only come once, looking uncomfortable. He said he was sorry, which they both knew was a lie. She kept the meeting businesslike and explained that she would call an attorney as soon as she reached New York the following week. She would give him the benefit of waiting to file for another three weeks, and he could keep his green card with her blessing. And then, looking at him with a look of bottomless revulsion, she asked him to go. He stopped at the door to say something to her, but he didn't say it. He only shrugged, and then walked out, softly closing the door. After that he didn't call her. Nothing more was said. And two days later, with Bettina still in the hospital, the road show moved on.

The rest of her hospital stay was uneventful. She felt sad and lonely, not for Anthony, but for the child who had died. It had been a baby girl, they told her, and day after day she lay in bed and sobbed. It wouldn't help, the nurses told her, but they understood she had to get it out. But by the end of the week Bettina realized that it wasn't just the baby. It was everything. She was crying for her father and the way he had left her, for Ivo and what she had done to him, and then the firm way in which he in turn had put her out, for Anthony and what he had done for his green card, and now at last for this lost child. Now she had nothing and no one. No baby, no husband, no home, and no man. No one wanted her. She had no one. And at twenty-six she felt like she was at the end of her life.

She still felt that way as she unhooked her

seat belt in the plane and slowly wandered down the aisle. For her everything seemed to be moving strangely slowly. She felt as though she were underwater and she didn't really care. She picked up her bag at the baggage claim, got a porter, and went outside to find a cab. Forty-five minutes later she was unlocking the door to Anthony's apartment. She had promised herself that she would pack in a hurry and go to a hotel, but as she looked around the apartment again it was awful, and she started to cry. She fumbled in drawers, emptied cupboards, and packed the mountains of clothes in her closet. The job was done in less than two hours. She hadn't lived there that long with him. Not quite six months. And seven years with Ivo. Two divorces. She was beginning to feel like used merchandise. . . .

She gathered all her bags near the doorway, and then slowly walked downstairs to find a cab. With luck she'd find one who could be bribed to climb up to the apartment and help her bring down all her bags. As it turned out, she was lucky and a young cabbie stopped when she waved. It took them four trips together, but they got everything, and when they reached the hotel she had asked for, she handed him a twenty-dollar tip. Leaving the loft had been oddly unemotional. Suddenly she just didn't care. All she cared about was herself. What a failure she was, what a fool she had been. Thinking of Anthony, she felt like a clown.

She should have been used to hotels by then after the road show, but she found as she sat in this one that all it did was make her cry more. She wanted to call Ivo, but she knew that wasn't right. There was no one for her to talk to, not even Steve, who was out of town. She tried to concentrate on the paper so she could find an apartment, but the paper blurred in front of her as she cried. Finally she couldn't stand it, she picked up the phone and dialed. She held her breath, feeling stupid. What if he hung up on her, what if he reproached her, what if — But she knew that Ivo wouldn't do that. She waited for Mattie's familiar voice, and then she was startled when she heard a voice she didn't know.

"Mattie?"

"Who is this?" the voice answered.

"I . . . it's . . . who is *this?* Where's Mattie?"

And after a pause, "She died two months ago. I'm Elizabeth. Who are you?"

"I . . . oh, I'm so sorry. . . ." Bettina could feel a fresh wave of tears coming on. "Is Mister Stewart there?"

"Who *is* this?" Elizabeth was obviously growing annoyed.

"This is . . . Mrs. Pearce, I mean Mrs. Stewart, I mean — oh, never mind. Is he there?"

"No. He's in Bermuda."

"Oh. When will he be back?"

"Not until the first of April. He's rented a house. Would you like the number?" But suddenly Bettina knew she didn't want it. It wasn't right. She hung up and sighed softly.

She spent a restless, anguished night in the hotel, and when she awoke the next morning, it had started to snow. It seemed odd to her because in the rest of the country, she had seen the beginnings of spring. Now she was suddenly plunged back into winter, with snowstorms, and nowhere to go. It made her suddenly reconsider. What if she left New York? If she went somewhere else entirely? But where would she go? She had no friends anywhere, no ties to any other city, and then, oddly, she found her mind wandering to California, to her fairy-tale week in San Francisco with Anthony, and suddenly she knew that what she wanted was to go there. Even without him, it was a place where she knew she could be at peace.

Feeling wildly adventurous, she called the

airline, and then half an hour later she went to the bank. Carefully she put all the jewelry she kept there in a leather tote bag, and she smiled to herself. Maybe this meant she was never coming back. This time it was she who was leaving, she who had made a decision.

She took all of her bags with her to the airport; she had brought everything that she owned. And before leaving the hotel in New York, she called the hotel where she had stayed with Anthony and asked for a room with a view of the bay. Maybe it was foolish to stay in the same hotel, but she didn't really think so. It had been so lovely, and it didn't matter what memories she had there. They no longer meant anything to her. And neither did he.

The flight to San Francisco was uneventful, and by now she was so used to changing towns every few days that it didn't strike her odd to have left the snow that morning and find herself now in the midst of a blossoming spring on the West Coast. San Francisco was as beautiful as she remembered it, and she settled into her room with a contented smile. It was only that night that the ghosts began to assail her. She took two aspirin and a glass of water. And then in desperation, an hour later, she went for a walk. She came back to the hotel and took two more aspirin. And finally at three in the morning she took a sleeping pill from the bottle they'd given her when she left the hospital. They had predicted that she might have trouble sleeping for a while. But even the sleeping pill didn't help her, and she stared at the bottle for what seemed like hours. And then suddenly she knew the answer, and she wondered why she hadn't thought of it before. It was crazy to have come all the way to San Francisco when what she had wanted she had had with her in New York. But she hadn't thought of it. And suddenly she smiled to herself. Now she understood it all. And it was so simple . . . so simple. . . . She walked into the bathroom, poured a glass of water, and then one by one she took all the sleeping pills in the bottle. There were exactly twenty-four.

24

There were bright lights overhead, which seemed to zoom down on her and then fade and disappear. There were machines whirring, and she could hear someone retching, and there was a strange sensation of something hard pushed down her throat. She couldn't remember . . . couldn't remember . . . and then at last she did. She was in the hospital . . . she was having a miscarriage . . . and then again she drifted off to sleep.

It seemed years later when she woke up and found herself staring into the face of a strange man. He was tall, dark-haired, brown-eyed, attractive, and he was wearing a pale-yellow button-down shirt and a white cotton coat. And then she remembered. She was in the hospital. But she wasn't sure why.

"Mrs. Stewart?" He looked at her questioningly, and she shook her head. She suddenly remembered, though, that she had not gotten around to changing her insurance card since she had married Anthony.

"No, Pearce." She answered hoarsely, surprised at her own voice, and then she shook her head distractedly again. "I mean . . . Daniels. Bettina Daniels." But that sounded strange too. She hadn't used that name in so long.

"Quite a collection of names you have, isn't it?" He didn't look disapproving, only surprised. "Mind if I sit down and we talk for a while?" And now she understood why he wanted to talk to her. "Let's talk about last night." Her eyes drifted away from his, and she looked out the window. In the distance all she could see was fog, hanging low over the Golden Gate Bridge.

"Where am I?" But she was stalling and he knew it. He mentioned Credence Hospital and she nodded with a small smile. And then nervously she looked at him. "Do we really have to discuss all this?"

But he nodded soberly. "Yes, we do. I don't know how long you've been out here, and I don't know what the procedures are in New York, but unless you want to be kept here for psychiatric treatment for a while, I think we'd better have a talk." She looked at him somberly and nodded again. "What happened last night?"

"I took some sleeping pills," she croaked. And then she looked at him. "Why is my voice so funny?"

He smiled at her and for the first time he actually looked young. He was very good-looking, but also terribly serious, and he didn't look like much fun. "We pumped your stomach. The tube we used will make your voice sound raspy for a few days. Now, about the sleeping pills, did you do it on purpose or was it an accident?"

She hesitated for a long moment, not sure what she should say. "I — I'm not sure."

He looked at her sternly. "Miss Stewart . . . Daniels, whatever your name is, I'm not going to play games with you. Either we're going to talk about this or we're not. I want to know from you what happened, or I'm simply going to put on your chart that you stay here for observation for a week."

Now she was angry. Her eyes blazed as she croaked at him, and he had to suppress a smile. She was really very pretty. "I'm not sure what happened, Doctor. I flew out here from New York yesterday, and the day before that I was released from a hospital for a miscarriage. They gave me some pills and I either took too many of them or they were too strong for me . . . I'm not sure." But she knew that she was lying. And suddenly she didn't care. It was none of his business what had happened. So what if she'd tried to kill herself? She hadn't succeeded, and it was still her own life. She didn't have to tell him everything. And it was none of his business either if she had "quite a collection of names," as he put it. So what?

"What hospital were you in for the miscarriage?" He sat there with her chart, pen poised, sure that she was probably lying, but she was quick to supply the information about the hospital in Atlanta and he looked surprised. "You certainly move around a lot, don't you?"

"Yes, I do." She croaked again. "I was Assistant Director of a Broadway play on tour, and I had the miscarriage on the road. I was in the hospital for a week, and I quit and went back to New York."

"Are you out here on business?" Now he looked curious and she shook her head. For a moment she was going to tell him that she was there on a visit, but she decided not to. She could at least tell him the truth about that.

"No, I moved out here."

"Yesterday?" She nodded.

"Married or single?"

"Neither one." She smiled at him slowly.

"Sorry?" He looked naive, and Bettina found herself wondering if he ever laughed.

"I'm in the process of filing for divorce."

"And he's . . . let me guess" — this time he actually smiled at her — "in New York."

Now she smiled too. "No. He's with the road show."

"Now I begin to see. Married long?" For a moment she was tempted to shock him and say Which time? but she shook her head noncommittally and let him think what he would.

He sighed for a moment, and then put down his pen. "Now about the miscarriage." His voice gentled, he knew how hard that could be. "Were there complications? Was it difficult? Did it take very long?"

She looked away and the light went out of her eyes as she stared at the bridge. "No, I don't think there were complications. They kept me in the hospital for a week. I . . . it — it happened one night. I woke up in the middle of the night, went to the hospital, and it was pretty bad by then. I don't know how long it took after that. Not very long, I think. And it" — she shrugged and wiped a tear from her face — "it was very painful."

He nodded gently, and suddenly he felt for this tiny redheaded girl. Not redheaded precisely, he thought to himself, her hair was more auburn, and as she looked at him he realized that she had bottomless emerald-green eyes.

"I'm sorry, Miss —"

He faltered and she smiled. "Bettina. So am I. But . . . my husband didn't want it anyway. . . ." She shrugged again, and he forgot about her chart.

"Is that why you left him?"

"No." She shook her head slowly. "There were some things I hadn't known about. A basic misunderstanding. . . ." And then suddenly she wanted to tell him; she looked deep into his brown eyes. "He married me to get a green card, his resident's permit. He was English. And apparently that was his only motivation." She tried to smile but the bitterness showed in her eyes. "It was something he didn't mention to me. Oh, I knew he needed the green card. But I didn't know that was why we got married, at least not exclusively. I thought that . . . well, anyway, it turns out that you only have to live together for six months, and" — she turned up both hands — "it'll be exactly six months next week. End of marriage. And as it so happened, end of baby. It all kind of happened at the same time."

He wanted to tell her that maybe it was for the best but he wasn't sure that he should. He had a way of being too blunt sometimes, and he didn't want to do that to her. She looked so small and so frail, propped up in the white hospital bed. "Do you have family out here?"

"No."

"Friends?"

She shook her head again. "No one. Just me."

"And you're planning to stay here?"

"Yes, I think so."

"All alone?"

"Not forever, I hope." She looked at him in amusement, and there was suddenly a twinkle in her eye. "I just thought it might be a nice place to start over." He nodded, but he was struck by her courage. She had come a long way from home.

"Your family's back East, Miss — er — Bettina?"

But she shook her head again. "No. My parents are dead, and . . . there's no one." Ivo didn't count anymore. For her, he was gone too.

"Tell me the truth now, and I mean it, just between us, was that why you did it? Last night?" She looked at him and for an instant, just an instant, she knew that she could trust him, but she only shrugged.

"I don't know. I started thinking . . . about

my — my husband . . . some other mistakes I've made . . . the baby . . . I got nervous . . . I took some aspirin, I went for a walk . . . all of a sudden it was like everything was closing in on me. But I've felt peculiar ever since I lost the baby, like I can't get my motors going anymore. It's as if I don't care about anything, as if nothing matters . . . and . . . I —" Suddenly she was looking at him and crying. "If I hadn't — if I hadn't gone on the road with that show, I wouldn't have lost it, I wouldn't . . . I felt so guilty . . . I. . . ." She was suddenly telling him things she hadn't even known that she felt, and unconsciously she had reached out to him, and he soothed her, holding her gently in his white-coated arms.

"It's all right, Bettina . . . it's all right. It's normal for you to feel like that. But I'm sure they told you that no matter what you'd have done, you'd probably have lost the baby. Some babies are just not meant to be born."

"But what if this one was? Then, I killed it." She looked at him miserably and he shook his head.

"When a baby is all right, you can do almost anything, ski, fall down the stairs, you can do just about anything and you won't lose it. Believe me, if you lost it, it wasn't right."

She lay back slowly in bed and watched him with troubled eyes. "Thank you." And then with a look of sudden worry, "Will you make me see a lot of shrinks now? Are you going to lock me up with the crazies because I told you about last night?" But he smiled at her and shook his head.

"No, I'm not. But I'd like to have you looked at by one of our gynecologists just to make sure that everything's okay, and then I'm going to ask you to stay here for a few days. Just so you can catch your breath, get on your feet, get some rest, and take some of those sleeping pills, if you need them, under our supervision, not your own. But what you're going through is normal. It's just that usually a woman has a husband or a family to turn to with this kind of anguish. It's very hard to handle this alone." She nodded slowly. He seemed to understand.

"And I'd like it if we could talk some more." He said it very gently, with a small smile. "Would you mind that very much?"

She shook her head slowly. "No. What kind of doctor are you, by the way?" Maybe he was a shrink after all. Maybe she was being tricked.

"An internist. If you're going to stay in

the city, you're going to need one of those too. And maybe right now, while you're settling down here, you could use a friend." He smiled at her then and held out a hand. "I'm John Fields, Bettina." She shook his hand firmly, and then he looked at her again. "And by the way, how did you come by so many names?"

She grinned at him then. If he was going to be her doctor and her friend, he might as well know the truth. "Pearce is my most recent married name; Daniels is my maiden name, which actually I suppose I'll take back now; and Stewart was" — she hesitated for only a fraction of an instant — "my first married name. I've been married once before."

"And how old did you say you were?" He was still smiling as he walked to the door.

"Twenty-six."

"Not bad, Bettina, not bad." He saluted and prepared to leave, and then for a moment he stopped and looked at her. "I think you're going to be just fine." He waved then, and as he left he smiled at her in a way that told her everything just had to be okay.

25

"And how are you today, Bettina?" John Fields walked into her hospital room with a smile.

"Fine." She returned the smile. "Better. Much better." She had slept like a baby the night before, without the nightmares, the ghosts of old faces, without even a sleeping pill. She had put her head down on the pillow and fallen asleep. Life in the hospital was wonderfully simple. There were mommies and daddies in white uniforms who were there to take care of you, to keep all the bad dreams and bad people away, so you could relax. She hadn't felt this peaceful in a year. And as she thought it she looked up at the attractive young doctor sheepishly. "I shouldn't say it, but I wish I didn't have to leave."

"Why is that?" For only an instant a trace of worry crossed his smile. He had taken a lot on his shoulders, not bringing a psychiatrist in on the case. But he didn't really feel that she had deep-seated problems.

She was looking at him now with that childlike smile of hers and those devastating green eyes, which seemed to dance. She certainly didn't look like a crazy, but nevertheless he was going to keep an eye on her after she left.

She lay back again against her pillows, with a little sigh and a smile. "Why don't I want to leave here, Doctor? Oh, because" — the eyes drifted toward him — "because it's so easy and so simple. I don't have to look for an apartment, find a job, worry about money, go to the grocery store, cook for myself. I don't have to find a lawyer." She looked at him, smiling again. "I don't even have to wear makeup and get dressed." But she had bathed for half an hour and there was a white satin ribbon in the long auburn hair. He looked at her and returned her smile. She looked pretty and young and as though life were terribly simple; she looked more like twelve years old than twenty-six.

"I think you've just given me all the reasons why some people stay in mental institutions for years, or even all of their lives, Bettina." And then more quietly, "Is that what you have in mind for yourself? Is it really all that much trouble to get dressed or to go to the store?"

She was suddenly startled by what he had just told her, and she shook her head. "No . . . no, of course not." And then she felt she had to explain to him. Just so he wouldn't really think her crazy after all. "I — I've been" — she looked for the right words as she watched him — "I've been under a lot of pressure for a long time." Jesus. Then maybe she did have a major problem. He wondered as he watched her, wondering also if he should send her home.

"What kind of pressure?" Quietly he pulled up a chair.

"Well" — she stared down at her hands for a long time — "I've been running houses, servants, kind of elaborate households for a lot of years." She looked up with a small smile. "Two husbands and a father have kept me busy for about the last fifteen years."

"Fifteen? What about your mother?" His eyes never left her face.

"She died of leukemia when I was four."

"And your father never remarried?"

"Of course not." And more softly, "He didn't have to. He had me."

The doctor's eyes grew suddenly wide in horror, and she quickly shook her head and put up a hand. "No, no, not like that. People like my father marry for all kinds of reasons, the convenience, someone to talk to or advise them, someone to keep them company when they're on tour, or to run interference for them while they're writing a book. I did all that for him."

He watched her, suddenly fascinated by something in her face. She seemed oddly knowing and much older as she spoke of it, and she also looked more beautiful than any woman he had ever seen.

She was nodding slowly. "I think most people marry for convenience and to combat loneliness."

"Is that why you married?"

"Partly." And then she smiled and lay her head back on her pillows with her eyes briefly closed. "And I also fell very much in love."

"With whom?" His voice was barely more than a whisper in the small room.

"A man named Ivo Stewart." She continued to talk to the ceiling, and then she looked back at him. "I don't know if it makes any difference, but he was the publisher of the *New York Mail* for years. He retired a little more than a year ago."

"And you married him?" The young doctor looked more surprised than impressed.

"How did you meet him?" He still couldn't place her, couldn't understand her. He knew she had been with a theatrical road show. Yet there was something still more worldly, more regal about her bearing, and how did a little girl with a road show come to be married to the publisher of the *New York Mail*? Or was she lying? Was she really crazy? Maybe he should have checked on her further. Who was this girl?

But Bettina was smiling at him now. "Maybe I should go back to the beginning. Have you ever heard of Justin Daniels?" It was a stupid question. Even she knew that.

"The author?" She nodded.

"He was my father."

Then she gave him the unabridged version of her life, sparing no details. She really needed to talk it out.

And when she was finished with all the details, the hopes, the dreams, he said, "And now what, Bettina?"

She looked him square in the eye. "Who knows? I guess I start fresh." But she still felt as though she had a load of bags on her back from years gone by. It was a heavy burden with which to travel into a new life, and even telling him hadn't really lessened the pain.

"Why did you choose San Francisco?"

"I don't know. It was a spur of the moment inspiration. I just remembered it as being very pretty and I don't know anybody here."

"Didn't that frighten you?"

She smiled at him. "A little. But by this time that was a relief. Sometimes it's nice to be anonymous, to go where you aren't known. I can start over here. I can just be Bettina Daniels and find out who she is."

He looked at her seriously. "At least you can forget who she was."

Suddenly she looked at him and knew he didn't understand. "That's not the point really. I've been several different people, but all of them meant something. All of them had a reason. In their own way each of those people was right at the time. Except maybe this last time — that was a mistake. But my life with my father —" She hesitated, looking for the right words. "That was an extraordinary experience. I would never give that up for anything else."

But John was shaking his head. "You've never had a normal moment in your life. No parents to love you, no simple home, no kids to bring home from school, no marriage to a boy you met in college, just a lot of nightmares, and odd, eccentric people, and show business, and old men."

"You make it sound so sordid." It made her sad to listen to him. Was that how it would sound to people now? Ugly and freakish? Was that what she was? She felt tears well up inside her and she had to fight them back.

And then suddenly he felt horrified at himself. What was he doing? She was his patient and he was badgering her. He looked at Bettina with guilt and horror in his eyes and reached out to touch her hand. "I'm sorry, I — I had no right to do that. I don't know how to explain it to you though. It frightens me when I hear all that. It upsets me that you had to go through it. I'm worried about what will happen to you now."

She looked at him oddly, the hurt still fresh in her eyes. "Thank you. But it doesn't matter. You have a right to say what you think. As you said in the beginning, if I'm going to settle down here, I'm going to need more than just a doctor, I'm going to need a friend." It was time she got out and discovered how the rest of the world lived, the "normal people," as John would have said.

"I hope so. I'm really sorry. It's just that you have had a very, very hard life. And you have a right to much better now."

"By the way, where are you from?"

"Here. San Francisco. I've lived here all my life. Grew up here, went to college at Stanford. Med school there too. It's all been very unexciting — peaceful and normal. And when you ask me what I think you have a right to, when I say that you have a right to better than you've had, I mean a nice, decent, wholesome husband, who's not four or five times your age, a couple of kids, a decent house."

She looked at him with hostility for a moment. Why wouldn't he understand that some of that life had been beautiful, and whatever it had been, it was part of her?

He read something in her eyes. "You're not planning to get a job in the theater again, are you?"

Slowly she shook her head, holding his eyes with a firm look of her own. "No. I was planning to start working on my play."

But he shook his head. "Bettina, why don't you get yourself a regular job? Something simple. Maybe something secretarial, or a nice job in a museum, or something in real estate maybe that lets you see nice, wholesome, happy people. And before you know it, you'll have your life back on the right track."

She had never thought of being a secretary or a real estate agent before. It wasn't really her cup of tea. The literary and theatrical worlds were all she knew. But maybe he was right. Maybe it was all too crazy. Maybe she had to get away from all that. And then she remembered something else.

"Before I do that, do you have the name of a good lawyer?"

"Sure." He smiled at her and pulled a pen out of his pocket. "One of my best friends. Seth Waterston. You'll like him a lot. And his wife is a nurse. We all went to school together as undergraduates at Stanford."

"How wholesome." She was teasing but he didn't laugh.

"Don't knock it till you've tried it." And then hesitantly he tilted his head. He paused for a long time as he considered, not sure if it was the right thing to do. But something was pushing him to do it. He had to. For her. "As a matter of fact, Bettina —" He seemed to hesitate for a long time as Bettina watched. "I want to suggest something to you that may not be entirely ethical, but it might do you some good."

"It sounds fascinating. What is it?"

"I'd like to take you to dinner with Seth and Mary Waterston. How does that sound?"

"Delightful. And why is that unethical? You said you were also my friend."

He smiled slowly then, and she smiled in answer. "Is it a date, then?" She nodded. "Then I'll call them and I'll let you know before you leave when they can make it."

"By the way, when am I leaving?" They had both forgotten as she told him her life story.

"How about today?" She thought briefly of the hotel to which she would have to return. It was not a very cheerful thought. It was the place where she had stayed with Anthony and suddenly she didn't want to go back there. "Something wrong?"

But she shook her head briskly. "No. Nothing at all." She had to work it out for herself. And he was right. What she needed was a normal life, a simple job. She could wait another six months to start her play. All she needed now was an apartment, a job, and a divorce. She'd work out the first two and hopefully John's friend would help her with the last one. Now she understood she was divorcing more than just a person this time. John helped her see that. She had to divorce a whole life.

26

Five days later Bettina had her own apartment, a tiny but quaint studio overlooking the bay. It had previously been the main parlor in a lovely Victorian owned by three men. They had fixed up the two top floors for themselves and had divided the bottom floor into two studio apartments, which they rented out. Bettina got the larger one, and it was a beauty. It had a fireplace, two huge French windows, a tiny balcony, a kitchenette, a bathroom, and a devastatingly beautiful view. She was enchanted when she first saw it, and the miracle of it was that it was something even she could afford. The rent was so low that she could have managed just on her monthly money from Ivo, which she would have, no matter what, for the coming years.

Two days after she found her apartment John Fields arrived to take her to dinner with his lawyer friend and his wife.

"Bettina, you're going to love them."

"I'm sure I will. But you haven't told me. How do you like my place?" She looked at him as they left her apartment. He had commented only on the view. But now he looked at her squarely as he opened his car door. He drove a small American compact, in a subdued navy blue. There was nothing flashy or ostentatious about his clothes, his car, or his person. Everything was attractive, but quiet, like the tweed jacket he wore, the button-down shirt, the gray slacks, the well-polished loafers. In fact it was oddly comforting. He was predictable, in his style and taste. He looked like every good American ought to, he was every mother's dream of the perfect son. Handsome, bright, attractive, well-mannered, a graduate of Stanford, a doctor. Bettina smiled at him. He was really a damn good-looking man. She felt suddenly awkward in his presence. As though everything she had on was too expensive, too showy. Maybe he was right. She did have a lot to learn. "Well, what about my apartment, Doctor? Isn't that some find?"

He nodded slowly with a smile. "It is and I like it. But it still has the look of 'Milady's Manor.' I kept waiting for you to tell me you'd rented the whole house."

He smiled to soften his words as he helped her into the car. The door slammed shut, and she wondered if she'd worn the wrong dress. She was wearing a white wool that she and Ivo had bought in Paris. It wasn't dressy, but it was easy to see that it was expensively made. It was a simple dress with long sleeves and a small collar, and she had worn it with a single strand of pearls and black kid Dior shoes. But when she reached the Waterstons' house in Marin County, she knew that she had made a faux pas again.

Mary Waterston came to the door, smiling broadly, her hair swept up on the back of her head with a leather thong. She was wearing a button-down shirt, a green V-neck sweater, bare feet, and jeans. And Seth arrived in almost the same costume. Even John looked overdressed, but he had come from the office. Bettina didn't have that excuse. She shook their hands with a faint look of embarrassment, but they were quick to put her at ease. Seth was a tall, handsome, sandy-haired man with a cowlick, a look of surprise, and seemingly endless legs. Mary was small, dark-haired, and pretty in spite of horn-rimmed glasses, and she was almost as thin as Bettina except that she had a somewhat noticeable paunch. A little while later she saw Bettina glance at her bulging midriff and she grinned.

"I know, isn't it awful? I hate this stage, everyone just thinks you're fat." She patted it fondly, and then explained. "Number two on the way. The first one is asleep upstairs."

"Is she?" John had just joined them, the two men had been outside for a moment and had just returned. "I had hoped we would see her." He looked warm and kind as he said it, and for an odd moment Bettina felt something pull at her heart. Why hadn't she ever had a man who felt that way about children? It had been a closed door with Ivo. And Anthony had hated the baby from the start. For a moment she felt a terrible flash of pain as she looked at Mary. Only a few weeks before she had been about as pregnant as that.

"When is the baby due?" she asked her softly.

"Not till August."

"Are you still working?" But Mary only laughed.

"No, that's a thing of the past, I'm afraid. I used to be an O.B. nurse until the first time I got pregnant. Now I seem to be a regular patient there." The three of them grinned. And somehow Bettina felt left out. John had been right. It all seemed so normal. And she suddenly longed to be one of them.

"How old is your first one?"

"Nineteen months." Bettina nodded and the other woman smiled. "Do you have children?" But Bettina only shook her head.

They all drank red wine and ate steaks that Seth barbecued for dinner. And after coffee John offered to go out to the kitchen to lend Mary a hand. He had orchestrated that earlier with Seth, who looked at Bettina as soon as they were alone and gave her a warm smile.

"I understand you want a dissolution?" She looked at him in confusion and he laughed.

"I'm sorry, I didn't understand. . . ."

"That's California legal jargon. I apologize. John mentioned that you're looking for an attorney to get a divorce." She nodded, and then sighed. "Can I help?"

"Yes, I'd like that very much."

"Why don't you come to my office tomorrow? Say around two?" She nodded gratefully. A few minutes later John was back, but somehow she felt degraded by her exchange with Seth, by Mary's gently bulging stomach, by all of it. She had such a long way to go to be like them. And if they knew the truth, they'd never accept her.

Look at them. Mary was thirty-five, the two men thirty-six, they all had respectable careers in medicine or in law. Seth and Mary had a house in the suburbs, one child, another on the way. How could she expect them to accept her? Later, when John took her back to her place, she told him mournfully what she had felt.

"You don't have to tell them. No one ever needs to know. That's the beauty of you starting out fresh here."

"But what if someone finds out, John? I mean, my father was very well-known. Conceivably one day I could come across someone who once knew me."

"Not necessarily. And that was so long ago, who would recognize you? Besides, no one needs to know about your marriages, Bettina. That's behind you now. You have to start fresh. You're still very young. No one would even suspect you had been married before."

And then she looked at him hauntingly. "Is it so terrible that I have?" But he didn't answer for a long moment.

"Bettina, it's just something no one needs to know." But he hadn't said that it wasn't awful. He hadn't told her what she had needed to hear. "Did you make an appointment with Seth?"

She nodded. "Yes, I did."

"Good. Then you can get that taken care of. And then you can find a job." But it was odd. She really didn't want to. Except that she knew she should. She had to have the job for respectability because John thought so. She suddenly knew just how much it mattered to her what this man thought.

27

A few weeks later she found a job in an art gallery on Union Street, and although it was neither exciting nor immensely profitable, it occupied most of her time. She worked from ten in the morning until six at night. And sitting at a desk smiling innocuously at strangers all day seemed to leave her exhausted, though she couldn't even remember what she'd done.

But she had finally become one of the great working class, working all day, and bored with it, and anxious to find a reason to get out of her job.

John took her out two or three times a week, for dinner or a movie, and they were beginning to spend some time together on the weekends. He loved to play tennis and sail. The time they shared was certainly healthful. Bettina was looking better than she had in a long time, and she had a deep honey-colored tan. It set off the reddish lights in her hair, and her eyes looked more like emeralds than ever. The four months in San Francisco had been good for her in many ways.

Tonight he had cooked at his apartment and they were lingering over coffee.

"Want to stop by and see the Waterstons tonight? Seth says Mary's getting antsy and the doctor won't let her come to the city anymore. She delivered last time in under two hours, and he's afraid that this time she won't make it to the hospital at all."

"Oh, Jesus." And then she looked at him thoughtfully with a half smile. "That whole baby thing scares me to death."

"But you were pregnant." He looked surprised at her reaction. Having a baby was so normal. Why would any healthy woman be afraid?

"I know, and I was excited about the baby. But every time I thought about the rest of it, it scared me to death."

"But why? Don't be silly. There's nothing to be afraid of. Mary's not afraid."

"She's a nurse."

And then he looked at her more gently. "If you ever had a baby, Bettina, I'd be there with you." She wasn't sure what he meant for a moment. As a friend? Or a doctor? Even though they'd been sleeping together for three months now, she wasn't quite sure what he meant. There was something so oddly uncuddly about their relationship that she was never sure if they were really lovers, or just friends.

"Thank you."

"You don't sound very excited at the prospect." He smiled at her and she laughed at him.

"It all seems very far off."

"What, having children? Why should it be?" And then he smiled at her more tenderly. "You could have one by next year." But she wasn't sure she wanted one anymore. She wanted to write her play.

"That doesn't mean I will." It seemed a safe answer, and he laughed.

"Well, you certainly could. Let's see . . . when is your divorce final?" Suddenly she felt her heart racing. What was he asking her? What did he mean?

"In two months. September." Her voice was oddly soft.

"We could get married then, get you pregnant immediately, and presto magic, next June you have a baby. How does that sound to you?" He was looking at her more closely now, and she felt his hand reach for hers.

"John . . . are you serious?"

And then very softly, "Yes, I am."

"But so — so quickly? . . . We don't have to get married the minute the divorce comes through . . . it's. . . ."

He looked at her in consternation. "Why not? Why would we wait to get married?"

And then, fearing his disapproval again, "I don't know." People like John Fields don't live with someone. They get married. They have babies. Bettina knew that for sure now. He was not going to fool around. And not complying with his wishes meant fresh failure. It meant not measuring up, not being "normal." And she didn't want to do that anymore.

"Don't you want to, Betty?" She hated the nickname, but she had never told him, because there were other things about him that she did love, his solidity, the way you could count on him, he was reliable and sturdy and handsome, and he made her feel like an ordinary, regular person, when they played tennis, or had dinner, or joined some of his friends for a Sunday sail. It was a life she had never known before. Never. Until she met Dr. John Fields. But marry him? Get married again? Now? "I don't know. It's too soon." It was only a whisper.

He looked at her unhappily. "I see." And then he seemed to pull away.

28

The next morning, on her way to the gallery, Bettina thought again about John's proposal. What more did she want? Why wasn't she ecstatic? Because, she answered herself slowly, what she wanted more than children or marriage was time. She wanted to find herself, Bettina, the person she had lost somewhere along the way while she was so busy changing names. She knew she had to find her, before it was too late.

She let her car idle at a stop sign, as she once again remembered his words, and the look on his face when she told him it was too soon. It *was* too soon. For her. And what about her play? If she married him now, she'd never write it, she'd get too caught up in his life and being Mrs. John Fields. That wasn't what she wanted now . . . she wanted — A horn bleated angrily as she remembered where she was and moved on. But she couldn't keep her mind on her driving, she could barely even keep her eyes on the road. She just kept thinking of the look on his face when she said — And then suddenly there was an odd thump against the front of her car, and she heard a woman scream. Startled, she stomped hard on the brake, and as she jolted forward against her seat belt she looked around. There were people standing, staring . . . they were staring at her . . . at . . . what were they looking at . . . oh, my God! Two men were bending down, talking to someone right in front of her car. But she couldn't see. What was it? Oh, God, it couldn't . . . she didn't . . . but as she flew from her seat she knew.

As she shakily ran to the front of the car, she saw him, a man in his early forties, lying prone on the street.

She felt panic rise in her throat. She knelt next to the man, trying to keep from crying. He was well dressed in a dark business suit, and the contents of his attaché case were strewn over the ground. "I'm sorry . . . I'm sorry . . . isn't there anything I can do?"

The police were quiet and courteous when a few moments later they arrived on the scene. An ambulance appeared only five minutes after. The man was removed. Bettina's name and license number were recorded. The police spoke to the eyewitnesses, their names written down in a careful little list compiled by a left-handed cop who looked barely older than a boy.

"Had you taken any medication this morning, miss?" The young policeman looked at her with wise eyes, but she shook her head and blew her nose in the handkerchief she had dug out of her bag.

"No. Nothing."

"One of the witnesses said he'd seen you stop a few minutes before, and you looked" — he gazed at her apologetically — "well, he said 'glazed.' "

"I wasn't . . . I was . . . I was just thinking."

"Were you upset?"

"Yes . . . no . . . oh, I don't remember. I don't know." It was hard to tell if she had ever been rational, she was so distraught over what she had just done. "Will he be all right?"

"We'll know more after he gets to the hospital, You can call later for a report."

"What about me?"

"Were you hurt?" He looked surprised.

"No, I mean —" She looked up at him bleakly. "Are you going to arrest me?"

He smiled gently. "No, we're not. It was an accident. You'll get a citation, and this will have to go to court."

"To court?" She was horrified, and he nodded.

"Other than the citation, your insurance company will probably handle most of it for you." And then more gravely, "You *are* insured?"

"Of course."

"Then, call your insurance agent this morning, and your attorney, and hope for the best." Hope for the best . . . oh, God, how awful. What had she done?

When at last they had gone, she slipped behind the wheel of her car, her hands still trembling violently and her mind whirling, as she thought of the man they had loaded into an ambulance only moments before. It seemed to take her hours to get to the gallery, and when she arrived, she didn't bother to throw open the door or turn on the lights. She rushed right to the telephone after firmly relocking the door behind her. She called her insurance agent, who seemed nonplussed. He assured her that her twenty thousand dollars' worth of coverage ought to be adequate to take care of the accident unless it were terribly serious.

"Anyway, don't worry about it, we'll see."

"How soon will I know?"

"Know what?"

"If he's going to sue me."

"As soon as he decides to let us know, Miss Daniels. Don't worry, you'll know."

There were tears rolling down her face as Bettina dialed Seth Waterston in his office. He came on the line only moments after she placed the call.

"Bettina?"

"Oh, Seth. . . ." It was a desperate, childlike wail. "I'm in trouble." She began to sob out of control.

"Where are you?"

"At the . . . gall . . . ery. . . ." She could barely speak.

"Now calm down and tell me what happened. Take a deep breath . . . Bettina? . . . Bettina! . . . now talk to me. . . ." For a moment he was afraid that she was in jail. He could think of nothing else to cause hysterics on that order.

"I had an . . . accident. . . ."

"Are you hurt?"

"I hit a man with my car."

"A pedestrian?"

"Yes."

"How badly is he hurt?"

"I don't know."

"What's the guy's name and where did they take him?"

"Saint George's. And his name is" — she

glanced at the little piece of paper given her by the police — "Bernard Zule."

"Zule? Spell it." She did, and Seth sighed.

"Do you know him?"

"More or less. He's an attorney. You couldn't have hit some nice ignorant pedestrian? You had to hit a lawyer?" Seth tried to joke, but Bettina couldn't, and then as a wave of panic washed over her, she held the phone tighter.

"Seth, promise me you won't tell John."

"Why not, for God's sake? You didn't do it on purpose."

"No, but he'll — he'll be upset . . . or angry . . . or . . . please. . . ." Her voice was so desperate that Seth promised, then hung up to call the hospital.

Four hours later Seth called her at the gallery. Zule was all right. He had a broken leg. It was a nice clean break. A few bruises. No other damage. But Bernard Zule was a very angry man. He had already called his attorney and he fully intended to sue. Seth had talked to him himself. He had explained that the woman who had hit Zule was a personal friend, she was terribly concerned, very, very sorry, and she wanted to know if he was all right.

"All right? That dumb fucking bitch runs me down in broad daylight, and then she wants to know if I'm all right? I'll tell her in court how all right I am."

"Now, Bernard. . . ." Seth's attempts at putting oil on the waters were of no avail, as Bettina learned three days later when she was served with papers for Zule's suit. He was suing her for two hundred thousand dollars for personal injury, inability to practice his profession, emotional trauma, and malicious intent. The malicious intent wasn't worth a damn, Seth assured her, she didn't even know Zule, after all. But it was a whopping big suit. He also told her that it could take a couple of years to come to court, by which time his fracture would be nothing but a dim memory. But it didn't make any difference. All Bettina could think of was the amount. Two hundred thousand dollars. If she sold every piece of jewelry she still owned, maybe she could pay it, but then what would she have? It reminded her of her panic after her father died, and it was all she could do to remain in control.

"Bettina? Bettina! Did you hear me?"

"Hmm? What?"

"What's wrong with you?" John stared at her in annoyance, she had been like that for weeks.

"I — I'm sorry . . . I was distracted."

"That's an understatement. You haven't

heard a word I've said all night. What is it?" He didn't understand. She had been that way since the night he had proposed to her. It hardly cheered him to acknowledge that. And then, finally, at the end of the evening when he brought her home, he looked at her sadly. "Bettina, would you rather we didn't see each other for a while?"

"No . . . I —" And then, without wanting to, she let herself be pulled into his arms, as long, terrified sobs wracked her soul.

"What is it? Oh, Betty . . . tell me what it is . . . I know something's wrong."

"I . . . oh, John, I can't tell you . . . it's so awful . . . I had an accident."

"What kind of an accident?" His voice was stern.

"In my car. I broke a man's leg."

"You what?" He looked at her, shocked. "When?"

"Three weeks ago."

"Why didn't you tell me?"

And then she hung her head. "I don't know."

"Isn't your insurance handling it?"

"I'm only insured for twenty thousand. He's suing me for" — her voice dropped still lower — "two hundred thousand?"

"Oh, my God." Quietly they both sat down. "Have you talked to Seth?" Silently she nodded. "And not to me. Oh, Betty." He pulled her closer into his arms. "Betty, Betty . . . how could something like this happen to you?"

"I don't know." But she did know. She had been thinking of the night before when he'd proposed, and of how much she didn't want to get married, but she didn't tell him. "It was my fault."

"I see. Well, it looks like we'll just have to face the music together, doesn't it?" He smiled down at her gently. She needed him, and that made him feel good.

But she looked horrified as her eyes met his. "What do you mean together? Don't be crazy! I have to work this out by myself."

"Don't you be crazy. And don't get yourself totally insane over this thing. A two-hundred-thousand-dollar lawsuit doesn't mean anything. He'll probably be happy to settle for ten."

"I don't believe that." But she had to admit that Seth had told her something like that the day before. Not ten exactly, but maybe twenty.

And as it turned out, they were right. Two weeks later Bernard Zule accepted the sum of eighteen thousand dollars to balm his nerves and his near-mended leg. The insurance company canceled Bettina's insurance, and she had to sell the small, inexpensive used car she had bought after she got her job. The sum of two hundred thousand dollars no longer shrieked in her head, but there was a feeling of defeat somehow, of failure, of having taken a giant step back, and not having been able to take care of herself. The pall of depression dragged on for weeks, and it was only two weeks before her divorce became final that John proposed to her again.

"It makes sense, Bettina." And then, with rare humor, he grinned at her. "Look at it this way. You could drive my car."

But she didn't even smile. He pushed on. "I love you, and you were born to be my wife." *And Ivo's, and Anthony's. . . .* She couldn't keep the thought from her mind. "I want you, Bettina." But she also knew that he thought she couldn't take care of herself. And in a way she had proven him right. She was incompetent. Perhaps dangerously so. Look at what she had just done. She had almost killed a man . . . she never let that thought slip from her mind. "Bettina?" He was looking down at her. And then very gently he kissed her fingers and her lips, and then her eyes. "Will you marry me, Betty?"

He could hear the sharp intake of breath,

and then, with her eyes closed, she nodded. “Yes.” Maybe he was right after all.

29

With small measured steps Bettina approached the altar on the arm of Seth Waterston. She had asked him to give her away. There were close to a hundred people in the church, watching them happily as Bettina's white moiré whispered softly against the satin runner as they walked. Seth smiled down at her as she walked beside him, her face concealed by the delicate veil and the Renaissance coif. She looked beautiful and stately, yet she felt strange in the white wedding dress, as though she were in costume, or as though it were a little bit of a lie. She had resisted John's suggestion to have a white wedding until the end, but it had meant so much to him. He had waited so long after medical school to get married that she knew she had to do it for him. And, in the two brief weeks after she decided, he had promised that he would take care of everything, and he had. All she had had to do was go to I. Magnin's to shop for her wedding dress, and he had done the rest. He had organized the ceremony itself in the little Episcopal church on Union Street, and the reception afterward for a hundred and twenty-five guests at the yacht club overlooking the bay. It was a wedding day that any girl would have died for, but somehow Bettina would have felt more comfortable going to City Hall. The divorce had come through only two days earlier, and as she walked down the aisle on Seth's arm she kept thinking of Anthony and Ivo. Suddenly she had a mad urge to giggle and shout at the dewy-eyed guests, "Don't get too excited, folks, this is my third!" But she smiled demurely as she reached the altar and took John's arm. He was wearing a morning coat for the occasion with a little sprig of lily of the valley on his lapel. Bettina's bouquet was made of white roses, and they had given Mary Waterston a beige orchid corsage. John no longer had either of his parents, so there were no families to contend with, only friends.

The words seemed to drone on forever in the pretty little church, and the minister smiled lovingly at them as he spoke.

". . . and do you, John? . . ."

As she listened, suddenly that strange feeling came back to her. What if she said the wrong name when she made the vows? *I, Bettina, take you, Ivo . . . Anthony . . . John. . . .* She wasn't going to louse it up this time. This was her last chance to do things right for herself. This was for real.

". . . I do. . . ." The words were barely more than a whisper as she said them. She was being given her last chance. Her eyes went quickly to John's and he looked at her seriously and repeated the same words loudly and firmly so the whole church could hear. He had taken her, Bettina, to have and to hold, to love and to cherish, in sickness and in health, for richer or poorer, until death did them part. Not misunderstanding, not boredom, not a green card or a road show, or a difference in age. *Until death did them part.* As Bettina listened she felt the impact of the words, she was aware of the smell of the roses. For the rest of her life she would smell those roses whenever she thought of those words.

". . . I now pronounce you man and wife." The minister looked at them, smiled at them both, and then leaned gently toward John. "You may kiss the bride." John did so quickly, while holding tightly to her hand.

The wide gold band was on her left hand now, the tiny diamond engagement ring on her right. She had wanted to show him her jewelry just before the wedding, but once he had given her the ring, she knew she couldn't do it, because she still had the nine-carat diamond from Ivo. And then, finally, she had decided to conceal his ring and show John the rest. The collection she had acquired from Ivo and her father was something she never showed anyone, and she never wore any of it anymore. It sat safely in the bank, it was her nest egg, all she had left now of her own. And showing it to John, or wanting to, had been her final act of trust. But when she had told him that she had something she wanted to show him, something she kept at the bank, he had looked angry and suspicious until she finally explained.

"It's nothing . . . don't look like that, silly . . . it's just some jewelry I have from my other life. . . ." She had grinned at him sheepishly and she had been stunned when he exploded in the tiny room at the bank.

"Bettina, this is disgraceful! It's outrageous! Do you realize how much money you have tied up here? . . . It's — it's —" He had actually spluttered. "It looks like a collection from some old hooker, for chrissake. I want you to get rid of it all!" But this time she had exploded. If he didn't like it, it was his business, and she would never wear any of it again. But they were beautiful pieces and they all meant something to her. And as they both stood there, angry, she promised herself again that she never would show him any part of her past. It was hers, just as the jewelry was, and it would stay that way, just as the jewelry would.

She had mentioned the money she still got from Ivo and would continue to get for her remaining years. But that had outraged John even more. What was wrong with her to stay on that man's payroll? Couldn't she live on her job? And she damn well better not plan to take any money from *him* after they got married, because he wouldn't stand for it. It was like a slap in his face. She didn't look at it that way and she tried to explain it to him, though unsuccessfully, that in some ways Ivo had always been like a father to her. He didn't give a damn, he told her. She was grown-up now, she didn't need a father anymore. And this time it was not like the jewelry, which went unmentioned ever again. This time he drafted a letter himself to Ivo's lawyers and explained that Mrs. Stewart — his teeth clenched as he wrote the word — did not wish to accept the monthly payment anymore. She signed it, tearfully, but she signed it. And that was the end of that. She had severed her last contact with Ivo, even if it was only through his attorneys. And now, after the ceremony, she belonged wholly to John.

John and Bettina stood side by side outside the church for almost half an hour, smiling, kissing cheeks, shaking dozens of hands. And through it all Bettina watched them, his cousins, his classmates, his patients, his friends. And remarkably they all looked the same. They all looked healthy, youthful, smiling, wholesome. It was all so pretty and bland.

"Happy?" He looked at her for a moment as they stepped into his car. He hadn't hired a limousine. He said it was expensive and silly. He would drive himself.

She nodded as she looked at him. And remarkably she was very happy. There was something very refreshing about this new world. "Very." She didn't have to be sparkling and witty. Didn't have to be charming, or give the best dinner parties in town. She just had to be pleasant and make inane comments as she stood beside John. In many ways it was restful and undemanding after the years she had spent of being eternally "on." "I love you, Doctor." She smiled at him, and this time she really meant it.

He smiled back at her. "I love you too."

They went to Carmel on their honeymoon and spent three heavenly days wandering through shops and walking along the beach. They drove down to Big Sur one afternoon and held hands as they looked at the surf. They had long romantic dinners and spent the mornings in bed. It was everything a honeymoon should have been. And two weeks later, as Bettina sat in the gallery on Union Street, she felt desperately ill. She went home early and went to bed, where John found her later, curled up, looking ghastly, and trying to sleep. He frowned as he looked at her, inquired about her symptoms, and then sat down gently on the side of the bed.

"Can I have a look at you, Betty?" It still seemed funny to her when he called her by that name.

"Sure." She sat up in bed and tried to smile at him. "But I don't think there's much to look at. I just have the flu. Mary said she had it last week."

He nodded and examined her gently: he found her lungs clear, her eyes bright, and no fever. And then he looked at her, wondering, and smiled happily. "Maybe you're pregnant."

She looked at him, startled. "Already?" It

didn't seem possible. Two weeks after they had stopped using birth control? That had been his idea.

"We'll see."

"How soon will we know?" Suddenly she felt anxious.

But John was smiling, pleased with himself. "We can find out in about two weeks. I'll have them run a test in the office, and if it comes out positive, I'll send you to an O.B."

"Can I go to Mary's?" Suddenly everything made her feel anxious. What was happening to her? Who had made this decision? She was terrified just thinking about it, and she didn't want it to be true.

He kissed her forehead and left the room. He was back a few minutes later with a cup of tea and some crackers. "Try this." She did and a little while later she was feeling physically better, but still very much afraid. But she didn't dare tell him that.

Two weeks later John came home with a small bottle and put it in her hand before they went to bed. "Use this tomorrow morning. First urine. Leave it in the fridge, and I'll take it to work."

"Will you call me as soon as they do it?" She looked at him grimly, and he patted her arm and smiled.

"I know you're excited, baby. Just hang in. We'll know in the morning. And I promise, I'll call you as soon as we know." And then after he kissed her, "I'm pretty excited too, you know." And she knew he was being honest. He had looked as though he had been floating on air for two weeks. It had made it that much more impossible to tell him how she felt. And then suddenly, in a burst, she had to tell him as they lay side by side in the dark.

"John?"

"Yes, Betty?"

She reached out and took his hand as she pressed herself into his back. "I'm scared."

He sounded surprised. "Of what?"

"Of . . . you know . . . of" — she felt like an ass as she said it, it was so normal to him — "of being pregnant."

"But what are you afraid of, silly?" He turned around in their bed and faced her in the dark.

"Of . . . well . . . what if it's like the last time?" It was hard to get out the words.

"You mean you're afraid you might lose it?" She nodded, but in truth she was afraid of much more than that.

"A little . . . but . . . oh, I don't know, John, I'm just scared. What if it's awful . . . if it's too painful . . . if I can't stand it . . .

I . . . what if I can't take the pain?"

There were tears in her eyes as she asked him the questions and he took her shoulders in both of his hands. "Now I want you to stop this, Betty. Right now. Birth is a perfectly normal occurrence, there is nothing to be afraid of. Look at Mary. Did she die of the pain? Of course not." He answered his own question with a smile. "Now, just trust me. When you have the baby, I'll be with you every minute, and it'll be nothing, you'll see. Really, I promise you. This whole pain in childbirth thing is immensely overrated. It just isn't that bad."

She felt comforted, but there was still a thread of terror running through her soul.

She leaned over and kissed him gently. "Thank you . . . for wanting the baby. Would we stay here?" She had moved into his apartment, which was spacious and pretty, but it only had one bedroom and a small den, which he used a lot. But there was a long silence after she asked him, and then a chuckle from his side of the bed. "What does that mean?" He didn't often tease, and she looked surprised. "Well?"

"It means mind your own business . . ." And then he couldn't resist. He had to tell her. "Oh, all right, Betty, I'll tell you, but don't get excited yet. Nothing is sure. But"

— he paused dramatically and she turned around to watch him, smiling — "yesterday I put a bid on a house."

She looked astonished. "You did? Why didn't you tell me? Where? John Fields, you're impossible!" He grinned proudly at her and she looked thrilled.

"Wait till you hear. It's in Mill Valley. And it's next door to Seth and Mary's house." He sounded triumphant and Bettina grinned.

"That's fabulous!"

"Isn't it? Just keep your fingers crossed that we get it."

"Do you think we will?"

"I think we might. But first, let's find out if you're pregnant, madam. That's a lot more important. At least to me." He put an arm around her and they snuggled in the bed.

Her old life forgotten, gone the penthouses, the lofts and the elegant co-ops, the quiet town house . . . all she could think of was her house in Mill Valley, her baby, her husband, and her new life.

30

"Do you realize that this is the hottest June they've had since nineteen eleven? I heard it on the radio yesterday while I was lying on the bathroom floor trying to cool off." Bettina looked at Mary in despair as she fanned herself in Mary's kitchen, and her friend and neighbor laughed.

"I have to admit, I can't think of anything worse than being nine months pregnant in the heat." And then she laughed again as she looked at Bettina with sympathy. "But I've done it both times." Her children were three years old, and ten months now, but both were mercifully down for their naps.

Bettina grinned halfheartedly and picked at the dry tuna fish salad she'd brought. "May I remind you that I am nine and a half months pregnant." With a dismal sigh she looked down at the tuna fish and made a face. "Yuk, I can't eat any more." She pushed it away and attempted to settle herself more comfortably in the chair.

Mary looked at her sympathetically. "Do you want to lie down on the couch?"

"Only if you realize that I may never be able to get up."

"That's all right. If we can't get you up, Seth can push the couch out our back door into yours."

And then Bettina smiled at her. "Isn't it nice being neighbors?"

Mary smiled back. "It sure is."

They had had the house for six months. And it had meant commuting to the city to her job at the gallery for the first four, but finally John had let her off the hook when she had complained that she'd never get the house done unless she quit and stayed home. He had eventually relented, and she was ecstatic to be free. But the ecstasy had only lasted for a few weeks. In her last month of pregnancy she had been so tired, so bloated, so uncomfortable that she hadn't been able to get anything done.

Now as she stretched out on the couch she looked at her friend. Although they were neighbors, they hadn't seen each other in weeks. "Is it always like this for you?"

Mary looked pensive for a minute. "It's different for everyone, Betty. And it's different for every woman each time."

Bettina grinned. "You sound like a nurse."

Mary laughed in answer. "I guess I still am. Everytime I see you, I find myself wanting to ask you questions about what's happening, are your ankles swollen, are you getting headaches, generally how do you feel? But I restrain myself. I figure you must be getting enough of that from John."

But Bettina shook her head, smiling. "Surprisingly he's very good. He never says much of anything. His feeling is that it's a natural process, it's no big deal."

"And what does your O.B. say?"

Bettina looked relaxed as she answered. It had taken her the full nine months to dispense with the last of her fears. Now she knew they had all been groundless. And she knew that she was well prepared. "He says pretty much the same thing."

"Is that what you think?" Mary looked stunned.

"Hell, yes. I've worked my ass off with those breathing exercises in the classes I've gone to. I know I've got it down pat. Now, if I'd just have the baby." She sat up awkwardly on the couch, and for a moment she flinched. "Christ, my back is killing me."

Mary handed her two more cushions and brought over a stool for her feet.

"Thanks, love." She smiled gratefully, and

carefully raised her feet. But even the pillows didn't seem to help her back. It had been killing her all day.

"Something bothering you?"

"My back."

Mary nodded and went on. "You know, I was scared shitless before the first one. And actually" — she smiled openly — "I was kind of scared before my second one too."

"And how was it?" Bettina looked at her frankly.

Mary smiled pensively in answer. "Not bad. I was pretty well prepared the second time, and I had Seth with me." And then she looked at Bettina pointedly. "But I was not in any way prepared for the first."

"Why not?" Bettina looked intrigued.

"Because even though I was an O.B. nurse and I'd seen it a thousand times, no one can really tell you what it's like. It hurts, Betty. Don't kid yourself about it. It hurts a lot. It's kind of like a long, hard race for a long time, and then you get to a point when you think you can't take it, from about seven centimeters on. Hopefully that doesn't last too long. And then you get to pushing. That's exhausting, but it's not so bad."

She wanted to ask her how John had let her go to McCarney. He was the coldest, cruelest doctor she had ever assisted in O.B.

Twice she had left the delivery room in tears after the patient had delivered. And after that she had always disappeared when she knew he was bringing someone in. "Do you like him?"

Bettina seemed to hesitate for a long time. "I trust him. I think he's a very good doctor, but I don't . . . I don't love him." She grinned sheepishly. "But John says he's an excellent doctor. He teaches at the university, he's done a lot of recent research papers. He's apparently working on some fancy new equipment too. John says he's really tops. But he isn't . . . well, he isn't warm. But I figured it didn't really matter. If he's good and John's there, so what?"

Mary thought for a moment. There was no point frightening her now. It was too late. "McCarney is certainly a very respected doctor, he's just not quite as warm and friendly as mine. And you'll have John with you." Thank God. "But try to be realistic about a first labor, Betty. It could take a while."

Bettina watched her in silence for a moment, and then shook her head. When she spoke, it was very softly, with an old memory still lingering in her eyes. "This isn't my first time, Mary."

"It's not?" Now she was shocked. "You've

had another baby?" But when? With whom? What had happened to it? Did it die? She restrained the questions and Bettina went on.

"I had a miscarriage at four months a year and a half ago, before I moved to California. In fact" — she decided to tell the truth now, she felt oddly close to her friend — "that was how I met John. I had the miscarriage and moved to San Francisco a week later, got depressed, and tried to commit suicide. They called John after they pumped my stomach, and" — she smiled softly — "we got to be friends."

"Well, I'll be damned. He never said a thing to us."

This time Bettina smiled more broadly. "I know. He didn't want me to either. But Seth knows."

"Seth?" Mary looked at her in disbelief.

Bettina grinned. "He handled my divorce."

"You were married before too? Well, aren't you full of secrets. Anything else?"

Bettina laughed and shrugged. "Not too many. Just a few . . . let's see. . . ." Suddenly she wanted to make a clean breast of it to someone, and she had never felt as close to her friend. "I've been married twice."

"Including John?" Mary checked it out.

"Before John." Bettina spoke softly. "Once to a much older man, and once to an actor. I used to work in the theater, my last jobs were as assistant director —"

"You?" Mary looked not only stunned but impressed.

"And my father was a writer. A well-known one." She smiled and sat back against her pillows as Mary watched.

"Who was he? Anyone I've ever heard of?"

"Probably." She knew Mary read a lot. "Justin Daniels."

"What . . . Of course . . . Bettina Daniels . . . but I never made the connection. Jesus, Bettina, why didn't you tell us?" And then she put both hands on her hips. "Or does Seth know all of this too?"

But Bettina shook her head firmly. "He only knows about my last marriage. He doesn't know all the rest."

"Then why didn't you tell us?"

Bettina shrugged. "John's not very proud of my checkered past, I'm afraid." Momentarily she looked embarrassed. "I didn't want to — to humiliate him."

"Humiliate him? How? By being Justin Daniels's daughter? I would think he'd be proud. And as for the rest, your two marriages, so what, I'm sure they made sense or you wouldn't have done it, and your friends would love you no matter what. People who love you will always understand, or at least try to. The others . . . who cares? Your father must have known that. I'm sure people didn't always approve of the way he lived."

"That was different. He was a genius in a way. People expect 'eccentricities' of someone like that."

"So write a book, your past will become exotic."

Bettina laughed, and then sheepishly hung her head before looking back up at her friend. "I've always wanted to write a play."

"Have you?" Mary looked thrilled, and then sat back on her heels. "Good Lord, Betty, do you realize I've always thought you were as dull as the rest of us, and now I find out you're not. When the hell are you going to write your play?"

"Probably never. I think it would upset John. And . . . oh, I don't know, Mary . . . that" — she seemed to struggle with her words — "that world isn't very respectable. In some ways maybe I'm lucky I escaped."

"Maybe. But you escaped with your talent. Couldn't you be respectable and exercise that too?"

"I'd like to try it someday." She spoke as though dreaming, and then shook her head.

"But I don't suppose I will. John would never forgive me. I think he would feel I was dragging something unsavory into his life."

"Didn't it ever occur to you that maybe that was only *his* opinion, that maybe he was wrong? You know, sometimes without even knowing it, people are jealous. We all lead boring, ordinary, mundane existences, and now and then a bird of paradise comes along, and we all get scared. It scares us because we're not like that, our feathers aren't brilliantly hued in red and green, we're brown and gray, and seeing that bird of paradise makes us feel ugly, or as though in some way we've failed. Some of us love to watch that bird, and we dream that one day we might be birds of paradise too . . . others of us have to shoot at the bird . . . or at least frighten it away."

"Are you saying that's what John did?" Bettina looked shocked.

But when Mary answered, her voice was infinitely kind. "No. I think what he did was run around to find you brown and gray feathers and dress you up like one of us. But you're not, Bettina. You're exotic and beautiful and special. You are a very, very rare bird. Take off the brown feathers, Betty. Let everyone see how rich your plumage is.

You're Justin Daniels's daughter, that in itself is a rare gift. How would your father feel about you hiding out here? Pretending you're not even his child?" Bettina's eyes filled with tears as she thought of it, and then suddenly she flinched. It was as though an electric shock had gone through her back. Mary leaned toward her and kissed her cheek softly, with a look of great tenderness in her eyes. "Now tell me about those pains you've been having. It's started in your back, hasn't it?"

Bettina looked up at her in amazement, still deeply touched by all she had said. It was the first hint she had that she was still acceptable, in spite of her somewhat exotic past. "How did you know about my back?"

"Because that used to be my business, remember? We can't all be birds of paradise, kiddo. Some of us have to be firemen and policemen and doctors and nurses." She was smiling and holding Bettina's hand as she flinched again.

"I'm glad."

"Do you want to start the breathing yet? Don't if it's not bad."

"It is." She was surprised at how quickly it had started to hurt her. An hour before, it had only been a vague twinge and she hadn't known what it was. Ten minutes earlier it had been uncomfortable once or twice. Now it was cutting off her breathing.

Mary was looking down at her now, taking stock of the situation and still holding her hand as she had a new pain. But this one wasn't in her back, it ripped through her stomach, pulling at everything in its wake and tying it in a long razor-sharp knot that had her gasping and clutching at Mary's hand. The pain went on for over a minute as Mary steadily looked at her watch. "That was a bad one."

Bettina nodded and broke into a sweat as she lay back against the couch. She was almost speechless but managed to whisper, "Yes." And then suddenly her eyes grew frantic and she spoke hoarsely this time. "John."

"It's okay, Betty, I'll call him. You just lie still. And when you get another pain, just start the breathing."

"Where are you going?" Bettina's eyes filled with panic.

"Just to the kitchen, to the phone. I'm going to call John and have him call your doctor. Then I'm going to call Nancy across the street and have her come over to sit with the kids." And then she smiled at Bettina. "Thank God they haven't woken up from their naps. And as soon as Nancy gets here, which should be in about two minutes, you and I are going to get in the car and drive over to the city and get you to the hospital. How does that sound?"

Bettina started to nod, but then she grabbed wildly at Mary's hand again. It was another long, rocky pain. "Oh, Mary . . . Mary . . . it hurts awfully . . . it. . . ."

"Ssshhh . . . now, you can handle it, Betty. Calm down." Without saying more, she went to the kitchen quickly and came back with a damp cloth, which she put on Bettina's head. "You just take it easy and I'll make those two calls."

She was back in two minutes, wearing espadrilles with her jeans and T-shirt and carrying her handbag. She had asked Nancy, the neighbor, to stop in at John and Betty's and pick up the suitcase that she knew was standing in the hall. It was only five minutes later when Mary eased Bettina slowly into the car.

"What if we don't make it?" Bettina looked at her nervously and Mary smiled. She almost hoped they wouldn't. She'd much rather have delivered Bettina on the front seat of the station wagon than handed her over to McCarney when they arrived.

Mary grinned at her as she started the car. "If we don't, then I'll deliver you myself.

And think of all the money you'll save!"

They drove on in silence for a while as Bettina breathed doggedly through all of her pains, but they were coming much closer together and there was a glazed look of determination now in her eyes. Mary was surprised that it had gotten so sharp so quickly, but she hoped that would mean a quick delivery. Maybe she would be lucky, after all. And it wasn't her first child. As they drove, Mary found herself thinking back to what they had been discussing. It was extraordinary how you could know someone, and not know them at all.

"How's it going, kid?" Bettina shrugged and panted determinedly as they drove on. Mary waited until the pain had subsided, and then gently touched her arm. "Betty, don't be a hero, love. I know you've prepared for natural childbirth, but if it gets to be too much, you ask for something, as soon as you want to. Don't wait." She didn't want to tell her that if she waited too long they wouldn't be able to give her anything at all.

But Bettina was shaking her head at Mary. "John won't let me. He says it'll brain-damage . . . the kid. . . ." Another pain was starting and Mary had to wait again. But when the pain was over, she pressed on.

"He's wrong. Trust me. I was an O.B.

nurse for years. They can give you an epidural, which is something like a spinal, and it will cut off all sensation below your waist. They can give you a little Demerol maybe, some kind of shot that will take the edge off the pain. They can do a lot of things that won't hurt the baby. Will you ask for it if you need it?"

Bettina nodded distractedly. "Okay." She didn't want to waste her breath arguing. She knew how John felt about it, and he had insisted that she would damage their child if she took anything for the pain.

Fifteen minutes later they drove up to the hospital, and Bettina could no longer walk. They put her on a gurney quickly, and Mary held her hand as she writhed in pain.

"Oh Mary . . . tell them . . . no! . . . Stop rolling!" She sat up, grabbing at the orderly, and then fell back and screamed. He waited patiently for the end of the contraction, and Mary tried to soothe her as she talked to her softly and held her hand. She was almost certain that she was now in transition and the pain was at its worst. But only three more centimeters, if that were the case, and she would be fully dilated, and then it would be almost over. She could start to push.

John was waiting for them at labor and

delivery, with a look of excitement on his face. He looked at Mary happily and smiled at her and then down at Bettina, dripping perspiration and groaning as she lay huddled on the gurney. She clutched at him wildly and started to cry as she held on to his white coat desperately. "Oh, John . . . it hurts . . . so much. . . ." She was almost instantly torn apart by another pain as he watched. But he held her hand quietly and checked his watch as Mary looked on. An idea came to her suddenly then, and she quietly signaled John. When Bettina's pain had ended, he came to her with a look of peaceful satisfaction.

"What's up?"

"I just thought of something. Since I used to work here, they might let me scrub up to just be with you two. I can't assist, but I could be there for her." And then she couldn't help adding, "John, I think she's going to have a hard time." Mary had seen it often. And things were rapidly getting out of control.

But John smiled gratefully at Mary, patted her shoulder, and shook his head. "Don't worry, everything's going just fine. Just look at her" — he cast a glance over his shoulder with a smile — "I think she's already in transition."

"So do I. But that doesn't mean it's over."

"Don't worry so much. You nurses are all alike." She tried to insist for a moment longer, but he firmly shook his head. Instead he signaled to one of the waiting O.B. nurses to push her into an examining room. But Mary went quickly to her head.

"It's going to be okay, kiddo. You're doing great. All you have to do now is hang on. Kind of like a roller-coaster ride." And then she bent down and kissed her gently. "It's all right, Betty, it's all right." But tears were pouring from Bettina's eyes as the nurse pushed her silently into an examining room. And a moment later Mary saw Dr. McCarney disappear through the door, with John striding alongside. Mary almost cringed as she watched them, sure that no one had warned Bettina that he was going to have to examine her midpain. And tears filled Mary's eyes a moment later as the nurse came hurriedly out of the examining room, shrugged her shoulders, and they heard Bettina scream.

"They wouldn't let me stay with her." The nurse looked apologetically at Mary, who nodded.

"I know. I used to work here. Do you know how dilated she is?"

"I'm not sure. They were guessing at seven

and a half. But she just won't seem to progress."

"Why don't they run an I.V. of Pitocin?"

"McCarney says there's no point. She'll get there in good time." After that all Mary could glean from the hurrying nurses was that she was eight centimeters dilated, and McCarney and her husband had agreed that she shouldn't have anything for the pain. They figured it would be over pretty quickly, and either way, she'd be better off without doping herself up. The nurses were ordered out of the room almost as soon as they entered, and Mary paced the halls, close to hysteria herself. McCarney and John had decided to handle this one themselves while she was in labor, and the great Dr. McCarney didn't want any nurses around until they went to the delivery room. Mary paced up and down the long halls, wishing she had Seth with her, wishing Bettina had a different doctor, wishing everything, and occasionally hearing the girl scream.

"She can't still be dilating, can she?" Mary looked woefully at the head nurse, who knew her well.

But slowly she nodded. "It's just one of those bad-luck ones. She got to eight in a hurry and now she seems to be stuck right there."

"How's she doing?"

There was a moment of silence before the head nurse answered. "McCarney had us tie her down."

"Oh, Jesus." He was as bad as Mary remembered, and finally she put a call through to Seth. But he wasn't able to join her until after six o'clock. By then Mary was crying when she explained what had gone on. He put an arm around her shoulders.

"John's in there, he's not going to let the old guy be too rough on her."

"The hell he's not. They tied her down three hours ago, Seth. And John told her he doesn't want her to have anything for the pain, or it'll brain-damage the child. What makes me crazy is that it doesn't have to be like that. You know that." He nodded and for a moment they both thought back to how beautiful it had been for them ten months before when they shared the birth of their second child. And even their first one had been nothing like this. "He's making it as awful for her as he can."

"Just take it easy, Mary." And then he looked at her gently. "Do you want to go home?"

But she was vehement as she shook her head. "I'm not leaving until that sonofabitch delivers her." The head nurse chuckled as she walked by.

"Amen, Waterston." The two women exchanged a small grim smile.

"How's she doing?"

"About the same. She's at nine now." It had only taken seven hours for one centimeter, with yet another to go. It was just after ten o'clock at night.

"Can't they give her something to speed it up?"

But the head nurse shook her head and walked on.

At last, another four hours later, just after two A.M., the door to her labor room opened, and John, McCarney, and two nurses hurried out. One of the nurses was pushing the gurney, where a strapped-down, restrained, hysterical Bettina whimpered as she lay there, almost insane from the pain. No one had spoken to her for hours, no one had comforted or explained. No one had held her hand, helped her move more comfortably. They had simply let her lie there, tied down, hysterical, agonized, frightened as the pains tore through her body and mind. At first John had tried to help her with her breathing, but McCarney had been quick to suggest that he stay down at the far end. "The work is happening down here, John." He had pointed to where he was working. They had had her tied into stirrups so they could check her with greater convenience, for the past eleven hours. Once or twice she had tried to tell them how badly her back was cramping, but after a while she didn't care. And when John had hesitated another time as he heard her crying, McCarney had shook his head firmly. "Just leave her alone. They all have to go through it. She won't even hear you if you talk." So John had done as McCarney told him, and when Seth and Mary saw her being shoved into the delivery room, it was obvious that Bettina was almost out of her head.

"Oh, God, did you see her?" Mary began to cry as the door to delivery closed behind them and Seth took her into his arms.

"It's all right, honey. She's going to be all right." But Mary pulled away from him, staring at her husband in horror.

"Do you have any idea what it's like to do that to a woman? Do you know what they've done to her mind? They've treated her like an animal for the last twelve hours, for God's sake. She'll never want to have a baby again. They've broken her, damn you! They've broken her!" And then, wordlessly, she reached for her husband and began to sob. He stood there, feeling helpless as he stroked her hair. He knew that what she was saying was right, but there was nothing he could do. He didn't understand how John had let McCarney deliver her. It seemed like a foolish thing to do. The man was competent, but he was a ruthless bastard. There was no doubt about that.

"She's going to be all right, Mary. By tomorrow she won't remember all this."

But Mary looked at him sadly. "She'll remember enough." He knew it was true, and they stood there together, feeling helpless and unhappy, for another two hours. At last at four thirty in the morning Alexander John Fields came into the world, lusty and crying, as his father looked at him proudly and his mother just lay there, staring blindly as she sobbed.

31

"Bettina?" Mary knocked softly on the open doorway, wondering if she was at home. At first there was no answer, and then there was a cheerful call from upstairs.

"Come on up, Mary. I'm straightening up Alex's room."

Mary mounted the stairs slowly and smiled when she found Bettina at the top. "I spend half my life doing that. Where's the prince?"

"Today's his first day at school." And then she looked at Mary in embarrassment. "I don't know what to do with myself, so I thought I'd clean up his room." But Mary nodded in answer.

"That does me in every time."

"What do you do to combat it?" Bettina smiled at her and sat on the brightly covered bed. The room was done in reds, blues, and yellows, with toy soldiers marching everywhere.

But Mary was suddenly laughing. "What do I do? I get pregnant." She was grinning broadly as Bettina looked at her.

"Oh, no! Mary, not again?"

"Yup." They had had their third child two years before, and now there would be a fourth. "I just got the call from the doctor's office. But I think this is going to be it for the Waterstons. Hell, kid, I'll be thirty-nine this month. I'm not a baby like you."

"I wish I felt like one." She had just turned thirty-one. "But in any case for me pregnancy is not the solution." She looked pointedly at her friend, and Mary looked at her sadly.

"I wish it was." The experience of Alexander's birth had marked her. And she had made her stand to John very clear. There were going to be no more kids. But he had been an only child too, and he was satisfied with just one. "You ought to rethink that decision some time, Betty. I told you three years ago it doesn't have to be the way it was." She remembered their conversation in the hospital right after Alexander was born. Mary had been tearful, angry, furious with John and McCarney. She had been the only one on Bettina's side.

Bettina shrugged. "I have enough with Alexander. I really don't want any more."

But Mary didn't believe her. For a woman who hadn't even been sure she wanted children, she was a marvel with the boy. Creative, loving, gentle. For three years Alexander and his mother had been best friends. Now she stood up and walked toward Mary with a smile. "But I must admit, I don't know what the hell to do without him today."

"Why don't you go into town and go shopping? I'd take you along with me, but I just got a sitter and I promised Seth I'd meet him to help pick out our new car."

"What are you getting?" Bettina wandered slowly downstairs in the wake of her friend.

"I don't know, something ugly and useful. With four kids who can drive anything lovely? We'll wait and buy our first 'nice' car when we're too old to drive."

"They'll be gone before you know it, Mary." The oldest one was already six, and she had seen how time flew with Alexander. It was hard to believe he was three. And then suddenly she looked at her friend with a chuckle. "Unless you keep having babies for another fifteen years."

"Seth would kill me." But they both knew that wasn't true. They enjoyed each other and their children. And after eight years of marriage they were still in love. Things were different with John and Bettina, they were very close, but they had never shared quite the same thing as Mary and Seth. And something had happened to Bettina. Part of her had closed up after the birth of the child. Mary had seen it happen to others. It came from being betrayed by people she had trusted. She would never trust anyone quite the same way again. It had often bothered Mary, but she had never dared to bring it up, just as she had never again dared to mention Bettina's play. But now that Alexander was starting school and Bettina would have more time on her hands, she wondered if now at long last she would start to write. "So? You going shopping?"

Bettina shrugged. "I don't know. Maybe I will go into town. Can I do anything for you?"

"Not a thing, Betty, but thanks. I just wanted to stop by and tell you the news."

"Thank you." Bettina grinned warmly at her friend. "When's it due?"

"April this time. An Easter bunny."

"At least you won't die of the heat for a change."

Bettina watched her leave, then got ready to go to town. She was wearing gray slacks and a gray sweater, and she put a raincoat over her arm before she left the house. It was one of those mottled days of autumn when it could turn out to be beautiful and sunny, or it could turn out to be windy and foggy and cold. For a moment Bettina hesitated, thinking that she might call John and ask him if he wanted to meet her for lunch. The nursery school where they had put Alexander kept him in school from noon until four. But she decided to call John from the city. After she decided what she wanted to do.

She parked her car downtown below Union Square, and then walked across the street to the solemn St. Francis and wandered through the elaborate lobby. She found a row of pay phones, called her husband, and discovered that he had already gone out for lunch. So she was left with a decision. To go shopping without eating, or stop somewhere for a sandwich by herself. She wasn't sure she was very hungry, and as she stood pensively for a moment she felt someone suddenly grab her arm. Startled, she jumped to one side, and then looked up to see who had grabbed her, and when she did, she fell silent, her eyes stunned and wide.

"Hello, Bettina." He had hardly changed in the five years since she had seen him. But just looking at him again, she felt like a little girl. It was Ivo, as tall, stately, and handsome as he had ever been, with as rich and full a head of snow-white hair. He looked scarcely older, and as she looked at him she was stunned to remember that now he had to be seventy-three.

"Ivo. . . ." She didn't know what more to say. She was stunned into silence, but then, without saying more, she felt herself hold out her arms. There were tears blinding her eyes as he held her, and when he pulled away again, she saw that he was crying too.

"Oh, little one, how are you? Are you all right? I've worried and worried about you."

But she nodded, smiling slowly. "I'm fine. And you?"

"Getting older but not wiser." And then, "Yes, darling. I'm all right. You're still married?" He checked her left hand quickly and saw that she was.

"Yes. And I have the most wonderful little boy."

"I'm glad." His voice was gentle as the crowds ebbed around them in the lobby. But as he looked at her, she felt ashamed. Three husbands. It was disgraceful. She looked at him and sighed. "You're happy?" he asked.

She nodded. In many ways she was. It was different than life had been with him. She wasn't a little girl living a fantasy life anymore. It was a real life with lonely moments and hard spots. But through it all was the knowledge that she was respectable now, and there was always the joy she derived from her child. "Yes, I am."

"I'm glad."

"And you?" She wanted to know if he had remarried, and he laughed when he saw her eyes.

"No, darling, I'm not married. But I'm perfectly happy as I am. Your father was right. A man should end his life as a bachelor. It makes a great deal more sense." He chuckled softly, but the way he said it did not deny what they had had. He put an arm around her now and drew her to him. "I always wondered what had happened when my lawyers told me what you'd done about the money. It took every possible ounce of effort not to set investigators on your trail to find you. For a while I was going to do that, then I decided that you had a right to your own life. I had always promised you that." She nodded, feeling oddly sobered and still overwhelmed to be standing there in his arms.

"Ivo. . . ." She looked up at him happily and he smiled. "I'm so glad to see you." It was like going home. For years and years she had almost forgotten what she had come from and who she was, and now here was Ivo in San Francisco, with an arm around her shoulders. She was so happy, she wanted to dance. "Do you have time for lunch?"

"For you, little one, always." He glanced at his watch, and then excused himself and went to the phone. When he came back, he was smiling. "I'm here to visit an old friend. Rawson. Remember him? He's the editor of the paper here now and I promised him some advice. But I have two free hours. Will that do?"

"Perfectly. After that I have to be home when my little boy comes home from school."

"How old is he?" He looked at her gently.

"Three, and his name is Alexander."

He looked at her for a moment. "Have you given up the theater?"

With a small sigh she nodded. "Yes."

"Why?"

"My husband doesn't approve."

"But you're writing?"

And then gently, "No, Ivo, I'm not." He waited until they were seated at a comfortable booth deep in the rear of the restaurant. Then he took a deep breath and faced her.

"Now what's this nonsense about your not writing?"

"I just don't want to."

"Since when?" He was scrutinizing her carefully as she spoke.

"Since I got married."

"Does this husband of yours have anything to do with that too?"

She hesitated for a long time. "Yes. He does."

"And you accept that?" She nodded again.

"Yes." She thought for a moment. "John wants our life to be 'normal.' He doesn't think that writing is." It was painful but true.

And then he watched her. He was beginning to understand. Slowly he nodded and reached for her hand. "You'd have been a great deal better off, my darling, if you had led a normal life from the first. If you had had a normal mother and father, if you had been allowed to be a normal little girl. But you weren't and you didn't. There has never ever been anything 'normal' about your life." He smiled gently. "Not even your marriage to me. But sometimes normal can mean ordinary, or boring, it can mean run-of-the-mill, or banal. And nothing that has ever touched you, from the moment you were born until now, has been any of those things. You were an extraordinary woman, right up until now. You can't pretend to be otherwise, darling. You can't be something that you're not. Is that what you're doing here, Bettina? Pretending to be some nice ordinary man's ordinary wife? Is that what he wants you to do?" Silently she nodded and he let go of her hand with regret. "In that case, Bettina, he doesn't love you. He loves a woman of his own creation. A painted shell in which he has forced you to hide. But you won't be able to do it forever, Bettina. And it isn't worth it. You have a right to be who you are. Materially your father left you nothing. All he left you was a piece of his genius, a flash of his soul. But those precious gifts you are denying each day you pretend to be someone you are not and refuse to write." And then after a long pause, "Can't you do both, Bettina? Couldn't you write and be this man's wife too?"

"I haven't allowed myself to consider that possibility." She grinned at him mischievously. "I'm considering it. What about you?"

"I'm doing my share. The intrinsic exhaustion you may remember turned out to be a bout of anemia, which, thank God, they cleared up. I've written a book, and now I'm writing a second. But nothing like Justin's, of course. This is all nonfiction." He smiled at her with pleasure.

"I'd love to read it."

"I'll send you a copy." And then, regretfully, he looked at her. Their two hours were over and he had to leave. "I'm leaving tonight. Do you ever come to New York?" She shook her head slowly.

"I haven't been back in almost five years."

"Isn't it time?"

"I don't think so. My husband doesn't like big cities."

"Then come alone." She rolled her eyes and laughed.

It gave him hope to see the spark in her eyes now. It hadn't been there before lunch.

"Maybe when I've written my play. I suppose it is time." Seeing him made her realize with a start how much she had sacrificed, all along, for the play. It would all be for nothing if she never wrote it.

He nodded. "What about your husband? Will you tell him you saw me today?"

She thought for a moment, and then sadly she shook her head. "I don't think I can." He was sorry for her then. She could always tell him everything. Except that foolishness she'd gotten into with the young actor at the end.

Bettina nodded slowly, and then she reached out and held Ivo close. "This is all like a dream, you know. It's as though you're some sort of deus ex machina dropped from the sky to change my course."

He chuckled softly. "If that's how you want to think of me, Bettina, that's fine. Just be sure you do it. None of this nonsensical housewife routine, darling, or I'll come back and haunt you, and then you'll be up the creek." They both laughed at that. "Now, you promise you'll send me what you've written?"

"I promise." She looked at him solemnly as they stood up and walked back to the lobby. If felt good to be with him again, to be tiny and elegant at his side. For a moment she longed for her old wardrobe, the expensive European clothes, and the jewels, and then as though he knew what she were thinking, he looked down at her and spoke softly.

"Do you still have the ring?" She knew he meant the big diamond, and she nodded with huge eyes.

"Of course, Ivo. I don't wear it. But I have it. I keep it in my vault at the bank."

"Good. Don't ever let anyone have that. You keep that for you. It's worth a small fortune now, and you never know if you'll need it." And then suddenly he remembered that he hadn't yet gotten her address or her new name. She gave it to him quickly, and then she giggled.

"They call me Betty Fields. Betty Fields." But Ivo didn't look amused as he watched her.

"It doesn't suit you."

And then in embarrassment, "I know."

"Will you write as Bettina Daniels?"

She nodded and it was obvious that he approved. And then he pulled her into his arms again and said nothing. He only held her, and for a moment she clung to him. It was Bettina who finally broke the silence. "Ivo . . . thank you. . . ."

His eyes were oddly bright when he looked down at her. "Take good care of yourself, little one. You'll be hearing from me." She nodded and he kissed her gently on the forehead, and she left him in the lobby, watching her go. He watched her until she had disappeared in the crowds outside the building, and at last with a small sigh he turned. How much she had changed in the five years he hadn't seen her. And how strong a hold this man must have on her to make her deny her other life, herself, and her old world. But Ivo wasn't going to let her disappear again so easily. On his way up in the elevator he took out a small black leather notepad and made several notes.

32

"How's it coming, Betty?" Mary smiled at her as she wandered slowly out into the yard. It was a warm, sunny April day.

"Not bad. How about you?"

"About the same." They exchanged a grin, and slowly began to walk. Mary was once again hugely pregnant, but she always looked peaceful and happy like that. Despite the jokes and her pretense at complaining, being pregnant was something she didn't really mind. "How long do you think it's going to take you to finish?" Only Mary and Ivo knew about the play. It was going well now.

Bettina squinted in the sunlight, thinking back on her afternoon's work. "Maybe another two weeks. Maybe three."

"That's all?" Mary looked impressed. Bettina had been at it for almost six months. "You might even beat me to it after all."

The baby wasn't due until the end of the month.

"Whoever produces first owes the other a lunch."

Mary grinned broadly. "You're on." They rambled on about the children then, and a little while later Alexander and Mary's two eldest came home. Bettina wandered slowly in after Alexander, confident that she had concealed all the pages of her work. But half an hour later she walked into her bedroom and found Alexander staring seriously down at her play.

"What's that, Mommy?"

"Something I've been doing." She tried to sound noncommittal. She didn't want him to tell John.

"But what is it?"

She hesitated for a long time. "It's a story."

"Like for kids?"

And then she sighed gently. "No. Like for grownups."

"Like a book?" His eyes widened in new respect, but she shook her head again with a gentle smile.

"No, sweetheart. And to tell you the truth, it's kind of a surprise for Daddy, so I don't want you to tell him. Think you could do that? Just for me?" She eyed him hopefully and he nodded.

"Sure." And then he disappeared into his bedroom and she thought to herself that one day she would have to tell him about his grandfather. He had a right to know that he was related to a man like Justin Daniels. Even people who hadn't liked him had admitted that he was a great man. And his books were so lovely. Lately Bettina had read many of them again in the evening whenever John was working. She concealed them from him. As she did the calls she got from Ivo now, from time to time. He only wanted to know how she was doing. And she assured him that she was working and everything was fine. He already had an agent anxious to receive her first draft when she was finished, and the last time she had spoken to him she had promised that it would be soon. But it happened even sooner than she expected. And suddenly, a week after she had talked to Mary, she realized that the play lay completed in her hands. She stared at it for a long moment, her hair ruffled, her face smudged with pencil, and with a broad grin. She had done it after all! She had never been so proud in her life. Her pride wasn't even matched by Mary, who gave birth to a baby boy the next day, easily as always.

After carefully rereading the play four

more times, Bettina put it in the mail to Ivo.

"How is it?" He sounded as excited as she felt.

"Wonderful! I love it!"

"Good. Then I'm sure I will too." He was going to send it to her agent.

A week later the agent called her and told her it needed more work.

"What does that mean?" She asked Ivo when she called to cry on his shoulder.

"Just what the man said. He told you where you should correct it. And it can't be news for you. You remember Justin doing his rewrites. It's not such a big deal. You didn't expect to have it right the first time, did you?" But he could tell from the disappointment in her voice that she did.

"Of course."

"Well, you waited almost thirty-two years to write it, now you can give it another six months." But she didn't have to. She had the corrections the agent wanted in three. She mailed it back to him over the Fourth of July weekend and two days later he was on the phone. Victory! She had done it! She had written a fabulous, wonderful, spellbinding play. She melted at the sound of his adjectives and lay on her bed for an hour, grinning at the far wall.

"What are you looking so happy about, Betty?" John came in from a game of tennis and looked at her with a smile.

She sat up on their bed and smiled at him, running a hand through his shining ebony hair. "I have a surprise for you, darling." She had had it bound for him when she'd had a copy made for the agent, but she had saved it until she heard if the play was any good.

"What is it?" He sounded intrigued as she walked across the room.

"Something I made for you." She grinned at him over her shoulder, not unlike Alexander when he brought something home from school.

With a look of curiosity in his eyes, John followed her as she reached rapidly into a drawer, and then turned to him, with a large book, bound in blue.

"What is this?" He opened it slowly, and then stopped as though he had been slapped when he saw her name. He turned to look at her angrily, snapping the thin volume closed. "Is this supposed to be funny?"

"Hardly." She looked at him and felt her legs tremble. "It represents nine months of work."

"What is it?"

"It's a play."

"Couldn't you have found something better to do with your time, Betty? The women's auxiliary at the hospital needs a chairman, your son likes going to the beach with you, I can think of a dozen things you could have done with yourself instead of that."

"Why?" It was the first time she had challenged him.

He laughed derisively at her. "This thing is probably drivel." And then in a sudden burst of fury, he threw it at her. "Don't give me this trash!" And then, without saying anything further, he slammed the bedroom door and hurried down the stairs, and a moment later she heard him slam out of the house. From their bedroom window she watched him drive away and wondered what he was going to do now. Probably drive for a while, or go for a walk somewhere, and then he'd come home and they wouldn't discuss it ever again. He'd never read it, never mention it. The subject would be taboo. But what if she sold it, she wondered, then what would happen? What would he do? Depressingly she realized that she'd probably never have to face that possibility, but it was still nice to dream.

33

Right after the Labor Day weekend Alexander went back to school. The neighborhood was suddenly oddly quiet. At least Mary had the baby, but Bettina had nothing to do. True to her silent prediction, John had never again mentioned her play, and the edition she had had bound for him in blue leather had been stuck back in her drawer for two months. He had never seen the dedication to Alexander and him. It had been two months since Bettina had sent it to the agent, and Ivo said it might take months before there was any news. But what news was there going to be? That someone had bought it? That there were a dozen backers? That the show was ready to go into production any day? She grinned at the unlikelihood of any of that happening and went down to the kitchen and put the dishes in the machine. From her kitchen window she could see Mary putting the baby in the carriage and she smiled to herself as she watched. Maybe Mary had the right idea. Because now that her play was written Bettina wondered what she was going to do with herself. As she put the last of the dishes mournfully in the dishwasher, she heard the phone ring.

"Hello?"

"Bettina?"

"Yes." She smiled happily out the window. It was Ivo. "I haven't heard from you in weeks." She felt dishonest talking to him now and never telling John, but there was no harm in it and she knew that. There were some things she decided that she had a right to do without telling him. And what could she tell John anyway? That Ivo was calling to discuss her play?

"I just got back from the South of France. And Norton was going to call you." Her heart skipped a beat. Norton Hess was his agent and now, of course, hers. "But I told him that I wanted to call you myself."

"What about?" She tried to sound nonchalant as she sat down on a chair.

But at his end Ivo was grinning. "What do you think it's about, little one? The weather in California?" She chuckled and so did he. "Not exactly, darling. As a matter of fact" — he drawled out the words and she almost groaned — "it's about your brilliant little play."

"And?"

"Not so impatient!"

"Ivo! Come on!"

"All right, all right. Norton has what looks like an army of backers. Some fluke happened and there's apparently an available theater and it sounds almost impossible but they're talking about opening in late November or early December. . . ." He was laughing happily. "Need I say more? Norton wants you to come to New York on the next plane. You can discuss it all with him when you arrive."

"Are you serious?"

"Of course I am. Never more so."

"Oh, Ivo. . . ." In all her writing and hoping and praying she had never really anticipated this. "What am I going to do now?" She didn't know if she should laugh or cry. But Ivo understood immediately.

"You mean about your husband?"

"Yes. What'll I tell him?"

"That you wrote a play, there's a producer on Broadway who's interested, and with any luck at all it's going to be a smash."

"Be serious."

"I am being serious."

"How soon do I really have to come?"

"The sooner the better. Norton will talk to you after I do, I'm sure. I just wanted the pleasure of breaking the news. But the fact is we're talking about an almost impossible opening date here, I gather. The only reason it's possible is because something happened to free this one theater, and your piece requires almost no costumes and scenery, so it only becomes a question of the financial backing, casting, and rehearsing. But the longer you drag your feet out there, the longer it will take to open here. How about coming tomorrow?"

"Tomorrow?" She looked stunned. "To New York?" She hadn't been there in five and a half years. There was a long moment of silence on the phone while Ivo let her digest it.

"It's up to you, little one. But you'd better pull yourself together right now."

"I'll talk to John tonight, and I'll discuss it with Norton tomorrow."

But Norton was not as gentle as Ivo. He called her half an hour later and insisted that she take the red-eye that night. "I can't, that's ridiculous. I have a husband and a small child. I have to make arrangements, I have to. . . ." He had finally settled on her arriving the next day, but that meant she had to reach John and tell him as soon as she could. She thought about going to see him at his office, but eventually she decided to wait until he came home. She wore something pretty, gave him a drink, and put Alexander to bed as soon as she could.

"What's on your mind, pretty lady?" He eyed her with interest and they both smiled, but Bettina's face grew rapidly serious as she put down her drink.

"There's something I have to discuss with you, darling. And no matter what you may think of it, I want you to know that I love you." She faltered for a moment as she looked at him, dreading having to tell him about the play. "Because I do love you very, very much. And this has nothing to do with loving you, it has to do with me."

"And what does all this mean? Let me guess." He was in a teasing mood tonight. "You want to bleach your hair blond."

But she shook her head somberly. "No, John, it's about my play."

"Is that what it is? What about it?" His face was instantly tense.

She couldn't tell him that Ivo had sent it to an agent, because she hadn't told him that she had seen Ivo again. "I sent it to an agent."

"When?"

"Last July. No, actually before that, and

he asked me to make some corrections and I did."

"Why?"

She closed her eyes for a minute, and then she looked at him. "Because I want to sell it, John. It's just . . . it's something I've always wanted to do. I had to. For myself, for my father. And in a funny way for you and Alexander too."

"Bullshit! All you have to do for me and Alexander is be here for us, in this house."

"Is that all you want from me?" She looked at him with enormous sad eyes.

"Yes, it is. You think that's a respectable profession, Madam Playwright? Well, it isn't. Just look at your father, the illustrious novelist. Do you think he was a respectable man?"

"He was a genius." She was quick to defend him. "He may not have been what you call 'respectable,' but he was brilliant and interesting, and he left contributions that millions have enjoyed."

"And what did he leave you, sweetheart? His lecherous old friend? His buddy? That old fart who married you when you were nineteen?"

"You don't know what you're saying." She was pale as she stared at him. "John, this isn't the issue. The issue is my play."

"Horseshit. The issue is my wife and the

mother of my son. Do you think I want you traipsing around with people like that? What do you think that does to me?"

"But I don't have to go 'traipsing.' I can go to New York, sell it, and come home. I live here with you and Alexander, and three thousand miles away in New York they put on my play. You never even have to see it." But as she heard herself begging she began to hate him for what he made her do. Why would she have to tell him that he would never have to see her play? Why wouldn't he want to see it? "Why are you so opposed to it? I don't understand." She looked at him unhappily and tried to force herself to calm down.

"The reason you don't understand is because you had such a lousy, fucked-up upbringing, and that's not what I want for my son. I want him to be normal."

She looked at him bitterly. "Like you? Is that the only thing that's normal?"

He was quick to answer. "That's right."

And suddenly she was on her feet. "In that case, John Fields, I'm not going to waste my time arguing with you. My God, you don't even understand where I come from, the fine people, the great minds. I spent my life before this among people that others would give their right arm to know. All except you, because you're frightened and threatened. Look at you, you won't even go to New York. What are you afraid of? Well, I am going back there now, tomorrow, to sell my play and come home. And if you can't accept that, then to hell with you, because by this weekend I will be right back here, doing what I always do, cooking your meals, making your bed, and taking care of our child."

He stayed in his study for the rest of the evening and he said nothing to her when he came to bed. The next morning she explained to Alexander that she had to go away to New York. She told him why and she told him about his grandfather. And the little boy was fascinated and awed.

"Did he write story books for children?" He looked at her with the same huge green eyes as hers.

"No, he didn't, sweetheart."

"Do you?"

"Not yet. I just wrote the play."

"What's that?" He sat down and looked at her in fascination.

"It's like a story that people act out on a big stage. One day I'll take you to a play for children. Would you like that?" He nodded, and then his eyes filled with tears and he reached out and clung to her legs.

"I don't want you to go, Mommy."

"I won't be gone for very long, sweetheart. Just a few days. And how about if I bring you a present?" He nodded, and she dried his tears as she disengaged herself from his grip on her thighs.

"Will you call me when I come home from school?"

"Every day. I promise."

And then, mournfully, "How many days?"

She held up two fingers, praying that would be all. "Two."

And then, sniffling loudly, he nodded and held out his hand. "It's a deal." He pulled her down toward him so he could kiss her cheek. "You can go." And together they walked out of the room hand in hand. She took him over to play at Mary's until the car came to take him to school, and half an hour after she left him, she was on her way to the airport alone in the cab. John had never discussed the matter with her further. And she left him a note, saying that she would be back in two or three days and leaving the name of her hotel. What she would never know was that when he got home that night he crumpled the note and threw it into the trash.

34

She hurried off the plane with the others, wearing a black suit and a pair of pearl and onyx earrings she hadn't worn in years. They had been her mother's and they were large and handsome, as of course was the choker Ivo had given her so many years before. Ivo was there to meet her, wearing tweeds and a smile. And she sighed with relief as she saw him. She had been tense during the whole flight. She couldn't imagine what it would be like to be in New York again, if it would be a nightmare or a dream. As the plane had forged through the skies crossing the country, a thousand memories had danced in her head . . . with her father . . . with Ivo . . . at the theaters . . . at parties . . . with Anthony in the loft. It had been an endless film she hadn't been able to turn off. But now seeing Ivo in the crowded terminal came as a relief. At least it was real.

"Tired, darling?"

"Not really. Only nervous. How soon am I seeing Norton?"

He smiled at her. "As soon as I get you to your hotel." But there was no nuance, no impropriety. Ivo had long since relinquished his old role. He was back to being a friend of her father's, who in a way now stood in her father's stead. "Are you very excited?" But he only had to look at her to know. She nodded nervously, and then giggled, and they waited for her bags.

"I can hardly stand it, Ivo. I don't even know what it all means."

"It means that you're going to have a play on Broadway, Bettina." He smiled happily with her, and then looked at her gently. "What did your husband say?"

For an instant she looked serious, and then she shrugged and smiled again. "Nothing."

"Nothing? You mean he didn't mind?"

But Bettina shook her head and this time she chuckled. "I mean he wouldn't speak to me from the time I told him until I left."

"And your son?"

"He was much more understanding than his father." Ivo nodded, not wanting to say more, but he had been wondering what Bettina planned to do with Alexander. If the play went into production, she would have to come to New York for several months. Would she bring the boy or leave him with his father? Ivo wondered, but he didn't want to stir up problems before the deal was closed. Instead they made idle chitchat as her bags turned up on the turntable and a porter took them out to Ivo's car. He had a new driver.

"Does it look very different?" He was watching her as they crossed the bridge, but she shook her head.

"Not at all."

"I didn't think it would." And then he smiled at her. "I'm glad." He wanted her to find it familiar, to feel at home in her old town. For too many years she had lived like a foreigner with people who didn't understand what she came from, and with an almost alien man. Without knowing him, Ivo didn't like him. He didn't like the feelings he had bred in her, her distaste for her background, her father, her history, and herself.

As they sped up Third Avenue and then Park Bettina watched the crowds, the cars, the people, the action swirling about them in the early evening, people leaving offices, going to parties or dinner, hurrying toward restaurants, or hastening home. There was a kind of electric excitement that, even in the sanctuary of the limousine, they could both feel.

"There's nothing like it, is there?" He looked around him proudly and she shook her head, and then smiled at him.

"You haven't changed a bit, Ivo. You still sound like the publisher of the *New York Mail.*"

"In my heart I still am."

"Do you miss it a lot?"

He nodded slowly, and then shrugged. "But eventually everything has to change." She wanted to tell him Like us, but she didn't. She sat very still, and a few minutes later the car swooped around the island of shrubbery and stopped at her hotel.

The facade was mainly gilt and marble, the doorman covered in brown wool and gold braid, the front desk marble, the concierge obsequious in the extreme. Only moments later Bettina was ushered upstairs and into her suite. She looked around her in astonishment. It was years since she had been anywhere like this.

"Bettina?" A short heavyset man with bright blue eyes and a fringe of gray hair walked toward her. He wasn't handsome, but dignified, as he rose from the chair in her living room and held out a hand.

"Norton?" He nodded. "I'm so glad to meet you after all these months on the phone." They shook hands warmly. She saw that her bag was deposited in the bedroom and that Ivo tipped the porter, so she called room service and ordered drinks.

And then Norton smiled at her. "If you're not too tired, I'd love to take you to dinner, Bettina." He looked at her questioningly with a warm smile. "And I apologize for intruding on you so quickly, but we have a lot to discuss tonight. And I know how anxious you are to get home. Tomorrow we have meetings with backers, the producer, and I want some time with you to myself. . . ." He looked apologetic and she held up a hand.

"I understand. That's perfect. And you're right. I want to do what I have to and get home." For a moment his eyes traveled to Ivo's. He wondered if she realized that she was going to have to spend several months in New York. But there was no point pushing her on the first evening. That much would become plain to her the next day. "As for dinner, I'd love it. Ivo, you too?"

"I'd be delighted."

The three of them smiled at each other, and Bettina sat down for a minute in one of the comfortable Louis XV chairs. It seemed extraordinary to be back in these surroundings after all those years. It looked like every hotel she had ever stayed in with her father. The only difference was that now they were there because of her. They chatted comfortably over white wine for Bettina and martinis for them, and an hour later she changed and ran a comb through her short chestnut hair. She once again wore her mother's pearl-and-onyx earrings, but this time she wore a new black silk dress. Seeing the new dress, Ivo noticed how plain her taste had become. The dress was good-looking, but compared to her old panache with a wardrobe, the little black silk dress was very dull.

At ten o'clock they went to La Grenouille for dinner, and as they sat down Bettina breathed a deep sigh of relief. It was as though for years she had lived in another atmosphere and now at last she was home. Ivo was thrilled as he watched her, and all she did was smile at him with her eyes. They all had caviar to begin with, rack of lamb, asparagus hollandaise, and soufflé for dessert. At the end of the meal both men ordered cognac and coffee and lit Cuban cigars. Bettina sat back and watched them, enjoying the sights around her and the familiar smells. It seemed years since she had eaten a dinner like this one or smelled the rich aroma of Cuban cigars. And as she looked around her for the hundredth time that evening, she marveled again at the women, their makeup, their jewelry, their costumes, and their hair. Everything was put together to perfection, everything was designed to capture the eye and keep it both pleased and aware. They were a pleasure to look at, and beside them Bettina felt unbearably plain. Suddenly she realized more than ever how much she had changed in five years.

It wasn't until after the cognac that Norton seriously brought up the play.

"Well, Bettina, what do you think of our little deal?" He looked at her with satisfaction, clearly a man who had succeeded and was well pleased. He had a right to be. What had fallen together for Bettina was a most remarkable deal.

"I'm very impressed, Norton. But I don't know all the details yet."

"You will, Bettina, you will."

And by the next day she did. A remarkable sum of money, the best backers on Broadway, a producer people killed or died for, and a theater that was nothing less than a dream.

It was one of those rare events in the theater when absolutely everything falls into place. Normally her play wouldn't have been put on until at least six months later, but because of the simplicity of the production, the availability of the theater, the backers, and the producer, everything was set to roll within three months. The producer was almost certain he could get the actors he wanted. The only thing lacking now was Bettina's okay. It all hinged on her.

"Well?" Norton asked her at the end of a grueling day. "Shall we sign it today and give everyone the green light, madam?" He beamed at her and waved at the mountain of contract forms on his desk. Technically she understood almost none of what was happening, all she knew was that if she agreed to accept a vast sum of money and come to New York until the play opened and the kinks had been worked out, and then kept an eye on what was happening with it for a little while, her play was in business and would open before Christmas. It was as simple as that. But she looked exhausted and nervous as she faced Norton across his desk. "What's the problem?"

"I don't know, Norton . . . I . . . have to talk to my husband. I don't know what I'd do with the baby. . . ." She looked terrified and he looked startled. The baby? She had a baby?

"The baby?"

She laughed nervously. "My three-year-old son."

Norton waved a casual hand and smiled again. "Bring the baby with you, put him in school in New York for three or four months, and after Christmas you all go home. Hell, if you want to, bring your husband. For God's sake, they're paying you enough to bring all your friends."

"I know . . . I know . . . and I don't mean to sound ungrateful. I'm not, it's just that . . . my husband can't come, he's a doctor, and —" She stopped, staring at Norton. "I don't know, for God's sake. I'm scared. What the hell do I know about Broadway? I wrote a play, and now I wonder what I've done."

"What have you done?" He looked at her for a moment with hard, beady eyes. "You have done nothing. Zero. Zilch. You have written a play. But if you don't let someone produce it, if you don't take your chance when you get it, then, my dear, you haven't done shit. Maybe what you'd like better" — he paused for a moment, and then went on — "is to take your play back to California and have it put on by some local playhouse, where no one will ever hear of it, or you, again." The silence in the room was deafening after his brief speech. "Is that what you want, Bettina? I'm sure if he could see it, it would make your father very proud." He smiled at her benignly, unprepared for what happened next so that he jumped slightly when she slammed a fist down on his desk.

"Screw my father, Norton. And Ivo. And John. Everyone is always wanting me to do what suits their purpose, and invoking whatever names they have to to get whatever they want done. Well, I'm not doing this for my father, or my husband, or Ivo, or you. If I do it, I'm doing it for me, Norton, for me, do you hear me, and just maybe for my son. And the fact is I can't give you an answer and I'm not going to sign a damn thing today. I'm going to go back to my hotel and think it over. And in the morning I'm going to go home. And when I've thought it out clearly, I'll call you."

He nodded calmly. "Just don't wait too long." But now she was tired. Of him and of them. Of everyone. And of being pushed around.

"Why not? If the play's any damn good, they'll wait to hear from me."

"Maybe. But they may lose the theater, and that could change the deal. You need everything going for you at one time, Bettina, and right now you have that. I wouldn't take too many chances with that if I were you."

"I'll keep that in mind." She looked troubled as she stood up and looked at him, but he smiled as he came around the desk to her.

"I know it's hard, Bettina. It's a big change. Especially after being gone for so long. But it's also a big chance, and good things are never going to happen to you if you don't take a chance. It could be a huge success, and I think it will be. I think it will make your career."

"Do you really think so?" She looked at him in confusion. She didn't understand any of it. "But why?"

"Because it's about a man and his daughter, because it says a great deal about our times, about men, about you, about dreams that get broken, and about hope that somehow pushes through the rocks and the shit and the weeds. It's a tough play, but it's a beauty. You said something you felt in your heart, Bettina. You paid a price for that understanding, and you felt every word you put down there, and the beauty of it is that others will too."

"I hope so." She whispered it as she looked at him sadly.

"Then give them that chance, Bettina. Go

home and think about it. And then sign the papers and come back here. You belong here, lady. You have a job to do right here in this town."

She smiled at him then, and before she left him, she kissed his cheek.

She didn't see Ivo again before she left New York, and she didn't speak to Norton again either. And as it turned out, she didn't stay in the hotel to sleep. Instead she called the airline and caught the very last flight home. She walked into their house in Mill Valley at two o'clock in the morning and tiptoed upstairs to their bedroom, where John was sound asleep in bed. Like all doctors though, he was a light sleeper and he sat up instantly as she closed the door.

"Something wrong?"

"No." She whispered softly. "Go back to sleep. I just got home."

"What time is it?"

"Almost two." As she said it she wondered if he appreciated the fact that she had hurried home to him and had made a point of spending only one night in New York. She could have stayed for another evening, another dinner, another night in a fancy hotel, but she wanted to get back to Mill Valley, to her husband and her son. As he lay back in bed slowly, watching her, she smiled and set down her bag. "I missed you."

"You didn't stay away for very long."

"I didn't want to. I told you I wouldn't."

"Did you make your deal?" He sat up on one elbow and switched the light on as slowly Bettina let herself into a chair.

For a moment she didn't answer, and then she shook her head. "No. I wanted to think it over."

"Why?" He looked at her coldly, but at least he was talking to her about the play. But she didn't want to tell him all the details. Not so quickly. Not in her first hour at home.

"It's more complicated than I expected. We can talk about it in the morning."

But he was wide awake now. "No. I want to discuss it now. This whole thing has been much too shrouded in secrecy from the start. You've been sneaky about it since you started writing that piece of garbage. Now I want it out in the open all around." So it was back to that, then.

She sighed softly and ran her hand tiredly over her eyes. It had been an endless day, and by New York time it was already 5 A.M. "I never meant to be sneaky, John. I didn't tell you about it, in part because I wanted to surprise you, and in part because I was afraid you'd disapprove, and it was something I had to do. It's in my genes maybe, what do I know. I wish you'd try to see this thing a little more broadly. It would make it a lot easier for me."

"Then you don't understand how I feel about this, Bettina. I have no intention of making it easier for you. I don't choose to. And if you were smart, Betty, you'd forget about all that. I gave you that chance five years ago. I don't understand why you have to go back now. Do I have to remind you that you tried to commit suicide, that you lost a baby, that you had been married twice and left destitute by your father, then you got swept up on the beach like an orphan out here." It was not a pretty picture he painted, and Bettina hung her head.

"John, why don't we just stick to the issue."

"What is the issue?"

"My play."

"Oh, that." He looked at her angrily.

"Yes, that. The problem, since you want everything out on the table, is that if I sell it, I'll have to spend the next few months in New York." She gulped hard and went on, avoiding his eyes. "Probably only until Christmas. I could come home right after that."

"No, you couldn't." His voice was like ice.

But her eyes flew innocently to his. "Yes, I could. Norton, my agent, said that I don't have to be there for long at all after it opens and they want to open in late November or early December. So by Christmas I should be home."

"You didn't understand me. If you go to New York to do this, I don't want you back."

She looked at him with horror as he sat in rigid fury on his side of the bed. "Are you serious? You'd give me a choice like that, John? Don't you understand what this could mean to me? I could be a playwright, for God's sake, I could have a career. . . ." Her voice trailed off as she watched him. He didn't give a damn.

"No, you could not have a career, Betty. Not and remain my wife."

"It's that simple, then? Go to New York with the play and you throw me out?"

"Exactly. So that takes care of it, doesn't it? It's a very clear-cut choice. I thought you understood that before this."

"I didn't or I wouldn't have bothered to go to New York."

"Well, I hope you didn't waste your own money." He shrugged and turned off the light, and Bettina went to undress in the bathroom, her shoulders silently heaving as she clutched a towel to her face to silence her tears.

35

"I'm sorry, Norton, I can't help it. It's my husband or you." She felt laden as she sat holding the phone. She had cried all night long.

There was a long pregnant silence, and then Norton told her the truth. "I think you ought to understand something, Bettina. I'm not the issue here, you are. It's your husband or you. That's a hell of a choice he's given you. I hope he's worth it."

"I think he is." But as she hung up the phone she wasn't as sure of it, and she was even less so as she wandered over to Mary's and stared forlornly into her coffee as she shed fresh tears.

Mary looked at her numbly. "I don't understand it."

"He feels threatened. He hates that part of my past. There's nothing I can do."

"You could leave him."

"And do what? Start over again? Find a

fourth husband? Don't be ridiculous, Mary. This is my life here. This is reality. The play is a dream. What if it's a bomb?"

"So what? Can you really give up your dreams for this man?" She looked at Bettina angrily. "He's my friend, Betty, and so are you, but I think he's being ridiculous, and if I were you, I'd take my chances and go to New York." Bettina smiled a watery smile and blew her nose.

"You're just saying that because you're tired of your kids."

"I am not. I adore them. But I'm not you. Remember that bird of paradise story I told you . . . well, you're starting to look ridiculous with a gray and brown beak. You don't belong here, Bettina. You know it, I know it, Seth knows, even John knows it, that's why he's busting his ass, and yours, to keep you here. He's probably afraid he'll lose you."

"But he won't." She said it with a mournful whine.

"Then tell him that. Maybe that's all he needs to hear, and if he doesn't shape up after that, screw him, pack your bags, take Alexander, and go do your play." But as she watched Bettina walk back to her place, Mary knew that she wouldn't do it. She wouldn't leave him. She was too sure that he was right.

Bettina spent the afternoon alternately trying to read one of her father's books and staring out the window, and eventually the phone rang and it was Ivo this time.

"Are you nuts? Are you crazy? Why did you bother to come to New York if you were going back to hide again?"

"I can't help it, Ivo. I have to. Please . . . don't let's discuss it. I'm unhappy enough."

"It's that moron you married."

"Ivo, please —" She faltered.

"All right, dammit, all right. But please, for God's sake, Bettina, reconsider . . . you've wanted this for your whole lifetime. Now the chance comes and you're throwing it away."

She knew what he was saying was true. "Maybe there'll be another chance later."

"When? When your husband dies? When you're a widow? In fifty years? My God, Bettina . . . think of it . . . think of it . . . your play could have been on Broadway, and now you've doomed it to silence. You did it. No one else."

"I know." Her voice was little more than a whisper, and then her eyes filled with tears. "I can't talk about it anymore now, Ivo. I'll call you tomorrow." But when she hung up, she was once again blinded by her tears. She wondered if John knew what it had cost her to deny her life's dream.

And then, pensively, wiping her tears on her shirtsleeve, she went back to her book. Oddly enough it was one of her father's that she hadn't read in years, and Mary had had it in her bookcase. Bettina borrowed it months before and never read it. But it seemed comforting somehow today. As though he understood, as though he had written it knowing what she was feeling. She felt his presence as she continued to dry her tears and read. And then she found it. A folksy passage he had liked so well that he had often quoted it to her. Something his father had long ago said to him. . . .

> Don't give up your dreams or your dreaming. Don't let life cut your line as you reel in those dreams . . . hold on tightly . . . keep reeling . . . don't give up . . . grab that net . . . and if they look like they're about to leap out of the net after you've caught 'em, jump in after 'em, and keep on swimming, till you drown if you have to . . . but don't ever let go of those dreams. . . .

Bettina slowly closed the book on her lap and this time she laughed as she gave way to her tears. She walked quietly to the kitchen and dialed Norton. And then she waited for her husband to come home that night. When he did, she told him, quietly, firmly, that her mind was made up.

36

"Promise you'll at least call me once in a while?" Mary looked at her mournfully, the car filled with children, her eyes filling with tears.

"I promise." Bettina held her friend tightly, she kissed everyone, then waved at them all as she scooped Alexander out of the car.

"Good-bye!" He waved at them frantically, and then marched into the terminal beside his mother, holding tightly to her hand. She had explained to him about going to New York for a few months and going to a new school, having a baby-sitter sometimes, and seeing a real play for children, and meeting some of his grandfather's old friends. He was sad that he couldn't take his Daddy, but he understood that Daddy had to stay to help sick people, and he was glad he was going with his Mom. He had left his Dad a big drawing, and then hurried to finish packing his favorite toys. And that had only been the night before. His Dad was already gone when he got up that morning. Someone must have been real sick for him to have to leave so early. And Aunt Mary from next door had driven them to the airport. It had been okay except that she and his Mom had cried a lot.

"You okay, Mommy?" He looked up at her with a hesitant smile.

"I'm fine, sweetheart. How about you?" But Bettina had been looking anxiously all over the airport on their way to the gate. John had been gone before she got up that morning also, and she was still hoping that he'd turn up to say good-bye. She had left him a letter telling him that she loved him, and she had called his office several times but even the nurse wasn't there, and the answering service hadn't been able to page him. He never showed up, and Bettina and Alexander boarded the plane.

It was Alexander's first trip on an airplane, and he had fun playing with the things they gave him and running up and down the aisle. There were three other children to play with, but eventually he fell asleep in Bettina's lap. This time when they arrived in the New York airport, Ivo had been unable to come, but he had sent his car.

Bettina was delighted with the comfort, and the driver took her to the hotel she had chosen, further uptown than the last one. She wanted Alexander to be able to go to the park. They had a pretty suite with bright-colored fabrics and paintings and lots of sunshine. The autumn afternoon sun was streaming in the windows as the porter set down her bags. There were flowers from Norton, and Ivo, and a huge arrangement of roses from the producer of the show, which said only WELCOME TO NEW YORK.

That night Bettina spent settling in with Alexander, and before he went to bed, they tried to get John on the phone, but he wasn't there when they called him, so they called Seth and Mary and their kids instead.

"Homesick already?"

"Not really. We just wanted to say hi." But Mary knew that Bettina was probably worried about John. She'd settle down once she started work on the play. And he would probably eventually come to his senses. And who knew, maybe he'd even go to see her in New York. She voiced her hope to Seth over dinner, but he only nodded vaguely.

Bettina tucked Alexander into his new bed in the suite's second bedroom, and then walked across the large pretty living room to her own and sat down on the bed with a small sigh. She had rapidly done all her unpacking. All that remained to do the next day was meet Alexander's baby-sitter and check out the school she had selected for him.

She managed to accomplish both of those tasks before noon and turn up in Norton Hess's office by one for a quiet lunch his secretary brought in on trays.

"You ready?"

"Absolutely. My son's new baby-sitter is adorable, and he loved his first morning at school. Now I can get down to business, when do we start?"

He grinned as he saw her, she looked like a pretty young matron from the suburbs as she sat there in a camel's hair coat, black slacks, a sweater, her Goldilocks hair, and a little black hat. She had style, even as she sat there in the clothes she had worn to take her kid to school, but there was something so subdued, so quiet about her. It made him wish that she would tear off her clothes and jump on his desk.

"You know, I never thought I'd see you here, Bettina."

"I know. I didn't really think I'd come."

"What changed your mind? It couldn't have been anything I said?" His eyes asked a question, but she laughed and shook her head.

"It wasn't. It was my father." His brows knit immediately in answer. What the hell did she mean? "I was reading one of his books and it was something I saw there. I realized that I had no choice. That I had to come."

"I'm awfully glad you came to your senses. You saved me an air fare." His eyes twinkled.

"I did. How?"

"I was planning to come out to San Francisco and jump off the Golden Gate Bridge. After I beat you up."

"I might have gotten there first. I was so depressed, I could hardly see."

"Well" — he sat back and lit a cigar he plucked from his humidor — "everything's worked out for the best. And tomorrow you get to work. Any other plans in the meantime? Anything you're itching to do? Go shopping, invite some friends in? My secretary will help you with anything you need." But Bettina had started to shake her head quickly, and then slowly her eyes lit up as she tilted her head to one side.

"It's been so long since I've been here. . . ." She mused happily. "Last time I was really only here for a day. I think maybe . . . Bloomingdale's . . ." She grinned.

"Women." He rolled his eyes. "My wife lives at Bergdorf's. She only comes home for meals." She chuckled as she left him, and it was four hours later before she got back to the hotel, feeling guilty about Alexander left to a new sitter after he had been to a new school, in a new town. But when she got back to the hotel, buried under a stack of boxes, Alexander was eating spaghetti and had chocolate ice cream all over his face.

"We ate the ice cream first, then the spaghetti. Jennifer says my tummy won't know which came first as long as I eat them both." He grinned happily at his mother, a portrait in red and brown. He certainly didn't seem to have missed her, and she had had a wonderful time.

A note from the desk told her that Ivo had left for London and that the producer would be at the hotel to see her at ten the next morning. It was obvious that John hadn't called. But she brushed her qualms away from her conscience and retired to her room to try on four new dresses, three sweaters, and a suit. She had spent almost a thousand dollars. But she could afford it now, and she had had a ball. Besides she would need the wardrobe. Now that she was back in New York nothing she had brought with her looked even remotely right.

And she was gratified the next morning when she met the producer in a wonderful cream-colored cashmere dress.

"My God, you look marvelous, Bettina. We ought to cast you."

"Hardly, but thank you." They had exchanged a warm smile and gone back to work. For the moment all she had to worry about was the smoothing of a few kinks; he had the mechanics to worry about and the hiring of everyone from actors to the director of the play. But they must have been living under a spell of magic, because all of the casting and hiring had been done by the end of a week.

"Already? That's a miracle!" Norton had told her when she called to report to him. She had seen all the final tryouts and she loved the actors they had selected for the play. For a while she had been nervous that Anthony might show up for the auditions, but she didn't even know if he was still in the States, and six years was a very long time. It had been that long since she'd seen him last. But whatever the reason he never showed.

It was two weeks later when she got a call from Ivo. She had just sailed in from the theater to dine with Alexander and she was wearing a comfortable old sweat shirt and jeans.

"Did you just get back from London?"

"Last night. How've you been?"

"Wonderful. Oh, Ivo, you should see how the play's going. It's just beautiful, and they've got the most marvelous actors to play the father and the girl." It was easy to hear in her voice that she was thrilled.

"I'm glad, darling. Why don't you tell me about it over dinner? I'm having dinner at Lutèce with a friend."

"Very fancy, Ivo. I'm impressed." It was still the most expensive restaurant in town.

"Don't be. You should be more impressed with whom I'm dining with. The new theater critic at the *Mail.*"

"Oh, God."

"Never mind that, you ought to meet him, and he's very, very nice."

"What's his name? Do I know him from way back when?"

"Unlikely. He's been at the *Los Angeles Times* for the last seventeen years. He just came to us —" He grinned at the slip and she laughed at him. "To them, sorry, about six months ago. His name is Oliver Paxton. And he's both too young and too sensible to have been one of your father's friends."

"He sounds dreary as hell. Do I really

have to meet him?"

"He's not and you should. Come on, darling, it'll be good for you. You didn't just come here to work."

"Yes, I did." She was being immensely careful not to make the same mistake that she had made on the road show with Anthony seven years before. She wasn't hanging out with the cast or the crew or the producer, and she wasn't soliciting any close friends. She was doing precisely what she had told John she would do. Working, taking care of Alexander whenever possible, seeing her agent — but that was about it. Except for Ivo, but he was a special kind of friend. She was not risking any involvements. She wanted to do her play, but she wanted to keep her marriage too.

"So, will you join us?" She was thinking about it and watching Alexander play with his food.

"I was just eating with Alexander."

"How exciting. Surely you can join us afterward, Bettina. Besides, his menu can't be as wonderful as all that."

"Not exactly." He had ordered hot dogs and chocolate pudding, with a double order for her. "As a matter of fact . . . what time are you dining?"

"I told Ollie I'd meet him at eight thirty.

He had some sort of meeting he had to go to at six."

"Sounds just like you in the old days, Ivo."

"Yes, doesn't it? But he's not nearly as handsome."

"And undoubtedly not as charming." She was teasing now and he was laughing.

"I'll let you judge that for yourself."

37

Bettina stepped out of the taxi on Fiftieth Street, east of Third Avenue, and hurried into the restaurant with an expectant smile. This would be the first time she had seen Ivo since she had agreed to do the play and had come to New York with Alexander. She was happy to see him, although she would have preferred to see him alone. But it didn't really matter. It was amusing to be out for an evening, instead of alone, poring over her notes in the hotel. She left her coat with the girl at the cloakroom, and then waited for the headwaiter so she could ask him if Ivo was already there. But before he could reach her, she noticed several men staring, and she wondered for a moment if what she had worn was all wrong. It was one of the dresses she had bought when she'd gone shopping, but she hadn't yet had occasion to wear it anywhere. It was a pale lilac velvet that did wonderful things to the creamy warmth of her skin and the color of her hair. It had clean, simple lines and it was a very pretty mid-calf length. And the simplicity and the color reminded her vaguely of the beautiful Balenciaga outfit she had owned years before, with a wonderful dark green velvet tunic coat. But this was much simpler, and she wore it with a single long strand of her mother's lovely pearls, and the matching earrings in her ears. She looked wonderfully fresh and demure as she stood there, tiny and delicate, with her eyes very large and green. Ivo was watching from a distant table and he signaled to her with a warm, friendly smile. She saw him quickly and slipped past the headwaiter, to where Ivo's table was, in a kind of canopied garden in the back.

"Good evening, little one, how are you?" He stood and kissed her and she gave him a warm hug, and then suddenly she noticed the giant standing next to him. He had the look of a friendly young man, with gray eyes, broad shoulders, and sandy California-blond hair. "And this is Oliver Paxton. I've been wanting you two to meet for quite a while." They politely shook hands and all three of them sat down at the table, as Oliver looked her over with considerable appreciation and wondered what lay between his friend and this girl. They seemed to have an odd, comfortable, almost familylike relationship, and then he remembered that he and her father had been close friends. And then suddenly he remembered what Ivo had told him before he went to London. This was Justin Daniels's daughter, the girl who had just written what was predicted to be the season's hit play.

"Now I know who you are!" He smiled broadly, and as she looked at him she grinned.

"Who am I?"

But he grinned. "You're Justin Daniels's daughter and you've just written what is supposed to be a wonderful play. Does anyone call you anything besides Bettina?" He looked at her warmly, but she shook her head with a laugh and a smile.

"Not in New York they don't. In California some of my close friends get away with a name I hate. But I won't tell you."

"Where in California?"

"San Francisco."

"How long have you lived there?"

"Almost six years."

"Like it?"

"I love it." Her face lit up with a warm smile and so did his. The evening was off and running. He was from Los Angeles but had gone to school at the University of San Francisco, and had a warm spot in his heart for that city, though it wasn't a sentiment that Ivo shared.

The three of them ordered a special dinner, and the conversation was fast and heavy for the next three hours. It was close to midnight when at last Ivo signaled to the headwaiter for the bill. "I don't know about you two children, but this white-haired old gentleman is about ready for his bed." He stifled a yawn as he smiled at them. But he had had a lovely evening, and it was easy to see that they were enjoying themselves too. But now Bettina was laughing and looking at him with a teasing eye.

"That's not fair, Ivo. You've had white hair since you were twenty-two."

"Possibly, darling. But by now I've earned it, so I can mention it as often as I like." Oliver looked at him with frank admiration. He was a rare specimen in journalism, and someone he had respected for all of his life.

Ivo bid them a warm adieu as he got into his car just outside the restaurant, where it had waited for him all night long. And Oliver assured Ivo that he would get Bettina back to the hotel.

"You won't kidnap her or do anything vulgar?"

Oliver laughed warmly at the suggestion and there was a definite gleam in his eye. "Kidnap her, no, Ivo, I promise not to, and I'd like to think that nothing I could do would be considered vulgar. At least not viewed by the right eye."

"I will leave that entirely up to Miss Daniels." He waved to them both, pressed the button that raised the window, and a moment later he drove off in his limo as the two of them waved and smiled.

Oliver looked down happily at Bettina as they walked slowly west, past brownstones, and then eventually apartment buildings, offices, and stores. "How long have you known Ivo, Bettina?"

"All my life." And then she smiled at him. Obviously he didn't know the rest of it. His next question seemed indicative of that.

"He was a friend of your father's?"

She nodded, still smiling, and then she sighed and decided to tell him the rest. But the smile hadn't fled. It was something she could tell easily now. It didn't shame her. It was something she remembered with tenderness and pride. "Yes, he was a friend of my father's. But we were also married for six years . . . a long time ago."

He looked at her in total astonishment, the handsome gray eyes amazed.

"What happened?"

"He wanted to think I outgrew him. But I didn't. In any case now we're just friends."

"That is the most extraordinary story I've heard all night. You know, I never had any idea of it tonight at dinner." And then he looked at her carefully. "Do you . . . still see each other? . . ." He floundered painfully and she grinned. "I mean . . . I didn't mean to . . . do you suppose he was angry when I said I'd take you home? . . ." He was in agony and all she could do was laugh.

"No, of course not." In fact she suspected that there had been an ulterior motive for the introduction, but she didn't say that to her new friend. Either Ivo wanted him to feel kindly toward her new play or he figured she needed an escort while she was in town.

"Well, I'll be damned." Oliver was still astonished, and for a while they walked along in silence, her hand slipped easily into his arm. And then he turned to smile down at her gently.

"Do you suppose it would be possible for us to go dancing?"

This time she looked at him in amazement. "Tonight? But it's almost one o'clock."

"I know it is." He looked at her in amusement. "But as Ivo said, things are different in New York. Everything is still open. Any interest?" She was about to say no to his outlandish offer, but something in the way he looked down at her amused her, and she found herself laughingly saying yes. They quickly jumped into a taxi, and he took her to a bar somewhere on the Upper East Side. There was live music and there were crowds of people, pressed together, swaying with the music, laughing and drinking and having a good time. It was a far cry from the elegant restraint of Lutèce, but Bettina enjoyed it thoroughly, and an hour later they left, with regret.

As they traveled back to her hotel they spoke of her upcoming opening.

"I bet the play is brilliant." He looked warm and solid as he looked down at her eyes.

"What makes you say that?"

"Because you wrote it — and you're a very special lady." She laughed appreciatively. "I wish you were something other than a critic."

"Why?" He looked surprised.

"Because I'd like you to come and see my play and tell me what you think. But since you are who you are, Ollie" — she smiled up at him as she used the name — "the producer would have a fit." And then she had a thought and looked up at him again. "Will you be the one who reviews it?"

"Probably."

"That's too bad." She looked woeful.

"Why?"

"Because you'll probably cream it, and then I'll feel awkward with you, and you'll be embarrassed, and it'll be awful. . . ." But he was laughing at her predictions of woe and despair.

"Then there's only one solution to the problem."

"What's that, Mister Paxton?"

"That we become fast friends before the play opens, so it doesn't matter when I review it what I write. How does that sound?"

"It's probably the only solution."

When they got back to the hotel he asked if he could take her for a drink. She told him her son was upstairs and she wanted to make sure he was all right.

"A son — you and Ivo had a son? Oh, my, this is confusing."

"No, the son is my child by my third husband."

"My, my, what a popular lady. And how old is this son?" He hadn't looked particularly impressed by her three marriages, and she was relieved as they walked on.

"He's four and his name is Alexander, and he's wonderful."

"And let me guess. He's your only child?" He smiled benevolently down at her as she nodded.

"He is."

Then he looked at her carefully. "And the young man's father? Has he been disposed of or is he in New York too?" The way that he said it made her laugh, despite her serious worries about John.

"Well, he's not too pleased about our coming to New York, which he is convinced is Sodom and Gomorrah. And he is furious that I'm doing the play. But I'm still married to him, if that was your question. He stayed in San Francisco. But I wanted Alexander with me."

"Can I meet him?" It was the only thing he could have said that brought him closer to her heart.

"Would you like to?"

"I'd love it. Why don't we make it a very early dinner before the theater tomorrow and take him. Then we can bring him back to the hotel and go out afterward. Sound reasonable?"

"It sounds wonderful. Thank you, Ollie."

"At your service." He bowed impressively,

and then hailed a cab. And it wasn't until she got upstairs that Bettina began having qualms. What was she doing going out with this man? She was a married woman, and she had promised herself she wouldn't go out with anyone while she was in New York. But he was a friend of Ivo's, after all.

She had heard nothing from John since the day they'd left. He answered none of Bettina's calls and letters, and his secretary always insisted that he had just gone out. Bettina let the phone at home ring again and again and again, but to no avail. He either never answered it or was never there. So maybe it wasn't so awful that she should have dinner with Oliver Paxton. And no matter how much she liked him, she was not going to have an affair.

And she told him that bluntly the next night after they left the theater and went to the Russian Tea Room for blini and drinks.

"So who asked you?" He looked at her in enormous amusement. "Madam, it's not you I want, it's your son."

"Have you ever been married?"

He smiled sweetly at her. "No, I've never been asked."

"I'm serious, Ollie." He was rapidly becoming a real friend. And whatever their attraction to each other was, they both understood that it would go no farther than the friendship they had. As far as Bettina was concerned, it couldn't. And Ollie respected that.

He was smiling at her now as their blini came and he dug in. "I was being serious too, and no, I've never been married."

"Why not?"

"There hasn't been anyone I wanted to get stuck with for the rest of my life."

"That's a nice way to put it." She made a face and tasted her blini.

He looked at her. "So Number Three doesn't approve of all this?"

She began by trying to defend him, which told Ollie its own tale. And then slowly she just shook her head. "No."

"That's not surprising."

"Why not?"

"Because it's hard for a lot of men to accept a woman with another life, either a past or a future, and you happen to have both. But you did what you had to do."

"But how do you know that?" She looked so earnest that he couldn't resist reaching out and rumpling her soft auburn curls.

He smiled at her slowly. "I don't even know if you remember it. But there's something in a book of your father's. I came across it one day when I was trying to decide if I should take the job at the *Mail* and come to New York. Your father would approve of your choice. . . ."

She looked at him and her eyes widened, and they quoted it together word for word. "My God, Ollie, that was what I read the day I told them I'd come here. That was what changed my mind." He looked at her strangely.

"It did that for me too." And then silently they toasted her father, finished their blini, and walked back to her hotel arm in arm. He didn't come upstairs with her. But he made a date for Saturday to go to the Bronx Zoo with her and Alexander.

38

By the end of October Bettina was working on the play almost night and day. She spent endless hours in the drafty theater, and then more hours late at night making changes back at the hotel. Then back to the theater again the next morning to try out the changes and change them again. She never saw Ivo, she hardly saw Ollie, it was all she could do to see Alexander for half an hour a day. But she always made time for him, and sometimes when she was at the theater, Ollie came by to play with him. At least it gave Alexander a man to relate to. And they still had heard nothing from John.

"I don't understand why he doesn't call me." Bettina looked at Ollie in irritation as she threw her hands up and hung up the phone. "Anything could have happened to him, or to us, and he wouldn't know. I don't know. This is ridiculous. He doesn't answer my letters or my phone calls. He never calls."

"Are you sure he didn't say anything more definite when you left home, Bettina?" She shook her head, and despite a strange premonition, he didn't dare say anything more. He understood that she considered herself married, and he respected what she felt. The subject changed quickly to her latest agonies about the play.

"We'll never be ready to open." She looked slightly tired and thinner, but there was something wonderfully alive about her eyes. She loved what she was doing and it showed. And Ollie was always encouraging when she told him her woes.

"Yes, you will be ready, Bettina. Everybody goes through this. You'll see." But she thought he was crazy as each week they drew nearer to the big day. At last there were no more changes to be made. They went to New Haven for three performances, Boston for two. She made half a dozen more changes after the tryouts, and then she and the director nodded in agreement. Everything that could be had been done. All that remained was to get one night of decent sleep before the opening and spend an agonizing day waiting for night to come. Ollie called her that morning, and she had already been up since six fifteen.

"Because of Alexander?"

But she only chuckled. "No, dummy, because of my nerves."

"That's why I called you. Can I help keep you amused today?" But he couldn't. For that day and that evening he was The Enemy, a critic, a reviewer. She couldn't bear to spend the day with him and then have him lacerate her play. Because she was certain that he would.

"Just let me sit here and be miserable. I love it."

"Well, tomorrow it'll be over."

She stared gloomily into space. "Maybe so will the play."

"Oh, shut up, silly. Everything's going to be just fine." But she didn't believe him, and after pacing nervously around her hotel suite and snapping at Alexander, she finally arrived at the theater at seven fifteen. They had more than an hour until curtain but she had to be there. She couldn't stand being anywhere else. She stood in the wings, she walked into the theater, she took a seat, she got up and walked down the aisle, she went back to the wings, then into the alley, back to the stage, back to the seat she had abandoned to roam down the aisle. Finally she decided to walk around the block and didn't give a damn if she got mugged, which she did not. She waited until the last of the stragglers were in the theater, and then she walked in and slipped into an empty seat in the back row. That way if she couldn't bear the tension, she could always leave without making the rest of the audience think that someone hated it so much, they had left.

Bettina didn't see Ollie in the theater, and when it was over, she didn't even want a ride in Ivo's car. She avoided everyone and left as quickly as she was able, hailed a cab, and went back to her hotel. She had the switchboard tell everyone she was already sleeping, and she sat in a chair all night, waiting to hear the elevator open and the man drop the morning paper outside her door. At four thirty she heard it and she leaped to her feet and ran to the door. Panicking, she tore open the paper, she had to see it . . . had to . . . what had he written . . . what had he . . . ? She read it over and over and over as tears poured slowly down her face. Trembling, she went to the phone and dialed his number, and shouting and laughing and crying, she called him names.

"You bastard . . . oh, Ollie . . . I love you . . . did you like it? I mean really like it? Oh, God, Ollie . . . did you?"

"You're a maniac, Daniels, do you know that? Crazy! Stark-staring crazy! It's four thirty in the morning and I tried to get you all night . . . now she calls me, now after I finally gave up and went to bed."

"But I had to wait to see the paper."

"You moron, I could have read you my review at eleven fifteen last night."

"I couldn't have stood it. What if you had hated it?"

"I couldn't have hated it, you silly ass. It's brilliant. Absolutely brilliant!"

"I know." She absolutely glowed at him, purring. "I read the review."

But he was laughing and happy, and he promised to meet her for breakfast in a few hours, whenever she called him after she got some sleep. But before she took off her clothes and went to bed, she asked the operator for another number. Maybe at that hour she'd find him at home, or he'd be caught unaware and he'd answer the phone. But still there was no answer. And she had wanted so badly to tell John that the play was a success. Instead she decided to call Seth and Mary, and they were thrilled for her as they sat over breakfast with their kids. It was a quarter to eight in the morning on the West coast. And at last, as the sun came up, Bettina settled into her own bed, with a broad grin on her face and the newspaper spread out all over the bed.

39

"So, kid, what now? Now that you're on the road to fame." Ollie grinned at her happily over poached eggs and a bottle of champagne. They had met in Bettina's hotel for their late breakfast and she still looked stunned and worn out and elated and shocked all at the same time.

"I don't know. I guess I'll stick around for a couple of weeks and make sure that everything goes smoothly, and then I'll go home. I told John I'd be back for Christmas, and I guess I will." But now she looked a little vague. She had had no contact with him for three months and she was seriously worried about him, and about what she would tell the child.

"And professionally, Bettina? Any other stroke of genius in mind?"

"I don't know yet." She grinned at him slowly. "I've been playing with an idea lately, but it hasn't taken hold in my head."

"When it does, can I read it?" He looked almost as happy as she.

"Sure. Would you really want to?"

"I'd love it." And then, as she looked at him, she realized that she was going to miss him terribly when she left. She had gotten used to their long chatty exchanges, their phone calls every day, their frequent lunches, their occasional dinners with Ivo and, whenever possible, alone. He had become almost like her brother. And leaving him was going to be like leaving home.

"What are you looking so morbid about all of a sudden?" He had seen the look of anguish on her face.

"I was just thinking of leaving you when I go home."

"Don't get yourself too worked up about it, Bettina. You'll be back here before you know it, and you'll probably see me more than you'll want to. I go back and forth to the Coast several times a year."

"Good." She smiled at him a little more happily. "By the way do you want to have dinner with me and Ivo, my last night in New York?"

"I'd love to. Where are we going?"

"Does it matter?" She grinned at him.

"No, but I figure it'll be some place wonderful."

"With Ivo it always is."

And it was. It was La Côte Basque, at his favorite table, and the dinner he had specially ordered was superb. There were quenelles to begin with, after they had had champagne and caviar; there was a delicate hearts of palm salad, filet mignon, wonderful little mushrooms flown in fresh from France, and for dessert a soufflé Grand Marnier. The three of them ate with a passion, and then sat back to enjoy coffee and an after-dinner liqueur.

"So, little one, you leave us." He looked at her with a gentle smile.

"Not for very long though, Ivo. I'll probably be back soon."

"I hope so." But as Ollie walked her back to her hotel she thought Ivo had looked oddly pensive.

She turned to look at her friend then. "Did you hear what he said to me when he kissed me good-bye? 'Fly well, little bird.' And then he just kissed me and got into his car."

"He's probably just tired, and he's probably sad to see you go." And then he smiled at her slowly. "So am I."

She nodded. She hated to leave him too. Hated to leave them both. Suddenly it felt as though she belonged here. She had put her roots back in the sod of New York in the last three months. It was cold, it was dreary, it was crowded, the cabbies were rude, and people never held doors open, but there was a bustle, a texture, an excitement. It was going to be tough to match in Mill Valley, waiting for Alexander to come home from school. Even Alexander had felt it, and except to see his father, he wasn't very anxious to leave.

Ollie took them to the airport, and he waved long and hard as Alexander reluctantly wandered toward the plane. He blew a kiss to Bettina, and then he left the airport and went home and got roaring drunk. But Bettina didn't have the same luxury. She had to be sober to face John. She hadn't sent him a note to warn him that she was arriving, and she hadn't even warned Mary and Seth. She wanted to surprise everyone. And their bags were filled with Christmas presents for John, Mary, and Seth, and all the kids.

The weather was mild and gentle when they reached the airport. It was five thirty in the afternoon. They found a cab that would take them to Mill Valley and they both got in. Alexander was beginning to get very excited. He was finally going to see his Daddy, after three long months. And he was going to tell him all about New York, and the zoo, and his friends, and what they had done in school. He hopped all over Bettina, and she grinned stoically as he elbowed and kneed her, preparing all that he was going to say.

It seemed forever before they pulled into the familiar driveway, and Bettina couldn't repress a smile. It did feel good to be home. The driver began to unload their luggage, and Bettina went to open the front door. But when she inserted the key in the lock, she found that her key would no longer fit. She turned it one way, then the other, pushed the door, jiggled the doorknob and then she looked up in astonishment, understanding what had happened. John had changed the locks. It seemed a very childish trick.

In a state of stupefaction Bettina hurried next door. She had paid the driver and told him to just push the bags into the garage. So she took Alexander by the hand and they crossed the backyard. She knocked on Mary's back door.

"Oh, my God! . . . Betty!" She took her quickly into her arms, and then Alexander, who was being loudly welcomed by his friends. "Oh, have I missed you!" And then she called out behind her. "Seth! They're back." He came to the doorway, smiling, and held out his arms. But the warm welcome was quickly over and she looked from one to the other and explained about her key.

"I don't understand it." And then softly, as they walked into the living room, she looked over her shoulder and faced them. "I guess John had the locks changed."

But Mary was looking unhappy, and Seth finally raised his eyes. "Betty, sit down, honey. I've got some fairly stiff news." Oh, God, had something happened? Had something happened to him while she was gone? But why did no one call her? She felt her face go suddenly white. But Seth shook his head slowly. "It's nothing like that. But as his attorney, I had to respect his confidence. He came to me after you left and he insisted that I not say anything to you. It's been" — he seemed to hesitate awkwardly — "it's been damn difficult, to tell you the truth."

"It's all right, Seth. Whatever it is, you can tell me now."

He nodded slowly, and then looked at Mary before he looked back at her. "I know. I have to. Betty, he filed for divorce the day after you left."

"He did? But I never got any papers."

Seth shook his head firmly. "You don't

have to. Remember when you divorced your ex-husband? In this state it's called a dissolution and all that's required is for one spouse to want out. He did. And that was that."

"How nice and simple." She took a deep breath. "So when is the final decree?"

"I'd have to look it up, but I think it's in about three more months."

"And he changed the locks on the house?" Now she understood why he never answered her letters or phone calls while she was working on the play.

But Seth was shaking his head again. "He sold the house, Betty. He's not there anymore."

This time she looked truly shocked. "But what about our things? My things . . . the things we bought together. . . ."

"He left you some boxes, and suitcases with your clothes, and all of Alexander's toys." She felt her head begin to reel as she listened.

"And Alexander? He's not going to fight me for him?" She was suddenly grateful that she had taken the boy to New York. What if he had disappeared with Alexander? She would have died.

But now Seth seemed to hesitate before he spoke. "He — he doesn't want to see the boy again, Betty. He says he's all yours."

"Oh, my God." Slowly she stood up and went to the doorway, where she met the eyes of her son.

He looked up at her, his eyes filled with questions. "Where's Daddy, Mom?"

But she only shook her head slowly. "He's not here, sweetheart. He went away on a trip."

"Just like us? To New York?" He looked intrigued and Bettina fought back tears.

"No, darling, not to New York."

And then he looked at her strangely, as though he knew. "Are we going back to New York, Mommy?"

"I don't know, sweetheart, maybe. Would you like that?"

He looked at her, smiling broadly. "Yeah. I was just telling them about the big zoo." It shocked her that he wasn't more anxious for his father, but maybe it was just as well. And then slowly she turned to face Seth and Mary, with tears in her eyes and a lopsided grin.

"Well, so much for Betty Fields." But she hadn't been that for three months now. In New York, as a playwright, she had been Bettina Daniels. And maybe, she realized, that was who she should always have been. She looked back at her two friends. "Can we stay with you for a few days?"

"As long as you like." And then Mary held out her arms and hugged her. "And baby, we're so sorry. He's a fool." But it wasn't the bird of paradise he had wanted. He had wanted the little gray and brown bird. Secretly Bettina had known it all along.

40

Bettina and Alexander left San Francisco the day after Christmas, and after much soul-searching she sent the boxes filled with their possessions ahead to her hotel in New York.

"But I've been here for six years, Mary."

"I know. But do you really want to stay here now?"

Bettina had thought about it endlessly for the two lonely weeks they were there, and by the time Christmas came, she knew that what Mary was saying was more than just a question of what city she wanted to live in. Everyone she had known in San Francisco was a friend of John's. Suddenly people who had been warm and friendly ignored her completely when they met her on the street. She not only wore the stigma of divorce, but of success.

And so, on the day after Christmas they got on the plane, and Ollie met them at the other end. It was odd, it didn't feel to Bettina as though she had just left home, instead it felt like she was coming back to it as she got off the plane in New York. Ollie swept Alexander into his arms and buried him in the folds of a huge raccoon coat.

"Where did you get that? It's super." Bettina looked at him with a broad smile.

"My Christmas present to me." And he had several for Bettina and Alexander in the backseat of the limousine he had rented to take her back to her hotel. It had snowed the day before Christmas, and there were still a few inches of snow along the side of the road.

But as they drove back to the city she had left only two weeks before, she sensed something different about Ollie, something quiet and tense. She waited until Alexander was busy with the teddy bear, the fire truck with the siren, and the set of battery-operated cars on the floor of the limousine, and then she looked over at him quietly.

"Is something wrong?"

Unconvincingly he shook his head. "How about you, Bettina?"

She shrugged, and then smiled. "It feels good to be back."

"Does it?" She nodded. But there was still something sad in her eyes. "Was it rough out there for you?"

She nodded slowly. "Kind of. I guess I just didn't expect it. None of it." She mused for a moment. "When we got in from the airport, we went to the house, and I thought he had changed the locks."

"Had he?"

She shook her head grimly. "No. He had sold the house."

"Without telling you?" Ollie looked horrified. "How did he eventually break the news?"

Ruefully Bettina smiled. "He didn't. My neighbors did." And then she looked long and hard at Ollie. "I never spoke to him while we were out there. Apparently he filed for divorce three and a half months ago, as soon as we left for New York."

"My God . . . and he never told you?" She shook her head. "What about . . . ?" He nodded his head toward Alexander and she nodded quick understanding.

"He says that's finished too."

"He won't see him?" He looked deeply shocked.

"He says not."

"Have you explained that?"

She looked pensive. "More or less." And then she sighed softly. "It was an interesting two weeks. And that was just the bad news.

The good news was almost worse. Every time I ran into someone I knew, acquaintances, or old friends, they stomped all over me, either bluntly or with kind of back-handed nasties." She chuckled softly, relieved to have left it. "It was a terrible two weeks."

"And now what?"

"I look for an apartment tomorrow, put Alexander back in school after the Christmas vacation, and I go to work on my new play."

Bettina watched while he stared out the window. At last she touched his arm gently and held his eyes with her own.

"Ollie . . . are you all right?"

He nodded slowly, but he averted her eyes. "I'm fine."

"Are you sure?"

This time he chuckled softly. "Yes, Mother, I am." And after a moment, "I'm awfully glad you're back, Bettina. But I'm sorry you had such a hard time."

"I suppose it was predictable. The only one who didn't predict it was me."

He nodded slowly. "I must admit, when he never got in touch with you here, I was afraid of something like that. But I just thought that maybe he was very angry. I figured maybe when he saw you he'd back off and you two would get a fresh start."

"No such luck." She looked glum for a moment and then looked back at him again. "By the way, have you seen Ivo?" He started to say something, and then shook his head. "I called him the day before Christmas and told him we were coming in. He said he was going to Long Island with friends for Christmas, but he's coming back tonight, and he asked me about lunch tomorrow." She looked at Ollie happily. "Want to come?" Again Ollie only shook his head. And he was spared further explanation as they pulled up in front of the hotel. The porter unloaded their bags, they reclaimed their old suite, which had been just vacated, miraculously, by two businessmen from London who had had it since she left.

"It feels just like coming home again, doesnt it?" Alexander had run off to his room, and Jennifer, his sitter, was due to return to them the next morning. Bettina was going to offer her a permanent job with them as soon as they moved. "Want some dinner, Ollie?"

"No, thanks."

She ordered a hamburger for Alexander and a small steak for herself, sat down on the long couch and ran a hand through her tousled hair. "Tomorrow I start to look for an apartment." But suddenly Ollie sat down next to her with eyes full of gloom.

"Bettina. . . ."

"Good heavens, what is it? You look like you just lost your best friend." Slowly he nodded, his eyes filling with tears. "Ollie . . . what is it? . . . Ollie?" She reached out to him and he took her into his arms, but as he did so she could feel that he was not seeking comfort, but offering solace to her. "Ollie?"

"Baby, I didn't want to tell you at the airport, but a terrible thing happened last night." He held her close and felt her tremble as gently she pushed away.

"Ollie . . . ?" And then she looked at him, horrified, understanding. "Oh, God . . . they closed my play?" He smiled gently, and then quietly shook his head.

"No, nothing like that." And then he took a deep breath and took her tiny, frail hand in his. "Bettina, it's Ivo." He closed his eyes for only a fraction of a moment. "He died last night."

"Ivo?" She jumped to her feet and stared at her friend. "Don't be silly. I talked to him two days ago, he was going to Long Island. He was —" And then suddenly, trembling, she sank to the couch and stared at her friend. "Ivo? . . . Dead?" Her eyes filled with an ocean of tears as she stared, and Ollie pulled her back into his arms where she cried. "Oh, Ollie, no . . . not Ivo . . . oh, no . . . not Ivo . . . not Ivo. . . ." He walked her slowly to the bedroom before Alexander could see her and gently closed the door, then he lay her down on the bed and let her sob. It was like losing her father all over again, almost worse because she was losing a lifelong friend, and he had always been so good to her, better than her father, and she had never stopped loving him, right till the end. "But I was going to see him for lunch tomorrow, Ollie. . . ." She stared at him, childlike.

"I know, babe . . . I know. . . ." Gently he stroked her hair as she buried her face again. "I'm sorry, I'm so sorry . . . I know how you loved him."

As she glanced down at the floor she saw the newspaper lying there and noticed Ivo's picture on the front page, with the story. She was glad she hadn't seen it before.

"He was responsible for everything good that ever happened to me," she said to Ollie as she swung her legs at last over the side of the bed and dried her eyes. "And now he's gone."

41

The funeral was two days later. Governors, senators, newspaper moguls, socialites, authors, playwrights, movie stars, everyone came. And in the front row was Bettina.

Ollie took her arm as they left the cathedral, and neither of them spoke a word after they got back into the car. She rode, silent and dry eyed, back to the hotel, holding tightly to his hand. She looked ivory-white as she sat there, her perfect features etched in cameo fashion against the gray silhouette of the sky.

"Do you want to come up for a cup of coffee?" She looked bleakly at Ollie, and then turned as he nodded and followed her inside.

But upstairs there was Alexander and she had to at least make the pretense of wearing a smile. And half an hour later after coffee and croissants and Alexander's stories to his mother about the joys of Central Park, the smile was more than just put on. Ollie was relieved to see her looking better.

"Bettina? How about a walk this morning? I think we could both use some air." And then maybe lunch, and after that coffee at his place. Watching her, he had just decided not to leave her alone. "How about it? You could put on some slacks, and we could go roam for a while. Sound inviting?"

It didn't really, but she knew he wanted to help her, and she didn't want to hurt his feelings by saying no. "All right, all right." She threw up her hands with a small grin.

They rode quietly down in the elevator and ten minutes later they were walking along the edge of the park. Traffic was less frantic than usual because it was Saturday, and now and then a hansom cab clopped slowly by. They wandered along for more than an hour, talking occasionally, and then falling silent for a while, and at last she felt a cozy arm around her and she looked up into his eyes.

"You're a good friend, you know, Ollie. I think that was part of my decision to come back to New York." And then she hesitated for a moment. "You and Ivo." She brushed quickly at a tear with a white-mittened hand. And then softly she spoke again as they waited to cross the street. "Life will never hand me another man like Ivo."

Slowly he nodded. "No, it won't."

And then hand in hand they walked on. It was almost an hour later when they finally stopped to catch their breath.

"Can I interest you in lunch at the Plaza?" But she shook her head slowly. She didn't feel fancy and festive. She still wanted to be left alone.

"I don't think so, love, but thanks."

"Too frenzied?" He understood perfectly.

"Kind of." She smiled.

"How about tea and sandwiches at my place? Does that sound all right?" She brightened at the prospect, nodded, and he quickly hailed a cab.

They hurried up the steps of his brownstone, and he opened the door with his key. He had the garden apartment, and as he filled the kettle with water she took off her jacket and looked out into the tiny garden filled with snow.

"I'd forgotten how pretty this is, Ollie."

"I like it." He smiled at her as he started to make their sandwiches.

"I hope I find something as nice as this."

"You will. It takes a while to find the nice ones, but it's worth the look." He had a beautiful beam-ceilinged bedroom with a fireplace, a cozy living room with the same, an old-fashioned kitchen with one brick wall, three wood-paneled ones, a wood floor, and a bread oven, and the garden, which was an unusual bonus in New York.

"How did you find it?" She looked at him happily as he worked.

He smiled at her. "Through the *Mail,* of course. What are you looking for?"

She sighed as she thought of it. "Something a lot bigger than this, I'm afraid. Like about three bedrooms."

"Why so many?" He handed her a plate with a handsome sandwich filled with salami, smoked ham, and cheese.

She smiled at him and picked up the sandwich. "I need a room for Alexander, someplace to write, and a room for me."

He nodded. "Are you thinking of buying?"

She looked at him in confusion and eventually put down the sandwich and stared at her plate. "I wish I knew." And then she looked up at him. "I don't know what's going to happen, Ollie. Right now I've got all this money from the play. But who knows if that's going to last." She looked at him soberly and he grinned.

"I can promise you, Bettina, it will."

"You don't know that."

"Yes, I do. You wrote a great play."

"But what if I can't write another one?

What if it all stops?"

He rolled his eyes in amusement but Bettina didn't smile. "You're just like the rest of them, kiddo. All writers seem to live with the same curse. They make a million bucks on their last book, they sit on the bestseller list for six months, and they cry to you about 'what about tomorrow,' can they still do it, what about the next one, what if . . . and on and on, and you're just like that with your play."

Slowly she smiled at him. "I'm not really sure anymore, but I think my father was like that too." And her eyes sobered again. "But look at him, Ollie. He died without a penny. I don't want that to happen to me."

"Good, so don't buy seven houses, nine cars, and hire twenty-three servants. Failing that, you should do just fine." He smiled gently at her. She had told him all about her father's undoing and the four million dollars of debt when he died.

She looked quietly at Ollie, her head tilted to one side. "You know, Ollie, all my life I've been dependent on men. My father, Ivo, that actor I was married to" — she didn't even like to say his name — "then John. This is the first time in my life when I haven't been dependent on anyone except me." She looked up at him with a small comfortable smile. "I kind of like it."

He nodded. "You should, it's a good feeling."

"Yeah," she sighed, still smiling, "and sometimes it's scary too. I've always had someone there, and now for the first time in my life, I don't." And then more softly, "I don't even have Ivo anymore. All I have is me."

He looked at her gently. "And me."

She touched his hand warmly. "You've been a good friend. But you know something funny?"

"What?"

"I don't mind having to rely on myself. It scares the hell out of me sometimes, but it's a nice feeling too."

"Bettina" — he eyed her with candor — "I hate to tell you this, but I think you've just grown up."

"Already?" She looked at him and started laughing, and he toasted her with his cup of tea.

"Listen, you're way ahead of the game. I'm nine years older than you are, and I'm not sure I've grown up yet."

"Sure you have. You've always depended on you. You've never been dependent like I have."

"Being independent has its drawbacks

too." He looked pensive as he stared into his garden. "You get so hung up on what you're doing, on where you're going, and how to get there, that you never get too close to anyone else."

"Why not?" She spoke very softly in the warm, cozy kitchen as he watched her.

"You don't have time. Anyway I was too busy getting important, wanting to be number one at the paper in L.A."

"And now you've almost made it here." She smiled gently. "Now what?"

"I haven't made it, Bettina. You know what I wanted? I wanted to be like Ivo, to be the publisher of a major newspaper in a major town. And you know what's happened? All of a sudden I don't give a damn. I like what I'm doing, I'm enjoying New York, and for the first time in forty-two years, I don't give a shit about tomorrow, I'm just enjoying myself right now, right here." She smiled at him in answer.

"I know just what you mean." And as she said it she leaned almost imperceptibly forward, without even knowing she had, and Ollie suddenly moved toward her, and without thinking they kissed for a long, heady time. She pulled away finally, looking startled as she caught her breath. "How did that happen?" She tried to make light of it, but he wouldn't let her. There was suddenly something very serious in his eyes.

"It's been a long time coming, Bettina."

She was about to deny it, and then she nodded slowly. "I guess it has." And then after a moment, "I thought . . . I kind of thought . . . we would always be just friends."

He took her carefully in his arms again. "We are. But there's a confession I have to make to you, Miss Daniels. It's something I've wanted to tell you for a very long time." He smiled gently down at her and she smiled.

"Really, Mister Paxton, what's that?"

"That I love you . . . in fact I love you very much."

"Oh, Ollie." She buried her face in his chest with a sigh, but he reached under and caught her chin with his finger and gently made her look him in the eye.

"What does that mean? Are you angry?" For a moment he looked almost sad, but she was shaking her head with a look of chagrin.

"No, I'm not angry. How could I be?" Her voice softened still further. "I love you too. But I thought . . . it just seemed so simple . . . the way it was."

"It had to be simple then. You were married. Now you're not."

She nodded, thinking, and then she looked him squarely in the eye. "I'll never get married again, Oliver. I want you to know that right now." She looked deadly serious as she told him. "Do you understand that?" He nodded. "Can you accept it?"

"I can try."

"You have a right to get married, you've never done it. You have a right to a wife and kids and all of that stuff. But I've done it, I've had it, I don't ever want that again."

"What do you want?" He held her loosely in his arms and caressed her with his eyes.

She thought for a long moment. "Companionship, affection, someone to laugh with and share my life with, someone who respects me and my work and loves my child. . . ." She fell silent and their eyes met and held.

It was Ollie who finally broke the silence. "That's not too much to ask, Bettina." His voice seemed gentler by the moment as he stroked her soft coppery hair.

She nestled in his hand like a cat near a fire in winter, her eyes sparkling as she looked into his. "And you, Ollie? What do you want?" Her voice was deliciously husky.

He seemed to hesitate for a long time. "I want you, Bettina." And as he said it his hands moved from the brilliant hair that framed her face and began to slowly peel away her clothes. She let herself be unraveled like a ball of twine, until at last she lay there, naked and shimmering, on his bed, a bare expanse of creamy satin beneath his soft, stroking hands. And then like a chorus to a song she had long dreamed of, he said it again and again and again. "I want you, Bettina . . . my darling . . . I want you . . . my love. . . ." And suddenly she felt the flames of her own long forgotten passion engulf her as he rapidly and expertly brought her body back to life. And suddenly she was leaping and surging in his arms, tearing at his clothes, until they lay there together, breathless and hungry, burning with an insatiable desire for each other's love. And at last the fires they had so quickly fanned burned gently to embers and they lay in each other's arms and smiled.

"Happy?" He looked down at her with a tender gleam in his eye that said that she was his now.

"Yes. Very happy." Her voice was a sleepy whisper as she laced her fingers into his and nestled her head into his neck. "I love you, Ollie." It was the smallest and sweetest of whispers, and he closed his eyes and smiled.

He pulled her gently toward him and let

his month hungrily seek hers once more, and his limbs and his soul and the very essence of his being reached out to her once again.

"Ollie. . . ." This time she smiled when he took her. It was their game now. And they were both having fun and enjoying making love to each other at last. "Is it really supposed to be like that?" She looked at him with a suspicious grin when it was over.

"Like what?" His smile was as mischievous as hers. "You mean lighthearted?" He was grinning broadly as he reached around and held her behind in both his hands. "Madam, has anyone told you lately that you have the best-looking fanny in town?"

"Do I?" She grinned wickedly at him. "Maybe they ought to put that on the marquee of my play. . . ." She appeared to ponder the possibility and Oliver laughed and tousled her hair.

"Come here, you. . . ." But the hands were gentle even when the words were playful. "Woman, you can't even begin to imagine how much I love you." He fell silent for a long moment, and Bettina gazed up at him with a lifetime in her eyes.

She nodded slowly. "Yes, I can, Ollie . . . oh, yes I can. . . ."

"Can you?" He was smiling again. "How?"

But she wasn't playing now. She reached out and held him with all of her strength, her eyes tightly closed, her heart held out to him as she whispered the words. "Because I love you with my whole soul." And as she said it she felt for a moment as though this were her last chance. Her eyes opened then and she looked at Oliver Paxton and smiled as he leaned down and kissed her again.

42

Bettina stared at Ollie gloomily in his kitchen as he poured her more tea. They had been spending long hours in his apartment for the past two weeks. She was renting her suite in the hotel by the month now, but Ollie's place still felt more like a home.

"Don't look so cheerful, darling. I promise, I'm honest, hardworking, and very neat." He waved at the total chaos around them, four days of newspapers, his bathrobe, and Bettina's clothes. "See?"

"Don't be funny. And that's not the point."

"Then what is?" He sat down comfortably at the oak table and reached for her hand.

"If we move in together, it's all going to start again, it'll happen. I'll get dependent, you'll want to get married. Now I have to think of Alexander. It's just not right." She looked miserable and his eyes attempted to console. They had been discussing it all week.

"I understand your concern about Alexander, and I share that concern too. But this doesn't make sense either. You're running back and forth to the hotel, you never have time to work, and it'll be the same damn thing if you get your own apartment. You'll be spending at least half your time here." He leaned over and kissed her and they both smiled. "Do you know how much I love you?"

"Tell me."

"I adore you." He whispered it softly.

"Goodie." She giggled and leaned forward to kiss him across the table as she felt his hand slide up her leg. It had been like that since the first time. He was so gentle and funny and easy to be with. He understood her, and her work, and he truly loved Alexander. But best of all, she and Ollie shared a special friendship. She wanted nothing more than to live with him, but she didn't want the same nightmares to happen again. What if he started to resent her work? What if Alexander annoyed him? What if he cheated on her or she on him?

"So? Do we get an apartment together?" He looked at her triumphantly and she groaned.

"Has anyone told you that you're pushy?"
"Frequently. I don't mind it at all."
"Well, Ollie" — she looked at him firmly — "I'm just not going to give in."
"Fine." He shrugged easily. "Then get your own apartment, don't get any sleep, stay here till five in the morning, and then rush home so your son doesn't know you were out, but that will mean another bedroom, you know."
"Why?" She looked puzzled.
"Well, you'll have to have Jennifer living in the way she does at the hotel, but I assume she'll want her own room. You can't just run off and leave Alexander in the middle of the night."
Bettina looked at him and rolled her eyes. "Damn you."
"You know I'm right."
"Oh, shit . . . well, let me think it over."
"Certainly, madam. Will five minutes be enough?"
"Oliver Paxton!" She stood up and shouted, but five minutes later he had her back in bed. "You're impossible!"
Two days later Ollie solved the problem. He arrived at her hotel suite with a broad grin. "It's perfect, Bettina." He looked victorious as he entered and Alexander immediately threw himself at the large man's

endless legs.

"Stop it, Alexander . . . what is?" Bettina was wearing two pencils in her hair. She was deep at work on the new play.

"I found the perfect apartment."

She eyed him evilly and sat down on a chair. "Ollie. . . ."

"Now wait a minute, just listen. It's sensational. A friend of mine is going away for six months to L.A., and he'll rent us his apartment. It's absolutely splendid, a duplex, four bedrooms, fully furnished, in a fabulous West Side co-op. The rent is a thousand a month. We can afford it easily. So we take it for six months while he's gone, and try it out. If we like it, we find our own place together at the end of the six months, and if we don't, we each go our separate ways. And if it'll make you less nervous, I'll sublet my own place while we try it, so you won't feel that you're stuck with me at the end of the six months. Sound reasonable?" He looked at her hopefully and she laughed. "Besides, how long can you go on paying hotel bills?"

"I don't know if you're a magician or a charlatan, Ollie Paxton, but one thing's for sure, you come up with some damn fine ideas."

"You like it?" He looked ecstatic.

"I sure do." She got up and went to him, wrapping her arms around his waist. "How soon can we take it?"

"I — uh — I'll have to ask him." But suddenly as she looked at him, she knew the truth.

"Ollie!" She tried to look outraged but she only laughed. "Did you already take it?"

"I — uh — of course not . . . don't be silly. . . ."

But she knew him better than that. "You did."

He hung his head sheepishly as she grinned at him. "I did."

"We already have it?" She looked at him in vast amusement.

"We do."

"But what if I'd said no to you?"

"Then I'd have had a very fancy apartment for the next six months." They both laughed for a minute, and then Bettina's face grew stern.

"I want you to understand something though, Ollie."

"Yes, ma'am?"

"We share the rent. And I have Alexander, so I'll pay two thirds."

"Oh, Christ. Women's liberation. Don't you suppose you could let me handle it?"

"No, if that's what you want, then it's no

go. Either we share or I won't move in."

"Wonderful. But how about if you just pay half?"

"Two thirds."

"Half."

"Two thirds."

"Half." And he firmly grabbed her ass. "And if you say another word about it, Bettina Daniels," he whispered as Alexander went back to his own room. "I will rape you right here." But they were both laughing and still arguing as they hurried to her room and closed the door.

43

"Do you like it?" He watched, hopefully.

"It's sensational, are you kidding?" She looked around her with delight and awe. It was one of those rare West Side apartments that was more than just elegant, it was absolutely grand. It was indeed a duplex, and the four comfortable bedrooms were all upstairs, but the living room and dining room were downstairs and the ceilings were the height of both floors. Both rooms were wood paneled, and even Ollie could walk in and out of the fireplaces with ease. The windows were long and handsome, and they had a view of Fifth Avenue across the park. There was also a small cozy den, which they could both use for their writing, and upstairs the bedrooms were all lovely and looked terribly French.

"Whose place is this?" She looked around again with fascination and sat on a beautifully sculpted French chair.

"A producer I knew years ago in the movies."

"What's his name?"

"Bill Hale."

"I think I've heard of him. Is he famous?" But she knew he would have to be to afford a place like this. When she looked at him, Ollie was grinning, and began reeling off the names of his movies and plays.

"He's not unlike you."

"Very funny."

"No, I mean it. He wrote one play and it was a hit, then he did several movies, then several more plays. Now he works mostly out of Hollywood. But it all started with one success, and then he was on his way." And then he reached out an arm for Bettina and took her in his big loving grip. "It'll happen to you. I'm just waiting to see it."

"Well, don't hold your breath. What's he doing in Hollywood now?"

He grinned at her. "Getting married. That's another thing he has in common with you. I think he's about thirty-seven, and this is his fourth wife."

"I don't think that's funny, Ollie." She looked suddenly very annoyed, and he tweaked her nose.

"Don't be so uptight, Bettina. You can't lose your sense of humor about it." He said it very gently and the smile returned to her eyes.

"Besides I only had three."

"I could help you catch up with him."

She looked over her shoulder despairingly. "Gee, thanks." She was on her way out to the kitchen, and when she got there she gasped. He heard her calling him as he was trying to help Alexander drag in a box filled with toys. "Ollie, come in here!"

"I'm coming . . . just a second. . . ." But when he did, he whistled too. The whole kitchen looked like a greenhouse, and there was a closed balcony outside filled with tulips, red, yellow, and pink.

"Isn't it gorgeous?" Bettina looked at him, enchanted. "I wish we could keep it forever."

But Ollie only smiled at her. "I'm sure Bill does too."

She nodded. "At least we've got six months."

But the months sped by amazingly quickly, and she finished her new play in late May. It was about a woman much like Bettina and she had called it *Bird of Paradise*. The title made Ollie smile.

"Do you like it?" She looked at him anxiously as he handed it back to her over breakfast. They were sitting in the kitchen, enjoying the spring sunshine and a bright blue morning sky.

"It's better than the first one."

"Do you mean it?" He nodded. "Oh, Ollie!" She threw her arms around his neck. "I'll have a Xerox copy made and send it to Norton today."

But as it turned out, he called her before the new play reached his desk.

"How about coming in to see me, Bettina?"

"Sure, Norton, what's up?"

"Oh, there's something I want to discuss with you."

"Me too. I was just about to send you my new play."

"Good. Then how about lunch?"

"Today?" She was surprised. He wasn't usually in a hurry, but by lunchtime, she knew why he was. They sat at a quiet table at 21, eating steak tartare and spinach salad, and Bettina looked at him in amazement as he told her what was on his mind.

"So, that's the offer, Bettina. What do you think of it?"

"I don't know what to say."

"I do. Congratulations." He held out a hand. "I suppose you'll have to go out there. But you could wait a few weeks. They don't want to start getting organized until July." It was perfect, that was when she and Ollie had to give up the apartment, but she still didn't know what to say. Everything Norton had just told her was still running around in her head. She managed somehow to get through lunch with Norton, and she hurried to the paper to find Ollie, writing his latest review.

"I have to talk to you." She looked anguished and he was instantly worried.

"Something wrong? Alexander . . . Bettina, tell me. . . ."

But she shook her head vaguely. "No, no, nothing like that. I just had lunch with Norton." And then she looked at him blankly. "They want to make a movie of my play."

"Which play? The new one?" He looked as stunned as she.

"No, the old one."

But suddenly he was grinning at her. "Don't worry, they'll wind up doing the new one too."

"Ollie, stop that! Listen! . . . What am I going to do?"

"Do it of course, you moron. Do they want you to do the screenplay too?" She nodded and he whooped.

"Hallelujah, you've made it! This is the big time, baby!" But she wanted to ask him What about you?

And then she looked at him sadly. "But

I'll have to go to Hollywood to do it, Ollie. They're making the movie there."

"So?" Then that was all it meant to him. Six months of pleasant cohabitation. Now she understood. And she had grown seriously attached to him in the last six months. "Don't look like that. It's not the end of the world."

"I know that . . ." She lowered her voice. "I just thought —"

"What?" He looked puzzled.

"Never mind."

"No, tell me." He grabbed her arm, and she raised her eyes.

"Ollie, I have to go out there to do it. And I — I didn't really want to leave you."

"Who says you have to?" He was speaking to her in a whisper as they stood in the busy room.

"What the hell does that mean?" She was whispering back at him. "What about your job?"

"Can my job. So I'll quit. So what? It's no big deal."

"Are you crazy? You're the lead theater critic, you can't just walk out on that."

"Oh, really? Well, watch me. I told you six months ago that all those boyhood ambitions of mine didn't mean a damn anymore. You're the one with the booming career, and I happen to love you, so I quit and we go."

She was shaking her head sadly. "That's not right."

But he grabbed her arm firmly again. "Remember that line of your father's about hanging on to a dream? She nodded and he increased the pressure on her arm. "This is mine."

She looked up at him gratefully. "But what'll you do for work?"

"Don't worry. I'll find something. I can probably even get back my old job."

"But do you want it?"

He shrugged easily with a smile as he looked at her. "Why not?"

It startled her that he would give up his job so readily for her, but she was grateful to him too. She had realized in the four months they'd lived together that she was far more ambitious than he. What he had said about his aspirations had been true. All he wanted now was a decent job and a life with a good woman, and maybe eventually some kids. He was marvelous with Alexander and she knew he wanted some of his own.

"So you think I should do it?"

"Are you serious, Bettina? Call Norton this minute and tell him yes."

But suddenly she hung her head sheepishly and grinned. "That's what I told him after lunch."

"Why, you little rascal. How soon are we going?" He lowered his voice as he asked her.

"Mid-July." He nodded, and she kissed him, and a few minutes later she left.

That evening when he got home, he called his old boss at the L.A. paper, and two days later they called him back with the offer of a job. It was better than his last one with them, but not as good a spot as he had in New York. For an instant Bettina felt guilty but he was quick to see the look in her eyes. He held her for a long moment as they sat alone in the cozy wood-paneled library and he gently stroked her gold-flecked hair.

"Bettina, even if I couldn't have found something else, I'd have come with you."

"But, Ollie, it's just not right." She looked up at him, her eyes filled with worry. "Your work is just as important as mine."

"No, it isn't, baby. And we both know that. You have a great career ahead of you, and all I have is a job."

"But you could have a great career too. You could be like Ivo. . . ." Her voice seemed to trail off, and with a small smile Ollie shook his head.

"I don't think so, babe."

"Why not?"

"Because that's not what I want. I'm forty-three years old, Bettina, and I don't want to knock myself out anymore. I don't want to kill myself sitting in an office until eight thirty every night. It's not worth it. I want the good life." So did she, but she wanted something more too. "But you're going to make it very big, baby." She smiled as she listened.

"Think so?" She liked the idea now. It was immensely appealing.

"Yes, I do."

44

At the end of July they reluctantly relinquished the apartment, and two days before Hale returned to take possession of it, Oliver, Bettina, and Alexander flew to L.A., where a real estate agent had already lined up a small furnished house.

"Oh, Jesus. . . ." Bettina looked around when they got there and grinned. "I don't know whether to throw up or faint."

Ollie looked at her, laughing. "How about both?"

The outside of the house had been painted purple and the inside was mostly pink. There were gold touches and bits of fake leopard, and everywhere were collections of artifacts interspersed with shells. The only advantages it boasted were that it was in Malibu and that it was on the beach. Alexander was enchanted and immediately hopped off the terrace to play in the sand.

"Think you can stand it, Bettina?"

"After what we had in New York, it may be rough. But I guess I'll have to." And then she looked at him blankly. "How could they do this to us?"

"Just be grateful it's only for six weeks." She nodded thankfully and wandered back inside, but in the weeks that followed they hardly had time to notice where they lived. Oliver was busy getting reestablished at the paper and Bettina worked twelve and fifteen hours at the studio, for the first few weeks, establishing what would go into the screenplay as opposed to what had been done on the stage. But by the end of August, things began to settle down and Bettina turned her attention to the house. She called the real estate agent and discussed it. She knew what she wanted, but the question was could it be found. One thing was certain, she had had enough of living at the beach, and she was anxious to find something so she could hide there and get to work.

For the first few weeks she was hopeful, and after that she sank back in despair.

"Don't tell me that, Ollie, there's nothing." She looked at him in desperation, and then barely missed sitting down on a shell. "And I can't stand this goddamn place any longer. I have to get to work, and I'm losing my mind." She looked at him desperately, and he held out his arms.

"Take it easy, baby. We'll find something. I promise." She had reestablished her friendship with Mary and Seth and commiserated with Mary over the phone one day about her problem finding a house.

"I'm beginning to lose hope. This place is crazy."

"You'll find a place, honey. Meanwhile you're the bird of paradise again." She smiled into the phone. She had seen houses that looked like palazzi with swimming pools indoors and out, places with Grecian statues, and one house with fourteen pink marble baths. But finally she found it, and she returned home with a gleam of victory in her eyes.

"I found it, Ollie. I found it! Wait till you see!"

He did and it was perfect. A beautiful but elegant house way at the back of Beverly Hills. It managed somehow to look both stately and lovely without looking pretentious, a rarity in that part of town. It was a little larger than she had wanted, but it was so pretty, she didn't care. There were five bedrooms upstairs, and a tiny den of her own; downstairs there was a solarium, a living room, a dining room, a huge kitchen, and another cozy den. Basically they could use all of it. She would work upstairs and Ollie down, and she had decided to hire someone to help her with Alexander, so one of the bedrooms could be for her, which still left two unused.

"What'll we do with all the bedrooms, kiddo?" Ollie smiled at her as he started the car.

"Just use them as guest rooms, I guess." And then she looked worried. "Do you think it's too much house?"

"No, I think it's perfect, but I had something in mind when I asked."

"I already thought of that." She looked at him proudly. "The downstairs den is for you."

But he only laughed softly. "That wasn't what I meant."

"It isn't?" She looked startled, and then confused as they drove back to Malibu. "Then what did you mean?"

For a moment he seemed to hesitate, and then quietly he pulled the car off the road. He looked at her seriously for a long moment, and then he told her what had been on his mind for so long. "Bettina, I'd like us to have a baby."

"Are you serious?" But it was easy to see that he was.

"Yes, I am."

"Now?" But she had to do the movie . . . and what if they put on her new play?

"I know, you're thinking about your work. But you said that you felt well when you were pregnant with Alexander. You could just write this screenplay while you're pregnant, and then I'll take care of it, and if we had to, we could hire a nurse."

"Is that fair to the baby?"

"I don't know. But I'll tell you one thing" — he looked at her in dead earnest — "I'd give that child all I have. Every moment, every scrap of laughter, every joy, every hour that I had to share."

"It means that much to you?" He nodded and she felt the pain of regret slice through her, but she slowly shook her head.

"Why? Because of your work?"

She sighed softly and shook her head. "No. I could probably manage that."

"Then what?" He pressed her, his desire for a child urging him on.

"No." She shook her head again, and then she faced him squarely. "No one is ever going to make me go through that again." For a long moment there was silence, and then gently he reached out and took her hand. He remembered the horror story she had told him only once.

"You wouldn't have to go through that,

Bettina. I'd never let anyone do something like that to you again." But she remembered too well what John had said. He was going to be there for her too.

"I'm sorry, Ollie. I can't. I thought I made that clear to you in the beginning." She sighed as he started the car.

"You did. But I just didn't realize how much it would bother me." He looked over at her with a halfhearted smile. He was hurt by her answer and he would be for a long time. "You're a hell of a woman, Bettina, and there's nothing in this world I want more than your child." She felt like a beast but there was nothing she could say as they drove home. Eventually the talk turned to the new house, and the next day she put in a bid. A week later it was theirs.

"A little expensive," as she said to Mary over the phone, "but wait till you see it, it's gorgeous and we love it. We've decided to stay out here."

Mary was happy for her. Whatever she did. "How's Ollie doing with his new job?"

"Actually it's his old job, but he likes it." And there was a silence, as a shadow crossed Bettina's eyes. She hesitated for a moment, and then she sat down in the kitchen, the phone resting on her shoulder. She was alone in the house in Malibu for the morning, and she looked sadly out at the beach. "Mary, I've got a problem."

"What is it, love?"

"It's Ollie." Mary frowned as she listened. "He wants a kid."

"And you don't."

"That is the understatement of the year."

"Why? Your career?" Mary didn't sound judgmental about it. She would have understood.

"No, it's not that, it's —"

"Don't tell me, McCarney." Mary said it and almost snarled. But Bettina had to laugh.

"Jesus, I think you hate him more than I do."

"I do." And then her voice softened. "But that's no reason not to have a baby. I told you five years ago it would never be like that again. Or, Jesus, Betty, even if it turned out to be a disaster, with a decent doctor he'd give you a spinal and a bunch of shots, you wouldn't even know what hit you; you'd be punchy and numb and the next thing you'd know you'd have a brand-new baby in your arms." Bettina smiled as she listened.

"You make it sound nice."

"It *is* nice."

"I know. I love Alexander, and I know I'd love Ollie's child, but I just . . . oh, Christ,

Mary, I couldn't. . . ."

"I'll make a deal with you. What you do about this is your business, but if you get pregnant, I'll come down and be with you for the birth."

"As a nurse?" Bettina sounded intrigued.

"Either way. As a nurse or a buddy. Whatever you want, and whatever the doctor says. I'd probably be more useful to you as a buddy, but whatever you like. And you could have Ollie with you. You know even in five years a lot of things have changed. With all this talk about babies, you two thinking about getting married?"

"Hell, no." Bettina laughed.

"I didn't think so, but I just wondered."

"That one, at least, he's given up."

"Then maybe he'll give this one up too."

"Maybe." But Bettina didn't think so, and she wasn't totally sure that she wanted him to give it up. She had just turned thirty-four, and if she was ever going to have another baby, it was time.

45

They moved out of the purple beach house a month after their six-week lease had expired and they moved into their lovely new stone one, and for a little while they lived with empty halls. But Ivo had left Bettina all of his furniture from the apartment in New York, so she called the place where it was in storage and had it sent out to the Coast. Then she and Ollie did some shopping, went to some auctions, bought some curtains, and spent a whole day picking out rugs. And three weeks later the place was off to a good beginning. Ollie's things had arrived from the little apartment he'd given up in New York.

He never again mentioned the baby, but Bettina thought of it as she closed the larger of the two extra rooms. She didn't have time to spend turning them into guest rooms, she had to sit down and get to work on the movie script of her play. It seemed to take forever, and four months later she was still buried beneath a mountain of notes, and changes, and rough drafts in her little sun-filled room. It jutted straight out from their bedroom, and Ollie could hear her typing late at night as he drifted off to sleep. But it wasn't till after Christmas that he noticed how tired she looked.

"You feeling okay?"

"Yeah. Fine. Why?" She looked surprised.

"I don't know. You look lousy."

"Gee, darling, thank you." And then she grinned at him. "What do you expect from me? I'm working my ass off on this damn thing."

"How's it coming?"

She sighed deeply and let herself fall into a comfortable chair. "I don't know. I think I'm almost finished, but I won't admit it to myself. I keep playing with it and playing with it, until I get it right."

"Have you shown it to anyone?" She shook her head. "Maybe you should."

"I'm afraid they won't understand what I'm doing."

"That's their business, baby. Why not try it?"

She nodded slowly. "Maybe I will."

Two weeks later she took his advice and gave it to Norton and the producers. They congratulated her on the completed script. But instead of looking better, she was looking worse.

"How about going to the doctor?"

"I don't need one. All I need is sleep." And apparently she was right. For the next five days she barely came out from between the covers, not even to eat.

"Are you that exhausted?" He looked frankly worried, but he had to admit that she had worked like a demon for four and a half months.

She nodded. "More so. Everytime I wake up, all I want to do is go back to sleep."

But two days later he got nervous and insisted that she go to the doctor. He made the appointment for her, and she grumbled mightily when he picked her up and took her there after work.

"What's the big deal about going to the doctor?"

"I don't need one." He had also noticed that she was snappish, and she hardly ever ate. "I'm just tired."

"Well, maybe he can do something to improve your mood." But she no longer laughed at his humor, and when she went into the doctor's office, for a moment Ollie had thought she was near tears. When she came out of the office, he was sure of it, and she didn't say a word. "Well?"

"I'm fine."

"Terrific. What made him decide that? Your charming disposition or the healthy glow in your eyes?"

"I don't think you're amusing. Can't you just leave me alone?" But when they walked into the house, he grabbed her arm and pulled her into the downstairs study so they could be alone.

"I've had enough of this bullshit, Bettina. I want to know what the hell is going on."

"Nothing." But as she looked at him her lip trembled and her eyes filled with tears. "Nothing! Okay?"

"No, not okay. You're lying. Now what did he say?" She started to turn away and he grabbed at her arm. "Bettina . . . baby . . . please . . ." But she only closed her eyes and shook her head.

"Just leave me alone." Slowly he turned her toward him. Maybe it was something awful. A tremor ran through him as he tried to hide from the thought. He couldn't bear to lose her. His life would never be the same.

"Bettina?" Now his voice trembled too, but at last she faced him, the tears streaming from her eyes.

"I'm three and a half months pregnant, Ollie." And then, gulping, "I was so wrapped up in that damn screenplay that I never noticed. All I did was work day and night, and I never thought . . ." She cried harder. "I can't even have an abortion. I'm two weeks too late."

He looked at her, momentarily in shock. "Would you have wanted one?"

But she only stared at him. "What does that matter now? I have no choice." And then, wrenching free from his grip on her, she ran from the room. A moment later he heard the door to their bedroom slam shut, and Alexander came running down the stairs.

"What's wrong with Mommy?"

"She's just tired."

But Alexander rolled his eyes in irritation. "Still?"

"Yeah, tiger, still."

"Okay, want to come play?" But Ollie was feeling distracted and he shook his head vaguely. All he wanted was to be alone.

"How about later?"

The boy looked disgruntled. "But later I have to go to bed."

"In that case" — Oliver stooped to give him a warm hug — "you're just going to have to excuse me. Shall I give you a rain check?" The boy nodded happily. That was one of the things he loved best. With a flourish Ollie took out paper and pen and gave him a rain check. "Will that do it?"

"You bet."

As Alexander left the room to find his baby-sitter, Ollie sank slowly into a chair. He was still stumped about what Bettina had said about an abortion. Would she really have done it? Would she have told him? How could she? But he forced himself to understand that that wasn't what was happening. She was having his baby . . . his baby. . . . He found himself smiling slowly, and then frowning again, agonized about her. What if it was as bad as the last time? What if she never forgave him? How could he do that to her? He felt himself begin to panic, and then almost without thinking, he looked for her phone book and dialed the number in Mill Valley. They hardly knew each other, but he knew that she would help.

"Mary? This is Oliver Paxton in Los Angeles."

"Ollie?" There was a moment of silence. "Is something wrong?"

"I . . . no . . . that is . . . yes." And then, with a sigh, he told her the whole tale. "I don't even know why I'm calling except that . . . oh, Christ, I don't know, Mary, you're a nurse, you're a friend . . . you were there last time . . . oh, Jesus, do you think it'll kill her? . . . I don't know what to say. She's hysterical. I have never seen her so upset."

Mary nodded as she listened. "She has a right to be."

"Was it as bad as she remembers?"

"No. It was probably considerably worse."

"Oh, my God." And then, hating himself for the words, he grabbed at the only straw. "Can't they do an abortion if she's three and a half months pregnant?"

"If they have to, but it's fairly dangerous." And then after a moment, "Is that what you really want?"

"It's what she wants. She said so." He sounded near tears.

"She's just frightened." And then slowly she told him what it had been like. It almost made him squirm. "She might have had a hard time anyway, but in essence it was all because of the doctor. He made it about as bad as it could get."

"Does she know that?"

"In her head, yes. In her gut, no. She's panic-stricken about it. I know. We've discussed it before. She decided right then she'd never have another one. And if I'd gone through what she did, I'd have made that decision too. But, Ollie, this time it will be entirely different."

"How do you know that?"

"Any doctor can tell you that. In fact hers probably did."

"She doesn't even have an obstetrician yet."

"Well, for God's sake, make sure she gets the right one. Have her talk to other women, other doctors, check the guy out in every way you can. Ollie, it's important. She shouldn't have to go through that again."

"She won't." He sighed softly into the phone. "And, Mary, thank you. I'm sorry to bother you with our problems."

"Don't be silly." And then, with a slow smile, "And Ollie . . . I'm so glad."

He sighed again. "So am I. But, God, I hate to put her through this."

"She'll calm down in a while. Just get her a decent doctor."

He took care of that the moment he hung up the phone. He called four of his close friends at the paper, who had recently had kids, or at least in the last few years. And miraculously three of the women had had the same doctor, and they all thought he was a dream. He hastily wrote the man's name down on a piece or paper, called information, and nervously dialed. Three minutes later he had him on the line.

"Doctor Salbert, my name is Oliver Paxton. . . ." Laboriously he told him his tale.

"Just bring her in in the morning. Say around ten thirty?"

"Fine. But what'll I do in the meantime?"

The doctor chuckled. "Give her a stiff drink."

"That won't hurt the baby?"

"Not if she just drinks one or two."

"What about champagne?" Oliver had never felt so ruffled and nervous, but the doctor only smiled.

"That'll be fine. See you tomorrow."

"Absolutely . . . and thank you. . . ." He hung up the phone and ran out the door.

"Where are you going?" Alexander called after him.

"I'll be right back." And he was, with a huge bottle of chilled vintage French champagne. Five minutes later he had put the bottle, two glasses, and some peanuts on a large tray and he was knocking softly on their bedroom door.

"Yeah?" He could hear Bettina's muffled voice within.

"Can I come in?"

"No."

"Good." He opened the door gently. "I love feeling welcome."

"Oh, Jesus." She rolled over in bed when she saw the champagne. "This is not a celebration, Ollie."

"Mind your own business, Daniels. I'll welcome my kid into this world any way I like. Besides which" — he put the tray down and looked down warmly at her — "I happen to be madly in love with the kid's mother." He sat down next to her and gently stroked her hair, but she pulled away.

"Don't . . . I'm not in the mood."

But he just lay there and watched her, a lifetime of loving in his eyes. "Baby, I know what you're feeling. I talked to Mary, and I understand what a nightmare it must have been. But it won't be like that again. Never, ever, I swear it."

"You called Mary?" She looked at him with surprise and sudden suspicion. "Why did you do that?"

"Because I love you, and I was worried, and I don't want you to be scared." And suddenly the way he said it brought fresh tears to her eyes.

"Oh, Ollie, I love you . . . oh, darling. . . ." She sobbed in his arms.

"It's going to be just fine."

"You promise?" She looked like a little girl and he smiled.

"I promise. And tomorrow we're going to see a doctor that everyone loves."

"You found me a doctor too?" She looked

stunned.

"Of course, I'm terrific. Hadn't you noticed that before?"

"Yeah . . . as a matter of fact I had. . . . How did you find this doctor?" She was smiling at him and she leaned over to kiss his ear.

"I asked some friends whose wives just had babies, and then I called him. He sounds nice."

"What did he say?"

"That you should drink some champagne." He sat up grinning. "Doctor's orders." He opened the bottle and handed her a glass of the sparkling wine.

"It won't hurt the baby?" She looked dubious as she held the glass and he smiled. John had forbidden her to drink while she was expecting Alexander.

"No, darling, it won't hurt the baby." And then he looked at her, glad that she cared. "It's going to be a lovely baby, Bettina."

"How do you know that?" She was smiling broadly, a look of relief slowly coming to her eyes.

"Because it's ours."

46

"Hey, fatso, it's for you!" Ollie waved to her from the doorway as she played with Alexander in the backyard. She had just bought him a new set of swings, and with her enormous belly in front of her she was pushing him as high as she could.

"I'll be back in a minute, darling." As best she could, she hurried to the kitchen door with a look of disapproval for Ollie. "Don't call me that, you big-mouthed giant. As it so happens, I've only gained fourteen pounds."

"You sure that guy knows how to read the scale?" But the doctor he had found her could do more than that. In the four months Bettina had been seeing him, he had established a relationship based on trust and confidence, and she was actually beginning to be less panicked by the birth.

"Never mind. Who's on the phone?"

"Norton."

"What's he want?"

"I don't know. Ask him."

She took the phone from him and they exchanged a friendly kiss. Their relationship was filled with joking and teasing. Ollie was ecstatic about the baby, and he was infinitely protective of her. Even Alexander had decided that maybe it wouldn't be bad after all, as long as it wasn't a girl.

"What?" Bettina was staring in disbelief at the phone.

Ollie glanced over at her, trying to mouth questions, but she shook her head and quickly turned her back. It seemed hours before she was finally off the phone. "Well, what was it? Don't keep me in suspense."

She sat down, looking pale. "They're going to do my second play. Not only are they going to do it, but he already has a movie deal."

"And you're surprised? I told you that months ago. The only thing that surprises me is that it took this long." It had taken almost a year to sell her second play. And then he looked suddenly worried. "When do they want to start?"

She looked at Oliver in amusement. "They had to be reasonable about it. Norton told them I was pregnant, so it's not for a while."

"What does that mean?"

"October." The baby was due in July. "The contract says I only have to be in New York for three months." And then she looked worried. "Can you take a leave of absence for that long?"

"If I have to." He didn't look concerned. "Can we take a baby that young to New York?"

"Sure. It'll be two months old."

"Not 'it,' 'she,' " he corrected. He kept insisting that he wanted a girl. He kept looking at Alexander proudly, saying that he already had a son. It was one of the reasons why he still wanted to get married, so he could adopt Alexander and give him his name. But Bettina was still firm in her refusal.

"It's more fun this way, we all have our own names, Daniels, Paxton, and Fields."

"It sounds like a law firm." But she wasn't moved.

Now she sat staring for a moment, thinking of her play, and Oliver smiled at her. "How soon will they want to start work on the movie?"

"After Christmas. And figure it'll take six months, so that will bring me through June. All in all, it'll be about nine months of work."

But he still looked worried. "That won't

be too much for you right after the baby?"

"It won't be 'right' after. I'll have two months to rest. Believe me, afterward isn't the hard part." She still had some fears. But they had gone to classes together and they shared each session at the doctor. Ollie had waited too long for this event to miss even a moment of it now. At forty-four, he called it the event of his life.

Bettina found herself dividing her excitement between the baby and the new play. It was only in the last month of her pregnancy that her excitement about the play was almost obscured. It seemed as though all she wanted to do was be with Ollie and sit peacefully in the shade, watching Alexander play. She went to bed early, she ate well, she read a little, but it was as though her mind was totally at rest. She didn't want to face any fresh challenges, didn't want to speak to Norton, or worry about making deals. Instead she was preparing for something very important that took all of her concentration. It seemed to absorb her whole life.

Two days before her due date Mary came down from San Francisco by plane. She had left all of the kids with her mother, and Seth had gone camping with a friend.

"Believe me, I'd much rather be here than out camping. So" — she looked at Bettina happily — "what's been happening with you?"

"Absolutely nothing. I've turned into a vegetable. I may never write another play." But she didn't even give a damn. All she could think about was the baby and the nursery. She wasn't even that concerned with Oliver anymore. Just with her belly and the soon-to-be child. It was an oddly self-centered existence, and Ollie understood it, because the doctor had warned him that it was like that at the end.

"What does the doctor say?"

"Nothing. Just that it could be any day. I don't suppose it'll come on my due date though."

"Why not?"

"Things just don't happen like that."

"Sure they do." Mary giggled as the three of them got in the car. "What you have to do is plan something fancy, like a nice evening, dinner somewhere or an evening at the theater, then you can count on it happening that night." The three of them laughed at the thought, but Ollie decided that he liked the idea.

"How about dinner at the Bistro?"

"On my due date?" Bettina looked appalled. "What if something happens?"

"If you ruin their carpet, then we never go

back." He chuckled and Bettina made a face. But he insisted when they got back to the house that he make a reservation for the following night.

"Oh, Jesus." Bettina looked at him nervously and took Mary upstairs to unpack her bags. The deal they had with the doctor was that she would be at the delivery, just as a friend. But he was amenable to as many observers as they wanted, within reason. "Just no small children or large dogs."

So the following evening the three of them trooped out to the Bistro to eat. It was as lovely as ever, with soft lighting, cut-glass panels, and elegant decor. Bettina looked radiant, in a floating white summer dress, with a gardenia tucked behind one ear.

"You look very exotic, Miss Daniels." And then he whispered softly, "I love you too."

She smiled and reached for his hand under the table, whispering the same thing. But it wasn't until they had ordered that Mary noticed an odd look on her face. At first she said nothing, but when it happened again five minutes later, she looked across the table and caught her eye.

"Was I right, Betty?"

"You might have been."

Oliver didn't hear them. He was ordering the wine. "Well, ladies? Everybody happy?"

"Absolutely." Mary was quick to answer and Bettina signaled her quickly. She didn't want to say anything yet. But when the dinner came, she only picked at her food. She didn't want to overdo it, if she really was in labor she wanted to keep it light.

"You didn't eat anything, baby. You feeling okay?" He leaned toward her again as they waited for dessert.

But she smiled at him brightly. "Not bad, for a broad about to have a kid."

"When?" He looked at her blankly. "Now?" He looked suddenly panicked and Bettina laughed.

"Not this minute, I hope, but in a while. I started having pains just before dinner, but I wasn't sure."

"And now you are?" He quickly grabbed her arm and she laughed.

"Will you stop that, Ollie? I'm fine. Have dessert and coffee, and then we can go home and call the doctor. Relax."

But it was impossible, and before the coffee had come, she was having trouble relaxing too. As they had the first time, the pains started to crowd her very quickly and grew rapidly intense.

Mary was timing contractions as they stood on the sidewalk, Bettina leaning heavily against Ollie, and she nodded her head. "We'd better take you to the hospital, Betty. You may not have time to go home."

"I should be so lucky." She smiled softly, but from the look in her eyes Ollie knew she was in pain, and suddenly he felt panic clutch him. What if this time was as bad as the first? But Mary saw what was happening to him and grabbed his arm firmly just before she got into the car. Bettina was already lying down on the backseat.

"She's going to be fine, Ollie. Take it easy. She's okay."

"Suddenly I couldn't help thinking —"

"She's probably thinking the same thing. But it's going to be fine." He nodded and Mary slid quickly into the car. "How's it going, Betty?"

"The same." And then a moment later as Ollie moved the car away from the curb: "I'm having another one."

He looked at Mary in terror. "Should I stop?"

"Christ, no." And with that the two women started laughing. Suddenly Bettina was no longer laughing, and by the time they got to the hospital, she no longer wanted to talk.

A nurse hurried away to call her doctor as two others ushered her gently into a small sterile-looking room. For a moment Bettina looked at Mary with a grim look in her eyes.

"I thought you said things had changed." It was a room just like the one where she had spent fourteen agonizing hours strapped down while she screamed.

"Take it easy, Betty." Slowly she helped her take off her clothes, but they had to stop constantly for the pains. And at last, as she held on tightly to Ollie, they helped her lie down.

"You okay, babe?" Suddenly he felt helpless and frightened, all he knew was that if they hurt her or his baby, he would kill them. He knew that for a fact. But slowly she smiled at him, holding tightly to his hand.

"I'm fine."

"Are you sure?" She nodded, and then gulped as she felt another pain coming on. But this time Ollie remembered what they had learned together, and he coached her as she breathed. When it was over, she looked at him in amazement with a small smile.

"You know, it works?"

"Good." He looked immensely proud and the next time they did it again. By the time the doctor joined them, everything was in control.

He told her that she was doing beautifully,

and only the brief examination reminded her for a moment of the past, but there was nothing else he could do. At least this time no one had tied her down. The nurses were gentle and pleasant, the doctor was smiling, and Mary was somewhere in a corner of the room. Bettina felt surrounded by people who cared about what was happening to her, and through it all Ollie was with her, holding her hand, helping her breathe, and helping her to keep control.

Half an hour later the pains got harder and for a few minutes Bettina didn't know if she could go on. Her breath caught strangely, she felt herself trembling, she felt sick to her stomach, and she was suddenly violently cold. Ollie looked nervously at Mary, who was sharing a knowing look with another nurse. Bettina was in transition, and they both knew that this would be the worst. Half an hour later she clutched desperately at Ollie's arm and started to cry.

"I can't . . . Ollie . . . can't . . . no!" She cried harder as another pain came, and then screamed as the doctor examined her with his hand.

"She's at nine." He looked pleased, and then suddenly he was encouraging her too. "Just a few more minutes, Bettina. Come on . . . you can do it . . . you're doing great . . . come on. . . ." As sweat dripped relentlessly down Ollie's sides, somehow they talked her on, and fifteen minutes later the doctor nodded and suddenly everyone around them began to run.

"Ollie . . . oh, Ollie. . . ." She was holding on to him desperately and Mary saw that she was starting to push; it was time. They got her onto the delivery room table, and she grabbed willingly at the handles on either side.

"Do I have to have stirrups?" She looked at the doctor desperately, and he smiled.

"No, you don't." He had a nurse on each side help with her legs and instructed Ollie to support her under her shoulders, and suddenly all she wanted to do was push. She had the feeling that she was climbing a mountain, shoving boulders out of her path with her nose, and now and then it all got too much for her and she slid a little way back down the hill. But all their voices were mingling, encouraging her and spurring her on, and then suddenly, with a last gasp and hard push, Ollie felt her whole body grow stiff as she strained and between her legs a little red face appeared and gave a wail. He looked at it in amazement, still holding her shoulders in his hands.

"My God, it's a baby!" And then everyone

laughed with relief. Two more pushes and the rest of their daughter had appeared.

"Oh, Ollie . . . oh, Ollie, she's so pretty!" She was laughing and smiling, and this time she was crying with joy, and Ollie and Mary were too. Only the doctor was dry-eyed but he looked as happy as they.

Half an hour later Bettina was in a room with the baby, and Ollie was still shaken by what he'd seen. His wife looked calm and unruffled, and proud of what she'd done. The whole birth had taken less than two hours, and she looked at them as she held the baby and grinned.

"You know what? I'm starving." Mary looked at her and laughed.

"I always was too."

But Oliver could only sit and stare in rapt fascination at his daughter. "I think you're both disgusting. How can you eat at a time like this?" But she did, she ate two roast beef sandwiches, a milk shake, and a doughnut. "You're a monster!" He laughed at her as he watched her devour the meal. But his eyes had never been as tender, and at last she held out a hand to him with a small gentle smile.

"I love you, Ollie. I couldn't have done it without you. A couple of times I thought I was giving out."

"I knew you never would." But once or twice he had been frightened too, only because it had seemed so painful and so much hard work, but there she sat less than an hour later, her face washed, her eyes bright, her hair combed. It was all a little hard to absorb. Mary had gone downstairs for a cup of coffee, and to leave them alone. "You were wonderful, darling. I was so proud." They watched each other in endless, mutual admiration, and for an instant he wanted to ask her to marry him. But he knew better. And even then, he didn't dare. They had already chosen the name for the baby. Antonia Daniels Paxton. And that was enough.

47

"Alexander, what do you think of your sister?" His mother looked at him in some amusement as he shrugged. She and the baby had been home for two days.

"Pretty cute, for a girl." He had survived his initial disappointment, after Bettina had let him hold her.

"Boy, is she small!" But he kind of liked her, and he handed her back with a smile. And then later, when he was alone with his mother, he let one thing slip. "I'm sure glad you were married to my Dad when I was a kid."

"Are you? Why?" Bettina looked at him curiously, wondering why he had brought it up.

"Because what if people knew? Maybe they'd say something funny." He looked at her, frowning. "I wouldn't like that." He had just turned six in June.

"I guess not. But would it really matter,

darling?"

"It would to me." Bettina nodded quietly and was lost in thought when Ollie came in to visit his wife and child. The doctor had let them leave the hospital quickly because the birth was so easy, but he wanted her to take it easy at home for about a week.

"What are you looking so serious about, madam?"

"Alexander. He just said a very strange thing." She told him and he frowned.

"Maybe he's just sensitive about that right now." He tried to look noncommittal but there was a light of hope in his eye.

"What if she is too, six years from now?"

"Then we'll tell people we're married."

She looked at him oddly. "Maybe we should."

"What? Tell people that we're married?" He looked confused, and she shook her head slowly.

"No, get married I mean."

"You mean like now?" She nodded and he looked stunned. "Do you mean it?"

She nodded slowly. "Yes, I think I do."

"Do you want to?"

She smiled at him more broadly. "Yes, I want to."

"Are you sure?"

"*Yes!* For heaven's sake, Ollie —"

"I don't believe it. I never thought I'd see this day."

"Neither did I. So shut up before I change my mind." Oliver rushed out of the room and a moment later they were laughing and drinking champagne. Three days later, after duly getting their license, with Mary and Seth in tow, Bettina and Ollie went downtown, and in City Hall they took their vows.

She looked at the certificate suspiciously afterward. "At least it doesn't say you're my fourth husband."

He grinned, but then he looked at her seriously. "Bettina, you don't have to be ashamed of anything you've ever done. You've done it all honestly. There's nothing wrong with all of that." He had always felt that way about her life, and she loved it about him. He made her feel proud.

"Thank you, darling." And then, hand in hand, they walked down the stairs of City Hall. But when they got home, he was looking pensive and he gently held out a hand.

"There is something else I want to take care of, Mrs. Paxton." But she knew he was only teasing. They had agreed that she would keep her own name.

"What's that, Mister Paxton?"

But he looked serious when he answered. "I want to adopt Alexander. Think I could?"

"If you mean would John let you, I'm sure of it." They had never heard from him. She looked tenderly at her husband. "Alexander would love it."

Ollie smiled at her slowly. "So would I. I'll call my lawyer tomorrow." He did, and four weeks later it was done. They were four Paxtons living under one roof.

48

On the first day in October all of the Paxtons flew to New York. Ollie had taken a three-month leave from work, they had found a nurse in New York to help Bettina with the baby, and they put Alexander back in his old New York school. By now he was a seasoned traveler. Ollie was quick to contact his old friends at the *Mail.* The play was hard work for Bettina, but she loved it, and she was fully recovered from Antonia's birth. When at last the play opened, it was another smashing success. They spent Christmas in New York in their suite at the Carlyle, and five days later they headed home.

"Feels good, doesn't it?" Ollie smiled at her happily as they lay in their own bed.

Bettina nodded happily. "Yeah, it does."

"I hope you wait awhile before you write another play."

"Why?" She looked at him in confusion,

he was usually so encouraging about her work. But he was laughing on his side of the bed.

"Because I'm tired of freezing my ass off in New York. Can't you stick to movies for a while?"

"For the next six months anyway." But she hated to tell him that on the plane home she had been thinking about a new play. Her career was booming, and she had recently had several offers just to do films. Most ardent among her pursuers was Bill Hale, the man who had owned the first apartment they had shared in New York, but she had no desire to work with him and had never answered his calls.

"When do you start work on the movie?"

"In three weeks, I think."

He nodded, and a little while later they were both asleep. And the next morning he went back to work while she reorganized their life. The baby was almost six months old and as cute as could be. Alexander was still on Christmas vacation and had turned out to be a big help with his sister. He loved to hold his little sister, and he was very proficient at feeding her and making her burp. Bettina was smiling, watching him do it at lunchtime, when she heard the phone. The sitter was hovering somewhere in the background, but Bettina nodded with a smile.

"I'll get it." She picked it up on the third ring, still watching Alexander hold the baby with a smile. "Yes, this is Mrs. Paxton." And then a long pause and, "Why?" And then suddenly her face turned gray and she turned around so Alexander couldn't see her cry. "Fine. I'll be right there." They called her from the paper, but when she got there, it was already too late. The fire unit was double-parked on the street, and everyone stood around him as he lay lifeless on the floor.

"It was a heart attack, Mrs. Paxton." The editor looked at her mournfully. "He's gone." She knelt gently next to him and touched his face. It was still warm.

"Ollie?" She whispered it softly. "Ollie?" But there was no sound, and the tears poured down her face. She heard someone urge the bystanders to go back to work or at least leave her alone, and she heard someone else say, "Isn't that Bettina Daniels? . . . Yeah . . . that was his wife. . . ." But the name of Bettina Daniels did her no good now. No success on Broadway, no movie, no screenplay, no money, no house in Beverly Hills would bring him back. At forty-five years of age, the man who wanted only the good life, who had wanted only to see the birth of his first child, had died of a heart attack on his office floor. Oliver Paxton was no more. It was the third man she loved that Bettina had lost in this way, and as she watched them bundle him carefully onto a stretcher, she sobbed in anger as much as in pain.

49

Mary and Seth Waterston came down for the funeral, and afterward Mary stayed with Bettina for another four days, while Seth went back to work. But there was very little they said to each other. She helped mostly with the children. Bettina seemed hopelessly withdrawn. She didn't move, she didn't talk, she didn't eat. She just sat and stared. Now and then Mary tried to bring her the baby, but even that didn't help. She just waved her away vaguely and went on sitting there, lost in her own thoughts. She was scarcely better the night before Mary left.

"You can't do this to yourself, Betty." As always she was honest, but Bettina only stared at her.

"Why not?"

"Because your life's not over. No matter how hard this is."

But then she looked at her friend angrily. "Why isn't it, dammit? Why not me instead of him?" And then, sadly, her eyes slowly filled as she stared at nothing. "He was such a good person."

"I know." Mary's eyes were damp too. "But so are you."

"When I had the baby" — her lip was trembling violently — "I couldn't have made it without him."

"I know, Betty, I know." She held out her arms and Bettina went into them and seemed to cry out her soul. But she looked better when Mary left the next day.

"What are you going to do now?" Mary looked at her piercingly as they stood at the gate.

Bettina shrugged. "I have to fulfill my contract. I have to write the screenplay for my second play."

"And after that?"

"God only knows. They keep hounding me to make other deals. I don't think I will."

"Will you go back to New York?"

But Bettina shook her head firmly. "Not for a while. I want to be here." Mary nodded, and they held each other for a long moment before Bettina kissed her cheek and Mary disappeared onto the plane.

Two weeks later, as promised, she appeared at the studio to begin discussing the initial work she was going to do in adapting her play. The meetings were dry, crisp, and exhausting. But Bettina never seemed to bend. She spoke to no one unless she had to, and at last she took refuge in her house to write the script. It took her less time than expected, and when it was completed, it was even better than they had hoped. They made her a lot of speeches about how gifted she was. And in short order Norton started getting an avalanche of calls. Bettina Daniels's reputation had been made.

"What do you mean you're not working?" He listened in shocked horror when he called her.

"Just what I said. I'm taking six months off."

"But I thought you wanted to start a new play."

"Nope. Not a new play. Or a new movie. Absolutely nothing, Norton, they can all go to hell."

"But Bill Hale's office just —"

"Screw Bill Hale. I don't want to hear it. . . ."

"But, Bettina —" He sounded panicked.

"If I'm that good, they'll wait six months, and if I'm not, then too bad."

"That isn't the point, but why wait when you can pull in anything you want at this point? Name the price, name the picture.

Baby, it's all yours."

"Then give it *all* back to them. I don't want it."

He couldn't understand it. "Why not?"

She sighed softly. "Norton, five months ago I lost Ollie." She sighed again. "The wind has kind of gone out of my sails since then."

"I know. I understand that. But you can't just sit there. It's not good for you." But she knew it was also not good for him.

"Maybe it is. Maybe all this bullshit isn't as important as I thought."

"Oh, Jesus, Bettina, don't do this. Don't do some kind of beachcomber routine. You are about to reach the summit of your life." But she had already done that. When the baby was born . . . when she married Ivo . . . when she had shared some of her father's great moments . . . there was more than just work and success. But she didn't want to explain to him. Just trying to made her feel tired.

"I don't want to talk about it, Norton. Tell everyone I've left the country for six months and you can't get in touch. And if they bug me, I'll make it a year."

"Terrific. I'll be sure to tell them. And look, Bettina, if you change your mind, will you call me?"

"Of course, Norton. You know I will."

But she didn't. She spent the time peacefully with her children. Once she went up to visit Mary and Seth. But she seldom left her house, or her children, and she seemed to have grown oddly quiet since Ollie's death. On Thanksgiving Seth and Mary noticed it when they arrived with the entire brood. It was a lovely family Thanksgiving, but Oliver's absence was sorely felt.

"How's it going, Betty?" Mary watched her closely as they sat in the garden. Something deep down inside her seemed to have changed. She was quieter, colder, more remote, yet she was also more sure of herself. She seemed much older than she had a year before.

Bettina smiled slowly. "It's going all right. I still miss him though. And there are things I still think about that I wish I could change."

"Like what?"

"I wish I'd married him sooner. It made him so happy, I don't know why I had to hold out till the end."

"You were still growing. He understood that."

"I know he did. Looking back at it, I realize that he understood too much. Everything was for my sake, everything he did was for me. He gave up his job in New York on the paper, took a leave of absence here so he could come to New York when I did the play. In retrospect it all seems so unfair." She looked at Mary unhappily as she thought of it, but Mary shook her head.

"He didn't mind it. He told me that once. His career wasn't as important to him as yours is to you." She didn't dare tell her that what she needed now was a man as powerful and successful as she. Even her face had changed. There was a kind of angular beauty that commanded attention, and the simplicity of her black wool dress and her jewelry spelled success. She had finally unearthed all her old jewelry, from her father, from Ivo, all of it, and she wore it almost every day. She looked down at the large diamond, smiling now as Mary watched her.

"I don't know. Maybe I'm spending too much time reliving my past."

"Are you just brooding about it, or do you understand it better than you did?"

"I don't know, Mary." Her eyes looked dreamy and distant. "I think I just accept it all better now. It has somehow become a part of me." Mary watched her with a small smile of pleasure and nodded her head. That was what she had always hoped for.

For Bettina to accept who and what she was. The only thing that made her unhappy was to see Bettina living a life behind locked doors.

"Do you see anyone?"

"Only you and the children."

"Why don't you?"

"I don't want to. Why should I? So they can gossip that they finally met me, the playwright with four husbands . . . Justin Daniels's eccentric daughter . . . ? Who needs it? For the moment I'm a lot happier living like this."

"I wouldn't exactly call it living, Betty. Would you?"

Bettina shrugged. "I have what I want."

"No, you don't. You're a young woman, you deserve more than solitude, Bettina. You deserve people and parties and laughter; you deserve to enjoy your success."

Bettina smiled at her in answer. "Just look at all this." She waved at the beauty of the garden and the house.

"That's not what I mean, Bettina, and you know it. This is pretty, but it isn't a substitute for friends. . . ." She hesitated, and then said it, ". . . or a man." Bettina met her eyes squarely.

"Is that what it's all about, Mary? A man? Is that the whole story? That life isn't complete without a man? Don't you think that maybe I've had enough?"

"At thirty-six? I hope not. What do you have in mind for yourself? To just sit here and give up?"

"What are you suggesting? That I run out and audition all over again? Don't you think four husbands is an outrageously high quota for anyone, or are you suggesting that I try for five?" She looked very angry.

"Maybe." And then after a moment, "Why not?"

"Because maybe I don't need one. Maybe I don't want to get married anymore."

But Mary wouldn't be put off that easily. "If I thought you meant that for the right reasons, I'd get off your back. No one has to get married, Bettina. That isn't the only name of the game. But you can't spend the rest of your life lonely because you're afraid of what people will say. And that's what it's all about with you, isn't it? You think that if you take your shirt off, someone will rush up and brand you with four letter A's. Well, you're wrong, for chrissake. Very much so. I love you, Seth does. I don't give a damn if you get married another twelve times, or if you don't, for that matter. But out there is someone, Bettina, someone who is as strong, as successful, as special, and as splendid as you. You deserve to find him, to let him know you, so you don't sit here for the rest of your life all alone. You don't have to get married if you don't want to, for God's sake, who the hell cares? But don't sit here, Bettina, behind your goddamn fortress doors." Bettina looked at her sadly, and Mary saw that there were tears in her eyes. She thought that maybe she'd reached her, and when Bettina went inside without answering, she was almost sure.

They left at the end of the weekend, and before they got on the plane, Bettina held Mary close.

"Thank you."

"For what?" And then she understood. "Don't be silly." Slowly she smiled at her. "One day you may have to give me a good kick in the ass too."

"I doubt it." And then she smiled broadly too. "But then again your life hasn't been as exotic as mine." And for an instant, only an instant, Mary thought that Bettina looked proud.

"What are you going to do now, Betty?" Seth leaned over to ask her.

"Call Norton and tell him I'm getting back to work. By now I'm sure he's given up on me."

"I doubt it." Mary was quick to answer, and then hurriedly they boarded the plane.

50

"Well, Rip van Winkle, coming out of hibernation, are you?"

"All right, Norton," she said, chuckling softly, "it was only six months."

"It might as well have been six years. Do you have any idea how many people I've turned away since you decided to 'retire,' temporarily, thank God?"

"Don't tell me." She was still smiling. It was the first of December and she was feeling good.

"I won't. Now what do you have planned before we cross wires again?"

"Absolutely nothing."

"You're not starting work on a new play?"

"No, as a matter of fact, I don't want to. I want to stay out here for a while. It'll be too hard on the children if I start dragging them back and forth to New York every year."

"All right, it doesn't make any difference. You have enough offers to write movies to keep you busy for the next ten years."

"Like from whom?" She sounded instantly suspicious and he went down the list. When he was finished she nodded, approving. "I'd say that's quite a few. Whom do you suggest I talk to first?"

"Bill Hale." He answered instantly and she closed her eyes.

"Oh, Christ, Norton, not him."

"Why? He's a genius. And he's doing producing now. As a matter of fact he's about as brilliant as you."

"Terrific. So find me someone a little less brilliant who wants to talk."

"Why?" He was intrigued.

"Because everyone says he's an asshole."

"In business?" Norton was stunned.

"No, personally. He collects women, wives, mistresses, who needs it?"

"No one asked you to marry him, for chrissake, Bettina. Just discuss this movie idea he has in mind."

"Do I have to?"

"Will you do it if I say yes?" He sounded hopeful.

"Probably not." They both laughed. "Look, I just don't want to put myself in an awkward situation. The guy has a legendary case of hot pants, which I hear he wears regularly to work."

"So carry a tray of ice cubes and bring a pair of brass knuckles, but do me a favor, Bettina, after six months on your ass and not answering the phone, at least go to lunch with the guy. You and he are the two hottest people in the business these days. It's insane for you not to listen to what he has to say."

"Okay, Norton. You win."

"Do you want me to set it up from here? Or will you?"

"You do it. I don't want to be bothered." Suddenly the voice of her father echoed in her own head. So that was how it had felt. . . .

"Any place special you want to see him?"

"No. If he's as big a phony as I think he is, he'll probably want to meet at the Polo Lounge at the Beverly Hills Hotel, so he can play Mister Hollywood and get paged every five minutes on the phone."

"So I'll call you every five minutes too, all right?"

"Fine."

And then suddenly he remembered something, but he didn't want to ask her. He was sure that she and Ollie had rented an apartment from him once, a long time before, in New York. But he figured it was just as well not to bring up Ollie. She had enough pain, and he knew that it had been a major blow when he died. She had had a lot of tough things happen, but on the other hand, he shrugged to himself as he dialed Bill Hale, she had had a lot of good things happen too. In some ways it was a story not unlike Bill Hale's.

He got through to Bill's secretary fairly quickly, and a moment later he was speaking to him. They agreed on the following Monday, but contrary to Bettina's prediction he asked if he might stop by her house after lunch.

"Is he kidding?" She was shocked when Norton called. "Why does he want to do a thing like that?"

"He said it is less distracting than trying to talk in a restaurant with waiters and phones, and he thought that maybe you'd feel uncomfortable going to his place to see him."

"So be it." She shrugged and hung up, and the following Monday, she dressed slowly an hour before he was due. She was wearing a deep purple suit that she had ordered from London, and it was a wonderful anemone color in a lovely thin wool. She wore a white silk blouse with it, and the amethyst earrings her father had given her. Her hair was soft and loose and the color of autumn in New England, and as she took a last look in the mirror she heard the bell. It didn't really matter what she looked like, but as long as she was going back to doing business, she might as well look like who she was. Not Justin Daniels's daughter, or Ivo Stewart's wife, or Mrs. John Fields, or even Mrs. Oliver Paxton. She was Bettina Daniels. And whatever else she was, she knew she was a damn good playwright, and after a hell of a lot of pain and mistakes she knew one other thing. She was whole.

"Mister Hale?" She eyed him archly as he stepped inside. Like her, he had dressed for the occasion and he was wearing a dark blue pin-striped business suit, a dark blue Christian Dior tie, and an especially starched white shirt. She had to admit to herself that he was well dressed and good-looking, but she didn't really care. He nodded politely when he saw her and held out his right hand.

"Bill, please. Miss Daniels?"

"Bettina." The formalities over, she led him into her living room and took a chair. Her housekeeper appeared a moment later with a large handsome lacquer tray. There was both tea and coffee, a plate of little sandwiches, and cookies that Alexander had eyed longingly that morning before school.

"Good heavens, I didn't mean to put you to all this trouble." She said something vague about it not being any trouble as she tried to decide if he was plastic or real.

After a few moments, as he drank coffee and she sipped her tea, they began to talk business, and it was two hours later when they stopped. She had to admit that she loved his idea and she was smiling as they slowly wound the meeting to a close.

"Should I call your agent and discuss the vulgar aspects of it with him?"

She laughed as he said it and nodded slowly, narrowing her eyes.

"You know, I like you a lot better than I thought I would," he said.

She looked at him, torn between amusement and astonishment and she laughed. "Why?"

"Well, you know, Justin Daniels's daughter. . . ." He looked apologetic. "You could have turned out to be one hell of a snob."

"And I didn't turn out to be?"

"No, you're not." And then, feeling bold as she looked at him, she chuckled too.

"I like you better too."

"And what strike did I have against me? I didn't have a famous father."

"No, but you have other sins from what I hear." She eyed him frankly, and he nodded, meeting her green eyes with his blue.

"The bluebeard reputation?" She nodded. "Charming, isn't it?" He didn't look angry, only lonely, and then he met her eyes again. "People love to catch tidbits, there's a lot they talk about that they don't understand." And then he told her honestly, "I've been married four times. My first wife died in a plane crash, my second left me after" — he seemed to hesitate for a moment — "after our life fell apart. My third was something of a dreamer, and six months after we got married she realized that what she really wanted was to join the Peace Corps, and my fourth," — he stopped with a broad grin — "was a raving bitch." For a moment Bettina laughed with him, and then slowly something gentle fell over her eyes.

"I don't have any right to quibble with all that."

"Why not? Everyone else does." She was oddly touched by his honesty and embarrassed at what she had thought. But suddenly she was laughing and she hid behind her napkin. All he could see were the dancing green eyes.

"I've been married four times too."

But suddenly they were both laughing. "Why, you . . . and here I was feeling guilty!" He looked like a kid who had discovered a friend with something in common, but she had sat up with a girlish look on her face too.

"Do you feel guilty?"

"Sure, I do. Four wives, are you kidding? That's not wholesome!"

"Oh, Jesus . . . so do I!"

"You should. And you should feel a lot guiltier for not telling me sooner." He nibbled a cookie, sat back in his chair, and grinned. "So tell me about yours."

"One lovely man who was a lot older than I was."

"How much is a lot? You were sixteen and he was nineteen?"

She looked faintly supercilious. "I was nineteen and he was sixty-two."

"Ooo . . ." he whistled. "That *was* older." But his smile was gentle and there was no reproach. Only interest.

"He was a marvelous man, a friend of my father's. Actually maybe you knew him." But he held up a hand as she started to say his name.

"No, no, please, this is marriage anonymous. Let's not blow it. The next thing you know we'll find out I was married to two of your cousins and you'll hate me all over again."

She laughed, and then looked at him more

seriously. "Is this what everyone in Hollywood does? Sit around discussing their last four husbands and wives?"

"Only the sickoes, Bettina. The rest of us just make human mistakes, not that anyone would believe it. I mean four is a bit much." They both grinned. "Anyway, continue. . . ."

"My second husband sounds like your wife who joined the Peace Corps. He wanted a green card. We were also married for six months." But her face clouded briefly as she thought of the baby she'd lost. "My third was a doctor in San Francisco, and for five years I tried to be a 'normal' wife."

"What does a 'normal' wife do?" He looked at her with intrigue in his eyes as he took another cookie from the plate.

"To tell the truth I was never sure. I just knew that whatever it was, I was never doing it. One of my friends says that you have to be a little brown and gray bird."

He looked at her, torn between laughter and compassion, as his gaze fell on the flaming hair and the deep-purple dress. "You are very definitely not that."

"Thank you. Well, in any case I blew it completely by writing my first play."

"He didn't like that?"

"He filed for divorce the moment I left for New York, sold our house, and I found out when I came home."

"He didn't tell you?" She shook her head. "Charming. And then?"

"Then I moved to New York and" — she seemed to hesitate for a moment, and then she went on — "I met . . . my fourth husband, and he was very special." Her voice softened as he watched her. "We had a baby, and almost a year ago he died."

"I'm sorry." They sat in silence for a moment, and then he looked at her gently.

"See, Bettina, that's what I mean. Other people, the rest of them out there, think that we just sit here laughing, collecting divorces, and paying alimony and that we're amused by our endless list of ex-wives, but what they don't understand is that it can happen to real people, tragedies and mistakes, and people you believed in who disappoint you . . . it's all terribly real, but no one understands." They looked at each other for an endless moment. "My second wife and I had two children, but she had a drinking problem I didn't know about when we got married. She spent most of our marriage in and out of hospitals, trying to deal with it, but eventually she lost." He sighed for a moment, and then went on. "She was driving one day with my two little girls in the car and —" His voice caught, and without thinking, Bettina reached out to him, knowing what he was going to say, and he took her hand. "She smashed the car up, and both of the kids died. But she didn't. And she was never the same after that. She's been in and out of institutions ever since." He shrugged and his voice drifted away. "I kind of thought we would make it, but . . . we never did." And then he looked up at her kindly and pulled away his hand. "How are you doing after losing your husband? Is that why you've been incommunicado for all these months?" Suddenly he understood.

She nodded slowly. "Yes, that's why. And I'm doing better. At first it seemed so — so unfair."

He nodded. "It is. That's the bitch of it. The good people, the ones you could make it with —" He didn't finish his sentence. "My first wife was like that. God, she was so good and so funny. She was an actress and I was a writer. She got her first damn road show, and . . . end of the road. I was twenty-three and I thought it would kill me. I almost drank myself to death for a year." And then he looked hard at Bettina. "Isn't that incredible? That was sixteen years ago . . . and there have been three other women in my life since who were important enough for me to marry. If someone had told me that after Anna died, I'd have killed them. It's odd, time does such strange things." He sat there musing for a moment, and then he smiled. "Interesting stories, yours and mine."

"I'm glad you think so. Once in a while I've thought it wasn't worth the trouble going on another day."

"But it is, isn't it?" He smiled at her softly. "The amazing thing is that it always is. There's always another event, another person, a woman you fall in love with, a friend you have to see, a baby you want to give birth to . . . something that makes you go on. It's been like that for me."

She nodded, loving what he was giving her, because his words were setting her free. It fit all the pieces together and made the picture not only whole, but it allowed her to see that there was still more of the picture, a part she had yet to see. "Do you have other children?" He shook his head slowly.

"No. Miss Peace Corps didn't stick around long enough to have a baby. And number four and I were married for three years, but —" He laughed softly. "They were the three longest years of my life." And then suddenly she remembered.

"I remember when you were getting married." She grinned broadly. "I lived in your apartment in New York."

"You did?" He looked baffled. "When?"

"When you got married. You were on the West Coast. It was a beautiful place on the West Side."

"My God." He looked at her in stupefaction. "I rented that to Ollie . . . Oliver Paxton . . . for chrissake. . . ." He looked at her, stunned. "That's who you are, Bettina! You're Ollie Paxton's wife!"

But as she looked at him, sitting very tall in her chair, she slowly shook her head. "No, I'm not. . . ." It was like hearing a dozen echoes and denying them all at last. Not even for Ollie could she be just that. "I'm Bettina Daniels."

For a moment he was startled, and then suddenly he understood, and he nodded, holding out a hand. She was not her father's or Ivo's or Ollie's anymore. . . . She was her own now . . . and he understood that, just as she knew it about him. Their eyes met as they shook hands carefully over the table. "Hello, Bettina. I'm Bill."

We hope you have enjoyed this Large Print book. Other Thorndike, Wheeler, Kennebec, and Chivers Press Large Print books are available at your library or directly from the publishers.

For information about current and upcoming titles, please call or write, without obligation, to:

Publisher
Thorndike Press
295 Kennedy Memorial Drive
Waterville, ME 04901
Tel. (800) 223-1244

or visit our Web site at:

http://gale.cengage.com/thorndike

OR

Chivers Large Print
published by AudioGO Ltd
St James House, The Square
Lower Bristol Road
Bath BA2 3SB
England
Tel. +44(0) 800 136919
www.audiogo.co.uk

All our Large Print titles are designed for easy reading, and all our books are made to last.